THRONES IN THE DESERT

A NOVEL BASED ON THE BOOK OF LUKE

DOUG PETERSON

O'Shea Books

For Jackson, Joshua, Tomás, and Sofía

NOVELS BY DOUG PETERSON

KINGDOM COME SERIES
Book 1: *Thrones in the Desert*

The story of Jesus, seen through the eyes of five fictional characters—a slave, a guard in Herod's palace, a Pharisee, the daughter of a Zealot, and a tax collector. They all encounter Jesus, who overthrows the thrones in their lives.

Book 2: *Swords in the Desert* (coming soon)

Book 2 follows Jesus's footsteps as He heads steadily toward Jerusalem. *Swords in the Desert* also continues to follow five fictional characters.

UNDERGROUND RAILROAD SERIES
Book 1: *The Vanishing Woman*

Ellen and William Craft escape when Ellen poses as a white man while her husband pretends to be her slave—a true story.

Book 2: *The Disappearing Man*

Henry "Box" Brown mails himself to freedom. He ships himself in a box from Richmond to Philadelphia—a true story.

Book 3: *The Tubman Train*

Harriet Tubman's name is legendary, but most people do not know her complete story. *The Tubman Train* is one of the first novels to tackle her remarkable life.

CIVIL WAR SERIES

Book 1: *The Lincoln League*

John Scobell, the first African-American spy for the U.S. intelligence service, operates deep within Confederate lines during the Civil War. Based on a true story.

Book 2: *The Dixie Devil*

André Cailloux is the forgotten first black hero of the American Civil War. This is the story of André and his wife, Felicie, as they try to survive in the turbulent world of New Orleans.

ANNIE O'SHEA MYSTERIES

The Puzzle People

A suspense novel that spans the rise and fall of the Berlin Wall. Inspired by real events.

HOLY LAND IN THE TIME OF JESUS

THE GREAT SEA

KING'S HIGHWAY

GALILEE

Capernaum
Magdala
SEA OF GALILEE
Gergesa
Sepphoris
Tiberias
Nazareth

Scythopolis

SAMARIA

DECAPOLIS

Jordan River

PEREA

JUDEA

Jericho

MOUNT OF OLIVES

Jerusalem ▲

Bethlehem

Machaerus

DEAD SEA

IDUMEA

NABATEA

KING'S HIGHWAY

CAST OF CHARACTERS

Main Characters

Eliana—The daughter of a Zealot freedom fighter

Asaph—A tax collector

Jeremiel—A priest and member of the Pharisee party

Sveshtari—A Thracian bodyguard for Herod Antipas

Keturah—A slave woman in the House of Herod Antipas

Supporting Cast

Nekoda—A priest and member of the Sadducee party

Chaim—Nekoda's younger brother

Malachi—Asaph's assistant, a fellow tax collector

Zuriel and Gershom—Childhood rivals of Asaph

Rufus—A guard in the House of Herod Antipas

Judah—A Zealot freedom fighter and father of Eliana

Lavi—Eliana's dog

FIGURES FROM HISTORY

Jesus—The Messiah, the Son of God

Mary—The mother of Jesus

Peter—A fisherman and disciple of Jesus

John the Baptist—A prophet and forerunner to Jesus

Joanna—Wife of the head of Herod's household

Herod Antipas—Tetrarch of Galilee and Perea

Herodias—Wife of Herod Antipas

1

LUKE, CHAPTER 1

ELIANA: THE MONTH OF ADAR (EARLY MARCH), 5 B.C.

"**G**O AHEAD AND THROW it," Zuriel urged Asaph.

Eliana glared at Asaph, daring him to hurl the rock at her. When Asaph picked up a stone, she noticed that it was small with rounded edges. Because Asaph had chosen a rock that wouldn't hurt as much as a sharp-edged one, Eliana took this as a good sign. Maybe he didn't want to destroy their friendship.

Zuriel folded his arms across his chest. "What are you waiting for, Asaph?"

"He's afraid," said Gershom, Zuriel's closest friend.

Eliana locked her eyes on Asaph as he jostled the rock in his right hand. She dug her sandals into the dirt, determined not to run. She would absorb the force of the stone, no matter how painful.

She and Asaph had been friends for many years, but now that she was nine and he was ten, they had been slowly separating, like stitches on an old garment. Her father said it was wrong for a girl to play with boys, especially at this age. Eliana didn't attend the school attached to the synagogue for this very reason; the school was meant for boys, while she was meant to help her mother.

But Eliana was determined to hold on to her friendship with Asaph. That's why she had decided to join him in climbing their favorite sycamore tree, even though Zuriel and Gershom also clambered among the branches. Eliana and Asaph used to spend hours climbing this tree, seeing who could reach the highest. But on this day, Zuriel guarded the lower limbs, preventing Eliana from getting a good handhold. He smacked her fingers whenever she tried to lace them around a branch.

Eventually, she gave up and stood at a distance, glaring at the three of them.

Zuriel kicked some dirt in her direction. "Eliana, we're tired of you following us."

She could care less what he thought. She cared only about Asaph, but she didn't dare speak this thought.

"You're a sickness we can't get rid of," added Gershom.

Zuriel and Gershom turned to Asaph, waiting for him to add an insult—or throw the rock. But he said and did nothing.

Zuriel laughed. "What's wrong, Asaph? Would you rather kiss her?"

"No!" Asaph's face reddened.

"Then hit her with that stone!"

Zuriel was a bit shorter than Asaph, but he overcame his lack of height with the aggressiveness of a jackal. He was a natural leader and expected obedience.

Asaph continued to jiggle the rock in his right hand while casting a look at Zuriel, then Gershom. Eliana realized that if he didn't hurl the rock, the others would—and they wouldn't choose a small, smooth stone. She swallowed, hoping Asaph would just throw the rock and be done with it.

Asaph cocked his hand back and paused, staring at her with a look that urged her to run before he let the stone fly. But she didn't even flinch. She stared back at him, her eyes dark with challenge.

Finally, he hurled the stone.

He aimed for her legs and didn't throw with full force. The stone fell far short, skipping past her foot. Eliana put a hand to her mouth and tried to hide her smile at the pitiful effort. Asaph was just being kind, going for her legs, but she couldn't help but laugh at his awkward throw.

"You fool!" Zuriel gave Asaph a two-handed shove, toppling him onto his rear end. Eliana rushed to help him to his feet, but Asaph shook her off, slapping her forearm. Eliana backed away, her face falling as she fought back tears.

Zuriel scoured the ground for a suitable stone. "I will do it myself." Eliana's heart began to race. Zuriel would probably hurl the rock at her head; he might even kill her. He once bragged about witnessing a woman being stoned to death. She thought he was lying, but still...

"Run," Asaph whispered, but Eliana acted as if she didn't hear.

Zuriel found an uneven rock with sharp edges—three times the size of the one that Asaph had chosen.

When Zuriel raised it high, every part of Eliana told her to run, but her stubborn streak was stronger than her fear. Instead, she held her ground and closed her eyes, waiting and wondering how it would feel. Would the rock sink deep into her skull like the one David slung at Goliath?

When Asaph screamed, she popped her eyes open in time to see him charge at Zuriel as the boy's arm moved forward. Asaph tackled Zuriel, knocking him clean off his feet and blocking his throw. Zuriel's face registered shock as he landed on his back, letting out an "Ooomph!"

Eliana smiled for a moment until she noticed Asaph's eyes darken, as if something in his mind snapped, like a branch breaking in a windstorm. He straddled Zuriel, his arms a fast-moving blur as he gave him a beating.

Eliana sucked in a sharp breath, her pulse spiking with each blow as Asaph bloodied Zuriel's face. Gershom made a weak attempt to pull Asaph off, but Asaph threw a wild punch that caught him hard in the left eye. Gershom ran for home, holding his face, whimpering.

Still, Asaph wouldn't let up.

"Asaph, that's enough!" She grabbed him by the shoulders, trying to peel him off. But he lashed out with the back of his hand, sending a flare of pain across her right forearm.

As Asaph battered Zuriel's face, first with his right fist, then his left, Eliana took a step back, eyes wide. It was as if he had a demon under his skin. Blood gushed from Zuriel's nose like red water from a spring, Asaph screaming with every punch.

Terrified, Eliana took off at a full sprint until she reached the safety of her house. She bolted into their courtyard, slowing to catch her breath, her heart going wild.

"What happened?" Her mother, who sat in the shade, spinning wool, gave her a quizzical stare.

Eliana followed her mother's gaze to her hand and was shocked to see traces of Zuriel's blood. She flinched. The flecks of red must have come from when she tried to stop Asaph.

"Just scraped it climbing trees." She wiped off the blood.

Life is in the blood. That is why they were taught to drain it all from an animal before they could eat the meat. Now, because of Asaph, she had been stained by Zuriel's lifeblood, and suddenly she felt impure and marked with guilt. She heard the blood cry out to her, like Abel's lifeblood shouting from the ground.

THE MONTH OF NISAN (LATE MARCH)

When Eliana and Asaph didn't see each other for the next two weeks, except in passing, she was certain their friendship was over. Then one morning, out of the clear blue sky, Asaph showed up at her house and challenged her to a footrace.

"Beat you to the market!" He took off running with Eliana right behind, her legs flying.

The only thing Eliana loved more than climbing trees with Asaph was racing him through the streets at breakneck speed. She was one step behind as they tore along the narrow paths that wound through clusters of white, cube-shaped homes. She skipped sideways to avoid colliding with a man coming out of his house, causing her to lose another step.

"Slow down!" the man bellowed, waving his hand in the air.

But Eliana ignored him, determined to beat Asaph to the town market—a race they had run many times before. While it was always close, this time, Asaph was a couple of steps ahead as they finished at the town gate.

"You got a head start!" Eliana leaned over, breathing heavily, and offered her complaint between breaths.

He grinned, his chest heaving. "And you're getting slower."

Eliana tried not to breathe too deeply, knowing the tanner's shop was at the very edge of the town. Even with shallow breaths, she caught whiffs of the foul odor.

Their small village, located in the hill country of Judea, was a day's walk from Jerusalem. A young family sat at the city gates—travelers waiting for an invitation to stay at one of the homes.

"We've had a traveler staying with us for several days now," Asaph whispered, glancing at the family. "He doesn't help with any of the chores, and he's not very friendly. Plus, he smells."

"The Torah says to take in strangers, even smelly ones." Eliana lifted her chin with an air of authority as they strolled by some women filling jars with water at the well.

They passed by the large sundial in the center of the square—a marvel. The shadow's movement along the dial broke the day into twelve equal parts, slicing it like a pie. They were in the early days of the month of Nisan, the time of the late rains, but today the sun shone, sharply defining the shadow on the sundial.

"My father hates this thing, but I think it's fascinating," said Eliana. Her father hated anything Roman, and this sundial had been given to the town by a wealthy politician.

"The Romans are even masters of time." Asaph's eyes locked on the shadow and the twelve numbers.

"Don't say anything like that around my father—and don't tell him I said it was fascinating."

"Of course, I won't."

At the sudden bray of a donkey, Eliana wheeled around and saw a young woman, perhaps fifteen years old, seated on the animal, entering the town. She was being led through the maze of whitewashed homes by a middle-aged man with skin like old leather.

The woman wore a white robe tied with a blue sash, and her raven-black hair peeked from beneath a blue and white headdress.

"Let's follow," said Eliana, but Asaph narrowed his eyes in return as if to say he didn't take commands from a girl.

At age nine, Eliana had three or four years before reaching a respectable age for marriage. In her eyes, they would always be friends no matter their ages, but Asaph acted increasingly awkward and distant.

With all her work at home—carrying water, grinding grain, helping her mother cook—there wasn't much time to play. So, why couldn't they enjoy what little time remained before adulthood when they would be consumed by duty? As adults, they would not even be able to talk together on the street without raising eyebrows. She wanted to put off that day as much as possible.

Shrugging at his stubbornness, she followed the woman on the donkey, staying about twenty paces behind. The next thing she knew, Asaph came running past, then slowed to a stroll a few steps ahead of her.

Eliana raised a brow with a scoff, wondering why they couldn't at least walk side by side. That's what friends did. But as she pulled alongside him, he hurried ahead two steps, then slipped in front. When she moved to the left, he cut her off again, determined to walk in front of her, the right of every boy.

She spotted a large stick on the ground and was tempted to use it to whack him in the back of the head. But she resisted the urge and continued in silence.

Twice, the woman on the donkey looked over her shoulder with a smile, her rich brown eyes sparkling. Eliana grinned. It was like they were sisters sharing a secret.

People peeked from windows with curious stares as the donkey wound its way through narrow pathways. Visitors were always big news in their small Judean town. Asaph increased his pace, putting a little more distance between them, but Eliana matched him stride for stride.

The two followed the donkey to the home of Zechariah and Elizabeth, who lived only a stone's throw away from Eliana's house. Zechariah was notorious throughout the region because he was the priest who had been struck mute while burning incense in the Temple in Jerusalem. Unable to speak, he communicated by writing on a tablet he carried in the folds of his robe. He made strange, muttering sounds, and his hands would flutter like small birds as he tried to make himself known. Eliana shuddered at the thought, finding it all a bit disturbing.

When the young woman reached the House of Zechariah, her companion helped her dismount. Eliana noticed how petite she was, barely taller than her.

Eliana paused, unsure if they should continue to follow. As if sensing their hesitation, the strange woman turned and smiled again, beckoning them with a subtle flick of her hand. This time, Eliana let Asaph lead the way as they entered the courtyard in the heart of Zechariah and Elizabeth's home.

Elizabeth appeared in the doorway but came up short, her face covered by a slanting shadow, like a veil. Her belly extended into the light, showing she was clearly with child. She was in the sixth month, but it was very odd for someone of Elizabeth's age to be in her condition. Something extraordinary was going on in the House of Zechariah.

Elizabeth stepped forward, her face revealing the strain of added weight, which was not easy on an older woman's back. But when she saw her visitor, she straightened up and brightened.

"Elizabeth, it is true!" the young visitor exclaimed. "You are with child!"

Elizabeth stopped short and put a hand to her swelling stomach. Her face filled with joy as she laughed. "Mary, come here quickly!"

The younger woman hurried across the courtyard; then Elizabeth directed Mary's hands to her round, ripe belly.

"Do you feel that? My child jumped when he heard your voice!"

Mary kept her hands in place and concentrated, like a blind woman trying to read the shape of a person's face. Then she broke into a smile. "Yes, I feel him moving."

Watching the two women embrace, Eliana wished she had someone to call sister, but her closest friend, Tamara, died a year ago of the ague. Tamara's parents had collected seven shavings from seven beams, seven nails from seven bridges, and seven ashes from seven ovens and hung them around the sick girl's neck with a white thread. But even that could not keep away the Angel of Death.

"Angel of Mercy, protect me," she whispered to keep her thoughts from Tamara's death.

She watched as Elizabeth took Mary's hands and stared into her eyes. "Blessed are you among women, and blessed is the child you will bear."

Eliana blinked, unsure if she heard it right. Shouldn't Mary be saying that to Elizabeth?

Elizabeth's eyes filled with emotion. "But why am I so favored, that the mother of my Lord should come to me?"

"Mother of my Lord?" Asaph whispered. "What is she talking about?"

Eliana had no answer. Yes, the House of Zechariah was an odd place indeed.

Then the woman, this Mary, kissed Elizabeth on both cheeks. "My soul glorifies the Lord, and my spirit rejoices in God my Savior, for He has been mindful of the humble state of His servant. From now on, all generations will call me blessed, for the Mighty One has done great things for me—holy is His name."

Mary spoke earnestly, with the eloquence of a rabbi reciting the Torah in the synagogue. Then old Zechariah, speechless Zechariah, strode into the courtyard, gesturing with his hands and grinning at Mary like a crazy man.

"Let's go." Asaph nudged her. He once told Eliana that he thought Zechariah was cursed. Asaph seemed afraid to be near such a man.

But Eliana remained, riveted by Mary's words.

When she didn't budge, Asaph glared. "Let's leave, Eliana. Now!"

As Eliana turned to follow Asaph, Mary said, "He has performed mighty deeds with his arm; he has scattered those who are proud in their inmost thoughts. He has brought down rulers from their thrones but has lifted up the humble."

Eliana stood transfixed. *Brought down rulers from their thrones.*

Those burning words branded Eliana's heart. Many in this town would like nothing more than to see the thrones of Herod and the Romans overturned and smashed with an iron fist. Her father especially would love to make it so.

Finally, Eliana followed Asaph from the courtyard, and once again, they raced back to the market, her legs flying. But just as they neared the edge of town, Asaph spotted another boy from the village and made a sudden sharp turn. The two boys ran off, leaving her stranded in the street, her face flushing.

She followed for a short distance, but the boys had already lost her in the maze of paths running through town like a dusty thread. Was Asaph taunting her? But why? What had she done to him besides being a girl? Her cheeks burned all the way to the tips of her ears as she stood in the center of the pathway. That's when she thought she heard a voice whisper in her ear, "You'll always be alone."

"Shut up," she said aloud as the throb of unshed tears welled behind her eyes.

THREE MONTHS LATER, MONTH OF TAMMUZ (LATE JUNE)

It was evening when Eliana and her family shared a meal in the open area outside their home. It was a pleasant night, so instead of eating in the upper room, her father had dragged a chest outside, and they used it as their table. Eliana's father covered a thick slice of barley bread with honey, the juice of the honeycomb as he called it—his favorite food.

Eliana's mother stood to the side, waiting to eat until her husband finished. "What do you make of their child?"

Eliana's father bit into the bread and closed his eyes as he slowly chewed, then licked at the dabs of honey clinging to his black mustache. His hair was tightly curled, his beard thick and oiled. His face shone like he was in the seventh heaven.

"Judah, I'm asking you a question!"

Suddenly, her father blinked, turning his attention toward his wife. "Did you say something?"

Eliana's mother sighed. "I was wondering what you thought about Elizabeth and Zechariah's new baby. They said he's going to be a prophet."

He smiled. "First, he'll have to learn to stop drooling and filling his swaddling cloths."

When Eliana and her four-year-old brother giggled, their mother shot them a look. Their mother had wanted an abundance of children, but God had given them only two—five years apart. Her mother was sad about this pitiful number, but her father said two was good. Only two were in the Garden of Eden, and animals entered two by two into the Ark.

Eliana watched as her father slathered more honey on his bread, using his knife—a large, wicked-looking blade. He noticed where her eyes had fallen. "Do not worry, my dove. I cleaned it thoroughly."

Leaning over, her father dribbled honey onto her bread and grinned. As he spread the last bit of honey on her bread, she wondered when he would leave them next, disappearing for days. Sadness dragged her down like heavy chains.

Closing her eyes, Eliana forced her mind toward comforting memories, like when they would walk in the fields together. Her father would take her by the hands and spin her around and around until she was too dizzy to stand straight. Those were the times when his protective spirit was strongest.

The meal was a lazy ending to an eventful day. Everyone was talking about Elizabeth and Zechariah and their newborn boy.

"I was shocked that Elizabeth announced they were naming the child John," said Eliana's mother. "No one in their family carries that name."

Eliana's father shrugged. "It is the father's choice. And Zechariah made it known that the child would be named John."

It was true. From what Eliana learned, poor mute Zechariah had motioned for a writing tablet, and then he wrote down those astonishing words: "His name is John."

But even more remarkable, Zechariah suddenly spoke for the first time since the day in the Temple when he lost his voice. He said their newborn son, John, would someday be a prophet and that he would prepare the way for the Lord, who would save us from our enemies.

"Abba, do you believe what he says about the baby John?" Eliana asked.

"All I know is we cannot wait twenty years for John to grow up and prepare a pathway for God to destroy the Romans." Her father waved his knife in the air. "This blade is sharp enough to clear a path right now." He laughed as he sliced into another chunk of barley bread.

Her mother sighed and glanced at Eliana, who shoved a large piece of bread in her mouth. "Eat slowly, Eliana. You don't want to choke."

Once the sun had gone, Eliana asked to sleep under the stars. With her parents' approval, she set her mat on their home's flat roof and lay on her back, staring up at the night sky. She marveled at the changing starscape, searching for the familiar shapes that people talked about.

Eliana squinted, trying to make out the lion. Pointing her finger, she traced the picture in the stars. She located the brightest star, the lion's heart, and sighed.

Eliana and Asaph once looked at the stars together; their parents would have been furious if they had known. She hadn't seen much of him lately, for Asaph had changed on the day he beat Zuriel. He seemed to enjoy his newfound power as other boys came to fear him. Her friendship with him was a dying vine.

Eliana tried to befriend a group of girls, but they wouldn't have her. They accused her of having a strange family, with an absent father who didn't have a normal occupation, like a carpenter or farmer. They treated her as one who was unclean.

Sighing, she refocused her eyes and sketched the lion in her mind. But she hadn't gotten very far when she heard a scuffling noise. She shot up, thinking it might be a wild dog. She leaned over the roof's edge, picking up movement in the narrow street leading to their home. A man began pounding on their door and hissing, "Open up. Judah, open up. Judah, open the door..."

She looked down as the door opened, and her father's voice sounded.

"What are you doing here at this time of night, Melech?"

"You must flee," Melech said.

"What has happened?"

"Take your family and run. You are all in danger."

"What has happened?"

"You have been discovered."

"By who?"

"I don't know, but the Romans are coming. If they find you, they will crucify you!"

The word "crucify" ran through Eliana like a spear.

"How can you be sure they are coming for me?" her father asked Melech.

"I saw them with my eyes, camped not far from the town. They plan to come in the night. You must leave now. All of you!"

Eliana's eyes adjusted to the dark as her mother appeared behind her father.

"Gather the children. We leave right now," her father said.

"Judah, what have you done?"

"This is no time to speak. We must act. *Now.*"

The next thing Eliana knew, she was being bundled onto the back of their donkey, along with her drowsy brother, and they were heading out of the town gate, their few possessions jammed inside a sack. They did not have an extended family, a *bet 'ab*, in the village, so it was only their small unit on the run.

As they passed the sundial in the town square, her father paused to stare at the stone slab. Suddenly, he picked up a large rock and smashed the gnomon, the piece sticking up from the sundial. Then they disappeared through the gate and into the Judean hill country.

Just like that, Eliana's life had been turned upside down faster than a star could shoot across the sky. Rocking back and forth on the donkey, she looked back at their small town, barely visible in the night. It disappeared into the darkness like a pebble, slowly fading as it sank into the black water of a deep well.

ASAPH

The man was huge, but that was typical for Roman legionnaires. The army recruited men who stood a full head taller than most. Several massive soldiers blocked any view of what was happening inside the home of Asaph's neighbor, a man named Melech.

As a crowd gathered around the house, they were being held at bay by about a dozen Roman soldiers. One soldier was so close that if Asaph dared, he could reach out from the crowd and touch the man's short sword strapped to his right side. The sword's grip was ivory, and the tip of the scabbard was gold with the image of an eagle. On the soldier's left side was the *pugio*, a dagger. He had heard that Roman double-edged blades were as sharp as lion claws.

Asaph looked up, and his heart skipped a beat when he realized the Roman legionnaire was staring down at him. The soldier grinned, pulled out the dagger, and held it close to Asaph's left cheek.

"Go ahead. Touch it if you like."

Asaph wondered if the man was teasing him. He started to obey but then pulled back, his heart pounding double-time.

The soldier leaned a little closer. "Touch the blade, boy. It won't hurt unless it touches you first."

Was that a threat? Carefully, Asaph put two fingers on the glimmering slice of silver, running his fingers down the cold, flat surface of the blade.

The legionnaire put away his knife and tousled Asaph's hair before returning his attention to Melech's home. Asaph couldn't see what was happening inside the house, but he heard a fist hitting flesh and the grunt of the unfortunate man, Melech. From inside, Melech's wife, Ruth, wept.

Asaph wondered if their children were also in there, witnessing his beating. It was the Roman way.

Then he thought he heard the muffled word "crucify" come from inside the house moments before a woman's scream. Suddenly agitated, the crowd muttered and shuffled about. Anger radiated from the men behind him like the heat of a fire. The Roman soldiers reached for their swords and moved into defensive positions.

Asaph knew Melech's children and was friends with the eldest, Bedad. He stretched high to see if he could catch sight of his friend as he recalled how King Herod had once put down a rebellion by crucifying six hundred Jewish men in one day, murdering their families at the foot of each cross.

Please let Melech's children be spared. Asaph stared up at the morning sky.

He still didn't know what Melech had done to stir up the wrath of Rome. He only knew that soldiers had arrived in the middle of the night and were hunting for Eliana's father.

Thankfully, Eliana and her family had disappeared like mist. If they hadn't, this commotion might have been happening outside *their* home, and he would be praying that the soldiers wouldn't kill Eliana at the foot of the cross.

The Roman soldiers pushed the crowd back, creating a pathway. Then Asaph saw Melech shoved through the door with his hands bound by cords. Blood streamed down his forehead, covering most of his face, and his right eye was already swelling so severe that it almost concealed his entire eyeball with purple, blood-gorged skin. When Asaph had beaten Zuriel, he had given the boy two black eyes, but nothing like this.

Melech was a friend of Eliana's family, but what had he done to deserve this punishment? Had he conspired with Eliana's father, who hated Romans? Asaph was afraid the Romans might start questioning *him* since he was a friend of Eliana, but a strange fascination kept him from fleeing the scene.

He followed the crowd as it flowed toward the town gate, moving in the wake of the soldiers and the condemned man. He noticed that someone had broken off a piece of the sundial in the town square.

Several women howled with grief as soldiers used the butt of their swords to strike some of the Jewish men to keep them passive.

The soldiers began to assemble a makeshift cross outside the town gate. Asaph shivered as they chose his favorite tree—the sycamore—to construct the base.

A large city like Jerusalem always had vertical beams set in place outside the city gates, ready for the next crucifixion. But in a small Judean town like this one, they had to make do with the nearest tree. One of the soldiers dragged a crossbeam out of the town—stolen from the local carpenter—and hammered it onto the tree trunk, creating the horizontal beam.

Asaph was sandwiched between two Jewish men, who didn't even seem to notice the ten-year-old in their midst. Asaph sensed their powerlessness and rage. He, too, once felt the same powerlessness in the presence of boys like Zuriel. But no more. He had fought back and won.

He straightened his back and stared daggers at these men, who were not battling back. They should at least try to help Melech! But they were all sheep, bleating sheep, like animals tied to posts in the Temple every day, waiting to be slaughtered. The soldiers, on the other hand, were lions. They were large, they were ferocious, and they were obeyed.

Asaph searched for his father, a shepherd, but he was nowhere in sight. His father would be furious to know he had come to watch the crucifixion. His father was more sheep than shepherd and didn't have the nerve to come close to these Roman soldiers.

At that moment, Asaph decided that as he got older, he would become a lion. Anything but a meek lamb. He would *not* follow in his father's footsteps, that much he vowed.

The Romans shoved Melech against the tree, facing the people. Although women were crucified facing away from the crowd, men had to stare their tormentors in the eyes. He watched with fascination as the Romans raised Melech, his arms draped over the back of the crossbeam and tied into place.

A soldier, mallet in hand, positioned the man's feet a hand's-breadth apart and drove in the nails through the sides of his ankles and into the flesh of the tree. When Melech didn't cry out, Asaph held his breath, astounded. He decided he would never climb this tree again. He wouldn't even step into the shadow of the sycamore. It was cursed by blood.

A man standing next to him bowed his head, his lips moving. The man was praying when he should be pulling out a knife and rushing these soldiers. *Such weakness!*

For one wild moment, he wished he had been born a Roman.

He watched, open-mouthed, as Melech struggled to push himself higher against the tree to ease his breathing. But then the man sagged back down and began to choke, making pitiful gurgling sounds. It was as if all the men of the village were as helpless as Melech, with their cowardice raised on a cross for everyone to see.

Soon, most of the Jewish men returned home, leaving only a few weeping women. This death would take a long time, and the Law forbade dead bodies from hanging through the night. If death didn't come before then, the soldiers would break his legs, which hurried asphyxiation, or they would drive a spear into his side.

Disgusted, Asaph turned and strode back to the town. He had seen enough. He had seen too much.

2

LUKE, CHAPTER 2

JEREMIEL: JERUSALEM

IT WAS JUST A small fire.

Jeremiel's wife, Martha, was saying the Sabbath prayers in their upper room when it happened. She moved her hands over the Sabbath oil lamp, drawing them in over the flames and creating a slight breeze. One pass of the hands. Two passes.

On the third pass, she nudged the lamp's handle. Just a nudge. But that was all it took to topple the lamp sideways, spilling hot oil and sending flames leaping from candle to cloth.

"Foolish woman!" Jeremiel burst.

When his wife moved to grab a nearby blanket to smother the flames, Jeremiel latched onto her arm. "Don't make this worse."

"But I—"

"Don't. It's the Sabbath."

Jeremiel released her and turned toward the flames, mesmerized as the fire advanced across the table, swallowing the linen stitch by stitch. Martha slunk back into the shadows, her face lit by flickers.

"Are you sure you cannot put it out?" Her voice was almost a whisper.

Jeremiel sighed. "You know we cannot."

When twilight had descended, and the first star appeared in the evening sky, the *hazzan* had blown the trumpet to signal the start of the Sabbath—two notes played three times. All work must cease on the second pair of notes, including the extinguishing of fires.

"Please, Jeremiel...the fire is so small."

"All work must cease on the Sabbath."

Jeremiel glanced over his shoulder at his wife, who used her eyes to urge him to listen to her. But Jeremiel was a priest, and he could do no such thing. Not on the day of rest.

"No one would know," said Martha, like Eve offering the fruit.

"Better an entire city should burn than break the Sabbath."

"But if lives are in danger..."

"We are not at risk—only our house is threatened."

The oral Law said you could put out a fire on the Sabbath if lives were at stake—but not to prevent property loss.

"Your father made that table." Martha's eyes locked on the flames and the blackening cloth.

"My father would understand."

His father had been a devout Pharisee, and his greatest desire was to see his son become a priest at the Temple—a priest who meticulously followed the Law, both the written and oral Torah.

Jeremiel turned away from Martha, watching the flame dance across the table and devour most of the cloth. The shimmering glow bounced off the stone walls. Above was the vulnerable roof, with its three layers—cypress beams covered by an interwoven mesh of twigs, topped by a packed-down layer of clay. The beams and mesh made good food for fire.

Please, Lord, let our house survive.

Their dwelling was a simple, four-room structure with shared exterior walls in the crowded city of Jerusalem. Jeremiel's extended family occupied several adjoining houses, all surrounded by a wall that enclosed their *bet 'ab*. He wondered if any of his brothers could smell the smoke and would come running over to fight the fire.

"Perhaps you can ask your brother Barnabas to put out the flame," his wife said as if reading Jeremiel's mind.

Yet another temptation. Martha was well aware that he could not ask another Jew to put out the fire.

The cloth curled inward, blackening into ash and smoke. Maybe the heat would not be intense enough to consume the table, the home's prize possession. The breeze caught a few fire-flecked ashes and carried them through the open window like glowing insects. The smell of burnt fabric stung his nose as sweat pooled on the back of his neck.

There were ways to extinguish a fire indirectly without breaking the Sabbath. Building barriers using water-filled containers was permissible to prevent the fire from spreading. But would that…?

"Out of the way, out of the way!"

Jeremiel spun to find his friend Nekoda climbing the ladder to their upper room. What was he doing here at this time of the evening?

Nekoda darted for the blanket, but Jeremiel leaped into his path, and the two men butted chests, their faces close.

"I said out of the way!" Nekoda tried to sidestep him.

"You cannot put out a fire on the Sabbath!" Jeremiel reached for his arm.

"Maybe *you* can't, but I can!"

Nekoda was also a priest, but he was a Sadducee, not a Pharisee, and his devotion to the Law did not burn as fiercely.

"This is my house, Nekoda!"

"And you need to preserve it! Do it for your wife's sake!"

How dare he! Jeremiel's eyes glowered with challenge, but Nekoda was taller and shoved him aside, snagging the blanket so fiercely that Jeremiel almost lost his balance.

When Jeremiel found his footing, he charged, latching onto the blanket and holding on like a wolf gripping the leg of a lamb.

"Don't be a fool, Jeremiel!"

Nekoda and Jeremiel tugged on opposite ends until the cloth started to slip from Jeremiel's grip, burning his palms. He squeezed all the tighter. Nekoda tried swinging him around, making him stumble, but he held firm. Behind Nekoda, an orange glow swelled. Soon, a blanket would be useless for battling the blaze.

Martha screamed.

As Nekoda backed up, he nearly set the loose folds of his robe ablaze. He hopped to the side and gave such a tug that the blanket tore. Jeremiel stumbled, pushing from the wall to keep from smashing his face against limestone. Nekoda ripped the blanket free in that instant, moments before throwing it over the flames.

Jeremiel made a move to charge again, but it was too late. Nekoda had already smothered the fire and broken the Sabbath. A cloud of smoke, like incense, filled the house, and Martha hurried down the ladder to the first floor, coughing.

Once the smoke cleared, Jeremiel and Nekoda glared at each other, panting like Greek wrestlers. Jeremiel pointed a finger, his hand shaking. "You had no right to barge into my house and break the Sabbath!"

"I just saved your house from fire, you fool!"

"A person who extinguishes a fire on the Sabbath is liable."

Nekoda just shook his head as he looked down at Martha, who had reentered the house, watching from the lower floor. Jeremiel sensed from her eyes that she approved of what Nekoda had done. That was the worst insult of all.

"Stupid Pharisee!" Nekoda tossed the scorched blanket on the floor, stormed down the ladder, and exited the house hotter than any flame.

ELIANA

Eliana's family moved across the brown, barren landscape. By this time, they were just west of the Dead Sea, a body of water so briny that nothing could live there. Even the land seemed dead, with little vegetation to conceal them. However, the hills of the oasis, En Gedi, were pocked with caves—great places for the family to hide.

They moved at night and slept in the caves by day to avoid detection by Roman soldiers. They were like nocturnal animals. At least, that's what it seemed like to Eliana. They had no home, no community, and no synagogue. Her father hunted at night, like the jackals that thrive in darkness.

But Eliana did not thrive in darkness. She loved staring at the star-swarmed sky when they lived in the village. But in the wilderness, that same darkness, that same sky, terrified her.

This morning, the sun was beginning to peek over the eastern horizon, so Eliana and her family hurried to a cave, where they moved deep into the shadows to sleep.

Darkness was always with them—inside a cave by day and surrounding them by night when they were on the move. Eliana's entire life had become an unending veil of cover. She wondered if she'd ever see broad daylight again.

To keep her company in the gloom, Eliana had created an invisible friend she named "Calev," which means both "dog" and "like a heart." She chose the name because she was inspired by her mother's story about the shaping of the human heart. Her mother pointed at a rock etched by the flow of water and said that if something soft like water could shape a stone, then the Word of God, which is fire, can create an even deeper impression in our hearts.

She pictured Calev as a strong young man who protected her heart and gave her courage. She sensed his presence by her side in the darkness and often conversed with him. Her father once overheard her and commanded her to stop, ordering her to live in the real world.

"I can't sleep," Eliana whispered to Calev as she adjusted on her stone bed. Her parents and younger brother breathed heavily—sound asleep in the cave's shadows.

"Then go for a walk," said Calev. "Go out into the light."

"I can't. Too dangerous. The Romans will see me."

"They gave up chasing your family many days ago," Calev said. "Move into the light."

Yawning, Eliana stood up, stretched her legs, and wandered toward the cave's entrance, which formed a bright circle. It was so tempting. Because En Gedi was an oasis, she could see a few lush trees in the sun framed by the cave's entrance. Out of nowhere, a deer wandered in front of the cave and just stood there, staring into the mouth of the cavern as if beckoning her.

Wide-eyed, Eliana stepped closer, but the deer was not startled. It remained in a halo of intense morning light.

"The deer is waiting for you." Calev's soft voice danced through the air.

Eliana was drawn closer and closer to the cave opening. Because she didn't make a sound in her bare feet, the deer stood statue-still. The only sign of life was a slight twitch of its ears.

Eliana moved within eight cubits, about the length of two men, and still, the deer stared back at her, unblinking. Was it sending a message telling her it was safe to step into the light?

Before she could contemplate further, the deer bolted, vanishing into the morning light. It happened so fast that Eliana thought at first it had been a ghost all along. But deer scamper when startled.

It was then that Eliana heard the sudden sound of men and hurled herself to the side, ducking behind a massive rock near the mouth of the cave.

"It's a hot one today," one of them said, speaking Latin.

A Roman.

Eliana knew Latin, although her father never allowed the Roman language in his house.

"Shall we cool off in this cave?"

"Good idea."

No, Eliana thought. *Not this cave.*

Were they ordinary Roman citizens, or could they be soldiers? She pressed flat against the rock, the only thing separating her from the men. Then she peeked around its edge.

The flash of gold armor and the red of a cape told her they were Roman soldiers. Her heart dropped. Their family had been discovered.

She shrunk back, closing her eyes as their voices moved further into the cave, their armor clanking. Sweat pooled down her back against the cool stone. She held her breath, not daring to move. Like the deer, she stood statue-still.

"Wonder how far back this cave goes," said one of the soldiers. "You think this could be a hiding place for Zealots?"

"Who knows? The area is riddled with caves. I heard that the old Israelite king, David, hid in them while being chased by a rival king named Saul."

"How do you know so much about Hebrews?"

"It helps to know the people you're hunting. If you want to catch Zealots, you must know their minds."

"I hunt wild pigs well enough without thinking like a pig."

The other soldier laughed. "Who says you don't?"

"Funny."

"Let's investigate. It'll cool the deeper we go."

Eliana's mind raced. She had to do something to draw their attention away from the cave's interior—maybe throw a rock, create a disturbance. She scoured the cave's floor for stones.

Then: a miracle.

Peering around the rock, she saw the deer reappear at the entrance. The men swung around at the sound, and one of the soldiers hurled his spear at the animal. Pulling back, Eliana squeezed her eyes shut.

"Good throw, Lepidus!"

Hearing the animal's anguished cry, Eliana envisioned the deer sprawled out on the ground, bleeding into the soil.

As she opened her eyes, she heard the men chattering about their next feast. One of them said he'd carry the animal, grunting as he heaved the animal over his shoulders. Then they trudged off, carrying their trophy back to their camp, wherever it might be.

Eliana poked her head around the rock, eying the fresh blood where the deer once stood and died. Her heart filled with regret, yet her family was alive because of its sacrifice. The soldiers were probably too busy thinking about cooking the animal over a fire to care about tracking Zealots on the run.

She hurried back into darkness, where her family continued to sleep—oblivious to the danger that had swept by their cave like the Angel of Death on Passover night.

JEREMIEL

The next morning, while it was still dark, Jeremiel rose from his mat, which he had laid on the roof. He liked to sleep under the stars on beautiful nights, but especially last night, with the smell of smoke so strong. The roof was flat and fine for sleeping, slanted just enough for water to drain into a barrel below. In a dry country, every drop was precious.

He rubbed the drowsiness out of his eyes. Sleep was a sixth-part death, say the rabbis, but this morning he felt at least a half-part dead to the world.

Climbing from the roof, he found his wife praying in the dark. The day before, she had prepared rounds of bread for the Sabbath meals, but he would be fasting through the morning, so he ignored the food on the burnt table.

When he leaned over to kiss Martha on the forehead, she said nothing. He sighed, wondering when she would speak to him again. She had said little since the fire the night before.

Jeremiel strapped a phylactery to his forehead, saying the blessing as he did. The phylactery, a little leather box, stuck out from his forehead like a lopped-off horn. Inside it were passages from Exodus and Deuteronomy, a constant reminder of God's wondrous deeds. He wrapped a second phylactery around his left arm and stepped into the dark street to meet the new morning.

Jerusalem was coming to life as he made his way from their home, west of the Siloam Pool by the city's southern wall. With Sabbath lights sparkling like stars all around him, worshippers streamed north toward the Temple—a glorious, massive structure. When the sun came out, the light reflected gold on the pure white stone of the Temple. For now, it was shrouded in shadows, and the sun hovered below the horizon.

"*Shalom aleichem*," called out Nekoda, who met him on many days walking to the morning sacrifice.

After what had happened the evening before, he didn't expect his friend to greet him, but he should have known better. Whenever they argued, Nekoda had a knack for forgetting, only hours later, that the conflict ever happened. But Jeremiel never forgot. The tension would remain bottled up in him for days, like an unruly prisoner.

Like many Sadducees, Nekoda came from a wealthy family in the Upper City of Jerusalem, close to the seat of power. The only reason they knew each other was that Nekoda's father did business at a market stall once operated by Jeremiel's father.

Jeremiel ignored Nekoda's greeting, not even looking at him. Still, he could hear his friend's footsteps behind him.

"Jeremiel, I know you want me to apologize for last night, but I would do it again."

Jeremiel wheeled around and shot out a finger, his jaw clenching. "You invaded my house and broke the Sabbath."

"But I did it for your sake—and Martha's. I am the one who broke the Sabbath, not you. Your purity remains."

"But it was my house!"

"It wouldn't have remained your house for long if that roof had caught fire."

Jeremiel rubbed the back of his head. "You dishonored me before my wife."

"Your devotion to the law borders on suicidal."

Jeremiel put up a hand. "Please. No lectures today."

When he walked away, Nekoda followed in silence.

The two men were a study in contrasts. Jeremiel was stocky and barrel-chested, Nekoda tall and lanky. Jeremiel had a thick, black, curly head of hair; Nekoda's was already thinning, even though he had just turned twenty.

As they passed through the colonnade, merchants opened their shops along the *stoa* and cluttered the pathway with tables overflowing with fruits and vegetables. Jeremiel glowered at the *agoranomos*, who ensured that shopkeepers used fair weights to measure out foodstuffs, even checking the quality of food and drinks.

"Gentile inspectors!" Jeremiel groused.

"On that, we can agree." Nekoda patted Jeremiel's shoulder. He had an annoying habit of doing that whenever driving home a point. "That Gentile inspector can ruin an entire barrel of wine with his impurity."

They passed through the Valley Gate, taking them into the oldest section of the city, which led north to the imposing Temple grounds. Jeremiel hated King Herod, but at least he had poured money into the Temple. Herod was a builder on a massive scale.

However, not all of the construction was good. Jeremiel abruptly stopped, noticing that construction had progressed on the Asclepion—a pagan place of healing dedicated to the god Asclepius. He narrowed his eyes as they adjusted to the dark. A woman wearing heavy makeup, much like an Egyptian, stood in the doorway holding two snakes.

"Do not even look," said Nekoda. Two more pats on the shoulder. "People who believe in the healing power of snakes are not worthy of our attention."

But Jeremiel continued to stare at the pagan with her serpents, the impurity drifting around him like currents of smoke.

"Herod should not allow this, especially so close to the Temple." Jeremiel finally turned away from the indelible image.

"I do not like it any more than you," said Nekoda, "but there is nothing we can do."

"Of course, there is much we can do."

Nekoda leaned closer. "Do not even speak it, my friend. Be pleased the Romans allow us to worship as we wish. This is not a fight we want to pick."

Jeremiel turned to face his friend squarely. "*We* do not pick our fights. God chooses them for us."

"Then perhaps God does not want us to fight a war with the Romans—a war we cannot win."

"*Perhaps*? Why is everything 'perhaps' to you? Why do you not *know* anything with certainty?"

"I know many things with certainty." But Nekoda conveniently offered no examples, and the conversation staggered into silence.

After safely passing the pagan temple, Jeremiel finally spoke what was on his mind. "Why did you even come to our house last night?"

Nekoda reached into the folds of his robe, pulling out a brand-new phylactery—a small, square box. He grinned and pointed at Jeremiel's forehead. "Your old phylactery looks like it is about to split open like an egg, so I thought you might like a new one. I was planning to give it to you last night as my gift."

Jeremiel stared, open-mouthed, at the beautiful black box. Its quality was a reminder that his friend was much wealthier. Still, Jeremiel couldn't argue that he needed a new phylactery, and this one was exquisite.

He plucked the box from Nekoda's hands.

"Everything has been done properly." Nekoda tucked his chin to hide a smile.

"It is made with twelve stitches?"

"Using threads from the veins of clean animals."

Without warning, Jeremiel's face lit up. "Thank you, Nekoda."

Nekoda beamed. "May this gift remind you that our friendship cannot be broken, even by disagreements, though they be many."

Embarrassed, Jeremiel diverted his eyes and turned on his heels. "Come, we will be late." Nekoda made it very hard to dislike him.

ELIANA: MONTH OF ELUL (EARLY SEPTEMBER), 5 B.C.

Eliana crouched behind a rock and listened to the piercing cry, the voice echoing across the land. By this time, she could distinguish it from the voices of other shepherds in the region.

She peeked above the boulder. In the distance, an army of sheep was scattered across the sun-drenched land. Just as she guessed, she spotted Noach, one of the shepherds. She wasn't the only one who knew his distinctive cry. So did his sheep, which turned to his call.

She loved to spend her mornings exploring the hilly country outside of Bethlehem, and she promised her parents she wouldn't wander too far from the cave where they had been holed up. She missed the bustle of town and a normal home, but she loved the freedom in these hills.

Once they settled in the caves near Bethlehem, her father finally allowed her to wander outside in the daylight. He figured that by now, they were no longer being pursued. Life in the hills had almost become ordinary. She even ventured into Bethlehem to experience the familiar surroundings of a small town.

Rising to her feet, Eliana sprinted down the hill. She no longer had Asaph to run with, so she raced her invisible friend, Calev.

"You're too slow!" Eliana said to the invisible friend as she leaped over a stone and raced down a hill toward Noach. The shepherd boy, six years older than her, looked in her direction and waved.

"Shalom!" Eliana called out as she neared Noach, whose name meant "tranquility." It fit him like a sandal because he was a quiet, peaceful boy.

However, he was anything but tranquil this morning. Eliana found him grinning and moving among the sheep with the uncontainable energy of a sheepdog.

Noach was lean and tall, and his hair was matted and cluttered with twigs from sleeping on the ground—as if he carried a bird's nest on his head like a crown. His cheeks were red from the wind that whistled through the hills, and he sniffed constantly. Surrounding him were hundreds of sheep, which the shepherds raised for sacrifice in the Temple in Jerusalem.

"Shalom, Eliana!" Noach tried to contain the grin that split his face.

"You seem happy this morning," said Eliana. She had struck up a friendship with several shepherds in the region near Bethlehem, but Noach was her favorite. Some of the older shepherds usually chased her away like a stray dog, but Noach was always welcoming.

"I *am* happy." He shifted his staff from hand to hand.

Crouching, Eliana petted one of the sheep, noticing its tail had been fastened to its leg to keep it from straying. She waited for Noach to explain his giddiness. Instead, he just leaned on his staff, smiling wide.

"And why are you so happy this morning?" she asked.

He shrugged. "Gidon said not to tell."

"Tell what?"

"If I told you, that would be telling."

Gidon, one of the old shepherds, didn't hide his dislike of her.

Eliana looked up the hill toward Bethlehem, nestled near the ridge road running between Jerusalem and Hebron. "Any signs of brigands last night?" The shepherds had been on the lookout for reported robbers after their sheep.

Noach's smile vanished. "Forget the robbers. Aren't you going to ask me again why I'm smiling?"

"Why should I ask? Gidon said not to tell, and you must obey your master at all times."

She knew this would rile up Noach, who was obviously itching to tell her his secret. If she ignored him, he would want to scratch that itch even more.

"Gidon is *not* my master."

Eliana looked up from the sheep, batting her eyes. "Oh. I always assumed he was. When did he give you your freedom?"

Noach frowned, drawing a line in the dirt with the tip of his staff. When he made eye contact, his gaze was filled with fury. "He's *never* been my master, and I've never been his slave!"

"Except when he tells you to keep secrets?" She pursed her lips, biting back the laugh that teased at the base of her throat.

Noach pounded his staff on the ground. "If I want to tell you about the angels, I will!"

His voice echoed off the hills. Eliana's brow furrowed as she straightened, standing tall. This was not the kind of secret she expected.

"Angels?"

Noach stepped on a rock and balanced using his staff. Once he steadied himself, he shot her a satisfied grin. His two crooked front teeth wrestled over the space in his mouth like Jacob and Esau in the womb.

"We saw angels last night."

Eliana stared at him in wonder. Was he teasing? No, he wasn't one to joke like this.

"Why would angels appear to you?" She didn't say what she was really thinking: *Why would angels appear before a huddle of dirty old shepherds?*

Noach shrugged. "They told us the Christ was born." He turned and pointed at the little town up the hill. "They told us we would find the Messiah in Bethlehem."

Maybe he was pulling her leg. "This isn't funny, Noach."

"I'm not trying to be funny. I swear to this. I swear by the altar."

Eliana stared at him. The only sound between them was the bleating of sheep and the whistle of the wind. While she knew Noach would never swear by the altar lightly, she began to wonder if her friend had lost his mind. That could happen when you spend most of the year outdoors with sheep.

"Did all of you see these angels?"

"Yes, just ask Gidon." Noach scratched his head, adding, "No, don't ask Gidon. He'll be angry I told you."

"When did these angels speak to you?"

"Last night. They said our Savior's been born, and we would find him, a baby, wrapped in swaddling clothes in a manger."

Insanity. He would seriously have her believe the Messiah was a baby and could be found in a nearby clay trough from which animals eat grain?

"Do you really think angels spoke to you?" Eliana crossed her arms.

Noach looked hurt, as if she had slapped him. "I'm not lying. If you go to Bethlehem, you can see for yourself." He pointed up the slope toward the town. "I'm not lying, and I'm not crazy."

"But are you sure they were angels? Maybe you just saw the star we've been seeing."

Like everyone, Eliana was aware of the new star in the heavens, bigger and brighter than any she had ever seen. Even more brilliant than the one at the heart of Leo, the lion.

"Stars do not talk." Noach raised a brow. "I know what we saw. The Messiah is in the cave behind the first house on the left. See for yourself."

"I will."

She continued to stare at Noach, who had lost his big grin and looked upset that she questioned his sanity.

"Noach, I do not think you lost your mind." She sighed, trying to make it seem she believed him. Her words soothed him, and his smile returned, a small smile but a look of happiness just the same.

"Go to Bethlehem and see for yourself," he repeated at her back as Eliana climbed the hill leading up to the town. "But don't tell Gidon that I told you!" he added just before she was out of earshot.

Eliana's legs burned when she finally reached the crest of the hill and was on level ground, entering Bethlehem by way of the single main road. The town was bursting at the seams due to a census. By Roman decree, citizens had returned to the towns of their fathers—in this case, the town of David—to be counted.

Her father said the emperor Augustus gave this order because the incoming taxes didn't match the number of people he ruled. So, the Romans would count every head to ensure they were milking everyone for money.

In Bethlehem, she found many people sleeping outside—some curled up against the houses as protection from the wind. Children ran around laughing, and mothers prepared food on open fires. The smell of smoke and animal stink was thick because most families traveling to Bethlehem had come on donkeys.

She found the house that Noach had mentioned, with a cave just behind it. The land around Bethlehem was honeycombed with caves, but this had to be the one he was referring to.

"Do you think it's true about the Messiah?" she asked her invisible friend, Calev. She was certain she heard him whisper, "It is *not* true."

She came to a stop and turned to face her invisible friend.

"Why would you say that?"

"The Messiah will not come as a baby," said Calev. "How can a baby save the world?"

"But how else would you expect the Messiah to come into our world? Do you expect him to be born as a fully grown warrior? That would be a difficult birth."

Calev started to argue with her, but she waved him off and continued forward. She noticed a man crouching in front of a fire by the cave, breaking bread into several pieces and placing them on a cloth next to some dried figs. He looked up and smiled, his warm eyes capturing hers. Something about him was special.

"Shalom," he said.

"Shalom."

He looked down at his meager serving of bread and figs and stared back at her, motioning at his food. "Are you hungry, little one?"

Eliana didn't like being called a "little one" but didn't say anything. She nodded and peered over the man's shoulder into the mouth of the cave, where a baby's gurgling sound came from the darkness. When she returned her gaze to the man, he was still smiling. He handed her a fig, and she bit into it, savoring its sugar.

"Thank you," she said, and he nodded and smiled again. "I talked to a shepherd this morning," she added, uncomfortable with his silence.

"Ah! We had several shepherds visit us in the night."

So, at least that part of the story was true.

Rising on her tiptoes, Eliana tried again to gaze into the black opening of the cave, but she could see nothing.

"Would you like to see our newborn child?" asked the man before taking a bite of the bread.

Eliana swallowed the last of her dried fig, wishing it was enough to fill her belly, and nodded.

The man grunted as he stood and motioned for her to follow. Eliana's heart skipped a beat, and she wondered why she was scared. What was there to fear? This was just a couple and their baby.

As she moved into the cave, she noticed several donkeys, a cow, and a few sheep. In the back, against a wall, sat the mother, her face hidden by shadow.

"We have a visitor." The man turned toward Eliana. "Her name is..." He waited for her to fill in the pause.

"My name is Eliana."

"Welcome, Eliana. I am Joseph, and this is my wife, Mary."

As the woman looked up, Eliana saw her features clearly, and she stifled a gasp with a hand to her mouth. She was the same woman from Elizabeth and Zechariah's courtyard—the one who spoke of her son who would bring down rulers from their thrones!

Mary's eyes crinkled as they filled with recognition. "I know you."

Eliana nodded, taking a small step forward, unsure of what to say. She stared at their child, wrapped tightly in swaddling clothes, just as Noach had said. The swaddling clothes covered the baby like a cocoon, revealing only his face. The clothes kept him immobilized and protected, allowing him to grow without deformity.

Without deformity. Like Noach's sheep, Eliana thought. The ones without deformity were chosen for Temple sacrifices.

"He is beautiful." Eliana started to reach out but then pulled back.

"His name is Jesus." Mary nodded at her child. "You may touch him if you like."

Eliana ran the back of her fingers against the baby's cheek. The skin was so smooth, so new. She could smell the oil rubbed on his skin, along with salt.

Mary leaned over and handed her the child, nesting Jesus in Eliana's arms. His nose seemed small and fragile, his eyelashes delicate like feathers. His eyes sought her face. It didn't seem possible she could be holding the Savior in her arms.

"Is it true—about Jesus?" Eliana asked.

Mary nodded with understanding. "It is true."

Eliana sprinted back down the hill so fast that she almost lost control. Like Noach, she seemed powered by unworldly energy. After leaving the cave, she wanted to announce to everyone within earshot that she had just seen the Messiah, the Anointed One. Leaping onto a boulder and pushing off, she launched into the air and sprinted down the slope. Breathless, she found Noach sitting on a rock, chewing on a piece of bread from his pouch.

"Did you see the child?" he asked.

"I did."

"And do you believe?"

"I do."

Noach smiled and scratched his head, dislodging a twig that fell to his shoulder and bounced to the ground. "I knew you would."

She explained that not long ago, she had met the mother of Jesus in her hometown. She also related the strange tale of Zechariah and Elizabeth as Noach's eyes widened with wonder.

"Gidon would probably like to hear the story of Zechariah and Elizabeth and their baby boy. You must tell him."

Eliana fidgeted, shifting from foot to foot. "Gidon doesn't like me all that much. And won't he be upset you told me about the angels and the child?"

"Not if you have this story to tell. He might even appreciate you—for once."

Eliana couldn't pass up a chance to get on Gidon's good side, so Noach told her she could find the old man in the watchtower by the sheepfold. She strode toward the sheepfold, skipping every so often and stopping to examine the sheep, whose wool coats looked healthy and full.

As Eliana buried her hand in the sheep's wool, it dawned on her that she hadn't sensed her invisible friend, Calev, since she had left Bethlehem. But now she felt the tingle of his presence, and she looked over her shoulder, imagining him standing several feet behind her.

"Do you believe now?" she asked him.

"I do not."

"But I saw the child."

"And he's just a child. I've seen millions of children."

"Millions!" Eliana scoffed. "You *haven't* seen millions."

"I have."

How could that be? Calev was *her* imaginary friend, no one else's.

"Gidon is waiting for you," Calev said. "He's in the sheepfold. Don't you want to see him and tell him what you saw?"

"Why do you care? You don't believe what I saw."

Eliana marched toward the sheepfold, sensing Calev two steps behind. The sheepfold was bounded by large stone walls—too high for her to climb—so she entered by the narrow gate. The pen was crowded with sheep, dumb animals, all of them, yet there was no sign of Gidon. He must be in the watchtower.

Eliana almost envied these sheep. They had several protectors, while she hadn't felt safe since the day they fled from their town. Families shouldn't have to live on the run, hiding in caves.

The morning chill gave way to a warmer afternoon, so Eliana removed her cloak and slung it over her shoulder. Once she told Gidon her news, she would head home to help her mother prepare the evening meal. Her stomach rumbled at the thought.

She trudged up a slight incline to the watchtower, where the shepherds kept an eye out for jackals, wolves, and robbers. Usually, Gidon would be on the roof, keeping an eagle eye, but the top was desolate. She sensed something wasn't right, but Calev urged her on.

"Gidon might be in trouble," he whispered. "Go on. Enter."

The entrance to the squat tower was on the opposite side, so she worked her way around and called out Gidon's name. No answer. The door at the tower's base was slightly ajar, and she thought she heard movement but was afraid to go in. She took one step back.

"Go on," Calev said. "Enter."

She stepped forward, stopping at the threshold. Extending her arm, she shoved open the door just a little, and a shaft of light shot across the room. The light revealed Gidon slumped against the far wall. At first, she thought he might be asleep, but when she saw the trickle of blood on his forehead, she rushed inside.

Someone lurking behind the door snatched her in his arms before she could take two steps into the tower. His unbreakable grip made it impossible to squirm free as he lifted her up in mid-stride. She kicked midair, yelling, "Let me go!"

"What do we have here?" He clamped an arm around her waist, hoisting her against his side.

Eliana shivered.

Although it was dark, she saw several men moving about in the watchtower's dim interior. She kicked one in the face as he came close, but he cursed and grabbed her legs. Her father often warned her to be careful of brigands, but the robbers usually operated only at night, so she didn't think she had anything to fear by day. She tried to twist her way free as panic galloped through her body.

"Looks to me like a pretty little lamb. She might be as valuable to us as twelve sheep," said one man.

Eliana let out a piercing scream—as piercing as the shepherd's cry when trying to get the attention of their sheep.

A large, hairy hand clamped over her mouth. "Keep quiet, or I'll slit your throat."

At first, she thought it was the robber's voice speaking, but it sounded strangely like Calev. She could no longer tell the difference. Everything seemed unreal—so strange and terrifying, as reality slipped away like sand beneath her feet.

JEREMIEL: 12 YEARS LATER, 7 A.D., PASSOVER, NISAN 15 (APRIL)

Jeremiel tossed the *chametz* into the fire and watched it burn until nothing was left but ashes.

Chametz was leaven—a grain like wheat, barley, or rye that had contacted water and risen. When the Jews fled from slavery and the Pharaoh, they had to leave in such a hurry that they didn't have time to wait for their bread to rise, or leaven. So, every Passover, Jewish families across the city cleaned their houses of all leaven—a symbol of the corrupting influence of sin, which could spread throughout a person's soul like yeast.

Surrounding him on the dusty ground just outside their home in the Lower City of Jerusalem was the rest of his family—his two sons, daughter, and wife, Martha. The night before, they had held the traditional hunt for *chametz* with all the family in the *bet 'ab*—cousins, aunts, and uncles included. He led the search using a candle, and they scoured every nook and cranny in their homes for any of these small grains. This was Jeremiel's favorite time of the year—the fifteenth of Nisan. Passover.

As the last of the *chametz* blackened in the blaze, Jeremiel ended the ceremony with the traditional prayer.

"Any *chametz* or leaven that is in my possession which I have not seen and have not removed and do not know about should be annulled and become ownerless like the dust of the earth."

Today, the morning of Passover, Jeremiel would take the lamb to the Temple to be slaughtered. He had chosen the lamb just as the Law required—a yearling with no flaws. Jeremiel helped his oldest son, Adam, select the animal, explaining that even the tiniest discoloration, the smallest wound, or the slightest hint of disease would make it an unacceptable sacrifice.

"Have you kept our lamb free from blemish?" he asked Adam.

"Yes, Father, he is perfect."

Jeremiel nodded without giving a hint of approval. He was especially tough on his oldest son because he expected Adam to follow in his footsteps and become a priest. Although his son seemed to be on the right path, Jeremiel's heart nearly stopped when Adam wrote an entire sentence on parchment on the Sabbath a few weeks ago. He thought he had made it very clear they were allowed to write only *one* Hebrew letter on the Sabbath.

Jeremiel would have struck him for this offense if his son had not shown him how he had written the sentence—*with his foot*. Jeremiel was relieved, for Adam understood he was permitted to write more than one letter on the Sabbath only if done with his foot or mouth.

Jerusalem was never more crowded than on Passover. As Jeremiel carried the sacrificial lamb toward the Temple, he squeezed through a tight group of worshippers. He stepped around a man on his knees, kissing the dirt. People flocked from far and wide, and he could pick out those who didn't live in the city because they gawked at the walls and towers, mouths open wide enough for a sparrow to roost. There had to be over a hundred thousand people jammed into the noisy city.

Jeremiel entered the Temple Mount and moved into the Court of Gentiles, which teemed with people selling their wares. Noisy vendors sold animals for burnt offerings, with moneychangers on hand so people could exchange their coins for the pure silver Tyrian shekel needed to purchase sacrifices. He moved parallel to Solomon's Porch, heading for the inner courts, when he spotted Nekoda walking with his younger brother, Chaim, and some other Sadducees.

Jeremiel narrowed his eyes, bile rising in his throat.

While he was no longer shocked by what Nekoda did, he didn't think the man would actually wear a purple robe on Passover. *Purple!* The color was a symbol of Roman royalty. Purple was also the pinnacle of fashion, so some Sadducees displayed it like proud peacocks. Nekoda was now a member of the Sanhedrin, the Jews' highest court, and his cloak was scandalous.

Jeremiel looked himself over. His cloak was simple, with four long fringes made with blue thread, reminding him to obey the Law. He smoothed out the folds.

Jeremiel tried to avoid Nekoda whenever he could. He curled his fist and shook his head because his former friend had bought his way onto the Sanhedrin. Jeremiel thought he should have been chosen for the ruling council, not someone like Nekoda. With one last heated glance, he retreated into the crowd until Nekoda and his rich Sadducee friends had swept past.

He cradled the lamb in his arms, planning to have it slaughtered straightaway. But he stopped to observe a crowd of priests gathered beneath the roof of Solomon's Porch—a row of colonnades that ran along the eastern side of the Temple Mount. He recognized some of his friends surrounding a young boy who sat among the teachers.

He pressed forward, curious.

It wasn't unusual for a boy this age to ask questions of the teachers of the Law; it was good preparation for the *bar mitzvah* at age thirteen. But the teachers' faces told him this boy was making a remarkable impression. Moving closer, he heard the boy asking deep, probing questions. He, too, had wondered about some of the same things but was too timid to voice his questions aloud.

The boy seemed particularly interested in what his elders had to say about the kind of water that comes from springs or groundwater—"living water." People could be cleansed by immersing themselves in any body of water, but some impurities required living water from springs.

Jeremiel felt a tug of jealousy because his oldest son—Adam—would never ask such perceptive questions, even if he were age twenty.

Jeremiel would have liked to hear more, but a commotion arose just to his left, and as he spun, a small figure barreled into him, nearly knocking him off his feet. He almost dropped his lamb, but he caught the animal under the front legs to keep it from tumbling to the ground.

The petite woman who had charged into him didn't even look at him or apologize. Instead, she stared at the ground, more worried about what she had dropped than the fact she had just run pell-mell into a priest.

"Watch where you are going, woman!"

Still, she didn't make eye contact to acknowledge his anger. Instead, she muttered unintelligible words and flapped her hands as if trying to shake them free of water. That's when Jeremiel followed her gaze to the ground.

There, sprawled out on the stone, was a dead rat.

The woman scooped up the rat, cradling it like a house cat. Jeremiel's jaw dropped. Was she mad? Demon possessed?

"What do you think you are doing?" Jeremiel's voice rose. "How dare you carry such a thing on Temple grounds!"

He was sure that the unclean vermin touched his person and maybe even contacted the blemish-free sheep cradled in his arms.

"You have made me ritually unclean!"

Still, the woman would not even recognize his presence. She stared at the dead rat in her arms and ran her hand across its bloodstained fur. The rat had a bloody slash near its neck, where the wound had blackened. A flurry of buzzing flies hovered over it, occasionally landing and flitting on the wound.

Meanwhile, several people had gathered around them, although some hurried off when they spotted the rat. A rodent was so unclean that if one should climb into your bowl, you had to break the dish.

Jeremiel jabbed a finger in the woman's direction while addressing the crowd, his voice shaking. "Remove this woman here before she defiles anyone else!"

An older woman emerged from the crowd, slipping an arm around the disturbed young woman, who had yet to acknowledge him.

"Come, Eliana, we must take that thing beyond the Temple Mount." The older woman looked at her with pity.

Eliana looked up into the eyes of the older woman, utterly confused. "But this is my sacrifice."

That settled it. Jeremiel drew in a breath with a shake of his head. This Eliana was utterly mad—or jiggered by demons.

"I'm sorry, Eliana, but you know that is not an acceptable sacrifice," the other woman said. "The rat is the Father of Impurity."

"But this is not a rat."

The older woman drew her away, casting a sympathetic glance in Jeremiel's direction. "Come with me."

"But I tell you...It is my sacrifice!"

Jeremiel tightened his hold on his lamb and watched the two women in disbelief as they disappeared into the mix of people. A woman like that should be kept far from holy ground. She needed to be removed like *chametz* during Passover.

He looked at the glossy eyes of his once pure lamb and sighed, his face twisting with disgust. There was a good chance the rat had made direct contact with the white fleece of his sacrificial lamb—not to mention touched his robe. He would be unclean until evening.

Shaking his head, Jeremiel left the Temple and strode for home with the unclean lamb nestled in his arms. The impurity clung to him like flies.

3
LUKE, CHAPTER 3

SVESHTARI: NINETEEN YEARS LATER, MONTH OF AB (JULY), 26 A.D.

IT WAS NIGHT, AND Sveshtari faithfully kept to his post in the Fortress of Machaerus, perched high on a remote hill overlooking the Dead Sea to the west. He stood guard in the palace's peristyle courtyard, with colonnades running along three sides. Straightening his spine, he stood before two cedar doors, behind which was the tetrarch, Herod Antipas.

It was Sveshtari's job to protect Herod Antipas, son of King Herod the Great. As a Thracian bodyguard, Sveshtari had become an expert in detecting threats against Herod. The only person he could not protect him from was the tetrarch's wife, Herodias.

Herod and Herodias seemed genuinely smitten with each other. While Sveshtari could see that Herod liked to please her, the couple fought constantly. Herodias nipped at him, and he nipped back, reminding Sveshtari of the behavior among foxes. Vixens and male foxes nipped and yipped at each other, even during courtship. Sometimes, it was hard to tell whether the foxes were fighting or flirting. The same was true for Herod and his wife.

When one of the maidservants walked by with a sly smile, Sveshtari shifted from one foot to the next, dropping his gaze. He had been pudgy as a boy, so he never knew what to do with the sudden attention from women. He'd grown into a trim man with dark, shoulder-length hair and added muscle, but female gazes still made him uncomfortable.

Sveshtari, equipped for a fight, stood with a tall bronze helmet and a breastplate and backplate cinched around his waist. His baggy woolen trousers were tucked into leather riding boots, and his sword remained ready at his side.

Suddenly, Herod Antipas threw open the door and marched into the courtyard.

"We must wait until the time is right," the tetrarch said, the hint of irritation bleeding through his words. He turned to face his wife, Herodias, who emerged from their quarters after him.

"When will that time be?" Herodias spoke in a calm, controlled tone.

Both talked as if Sveshtari was invisible.

Herodias folded her arms with a lift of her chin. "It is not in our interest to wait for John the Baptist to rally every Jew in Judea against us before you act, my husband. But I am confident you are too wise to let that happen."

"If we kill John, people will rise up."

"Making him a martyr is not the only option. But I am sure you have weighed all the choices before you."

When Herodias moved toward her husband, Sveshtari breathed in her strong perfume.

"If you are suggesting that I imprison John, I am already considering it," Herod Antipas said. "But I do not wish to act rashly. I believe the people's love for him will soon die down. Then perhaps he too can die."

Sveshtari continued to face forward, but he caught sight of Herodias in his peripheral vision. She was beautiful with black hair, the darkest shade of night, with eyes to match. She had heavy eyelids, the kind that either looked sleepy or inviting. He wasn't sure which. Her small mouth, Roman nose, and long neck, adorned with jewels, were regal. She even wore a purple robe of the finest silk to prove it.

"I understand," she said. "But we do not want your brother Philip taking smug satisfaction in what John the Baptist is saying about us publicly."

Herod Antipas divorced the daughter of King Aretas to marry Herodias, his brother Philip's wife. John the Baptist declared their marriage a sin.

"I refuse to act rashly," the tetrarch insisted. "Some people believe John is the Messiah."

"Messiahs die like the rest of us."

"Give it time, my doe."

Herodias suddenly turned her gaze on Sveshtari. "What if this man here insulted me?" Sveshtari's knees went soft as he melted under the heat of her eyes. "What if this man publicly denounced us for our marriage?"

Herod's stern gaze raked Sveshtari from head to toe. "I would crucify him."

A trickle of sweat slid down Sveshtari's neck beneath his thin breastplate. Herodias placed her hand on Sveshtari's chest and slid it upward until she caressed his cheek with the back of her hand. She was so close he could smell the wine on her breath.

He did not move a muscle. When cobras get this close, it is best to remain as still as humanly possible.

"What if he called me Jezebel?"

Jezebel. The evil queen of long ago. Sveshtari kept his eyes straight ahead.

"If he called you Jezebel, I would not even bother taking the time to crucify him. I would slit his throat before he could blink."

Herodias touched Sveshtari's throat before gently squeezing him around the neck. "Such a nice neck, though."

Herod glared at the bodyguard as if he was the one who had touched his wife—not the other way around. Sveshtari wet his lips and swallowed hard.

Finally, mercifully, Herodias withdrew her touch and stepped back from Sveshtari. "You speak like a true husband."

"I believe you are worth fighting for."

"And killing for?"

"Of course."

"Remember that when you consider the fate of John the Baptist."

Sveshtari heard the swish of Herodias's garment and sensed that she had returned to their sleeping quarters. Out of the corner of his eyes, he noticed Herod Antipas move alongside him, glaring. The oil on his beard glistened in the torchlight.

The tetrarch stepped in front of Sveshtari and stared into his eyes. The bodyguard did not return the stare but let his gaze drift over Herod's left shoulder.

"My wife admires your neck. I hope that is all she admires."

Sveshtari started to speak, but what could he say? His mouth opened and closed.

"What have you done to attract her attention?"

"Nothing, tetrarch. I never move from my appointed spot."

"Has she ever touched you before?"

"No, I swear it."

"By your neck, do you swear it?"

"By my neck, I swear it."

Herod broke into a grin. "Such a lovely neck."

After the tetrarch followed his wife into their sleeping quarters and the door closed with a gentle click, Sveshtari exhaled, sagging with relief. He rubbed his neck and put his fingers to his nose, smelling the lingering scent of her perfume.

ASAPH

Life was good for Asaph. He leaned back in his chair like a king on his throne and took in his surroundings.

Asaph's tollbooth was directly below a date palm tree that gave him plenty of shade on this hot day in the summer month of Ab. Jericho's weather was tropical, and the city had plenty of water, thanks to its abundant springs. Jericho was also an excellent source of balsam, used to make medicines. Balsam, in turn, was a useful source of taxation.

Taxes.

Asaph loved the very sound of the word. It sang to him every day.

When he first arrived in Jericho, he made a point of befriending the wealthy and powerful chief tax collector, Zacchaeus. Eventually, Asaph was put in charge of one of the strategic tollbooths at a gate leading into Jericho. He could not have been better positioned for collecting taxes unless he was at a gate leading into Jerusalem. The road between Jerusalem and Jericho was well traveled by traders, so there was plenty to tax—especially when you could invent your own taxes. All it took was a bit of imagination.

"John the Baptist is drawing huge crowds along the Jordan River," said Malachi, Asaph's twenty-year-old assistant. Malachi lounged in a nearby chair, his feet propped on a footstool. He made a good assistant because he lacked ambition and posed no threat to Asaph's position. He took orders with an easy-going smile.

Asaph rolled his eyes, bored by all the self-appointed prophets swarming the land. "John is just another Messianic huckster."

In contrast to Malachi, he preferred a smooth chin—partly because it was a Roman look and partly because, at age thirty-nine, he knew his beard would soon turn gray. He was a stocky man with a round face and receding hair that he kept meticulously trimmed to help hide the gray patches.

Malachi laced his fingers behind his head. "People say John is the Messiah's forerunner."

"Ridiculous. Herod will circumcise John's head from his shoulders if he's not careful."

Before Malachi could answer, Asaph heard the squeak of rickety wheels—music to his ears. A wagon was something he could tax. As it pulled closer, Asaph was shocked to see a familiar face driving the loaded cart. Asaph rose from his post, a smile blooming on his face.

"Well, if it isn't my good friend Zuriel!" He had not seen his boyhood enemy, Zuriel, for many years.

The man leading the cart stopped in his tracks. His eyesight must not have been good because Zuriel squinted at him from about twenty paces away.

"Is that you, Asaph?"

"It is!"

"I didn't know you collected taxes."

"Then you must not come to Jericho very often."

"It is a new trading stop for me."

"Welcome!" Asaph beamed, even though he knew Zuriel still hated him.

Asaph had beaten Zuriel as a boy to protect his friend Eliana. As they grew up together, Zuriel made a few feeble attempts at revenge, but Asaph was always one step ahead.

Once, when Zuriel lay in wait in some bushes, planning to jump out and pummel him with a stick, Asaph sent a dog into the bushes to flush him out like a bird. Asaph could still see the scar where the dog tore into his cheek.

Zuriel tried to smile, but Asaph could tell it was forced. Asaph took pleasure in knowing he could still make him squirm.

Asaph clapped his hands. "So, let me have a look at what you are bringing into the city."

"Nothing of great value, my friend," said Zuriel, resurrecting his smile.

"I will be the judge of that...my friend."

Asaph circled the wagon, pretending to take a serious look at it. "To begin, there is a tax on each of the wheels of your cart. Mark that down, Malachi."

Malachi grinned as he used a bone writing tool to mark his wax tablet.

Zuriel looked from Asaph to Malachi, then back to Asaph. "You're joking, right?"

Asaph patted Zuriel on the shoulder. "I never joke when it comes to collecting taxes."

Zuriel glowered. "I have heard of tax-gatherers charging for two axles but never *four wheels*!"

"Welcome to Jericho."

Asaph moved to Zuriel's donkey, a shabby-looking beast with a white nose and mottled brown body. He ran his hand along its tangled mane.

"There is a tax on each of your animal's stubby legs as well."

Zuriel's mouth opened, but no words came out. Asaph noticed that Malachi had to smother his laugh.

Next, Asaph opened one of the sacks and dug his hands deep into a load of figs.

"And what do you suppose you are doing?" Zuriel asked.

"Just making sure you are not trying to smuggle in valuables without paying a tax on them."

Zuriel muttered something under his breath. Asaph was enjoying himself a little too much.

Asaph looked up to see Zuriel wiping his brow with the back of his hand. Asaph smiled to himself as he moved to the next sack—a bag of grain. Once again, he dug in, plunging his arms into the grain past his elbows, making it possible to slip a silver lamp from his long sleeve, where he kept it hidden.

"And what, my friend, is this?" With the flourish of a magician, he held up the lamp, which flashed in the sunlight.

"That is not mine!" Zuriel paled.

"You mean to tell me it just happened to spontaneously grow inside your grain? Perhaps I should increase the tax if you're carrying magic grain."

"No!" Zuriel shouted, waving his arm.

"So, you *don't* think it magically grew in your grain?"

"Of course not!"

"Then you admit you hid it there."

"No! You put it there!"

"I don't think so. Hiding a vase to avoid tax is a serious offense, my friend."

Zuriel was a skinny man, but his fist would still carry power behind it. Asaph had to be careful here. He moved within whispering distance.

"But if you paid me a little extra coin, I could overlook this small crime."

Zuriel staggered to his left, looking around for help. Besides Asaph and Malachi, there was no one around except for a Roman guard; his job was to ensure no harm came to tax gatherers for the Empire.

"This is thievery," Zuriel hissed.

"You can pay the price or spend time in Jericho's finest prison."

Zuriel glanced over his shoulder at the Roman soldier, who stood about thirty paces away, smiling big.

Zuriel grumbled as he pulled out his money sack and began counting coins into Asaph's outstretched hands. "Someday, you'll wind up in the Jordan River."

"I have no intention of ever being dunked in the river by John the Baptist." Asaph laughed.

Zuriel made eye contact, staring for a beat too long. "I'm talking about a baptism in which you remain face down in the water. The baptism of Thanatos."

Thanatos. The god of death.

Asaph's forced smile tightened as the meaning sunk in. He was tempted to add another tax for the death threat alone but thought Zuriel might go berserk if he demanded anything more. He had tortured this insect long enough.

"You may pass." He waved an arm and stepped back. "Enjoy your time in Jericho."

Zuriel drove his donkey forward, glaring at him with unspeakable hatred.

SVESHTARI

Sveshtari and Keturah met in the shadows, near the storerooms of the Fortress of Machaerus, by the southern bastion and as far as possible from Herod's sleeping quarters. It was night, and Sveshtari had just finished his duty, his bronze helmet tucked beneath his right arm. They had only a few moments together before he returned to the barracks.

Keturah looked up at him, much shorter than him and four years younger than his twenty-three years. Her mahogany eyes complemented her umber skin. Her long black hair flowed down her back and was framed by her red headdress.

When Sveshtari leaned in to give her a kiss, Keturah put a finger on his lips, gently pushing back to stop his advance.

"Sveshtari, do you think you can find out how my mother died?"

The moment she asked, the air changed between them.

Sveshtari hoped that Keturah had given up on her attempts to find the cause of her mother's death. Pursuing secrets in the Herod household could be extremely dangerous.

"You are still thinking about this?" He stared into her troubled eyes.

"How can I not? My father talks about it all the time."

First, she brings up her mother, and now her father. It was as if her parents hovered in the air around them.

Sveshtari placed a hand against her cheek. "I'm concerned for your safety. For your sake, please drop this matter."

"You want me to drop my search for the truth of my mother's death?"

"The truth will not raise her from the dead. It will only put you in danger."

"It's a risk I'm willing to take."

Sveshtari withdrew his hand. "Does your father give you any idea why he thinks your mother was poisoned?"

Keturah wiped a tear lingering at the corner of her eye. In the distant hills, the high-pitched sound of a yelping jackal penetrated the darkness.

"My father doesn't trust Herod Antipas."

"Not many do. But that doesn't mean he poisons for no reason. Did the tetrarch believe your mother was disloyal? That would be his only reason to..." His voice trailed, leaving the sentence hanging in mid-air.

"No. I am not sure Herod even knew of my mother's existence."

Sveshtari ran his hands along her arms as if to warm her. She wore a shawl and headwrap, out of which her perfect face emerged, looking for answers. He had none, but he wouldn't admit it. Instead, he responded with more questions.

"As Herod's cupbearer, wouldn't your father know better than me if and how your mother was poisoned?"

"But my father is not in his right mind. He sees plots everywhere," Keturah said. "I need to know what happened to my mother, and I thought you might be close enough to Herod's inner circle to know what—or who—killed her."

"Is there anyone in the household who might want your mother dead?"

"I don't know of anyone. But if she was poisoned, it must have been Herod's doing."

Sveshtari couldn't share his real thoughts—that Keturah's mother had been struck down by sickness. It happened all the time, but he knew she wouldn't want to hear it.

"Does Herod know of your father's suspicions?"

"No, and it must remain that way."

"I agree. For your sake, I will keep your secret and see what I can learn about your mother."

Finally, Sveshtari had earned an embrace, and Keturah buried her face in his chest. As he breathed in the cinnamon scent of her hair, guilt nagged at him for meeting Keturah in secret. He feared he had displeased Dionysus, the god of pleasure, by focusing all his attentions on one woman. If the other bodyguards discovered his love for Keturah, he would be ridiculed without mercy. Bodyguards never marry nor keep to one woman. It would be as ridiculous as keeping to one god.

"I will protect your secret." He nuzzled the crook of her neck. "And I will see what I can learn about your mother."

"Thank you."

She lifted to her toes, brushing her lips with the briefest touch to his before she broke away and disappeared, the moment gone. Once again, the jackals in the distance let loose with their high-pitched yelps. These animals always sounded like they were in such pain.

ASAPH

"You brood of vipers! Who warned you to flee from the coming wrath?" the wild-haired prophet shouted to the masses. He stood thigh-deep in the brown, silty water of the Jordan River, flanked on either side by brown, barren hills.

So, this was the infamous John the Baptist. Asaph studied the man, born of Zechariah and Elizabeth. He recalled the bizarre incidents leading to the prophet's birth when Zechariah was struck mute. He wished John the Baptist had been the one struck mute.

With the stream of stories about this rough-and-tumble prophet who urged people to turn from their wicked ways, he finally had to see for himself. He laughed at the crowd's naiveté. If he could tax people on their gullibility, he would become even richer than he already was.

The Jordan River was east of Jericho, flowing south from the Sea of Galilee to the Dead Sea. It mainly ran straight along a cleft, cutting through the land like a crack in pottery. Throngs of people flocked to its banks, straining to hear. Asaph and Malachi edged a little closer, standing on tiptoes for a better view of the Baptist, who was dressed in animal skins.

John flung both hands to the sky. "Produce fruit in keeping with repentance! And do not begin to say to yourselves, 'We have Abraham as our father.' For I tell you that out of these stones God can raise up children for Abraham!"

Asaph noticed his tax-gathering assistant, Malachi, gawking at John the Baptist in awe.

"Wipe that look off your face. Surely, you don't believe this nonsense."

Malachi reddened at the rebuke. "The Baptist's voice carries authority."

"He's a good actor, that's all."

As Asaph and Malachi worked their way to the front of the crowd along the riverbank, Asaph noticed that everyone had the same sheep-like expression.

"John the Baptist comes from your hometown, does he not?" Malachi said to Asaph.

"I am sorry to say, but yes."

"So, you know him?"

"Not really. John was much younger than me, and I left my hometown before he came of age. He was always a strange little boy and became an even stranger man."

Asaph was happy to have escaped his hometown for Jericho, where he became a taxman, a *telone*. He hoped to make enough money to start a new life in Rome, escaping these sheep bleaters once and for all.

"The ax is already at the root of the trees, and every tree that does not produce good fruit will be cut down and thrown into the fire!" John called out.

Asaph had to hand it to John. He was unafraid of stirring up trouble. The ax was the perfect metaphor because John wielded words like they were cutting tools, swinging them recklessly and chopping away at the hypocrisy around him. He even swung at Herod Antipas for marrying his brother's wife, Herodias.

Asaph shook his head, surprised the ax hadn't yet been turned on John. With his long, Samson-like hair, the Baptist was a remarkable sight. He had taken the Nazirite vow and lived on nothing but locusts and honey. Asaph had tasted locusts cooked in salt water many times. He even had biscuits made from locust powder. But to eat locusts and honey *every day*. He supposed that qualified John as a very holy man. Or a fool.

Asaph's eyes flitted over the crowd in disgusted amazement. There had to be hundreds of people here by the Jordan River listening to the wild man, eating up his words as if his sentences were slathered with honey. He nearly laughed aloud.

Then John went silent and scanned the faces as if looking for someone. Asaph gave a visible start when the Baptist stopped, his eyes boring into his. Asaph held his gaze steady, unwilling to be intimidated by a prophet's staring match. He could stare an owl into submission.

A voice from the crowd shouted, "Teacher, what should we do?"

John continued to stare at Asaph as he answered. "Don't collect any more taxes than you are required to!"

Asaph tried to mask his discomfort with a smile, but he sensed that his grin had become an uncomfortable half-smile—and a shaky one at that.

"Don't collect any more taxes than you are required to!" John repeated, still staring at Asaph.

Asaph's awkward grin morphed into a scowl. *Don't collect any more taxes than you are required to? Is he insane?*

The Romans had built the entire system on collecting more than necessary. As a *telone*, it was his right to charge whatever he thought necessary, anything from one to twenty percent of a product's value. If John the Baptist had a problem with the system, he should take it up with the *equites* in Rome, who counted the money.

Asaph crossed his arms with a short nod. *Or better yet, Baptist, swing your ax at the publican, who sits at the top of the mound of money in this province.*

"How did he know you collect taxes?" Malachi whispered, his eyes widening as if he had just seen a magician do a mind-reading trick.

"He's probably seen me at the gates of Jericho. Do not be so easily impressed."

Malachi laughed. "But you have to give him credit for picking you out of this crowd."

Before Asaph could tell Malachi to stop being stupid, another voice called from the crowd. "And what should we do?"

Asaph did a double take when he realized the question came from a Roman soldier standing to the Baptist's right.

John turned to face the soldier. "Don't extort money and don't accuse people falsely. Be content with your pay."

"Money again...For a holy man, he's obsessed with mammon," Asaph said. "Come. We've seen enough."

Asaph retreated, shoving his way through the crowd and casting a final glance over his shoulder. He could not believe the soldier had stepped into the water, asking to be baptized! The lion allowed his mane to be shorn, voluntarily becoming a sheep.

"What a fool," he mumbled under his breath.

Asaph was about to continue walking away when he spotted someone standing on the shore, watching as John baptized the soldier. Out of over a hundred men along the shore, for some strange reason, this one caught his eyes. Maybe it was the brilliance of his clothes that made him stand out, for the man wore a bright white robe.

When the stranger stepped into the water, John the Baptist knelt before him. *That's odd*, Asaph thought. He frowned, transfixed by the sight.

Then the man put a hand on John's head, and the Baptist rose back to his feet, shedding water.

"Who could John be kneeling before?" Malachi asked.

Shrugging, Asaph turned. "Another charlatan. They swarm like locusts."

Asaph walked away, deciding that the sooner he returned to Jericho, the sooner he could make more money. But he hadn't gone far when he heard shouts and whistles coming from the crowd near the river. What's more, he could have sworn he heard the rumble of thunder. He looked up at the sky, but there weren't any clouds, let alone a thundercloud.

Stranger yet, he thought he could hear words in the rumble as if a rockslide were trying to speak.

He shook his head, obviously imagining things. Still, whatever had occurred by the river stirred up the crowd's excitement.

Fools. Asaph turned his back.

KETURAH

Keturah stood behind her mistress and used a bodkin to separate Joanna's long, oiled hair in the back from the hair in front, creating a part at each ear. Then she combed out the back, separating the strands by the nape of Joanna's neck, concentrating on the hair higher atop the back of her head.

"And how is your soldier?" asked Joanna.

Keturah gave a start and paused in her work. "My soldier, *Domina?*"

"Yes. How is Sveshtari?"

Keturah thought she had been discreet in her meetings with the bodyguard. "I am sorry, *Domina.*"

"You needn't apologize, Keturah. Your secret is safe with me—although you know about the ways of mercenaries, do you not?"

"I do."

Keturah swallowed, aware of the loose living of mercenary soldiers, especially those from the client state of Thrace.

"But you believe he is different?" Joanna asked.

"I *know* he is, *Domina*."

Keturah ran the silky strands of Joanna's hair through her hands repeatedly before twisting it into a tightly coiled bun.

"A man who does not devote himself to one God is a man who does not devote himself to one woman," Joanna said. "I must speak honestly."

"I understand, *Domina*."

Joanna had mentioned this philosophy before, but in Keturah's mind, there were exceptions to everything. Sveshtari was much more civilized than the brutes lining the fortress hallways.

Joanna, a Hebrew, did not practice the faith of her Fathers when Keturah first became her slave in the House of Herod. But recently, things began to change. Joanna's long-dormant beliefs started to spark and sputter like a fire suddenly breaking out from smoldering ashes.

Joanna sighed, changing the subject. "I do wish we could have stayed in Galilee. This fortress is so forbidding."

"Will the tetrarch be moving his household back to Tiberias soon?" Keturah asked.

"With Herod Antipas, anything can happen."

Keturah agreed with her mistress that the Fortress of Machaerus was remote and depressing, despite Herod's renovations.

Joanna lowered her voice. "I wish the fortress was closer to the Jordan River. I hope to see John the Baptist at the Jordan."

When Joanna dared to mention the prophet's name in Herod's palace, Keturah's lips parted with a soft gasp.

Joanna held a favored position because her husband was Chuza, the manager of Herod's household. But even a favored status would not protect you from Herod and Herodias's wrath if you showed any sympathy to John the Baptist.

Joanna touched the back of her neck with a smile as the hairstyle began to take shape. "You are doing a fine job—as good as your mother once did."

Keturah thanked the gods she had a mistress as kind as Joanna. Keturah's father, as Herod's cupbearer, was not as fortunate.

After fixing the bun on the back of Joanna's head with a bodkin, she twisted some hair at the nape of her neck into a tightly wound strand, draping it over the bun. Using a needle and thread, she stitched the strand around the base of the bun.

Joanna turned around when the hair was ready. "I pray for your father every day."

"Thank you, *Domina*." Keturah's heart began to race. Did Joanna know her father suspected that her mother had been poisoned?

"Your father has been acting unusual of late. Do you know what is bothering him?"

Keturah shook her head, relieved that her mistress was unaware of the reason for her father's behavior. "He frets about me."

Joanna took Keturah's hands. "I worry about you as well. You and your soldier need to be more careful. One of the slave boys, Tullius, saw you and Sveshtari in the courtyard the other night."

Keturah pulled one hand free from Joanna's gentle grip and covered her mouth.

"But if Herod learns..."

"Tullius will tell no one." Joanna raised her brow with a sharp nod. "I can assure you, but be more careful."

"Yes, *Domina*."

Keturah wrapped her hands in the fabric of her dress to keep them from trembling. When she was sure they had stopped shaking, she began the finishing touch to her mistress's hair.

SVESHTARI: ONE YEAR LATER, THE MONTH OF TISHRI (LATE SEPTEMBER), 27 A.D.

Sveshtari prayed for strength from Mars, the god of war, as he led a small contingent of soldiers to the Jordan River. It was a gray and windy day, the kind that could unleash torrents of rain without warning.

Sveshtari always prayed to Mars when marching into battle—or any other confrontation. What he had to accomplish today was not a battle by any means. Still, it could easily get out of hand if not handled properly.

Herod Antipas had ordered him to arrest John the Baptist, which sounded simple enough. John was just one man, but the Hebrew people could be as unpredictable and tempestuous as the weather. So Sveshtari prayed to Mars, the son of Juno, Queen of the gods. Juno gave birth to Mars in Sveshtari's home country of Thrace, so the god of war held special meaning.

A large crowd gathered by the river, several hundred by his estimates, but people parted as soon as the soldiers approached on horseback. Sveshtari kept his eyes peeled for any weapons. When someone picked up a large rock, Sveshtari sent him a hardened look, and the man tucked his head, dropping the stone.

Everyone stared at them with knowing eyes. Even John the Baptist didn't look at all surprised to see them.

As the soldiers spurred their horses through the crowd, Sveshtari overheard a Jewish man asking John a question.

"Rabbi, the man who was with you on the other side of the Jordan—the one you testified about—well, now he is baptizing, and everyone is going to him. What do...?" The man's question trailed off as the soldiers, armed to the teeth, dismounted.

John the Baptist ignored the commotion and smiled. The appearance of eleven armed soldiers was not about to disrupt his normal give-and-take with the people.

"I am not the Messiah but am sent ahead of him," John said. "The bride belongs to the bridegroom. The friend who attends the bridegroom waits and listens for him, and is full of joy when he hears the bridegroom's voice."

Sveshtari had no idea what the Baptist was babbling about. Brides? Bridegrooms? It made no sense.

"That joy is mine, and it is now complete." John paused, turning to fully face Herod's soldiers. "He must become greater."

John smiled directly at Sveshtari.

"I must become less," he added with a slight nod.

John was becoming less, all right, Sveshtari thought. The prophet's ministry was over, and by nightfall, he would either be dead or rotting in the Fortress of Machaerus.

Sveshtari and ten other soldiers plunged into the water up to their knees, their armor clanking. He could sense the crowd's agitation, like a hive about to explode. He and his men formed a semi-circle around the Baptist, allowing Sveshtari to bind his hands behind him. The Baptist gave no resistance. This was easier than Sveshtari expected. Thank Mars.

The Baptist smelled of fish and soil, and his long hair was tangled in knots. He was a large man, broad-shouldered, and Sveshtari thought he might have made a good soldier.

"Whoever believes in the Son has eternal life!" John bellowed to the crowd as Sveshtari finished tying his hands.

Sveshtari scoffed. "You prophets are all the same...getting in your last-minute preaching."

Sveshtari never could make sense of Jews. They believed in one God and didn't even carve images of this singular deity. Whoever thought of a God you couldn't see—in wood, stone, or even flesh? He knew exactly how Mars appeared. His god wore gold armor and a helmet that stood tall on his head, like the peak of a powerful mountain. The invisible God of the Jews was like speaking to air.

"But whoever rejects the Son will not see life, for God's wrath remains on them!" John shouted as he was led away as a prisoner of Herod.

Sveshtari had no idea who this Son might be, and he didn't care. Give him a god who hurled a thunderbolt any day.

The soldiers met no resistance back to the fortress, where they cast John into darkness.

Several nights later, the meal in Herod's palace was more splendid than ever. A slave brought out the tail of a sheep, dripping with fat, in a small cart specially designed to carry heavy delicacies. There were also braised joints of beef, soft-boiled eggs, dormice, minced nightingales, black pudding, and large pieces of bread to sop up everything from the silver plates.

Sveshtari had to stand by watching, his stomach growling. Herod was eating himself half to death. Although Sveshtari's job was to keep him from harm, that didn't include protecting him from gluttony.

Herod reclined at the center table, stretching out on cushions, with his wife to his left. Two side tables branched off on either wing, where guests feasted. Herodias's young daughter from a previous marriage, Salome, sat nearby, batting her eyes and flaunting herself before the middle-aged Roman across the table. Salome was only fourteen years old but looked much older.

When the Roman sent Salome an amused smile, his wife jabbed him with an elbow—not once but twice. Salome looked away, a guilty pleasure spreading across her cheeks.

Just then, Keturah's father, Obed, entered carrying Herod's silver wine cup, filled to the brim. Sveshtari still did not understand why Obed thought someone in the fortress would want to murder his wife. Herod and Herodias were quick to kill slaves they suspected of treachery, but Obed's wife was a trusted servant. Besides, if Herod wanted to kill her, he would do it openly. He wouldn't use poison, the weapon of palace intrigue.

Sveshtari stood behind Antipas, off to his right. The tetrarch was in good spirits, dressed in a purple tunic lavishly ornamented with designs. A golden diadem rested on his head, his eyes were slightly darkened with paint, and his beard was neatly trimmed. His appearance was a mix of both Roman and Jewish styles—appropriate for a man who tried to walk the balance beam between two rival cultures.

Obed sampled Herod's wine to ensure no one had laced it with poison. Once a few moments passed and he was still standing with breath in his lungs, Herod Antipas guzzled his red wine, some trickling down to his chin.

"What is the news from Nabatea?" Herod's voice boomed above the clamor as he aimed this question at the Roman enjoying Salome's flirtations. Sveshtari had no idea who this Roman might be—just that he was important enough to dine with the tetrarch.

The table went still.

"We do not need to think about Nabatea tonight, dear husband," said Herodias. "It is not good for the digestion."

Sveshtari cut his eyes to the side. The foxes were nipping at each other again.

By now, the wine had loosened Herod's tongue, and he ignored his wife. "I asked a question! What is the news from Nabatea?"

The Roman delegate dabbed a cloth at his mouth, giving himself time to form a tactful response. "Aretas is still unsatisfied."

Herod chuckled. "I am well aware that Aretas is not happy. I divorced his daughter, but he should be pleased I have not killed her! Tell me something new. Will he make a move on us?"

"I do not believe Aretas dares to attack," said the Roman.

"Will Emperor Tiberius support me if he does?" Antipas set down his cup and stifled a burp.

"I said you are unlikely to face a threat from Aretas."

"But can you guarantee it?"

Listening to the political bantering, Sveshtari almost lost all focus until he spotted a glinting flash of steel. Obed had pulled out a blade!

Sveshtari had been trained to move swiftly if someone drew a knife in the tetrarch's presence. Without thought, he moved on pure instinct.

Obed was a feeble man, and his blade momentarily caught in the folds of his garments, giving Sveshtari time to pounce. He clamped down on Obed's wrist, twisting it savagely, like breaking the wing off a roasted bird. As the man's wrist bones popped, Sveshtari sliced Obed's neck, leaving a thin scarlet strand like a red grin. Eyes wide with the shock of death, Obed dropped his knife, and his entire body crumpled like a fast-emptying sack of grain, collapsing on itself.

Most of the guests sprang from the table, backpedaling from the corpse as Herodias shrieked. Herod and the Roman were the only ones who remained seated. Herod's eyes darted back and forth as he struggled to gain composure and remain unshaken by death so close.

As Sveshtari stared at Obed, it dawned on him that he had just killed the father of the one woman he loved. His heart sank. There were no words to defend himself to his beloved. Although it was a reflex action, an unconscious decision, it was still done by his hand.

Imagining Keturah's face, Sveshtari put a hand to his churning stomach.

"You're turning white." Herod studied Sveshtari, his eyes narrowing. "Since when has gore made you sick?"

While everyone else stared in shocked silence at Obed's body, still bleeding on the floor, Herod continued to lock eyes on Sveshtari.

"Remove this body immediately and take it beyond the city gates!" Herod pointed to the exit. "Jackals deserve to feast tonight as well."

Then Herod returned to his meal and ate with obvious relish.

JEREMIEL

Jeremiel tried to look calm as he moved through the Royal Stoa, an open-air meeting place that looked onto the Temple's Court of Gentiles. A forest of massive white pillars surrounded him. In the midst of this stone forest sat Azriel, the sixty-year-old Pharisee leader.

Jeremiel paused. Azriel hated mindless chatter, so he said nothing more than "Shalom" before taking his seat. Azriel stared at him for the longest time as if to test whether he might try to fill the silence with blabber.

Jeremiel didn't take the bait.

"We want to send you to Galilee to look into the matter of a new prophet," Azriel finally said.

Jeremiel turned his face just out of sight, so Azriel could not see his disappointment. He had been hoping that Azriel would announce his appointment to a high position.

After a pause, he cleared his throat and faced him with a smile. "When you say a 'new prophet,' are you speaking of John the Baptist?"

"I do *not* speak of John—obviously. He is in Judea, not Galilee. He is not a new prophet, and he has been arrested. Why would I send you to see a condemned man?"

Blushing, Jeremiel rebuked himself for such a blunder. Azriel had a low tolerance for mistakes. "I'm sorry."

"There is a new prophet in Galilee, and people say he is greater than John the Baptist. They say that John is only his forerunner."

Jeremiel nodded, offering his most studious expression, stroking his chin. A forerunner is a humble position, clearing the path for the entrance of a king into a city. If people viewed this new prophet as a king, the man would not survive long under Herod's wrathful eye.

"The prophet's name is Jesus," said Azriel.

"A common enough name."

"For a common enough man—a carpenter from Nazareth."

Jeremiel snickered. "Nazareth! Whatever came out of a backwater town like Nazareth?"

Azriel scowled. "Sometimes the greatest threats come from the humblest of places. Have you forgotten about Simon of Perea?"

"You're right." Jeremiel nodded and blushed, praying he hadn't botched this interview. "Is this Jesus raising up an army?"

Azriel shrugged. "We don't know. That's why we decided to send you to learn what you can. Perform well, and you will be rewarded."

Jeremiel shot a look at Azriel. "With a position on the Sanhedrin?"

"I cannot promise that. But who knows what a successful job might bring." Azriel let the hint of reward sink in for a moment. "But if you do not give us the information we seek, there is also the risk of great disgrace."

Jeremiel understood perfectly. This assignment could make or break him. At his age, he was willing to take the risk.

"How soon do I leave?"

"In two days, a caravan carrying spices is heading for Sepphoris. Jesus is from Nazareth, not far from there, so you can travel with them."

"That does not give me much time to prepare."

Azriel shot to his feet. "Shall I pass the assignment to someone more ambitious?"

Jeremiel stood just as fast, a hint of desperation clinging to every move as he stepped forward, closing the gap between them. He should have remembered that Azriel didn't tolerate indecision. He wanted immediate answers, confident answers. "That is not necessary. I welcome the task."

"The Pharisees in Nazareth will be expecting you."

"Thank you, Azriel, for your confidence in me," Jeremiel said, but the Pharisee leader was already walking away.

ELIANA

Eliana wandered through the maze that was Lower Jerusalem. She had no idea where she was going, but Calev was leading her, and that was enough.

With a sack of clothes slung over her right shoulder, she turned down a narrow, twisting alley, where she came upon a man lugging a long, heavy wooden beam on his shoulder. As he attempted to turn a corner without smashing the beam into a building, a man with a huge jar strapped to his back came directly at him. There was no room for both to pass.

"Stop and turn around!" one of the men shouted, hunched beneath the load on his back.

"I had a hard enough time getting my beam this far down the street! You back up!" The man carrying the heavy wood struggled to speak, gasping for air with each word.

As the two continued to shout and curse, Eliana squeezed sideways to pass, unable to keep from chuckling. Her soft giggles soon became belly laughs, bringing both men's hard eyes to her and halting their shouting match.

"Shut your face, wench, or I'll drop this beam on your head!"

That ignited another wave of laughter, and Eliana stuck out her tongue and ran. They were in no position to chase her, being weighed down by their loads.

Eliana also carried a heavy load, but hers was of the mind and spirit. In recent days, Calev's voice had become stronger; he existed no longer as a whisper, floating a few feet away. He now merged with her thoughts, blending like wormwood in a drink.

Sometimes, she could escape Calev with pleasant dreams of her father taking her by the hands and swinging her around and around as he once did in the fields when she was a girl. In those moments, she was convinced she was being physically transported back in time. But then her father's image would transform into one of the brigands who captured her outside of Bethlehem so long ago. One brigand had her by the hands and the other by the feet. Together they swung her over a bottomless abyss, toying with her, acting as if they might let her fly into the infinite ravine.

Then she would wake up, heart pounding, relieved it was all a dream.

Today, Calev told her he was leading her to some Nabatean spice traders in Jerusalem. Just as he promised, Eliana came upon one of the traders behind an inn, strapping supplies onto their camels. When the smell of spices wafted over her, she held out her arms to the side. It was like standing in a perfumed rain shower.

"Can I help you?"

She turned to find a man with long, unruly gray hair wiping his hands on a rag. "My name is Eliana, and I need to reach Galilee."

Two other traders, crouching nearby and sharing a wine jug, perked up at her voice. One stood, his knees cracking, and he stared, raking his eyes over her body.

"You want to travel with our caravan?" said the bearded man.

"Calev says I should ask you."

"Never heard of him. Who is Calev?"

"You don't know him, but he knows you and says I should travel with you to Galilee."

"Did it occur to him to ask me in person?"

Eliana laughed. This fool thought he could speak with Calev! Didn't he know that only she could enter Calev's kingdom?

"I can pay you." Eliana said, shrugging.

Money had a way of heightening a man's senses. The spice trader's eyes widened ever so slightly.

"How much?"

"I have no money."

The man threw up his hands. "Then why are you bothering me?"

"I can pay you with my services."

This phrase also had a way of catching a man's attention. Although she meant cleaning up after animals and feeding them, men usually couldn't think past her body. It didn't matter either way. She carried a knife to settle any misunderstandings. She had used it before, killing the man who had enslaved her for many years.

The other two traders sidled over to the hairy one, and one of the men looked her up and down. He had a mouth of mostly missing teeth and smelled like a donkey. Looked like one, too.

"Let's bring her along, Rabbel," he said.

Rabbel ignored the younger man's eagerness. "Listen, I don't want to cause any trouble with this man, Calev. Are you running from him?"

"Calev is not my master. He's my adviser."

For some strange reason, the men found this hilarious.

"Calev says I have to leave Jerusalem," Eliana continued, "to find a prophet in Galilee."

"In Galilee, you can throw a stone in any direction, and odds are you'll hit a prophet."

"I don't want to hit this prophet with a stone." Eliana crossed her arms. "I want to kill him. Calev told me to."

The men initially looked stunned until they burst out laughing. She didn't understand what was so funny and wondered if she was signing on to travel with madmen.

"It's true we are heading to Galilee—to Sepphoris," Rabbel said. "You say you can pay us through your services?"

"I can. I will."

"What do men call you?"

"Eliana. Women call me that too."

Rabbel turned to the other two men, who continued to stare at her body, their eyes appreciating what they thought was to come. At nearly forty years of age, Eliana's skin was sun-beaten, and while she was short, she was strong from a life of hard work. Men still found her face open and appealing, even with a thin scar trailing down her left cheek. Some found it attractive in a strange way.

"We leave before midday but wash yourself first." Rabbel wrinkled his nose. "You smell like you've been living with pigs."

"Cattle," said Eliana.

"What?"

"I live in a stable with two cows. And one donkey."

When they burst out laughing again, Eliana scrunched her brow. What was so funny? She moved her lips in silent prayer, asking Calev to protect her from such crazy men.

As the traders returned to preparing their packs for the journey, she found a dry spot on the ground covered in hay. She sat down, placing her sack beside her, and watched them work.

Soon, others began to arrive—travelers who had paid to join the caravan for protection on the road.

People think there is safety in numbers, but they're fools. Eliana pursed her lips. *There is no such thing as safety anywhere in the world.*

A couple of families arrived, but most travelers were men who didn't even bother hiding their curious stares. It wasn't until a priest arrived that everything changed.

JEREMIEL

Jeremiel was stunned to see the woman sitting on the ground, her knees drawn up to her chest and rocking forward and back, muttering. She looked strangely familiar, yet he couldn't place her.

When the woman noticed him staring, she snapped, "What are you looking at?"

As she stuck out her tongue, it hit him. She was the mad woman who had occasionally been tossed from the Temple. Their first encounter was when she collided with him, carrying a rat!

Jeremiel wheeled around and spotted Rabbel readying one of the camels. "What is this woman doing here?"

Rabbel scanned the gathering crowd to determine who he was referring to. When Jeremiel pointed a finger at the crazy woman sitting on the ground, she glared back.

"She is traveling with us," said Rabbel. "This is a caravan. You didn't think you were the only one coming with us, did you?"

"But this woman is possessed by demons. I have paid good coin for this journey to Sepphoris. I did not pay to travel with a devil."

Rabbel stroked his beard and stared at the woman. "Demon-possessed, you say?"

Jeremiel could see that his words hit home. The woman continued to rock back and forth, muttering to herself, offering compelling evidence to back Jeremiel's claim.

Rabbel bowed his head with a soft nod before approaching the woman. "I'm sorry, Eliana. You cannot travel with us."

Eliana. That was her name.

Eliana stared back at Rabbel with eyes like hot coals. Then she leaped to her feet and became a living fury. "Did that priest change your mind?"

"I am in charge of my mind, and I say you cannot travel with us."

"But you promised!"

"I promise nothing to people who do not pay us in coins," Rabbel said. "Ours is not the only caravan traveling north. Another one is heading toward Jericho and then to the King's Highway leading north."

"The King's Highway? But I want to go to Sepphoris, closer to Nazareth!"

"You cannot be choosy when you have no money. The other caravan runs through Capitolias, where you can travel west to Nazareth."

"Traveling the King's Highway will add days to my trip!"

When Rabbel laughed, Eliana looked ready to cat-scratch his face. She spun toward Jeremiel and hissed, reinforcing his belief that he had done the right thing to keep her from this caravan. Being in the same group of travelers with this creature would be unnerving.

"But you can't do this!" Eliana's face flushed.

Rabbel sighed and shook his head. When she started to open her mouth to protest again, he grabbed her and slung her over his shoulder as he would a sack of grain.

"My bag! My bag!" Eliana screamed as she hung over his shoulder, her outstretched arm straining for her sack on the ground.

Rabbel waited for Jeremiel to pick up the woman's sack and hand it to her, but he was not about to touch such an unclean object. He looked away and frowned.

Eventually, one of the children from a family of travelers picked up the sack before Jeremiel could warn him not to touch the foul thing. As the little boy handed Eliana's belongings to her, his act of goodness seemed to calm her.

Still draped over the back of the spice trader, she smiled at the child. "Thank you."

Jeremiel cocked his head, thinking she almost looked human.

As the spice trader carried her into the streets to drop her off with another caravan, Jeremiel gave silent thanks that she was out of his life, hopefully for good.

SVESHTARI

Sveshtari rushed up the cold, dark stairs of the Fortress of Machaerus, sword drawn. He wondered if he was being a fool, doing what he was about to do. Torches lined the staircase, sputtering and throwing light just beyond his steps.

Heart pounding, he paused, placing a hand against the cool stone wall. Could he really do this?

Herod had just ordered him to kill Keturah, the woman he loved.

"None of Obed's family must be allowed to live," the tetrarch had declared.

Keturah was Obed's only remaining relative within Machaerus—the only one with the cupbearer's blood pulsing in her veins. Before the night ended, it was up to Sveshtari to finish off Obed's family.

He started up the steps once more, wondering what god he had displeased to be given this bloody business. Something sinister pushed against his heart, bringing up bile and making his mouth taste like the metal of his blade. He looked at his sword and gripped it harder.

Had he offended Dionysus? Had he offended the god of pleasure simply because he had chosen to love one woman?

When Sveshtari swept into Joanna's chamber, Keturah was there, getting ready for the night; she slept on a mat near the threshold of Joanna's room, always available to serve. Joanna stood at Keturah's side, and her eyes went immediately to Sveshtari's sword before swinging her gaze to him.

"Why is your sword unsheathed?" Joanna asked, breaking the stunned silence.

"I need to make this look real," Sveshtari said.

"Ah. I understand."

Sveshtari unhooked a goatskin pouch from his belt and removed the stopper. His eyes moved to Keturah. "Are you prepared for this?"

Eyes wide, she nodded and lay on her mat.

"It's just lamb's blood." Sveshtari gave her a reassuring look, tipping the pouch, splashing some of the blood across her robe and letting it pool at her side. "I'm sorry."

"It must be done," said Joanna, guarding the door. "Move quickly before anyone else comes to the chamber."

Sveshtari sprinkled some blood on the floor, then dipped his fingers in the gore and smeared it against the stone wall. He had just enough blood left in the pouch to splatter across his sword.

Joanna hissed a warning from her position by the door. "Someone is coming. Lights approach." Then she fell to her knees and let out an ear-splitting scream. *"Murder!"*

Sveshtari snatched a blanket from Keturah's bed and tossed it over her head, hiding her face.

"Go limp," he whispered as he lifted her into his arms like a dead girl.

He heaved her over his shoulder, wheeling around just in time to see two other guards arrive. The soldiers paused in the doorway, taking in the entire gory scene. Their eyes flitted from the blood on the bed and smeared against the wall to the blanket covering Keturah's listless body slung over Sveshtari's shoulder.

Joanna was still on her knees, her face buried in her hands, sobbing, chest heaving. For added drama, she let out one last anguished scream, leaped to her feet, and pummeled Sveshtari's back. One of the guards restrained her as she continued to scream.

"It is finished," Sveshtari said, looking over his shoulder at the blood before moving toward the door.

"Another fresh corpse," said one of the guards, stepping aside to let him pass. "The jackals will eat well tonight."

Sveshtari put on a stoic face and carried Keturah from the room. He could feel the beating of Keturah's heart as he descended the stairs, trying not to slip on the slick blood coating the bottom of his sandals.

Two sentries at the fortress gate noticed Sveshtari approaching and stepped back, allowing him passage. One sent him a sly grin with a nod of approval as the other offered him a torch. Since he had already disposed of Obed's body beyond the walls, they assumed he was on his way to deposit Keturah by her father.

"You are a busy man," said Rufus, one of the sentries. "Another body as food for the—"

"Shut your mouth, or the tetrarch will hear that his sentries have nothing better to do but chatter on duty!" Sveshtari snapped as Rufus's face hardened.

Sveshtari could sense his glare at his back as he passed through the gate, his torch flickering in the wind. The jackals howled in the dark, much closer than the other night. They had already feasted on Obed's body and wouldn't stray from a known feeding ground.

Beyond the fortress walls, Sveshtari's torchlight flickered along the narrow path down the steep hill on which the fortress stood. When they reached a boulder, he rounded it and found a young man of about fifteen, skinny as a reed, waiting for them and holding the reins of a donkey.

"Peace be upon you," said the boy, bowing.

Sveshtari handed the torch to him before lowering Keturah to the ground. He gently unwrapped the blanket, resurrecting her from her untimely death.

Taking Keturah by the hand, he helped her to stand. She trembled and clung to him. Then she looked over her shoulder at the young man with his donkey.

"Is this the one you told me about?" she asked.

"Peace be upon you," the boy said again, bowing to Keturah.

Sveshtari motioned in the direction of the boy. "Haran will lead you east to the King's Highway. You'll be covering dangerous ground."

Keturah wrapped her arms around Sveshtari's neck, pulling him closer so their foreheads met.

"Couldn't you come with me?" she whispered.

"If I do not return to the fortress tonight, Herod will know we tricked him, and he will send men after us. Your greatest hope is to go without me."

"But there are animals..."

"The most dangerous beasts are in the fortress, and they move on two legs. You must go with Haran. He will protect you."

Keturah pulled away, wiping her tears with the back of her hand. Sveshtari began to have second thoughts about sending her into the wilderness. He had to keep reminding himself that she would be in greater danger if he went with her.

"Will I ever see you again?" she asked.

"If the gods allow. Herod will eventually move his household back to Tiberias."

"Then I will head to Tiberias and wait for you there."

Sveshtari draped his cloak around her shoulders and kissed her lightly. After helping her onto the donkey, he handed her his sword.

"Head for the King's Highway, where you can find protection in a passing caravan."

Keturah stared at the sword, running a finger along the steel.

"Sveshtari, who killed my father?" Her solemn eyes bore into his.

The bodyguard let the question hang in the air.

"Herod," he finally said.

"I know he commanded it. But who spilled my father's blood?"

Sveshtari tried to silence her questions with a kiss, but she pushed him back. "Please tell me."

"One of the bodyguards," he said, looking away.

"But what is his name?"

"You do not know him."

"I need to know his name."

"Rufus," he said, using the name of the sentry they had just passed.

"Rufus." She repeated the word as if imprinting it in her mind. "*Ru-fus.*"

Sveshtari took her hand and caressed it.

"When you come to Tiberias, will you help me get my revenge on this man?" Keturah asked, wiping away a tear.

"I will." He gave her the words she wanted to hear.

"Will you also pray to Nemesis on my behalf?" she asked as the young boy took the donkey's reins.

"Every day."

Nemesis: the goddess of revenge. Sveshtari always found it intriguing that Nemesis was a woman. She carried a sword and a sand timer, which indicated how much time remained before she caught up with you and wreaked vengeance. He wondered how long it might take before Keturah learned the truth about what happened to her father.

He studied Keturah sitting high in her saddle, her back stiff and her chin held high. For one wild moment, he wondered whether Keturah was Nemesis come to earth. Was the goddess toying with him until she eventually killed him?

He shook off the notion. She was his Keturah, and he knew her heart.

"I promise," he said.

"Thank you, my love."

She leaned from the saddle to kiss his lips. As they separated, he watched his goddess depart into the darkness carrying his sword, which was still stained with the blood of the lamb.

4

LUKE CHAPTER 4

ASAPH

A SAPH WOKE TO THE smell of baking bread. One of his slave girls, Calliste, was already hard at work preparing his first meal of the day. He savored bread and honeycomb every morning, indulging his sweet tooth whenever possible.

He scooped some water from the basin outside his sleeping chamber and splashed his face before rising to full height and stretching the stiffness from his back.

Asaph had one of the better houses in Jericho; it was built around a large and lavish central court where Calliste prepared his meals. She had already set up the *trapeza*, a four-sided table, on which he spotted an unfamiliar vase with ornate yellow trim on the top and bottom. He narrowed his eyes, studying the art depicting men hunting with bows, arrows, and spears. It seemed to be of Greek origin.

"What's this?" Asaph motioned toward the mystery vase.

"It was there when I woke, *Dominus*," said Calliste. "Didn't you place it there?"

He shook his head. "Do you know where it came from?"

"No, *Dominus*."

"Was it here yesterday?"

"No, *Dominus*. I would have noticed."

"The gift of a friend, perhaps?" came a voice from behind.

Asaph spun around to see his fellow tax collector, Malachi, enter the courtyard with a big grin. He often strolled into his house unannounced.

"So...is this a gift from you?" Asaph pointed at the vase.

"You know I cannot afford such a thing. Perhaps one of the wealthy merchants in the city found it beneficial to offer you a present."

"When I receive bribes, I usually know who is behind it. What good is an anonymous bribe?"

"Maybe your benefactor is waiting for the right moment to reveal his identity—when he needs a favor. Maybe he didn't want you to turn down his bribe and return the vase."

Asaph scratched his scalp. "Then this mystery man does not know tax collectors. Who would turn down a bribe?"

Laughing, Malachi approached the table, stretched out on a couch, and began to slather honey on a piece of warm bread. "You have a point."

Asaph rolled the vase in his hands, studying every detail. "It is beautiful. But I don't like that someone crept into my house and placed it on my table without my knowledge."

"A thief in reverse?" Malachi dropped his voice with a gleam in his eye. "He breaks in to leave gifts. Most unusual."

Asaph returned the vase to the table and motioned to Calliste, who continued to set food and wine before them. "Did you hear anyone enter in the night?"

"No, *Dominus*." She frowned.

"Tonight, sleep on the threshold of the courtyard entrance. Any intruder will trip over you."

"Yes, *Dominus*." She nodded with a sigh.

Malachi laughed so hard that he spilled wine down his tunic. "Why do you even want to catch such a thief? I wish I had a burglar who came bearing gifts. Consider it a gift from the gods!"

Asaph grunted and shrugged. He collected artwork, including Grecian vases, and this addition would look good on the table along one wall of the courtyard. He bit into the honeycomb and closed his eyes, savoring the sweetness. But he also had a sour sense that this vase "from the gods" might be more trouble than it was worth.

KETURAH

The moment Keturah opened her eyes, her fear was instantly present, saturating the atmosphere. She breathed it in.

Even though the rising sun glowed red-orange over the hills, she was every bit as frightened as last night when she followed Haran in the dark, listening to the jackals in the distance. The entire time, she had been terrified of encountering a prowling lion with only a skinny boy and Sveshtari's sword for protection.

Keturah rubbed her aching neck. She had nodded off a few times during the ride, slumping at an odd angle, and paid the price for it this morning.

She soon forgot about her neck when a child's scream erupted from the surrounding rocks. She grabbed her chest, her heart racing. When she looked around, she spotted several large, rodent-like creatures before they vanished into the crevices of nearby rocks. They resembled large rabbits without the long ears.

Haran laughed. "Just a pack of hyraxes. Probably feeding nearby."

She smiled as one of them poked from its hiding spot and shrieked a warning. The Hebrews called them *damans*, which means "he who hides himself." Now that light was creeping across the wilderness, she sympathized, wishing she, too, could hide in the rocks.

An early morning mist partially concealed the hills in the distance. Keturah closed her eyes and tried to focus on anything other than her current condition. Her clothes, now covered in dust and dew, were still stained with dried blood. She feared the scent would attract animals. Licking her lips, she winced at the pain from the crack etched into the corner of her parched mouth.

Haran studied her for a moment before extending a bladder filled with water. "Drink."

As the cool water cascaded down her desert-dry throat, she sighed. Water rarely tasted this good.

"Thank you," she said, handing Haran the bladder.

Haran bowed and began packing their gear to continue their journey. They had reached the King's Highway, the famed trading route leading north—away from the Fortress of Machaerus and Herod. She prayed to the gods that Herod would not discover that Sveshtari had helped her escape.

"You are safe with me," Haran said, as if he had read her thoughts. "I have prayed to Isis for your protection."

"I will pray to her too."

Isis, the Egyptian goddess of the throne, had great magical powers. The Jewess Joanna would be disappointed she was praying to an Egyptian goddess, but she could use all the magic she could get.

"Isis knows what it is to wander." Haran grinned, displaying his stained teeth. "She wandered the world looking for all of the pieces of her husband, Osiris."

Keturah knew the story of how Osiris was chopped into fourteen parts and scattered throughout Egypt. Her life had been similarly ripped to pieces. First, her mother died mysteriously, and then her father was slaughtered in Herod's presence. She had two brothers, but they were sold off many years ago. Who knew where they lived—or if they even drew breath?

After saying her prayer to Isis, she called upon Nemesis, the winged goddess of vengeance and justice, when she spotted movement to her left. About fifteen paces away stood a wild dog, panting rapidly. Its ribs showed through parchment-thin skin.

"Yah!" Haran picked up a rock as big as his hand and hurled it at the animal. The dog squealed, turned tail, and ran away.

As Keturah and Haran continued north, she suddenly sensed a presence behind her. Turning, she discovered the same dog about twenty paces behind them.

When Haran noticed, he halted the donkey and searched for another stone. The dog stopped and stared, cocking its head. Its dirty and tattered coat was stained with dried blood from what looked to be an old wound on its shoulder. Keturah's heart went out to it. The dog's coat looked as pitiful as her clothes.

As Haran reached for a stone, Keturah raised a hand. "No! Leave him be. Isis or Nemesis might have taken on the form of this dog."

Haran stared at her as if she had lost her mind. Then, shrugging, he let the stone drop, and they moved on. Keturah peeked over her shoulder to find the dog following once again.

ELIANA

Eliana rocked back and forth on the spindly-legged camel, touching the handle of the knife hidden in her robes while staring at the man directing this small caravan to Tiberias in Galilee. After what she experienced while a slave, she didn't trust *any* man.

"You killed a man once; you can do it again," Calev said. His voice hovered and buzzed before her like a swarm of flies.

She swatted the air to rid it of Calev's presence. "You can shut up now."

The man on the camel in front of her turned and squinted. When she stuck out her tongue and wrinkled her nose, he chuckled.

"Kill these men when you have a chance." Calev's whisper sounded between her ears.

She closed her eyes. *Don't be a fool. There are too many of them. Besides, where would I go along this road alone?*

When Calev didn't argue back, Eliana opened her eyes. She didn't like the looks of the men leading this caravan but had little choice if she wanted to get north to Galilee. She swallowed the bitter taste, still lingering from how she was treated in Jerusalem. Getting slung over a man's shoulder and dumped with this caravan like a sack of grain was not the plan.

But at least this caravan made good time, passing through Jericho and crossing the Jordan River before reaching the King's Highway. Without the protection of these men, brigands and animals would have her for dinner.

As sand kicked up around them, so did the heat. Eliana tightened a veil over her mouth to keep from swallowing the grit.

"Don't hide your pretty face," said the man on the camel in front of her. Eliana wasn't sure if he was joking.

Someone whistled for the caravan to halt. Then, as the group stopped, one of the men asked, "What do we have here?"

Eliana peered around the caravan leader, shocked to find a younger woman sitting on a donkey by the roadside. Next to her stood a skinny young boy holding the animal's reins and grinning.

Eliana raked her eyes over the young woman, whose clothes were simple—and bloodstained. Yet she had no apparent wounds.

"Please, *Dominus*, my guide and I would appreciate the protection of your caravan." The woman bowed her head.

One of the men shifted his eyes from the bloody woman to Eliana. "I always wanted a harem. Besides, she's much prettier than the one we already have."

It was true. This woman was not only younger but also beautiful. While the insult stung, the other woman's charms might keep her safe from the men.

"The boy has money, *Dominus*," the woman said, motioning toward the skinny boy, who held out a sack of jangling coins.

"What are your names?" one of the traders demanded after taking the coins.

"Keturah."

"And Haran."

"An escaped slave?" The trader circled Keturah, sizing her up. He probably assumed she was a slave because she had used the term *Dominus*.

"Our master was killed by a jackal. We had nowhere else to go."

The trader lifted her robe, revealing her thigh, and examined the bloody fabric. "Your master's blood or the jackal's?"

Keturah's cheeks reddened as her mouth drew into a firm line. "Both."

The trader dropped the edge of her robe and leaned in, studying her long enough that she adjusted in her saddle and cleared her throat.

He laughed at her discomfort and gestured toward Eliana. "We are bound for Tiberias. Take your place riding at the back, just in front of *her*."

Keturah's mouth parted, and her eyes widened when she discovered another woman amidst the men. Eliana glowered. She assumed they would place Keturah behind her in the procession. Yet, this stranger ranked higher by being positioned in front of her, leaving Eliana easy pickings for any attackers coming from behind.

"Thank you, *Dominus*." Keturah bowed.

As the boy pulled their donkey into the caravan, Keturah smiled at Eliana and greeted her with "*Ave*."

Eliana grunted and tightened the veil over her nose. The blood smell on this woman was foul. Once the caravan began to move again, Eliana noticed several flies flitting around the slave girl's bloody headdress.

"Kill her." Calev's voice emanated from the swarm of flies.

"No," Eliana said out loud.

Keturah turned with a puzzled look. "I am sorry. What did you say?"

"I'm not talking to you." Eliana swatted at a few more flies. Frowning, Keturah turned back in her saddle.

"Kill her," said Calev. "You have a knife in your robes. Use it."

"Not now. Maybe later."

At the sound of Eliana's voice, Keturah straightened her back, tightening her legs around her donkey, urging it forward a bit faster. When Eliana realized she had spooked Keturah, she burst into laughter.

SVESHTARI

"So, what will you do now that Keturah is dead?" asked Rufus with a devious gleam in his eye. "Find yourself another woman?"

"What are you talking about?" Sveshstari looked across the threshold, where Rufus stood guard on the opposite side of the closed door. Behind it lay the *triclinium*, the banquet room in the Fortress of Machaerus.

Rufus whispered out of the side of his mouth. "I know you were seeing Keturah in secret."

Sveshtari cursed himself for being so reckless. Rufus had spies all over the palace grounds. If Rufus had discovered he was seeing Keturah, did he also know he had spared her life?

"Whoever you got your information from, he is feeding you lies," Sveshtari said, his voice laced with warning. "But if you want to pay your spies for fabricated information, that's your business."

Rufus snorted and lifted his chin with an air of confidence. He had a large but not grotesquely oversized nose, and he kept his hair trimmed close to the scalp, giving him a primitive and powerful look. His thick eyebrows added to the brutish air about him.

Sveshtari rolled his eyes. Rufus was a member of the *doryphoroi*, a guard unit that drew young men from prominent families. Most in this unit knew they were a cut above the Thracian or Celtic guards, and Rufus flaunted his position shamelessly.

"Now that you fed her body to the jackals, will you behave like a normal man?" Rufus said. "There are too many women in this world to keep to only one, especially a sordid slave like Keturah."

Sveshtari glared, trying to come up with a suitably severe response, when he spotted two men coming down the pathway to their left. Sveshtari recognized them from earlier visits—the priest Nekoda and his brother, Chaim. They were Sadducees, and they regularly reported to Herod.

The brothers, one tall and bald and the other shorter and rounder, started to quarrel, but they were too far away for Sveshtari to hear. Nekoda, the taller one, was especially angry. He kept giving his little brother gentle taps on the left shoulder until Chaim slapped away his hand.

Finally, they finished their argument and proceeded toward Sveshtari and Rufus.

"We are here to see the tetrarch," said Nekoda. While the man was just as tall as Sveshtari, soft living had given him a paunch, obvious beneath his robes.

"Not now, you aren't," said Rufus. "The tetrarch is entertaining guests."

"He will want to speak with us."

"I said he's busy. Wait for him in the *peristillum*."

"How long will he be?"

"As long as it takes."

Nekoda stepped toward the ornate closed doors, but Sveshtari blocked him.

"We can wait," said the younger brother, Chaim. Sweating heavily, he dabbed the sheen on his forehead with a cloth.

And so, the brothers departed the way they came, toward the manicured garden, where they sat by a fountain, glaring at one another. The two brothers looked ready to kill each other.

Sveshtari fully understood. He ached to kill Rufus.

ASAPH

When Asaph came to, everything around him seemed to be moving in slow motion. The edges of his vision blurred, and he had trouble focusing. He blinked through the darkness as someone, a man, took him by the tunic and shook him.

Realizing it might be the thief in the night, this time coming to murder him in his sleep, he shot up from his mat and reached beneath it to fumble for his knife.

Blade in hand, Asaph lunged for the housebreaker, dimly lit by lamplight.

"Asaph, it's me!" His assistant, Malachi, leaped back and put up his hands. Standing several paces behind him was his slave girl, Calliste, holding an olive oil lamp.

Malachi tugged again on Asaph's sleeve. "Soldiers are coming!"

"What are you talking about?" Asaph was so confused, so sleepy.

"They're coming to arrest you!"

Asaph gasped, and his heart raced, more awake now than if someone had doused him with a splash of cold water.

"Arrest me? What for?"

Sure, he gouged people with taxes, but that was perfectly legal. It was part of the game.

"I was in the drinking house tonight," Malachi said.

"Why does that not surprise me?"

"Zuriel was also there, along with Tarquinius."

Tarquinius was among the wealthiest merchants in Jericho—and the most dangerous.

"I overheard Zuriel telling Tarquinius he knew where he could find his stolen vase," Malachi said.

"*Stolen vase?*"

"Zuriel is setting you up. And they're coming here *now* to arrest you for theft!"

Heart racing, Asaph rushed into the courtyard, where the new vase stood proudly on display. Zuriel, his boyhood enemy, must have been the one who snuck it into his house—not as a bribe, but as a set-up.

Snatching the vase, Asaph thrust it into Calliste's hands. "Hide this! Take it somewhere else in the city!"

Calliste stared at the stolen vase as if he had placed a ball of fire in her hands. "Right now?"

"Of course! Do you want to be arrested along with me?"

Calliste paled and rushed toward the door with the vase tucked under her arm. Asaph sagged with relief, watching her escape into the night.

"And *you* need to leave the city!" Malachi slipped an arm around Asaph's shoulder and directed him toward the door.

"I can't leave my house!"

"Yes, you can. It would be best if you left Jericho until this blows over. I will keep an eye on your house while you're gone."

"But when they get here, they will know I fled. I will look guilty."

"I will tell them you left on a trip three days ago. My testimony will clear your name of any suspicion of guilt."

Asaph clamped his lips. Rage bubbled beneath the surface, just like when they were boys, and he pounded Zuriel's face to mush. He wished so badly he could grab Zuriel right now and smash his fist into flesh.

But this time, Zuriel was bringing soldiers. If any fists were going to swing, it would be those of soldiers beating on his bones. Asaph stood in the center of his courtyard, shaking violently, mostly out of rage but partly out of fear.

"You don't have time to think." Malachi took his friend by the arm. "If they find you, they will imprison you until they dig up the evidence they seek. The vase belongs to Tarquinius! He has influence!"

Asaph nodded. There was sense in that.

He could do this. He would leave for a few days until the storm passed, and then he would return to tax Zuriel into oblivion.

Rushing into his sleeping quarters, Asaph jammed a few extra tunics into a sack, along with some bread and figs. Then he grabbed his cloak and sword and rushed into the street. He spotted two soldiers making a beeline for his house, flanked by Zuriel and Tarquinius.

Hidden by the shadows, he ducked down an alley and paused, watching. Should he stay and face his accusers, declaring his innocence?

He shook his head. Malachi was right. Tarquinius was powerful and would toss him in jail, keeping him there until they found the vase or fabricated some evidence against him. Heaven forbid, they might even torture a confession out of Calliste.

Asaph sprinted through the dark city, nearly ramming into an old drunk who staggered into his path.

"Watch where you're going!" the drunk shouted, swaying and waving his cup as it sloshed wine over his clothing.

Asaph tossed a choice curse over his shoulder, sprinted through the city gate, charged by his tax booth, and fled into the wilderness. He hadn't run this fast since his youth when he used to race Eliana through the winding streets of their small town.

JEREMIEL

Jeremiel was hit by the scent of mint when he stepped inside the door of the small synagogue in Nazareth. He inhaled deeply the mint used to purify the air. Nazareth may have been a backwater town with a small synagogue, but at least it smelled familiar.

Jeremiel straightened his back and walked further inside. He was proud that the Pharisee leaders in Jerusalem selected him to travel to this Galilean town to gather information on this "Jesus."

Between the rumors of miracles and the rapidly growing followers that Jesus attracted, the Pharisees were on high alert. Would-be prophets popped up like weeds, and if you didn't tear them out by the roots, they could choke out the Truth.

The synagogue was perched at the town's highest point, not far from a bluff, because no man should live in a home above the synagogue.

As Jeremiel's eyes adjusted to the darkness inside the rectangular hall, his gaze bounced around the room, landing on the chief seats. These were ornate chairs just in front of the ark, which contained the scrolls of Scripture. His heart dropped when he saw that each of the chief seats next to the ruler of the synagogue was claimed. He had taken it for granted that one would have been reserved for him.

Jeremiel glared at the influential men who occupied the chief seats. But when his eyes landed on the two men sitting on the right side of the synagogue leader, he had to stifle a groan.

It was Nekoda and his younger brother, Chaim.

What were they doing in Nazareth? Had the Sadducees sent them on a similar mission to learn what they could about Jesus of Nazareth?

Nekoda caught his eye and gave him a slight smile and nod. Jeremiel shifted his glare toward the center of the synagogue. He searched for a front-row seat among the benches on either side of the raised wooden platform, the *bimah*, where the scrolls would be read. But every spot was also taken, except for one narrow space at the end. He decided he would squeeze into that seat, even if by force.

He made for the open spot, but before he could reach it, another man dropped onto the seat, forcing the entire line of men to shift right. Jeremiel came up short, his mouth dropping open. He was tempted to demand the seat but clamped his lips and held his tongue.

Didn't these people know he was a priest from the Temple in Jerusalem? Who did these bumpkin Nazarenes think they were?

By the time he squeezed into an open seat in the fourth row, Jeremiel was so angry he almost forgot why he was there. He closed his eyes and counted to ten. When he finally got a hold of himself, he scanned the crowd, wondering which one might be Jesus.

A man who appeared to be in his thirties stood to begin the service. Jeremiel looked him over, thinking it had to be Jesus. He'd learned that the famous son of Nazareth had been given the honor of being the *Sheiliach Tzibbur*—the person who leads the prayers. From the raised platform, Jesus began the service with two prayers, followed by the *Shema*, the words of Deuteronomy.

"Hear, O Israel: The Lord our God, the Lord is one. Love the Lord your God with all your heart and with all your soul and with all your strength. These commandments that I give you today are to be on your hearts."

The moment Jesus began to speak, something about his voice and manner drew Jeremiel deeply into the text. Jesus had charisma, but for Jeremiel, that was not necessarily a good thing. The service should focus on the Lord and the Law, not on a man.

Jesus followed the *Shema* with more prayers before other readers recited from the Torah, leading to a reading from the prophets. Jesus stepped onto the *bimah*, where he unrolled the scroll of the prophet Isaiah and began to read aloud.

"The Spirit of the Lord is on me, because He has anointed me to preach good news to the poor. He has sent me to proclaim freedom for the prisoners and recovery of sight for the blind, to release the oppressed, to proclaim the year of the Lord's favor."

Jesus raised his eyes from the scroll and swept the crowd, lingering momentarily on Jeremiel. Then he rolled up the scroll, handed it back to the attendant, and took a seat. Everyone's eyes fastened on him, waiting in anticipation for him to begin teaching, as was the tradition.

"Today this scripture is fulfilled in your hearing," Jesus declared.

Jeremiel bolted upright as if stabbed from behind. *This scripture is fulfilled*? Who did Jesus think he was? He must have misspoken. Does he think he is the Messiah, bringing sight to the blind and freedom to prisoners? Jeremiel picked at an itch on his right forearm, watching those around him become agitated, whispering to each other.

Then Jesus continued, and there was a slight easing of tension because his words were rich and smooth. Too smooth in Jeremiel's mind, too rich. Jeremiel liked his teaching plain and basic, like a crust of bread. Jesus's words were honey, and Jeremiel spurned honey as a decadent delicacy. But many around him seemed taken in by his teaching; he heard murmurs of approval as men nodded their heads.

"Isn't this Joseph's son?" one man within earshot whispered.

Just as Jesus seemed to have the men eating out of his hands, he slapped them back with his next words.

"Surely you will quote this proverb to me, 'Physician heal yourself!' And you will tell me, 'Do here in your hometown what we have heard that you did in Capernaum.'"

Jesus paused to let the words seep in. He was right. Many in this room probably thought they deserved to see a miracle like the ones he supposedly performed in places like Capernaum and Cana. They, too, wanted to witness a wonder.

"This is his hometown. Why shouldn't we see the proof in front of our eyes," one man whispered.

As if Jesus heard the whisper, he nodded. "Truly I tell you, no prophet is accepted in his hometown."

That statement wiped the smiles from the faces of these uneducated Nazarenes and nearly put a grin on Jeremiel's face. But he held back.

No prophet is accepted in his hometown.

He had to hand it to Jesus. The teacher had seen through the motivations of these small-town, small-minded men. They only admired him because of his miracles. They wanted to taste the honey of his healings.

Jesus looked from one side of the room to the other. "I assure you that there were many widows in Israel in Elijah's time when the sky was shut for three and a half years, and there was a severe famine throughout the land. Yet Elijah was not sent to any of them but to a widow in Zarephath in the region of Sidon."

Now, he had *really* angered them. Jesus said Elijah had used his miracles for a widow in Zarephath, a *Gentile*. While Elijah could have done a miracle for a Jewish widow in Israel, he chose a non-Jew instead! Was Jesus saying he would rather perform miracles for unclean Gentiles than for the Jews in Nazareth?

Friendly murmurs soon became frustrated mutterings. This prophet was going to get himself killed if he continued hurling insults. Jeremiel despised showing favoritism to unclean Gentiles, but he had to admit he enjoyed seeing the growing agitation among the Nazarenes. It served them right.

"And there were many in Israel with leprosy in the time of Elisha the prophet, yet not one of them was cleansed—only Naaman the Syrian," Jesus said.

Again, his words struck them with the force of a rock. The prophet Elisha did not use God's power to heal Jewish lepers, Jesus said. Instead, Elisha had cured Naaman, an unworthy, unclean soldier—*a Gentile.*

This was too much for the people of the synagogue. They rose to their feet and closed in on Jesus.

"Who are you to say we are not worthy of healing?" one man shouted, raising a fist.

"Do you dare tell us that God has sent you to the outsiders?"

Jeremiel was nearly knocked over as the man behind him rushed toward Jesus. The carpenter's son stood to his feet, but he said nothing to the men who suddenly encircled him like wolves. Jeremiel wondered if he might be heading back to Jerusalem sooner than expected because this prophet might not make it out of the synagogue alive.

When Jesus turned and walked slowly for the synagogue exit, Jeremiel was sure the men would not let him leave. They formed a human wall, but Jesus kept striding toward them, oblivious to the barrier. Jeremiel held his breath, waiting. But at the last moment, the group parted like the Red Sea, letting him pass.

Almost two dozen followed Jesus from the synagogue with Jeremiel at their heels. He watched the crowd outside, wondering if Jesus's mother was amongst them, about to see her child murdered. He felt a twinge of compassion but ignored it.

"Are we not holy enough to receive a miracle?" one of the men shouted as they continued to dog Jesus's steps.

Two men snatched up rocks while another plucked a thick stick from a pile of kindling. A fourth man pushed Jesus from behind and nearly knocked him off his feet as the crowd pressed him toward the edge of the bluff.

The Nazarenes were behaving like sheepdogs in reverse. Typically, one sheepdog could keep an entire flock *away* from danger. But in this case, dozens of howling dogs directed a single lamb closer to his death. It was against Jewish law to execute someone on the Sabbath, so would they really do it?

When the mob reached the brow of the hill, Jesus had nowhere to go. The dusty day turned the air a hazy brown as the wind snapped at the men's robes. Jesus's long hair seemed alive with the wind as he turned to face the crowd, which had gone silent.

The men had reached a tipping point in their fury. If they were going to kill this prophet, they need only give him a few more shoves, and he would be airborne, dying on the crags below.

Jesus looked from face to face, daring them. No one moved. Jeremiel rubbed his eyes as a bit of dust stung his vision.

Then Jesus strode away from the cliff edge toward the cluster of men, his piercing eyes making contact as he approached. Once again, the wall of men parted to let him pass in silence through the heart of their hatred. Then Jesus made a right turn to head toward the edge of town.

"*Yeshu!*" one of the men shouted, and several others picked up the taunt: "*Yeshu! Yeshu!*"

Yeshu was Hebrew for "may his name and memory be blotted out"—a clever play on the name of Yeshua, or Jesus.

Several men spit on the ground as Jesus vanished into the brown haze.

KETURAH

Keturah cast a quick glance over her shoulder at Eliana. Her skin crawled at the thought of being so close to this weird woman, but she had no choice. She was forced into line in front of Eliana, whether she liked it or not.

Keturah had to listen to the woman's constant babble at her back. Equally annoying was Eliana's camel, which let out a throaty moan almost non-stop. This creature, with its long neck and large, yellow teeth, could easily bite her from behind. Notoriously grouchy, camels were also known to draw stomach acid into their mouths and spit it at anyone at any time.

Keturah wouldn't be surprised if Eliana also bared her teeth and tried to take a bite out of her.

Keturah sighed as the sun dipped below the horizon. The caravan leaders didn't seem in any hurry to reach Tiberias, stopping at every chance.

Tonight, they settled at a spring to water the camels while Haran watered his donkey. The setting sun colored the ground with splotches of red, like the bloodstains on Keturah's clothes. Small scattered clusters of vegetation protruded through stony soil, giving some shelter from the breeze.

When a tingling sensation ran along Keturah's spine, she turned to find a few of the traders staring at her.

"Let's rest over here." Keturah pulled Haran toward a spot farther away, hoping to stay out of the sight and minds of the men. She noticed Eliana doing the same, finding a place all to herself, even farther from camp.

"These will give you strength," Haran said, producing figs from a sack, along with a round of bread.

"Thank you."

Keturah glanced again at Eliana, who had nothing to eat, and her servant's heart began to stir.

Eliana sat there, staring into the bleak distance, occasionally sifting sand through her fingers and watching it fly off with the breeze. While Keturah hated the thought of approaching this odd woman, she couldn't let her starve.

"Don't." Haran raised a hand, warning her not to help.

Keturah stood with a soft shake of her head. She couldn't believe it, but she found herself walking up to this strange soul.

"Are you hungry?" She held out one of the figs.

Eliana eyed the fig but made no move to take it. When Eliana licked her dry lips, Keturah pushed the food closer. Surely, the woman was famished. Suddenly, Eliana growled, followed by a quick hiss. As Keturah jerked her hand away, Eliana smiled triumphantly.

Undaunted, Keturah extended her other hand, which held a round of bread. Eliana paused before leaning forward to smell the food.

Keturah held out the bread until her arm began to tire. As she made a move to draw back, Eliana pounced, her hand striking like a snake, snatching the bread.

Then Eliana turned, hunching over and hiding the bread from view while nibbling on the edges. Keturah returned to her spot and sat cross-legged, biting into the sweet fig.

Keturah cocked her head. Why was Eliana traveling alone? It was dangerous, especially for a woman. Was she a widow? And if so, why hadn't she remarried?

The emperor Augustus recently passed a law requiring all widows to remarry within two years—although the government did not consistently enforce it among Jews on the outskirts of the empire. Besides, who would consider marrying someone like Eliana?

Keturah considered her own predicament. While slaves could not legally marry, a mistress like Joanna could have freed her to make it possible—assuming the magistrates allowed it. But who knew what would happen now? Could she pass as a free woman?

As shadows lengthened across the rocks, something drew Keturah's attention deeper into the gloom. It was a shadow of the wild dog she'd seen earlier, now peeking around a rock.

Eliana also spotted the dog. She and the animal stared at each other like they were in a contest of wills. Keturah was taken aback. Eliana rarely made eye contact with humans, yet she had no problem locking eyes with this dog.

Finally, Eliana scrambled to her feet and walked toward the dog. When it backed up and cocked its head, wary of human contact, Eliana halted. After a moment, the dog stepped forward, curious. Then Eliana closed the gap once more before the animal retreated. They repeated the same dance until, finally, Eliana held out a piece of the bread so tantalizingly close. The dog sniffed, edging closer.

"We don't have bread to spare, and she goes and gives it to a dog," Haran grumbled, but Keturah shushed him. She was mesmerized by Eliana's magic hold over the animal.

Eliana eventually had the wild dog eating out of her hand. She smiled at the animal, one of the first times Keturah had seen anything on her face other than a scowl. Even more amazing, Eliana tossed a look over her shoulder, sharing another smile with her.

When Keturah woke in the dark, a large hand smelling of dung covered her mouth. Keturah struggled with a muffled scream, but the hulking shadow put a knife to the corner of her eye.

"Try to scream again, and I'll give you something to scream about," a gruff voice whispered.

When the man released his hand, Keturah tried to scream, but he jammed a dirty rag inside her mouth, shoving it in so far that she almost vomited. When he realized she was choking, he adjusted the rag before wrapping another piece of cloth around her head and jaw to keep the gag in place.

As her eyes adjusted to the darkness, she recognized her attacker. It was the brute Ithamar. She began to wish that Sveshtari had really killed her back at the fortress.

Ithamar was strong, so she had no hope of squirming out of his grip—especially with that knife still pressed against her throat. He finally yanked her to her feet.

Maybe I should try to run, and if he kills me, so be it.

Her shoulders sagged. Why did Sveshtari send her out with only the protection of a boy too young to shave? Some help Haran was. He was sound asleep a good distance from her, and she could still hear him snoring. Even if she could scream, she had a better chance of waking up the rock he used as a pillow than him.

As Ithamar dragged her into the darkness, she let her body go limp, hoping to make his job as difficult as possible. Keturah's mind spun. She should do something now before Ithamar took her too far from camp. She should gouge out his eyes or scratch the skin from his face. Something. Anything.

But she did nothing. Like her body, her spirit had gone limp. She sensed she was already dead. Keturah squeezed her eyes shut, burying herself deep inside her soul.

Soon, they were too far away for any of the other men to hear. Tears stung Keturah's eyes as she thought of the strangers back by the fire. If the others heard her scream, would they even care?

She crawled deeper into herself, burying herself alive.

Then something charged from the dark at full tilt, barreling into her attacker. She caught sight of this someone in the moonlight, caught up in a frenzy of uncontrollable motion. At first, she thought it was Haran coming to protect her.

When Keturah wiped away the tears blurring her eyes, she found it wasn't Haran or any other man. It was a woman.

As Eliana knocked Ithamar on his back, Keturah tumbled in the opposite direction. Once Keturah was able to steady herself, she yanked out the gag, gulping deep breaths.

Eliana straddled Ithamar, plunging her hand downward repeatedly. Keturah blinked, unsure of what she was seeing in the dark, but it seemed that Eliana was stabbing the attacker with a wild pumping action.

As Ithamar let out a gurgling gasp, struggling to defend himself, Keturah maneuvered around the tangled mass of shadows. She thought about running to Haran for help, but there wasn't time. She had to do something to help, but she had never dared to attack a man before. Before she could locate Ithamar's head to gouge the man's eyes, the man wrapped his legs around Eliana's neck, jerking her backward. The next moment, he was on top of her.

Pinned on her back, Eliana had her right hand raised in the air, still clutching the knife, and she tried to stab him again. Ithamar grabbed her wrist, trying to break her sparrow-thin bones.

On instinct, Keturah leaped on Ithamar's back and looped her arm around his neck, a stranglehold, but he elbowed her in the stomach, knocking the wind out of her.

As she fell on her back, gasping for air, she rolled to her side. The knife was now in the man's hand, and he was about to kill Eliana. Keturah put a hand to her throat, knowing she'd be next.

5
LUKE, CHAPTER 5

KETURAH

A S ITHAMAR RAISED THE knife over Eliana's body, another shadow hurtled out of the dark and pounced on his back.

Keturah gasped as the wild dog tore into Ithamar's neck, blood spurting. She jerked backward, falling to her elbows, and rolled out of the way as Ithamar toppled to the side. The man tried to cover his head, but the dog was relentless. When Ithamar squirmed onto his back, the animal leaped onto his chest, ripping, biting, and growling.

Eliana pushed to a sitting position, watching the mauling in the dark while Keturah scrambled to her feet. They both stared as the dog continued his frenzied attack, even after Ithamar was no longer of this world.

Finally, the animal ceased and nudged the body with its nose, still growling. Eliana approached the dog and put a gentle hand on its back. As she stroked its matted fur, the animal began to calm. Keturah came to Eliana's side, also placing her hand on the dog's back.

"You're nothing but skin and bones," Keturah murmured.

Eliana knelt, resting her head on the dog's back as if listening to its heartbeat, and wrapped an arm around its side.

"Thank you," Keturah whispered, unsure whether she was directing her thanks at Eliana or the dog. They both deserved her gratitude. "You saved my life. I won't forget that."

Eliana didn't respond unless a grunt qualified.

"We should drag his body even farther from the camp," Keturah said, motioning for Eliana to help.

While she took hold of one of Ithamar's legs, a silent Eliana grabbed the other, and they dragged the body to a clump of bushes.

"If the traders find him, they'll assume he was done in by wild animals," said Keturah.

"He *was* done in by a wild animal."

The dog stood about ten paces away, observing them with a curious stare, and waited. With the job done, Keturah approached the dog and gently petted it with one hand. The dog licked her other.

"I think he deserves a name, don't you?" Keturah said with a nod.

"Lavi," Eliana answered instantly as if she had already chosen the name long before this moment. "He is Lavi."

Lavi meant "lion."

"I like it." Keturah grinned, her chest warming with emotion. "He's our lion, our protector."

A small smile flickered on Eliana's face, or so Keturah thought. The moment she saw the smile, it was gone, and she convinced herself she must have been imagining things in the dark.

ASAPH

Asaph counted six men, but who knew how many might lurk behind the rocks. He checked his surroundings like he really had anywhere to run.

While it was dangerous to travel alone, he had no choice. He intended to trek the relatively short distance west from Jericho to Jerusalem—a painfully steep road. He made it most of the way under the cover of darkness and was not too far from his goal when the sun arose. This band of brigands appeared on horseback, in sync with daybreak.

Typically, only Romans rode horseback, but these were no Romans. They were well equipped for speed and combat, so Asaph guessed they were Zealots—Jewish freedom fighters.

As the men blocked his path, one leaned forward on his horse, peering down at Asaph. "Where are you bound for?" said the muscular man with a long, black beard.

Asaph glanced at the men with a hint of hesitation. How he answered could determine his fate. Although they all donned smiles, they were not what Asaph would consider welcoming expressions.

No matter. Asaph put on a friendly front.

"Shalom! I am bound for Jerusalem." He extended his arms out to show he was not carrying a weapon.

"Alone?"

Asaph wondered whether he should fabricate a story about friends close by, but something told him these men could spot a blatant lie.

"It's just a one-day walk...from Jericho."

"Don't you know better than to travel by yourself? There are some unsavory people along these roads."

Such as these men.

Asaph covered his eyes as the sun continued to rise. "I have the Lord's protection."

Asaph hadn't prayed for the Lord's protection since his childhood. Still, these Zealots might appreciate a show of devotion.

"Does the Lord really protect a tax farmer?" asked a young man in the group. Asaph's stomach dropped.

Maybe it was time to start praying.

"He's a tax farmer?" The one with the thick black beard adjusted in his saddle to get a closer look at Asaph.

"When he mentioned coming from Jericho, I remembered," said the young man, not even twenty years old from the look of it. He nodded with assurance and pointed at Asaph. "He operates the tax booth as you enter the city."

Asaph gave a nervous chuckle, waving a hand in denial. "No, no, you must be mistaken. I know of the man you speak of, and I can see a slight resemblance. But I'm not him."

"He's lying," said the young man.

It was the black-bearded man's turn to laugh. "A liar and a tax collector. That's one and the same thing, isn't it?"

Asaph took a step back. "I despise tax collectors as much as the next man. I was going to the Temple in Jerusalem to worship."

"Dressed like a Roman?" Black Beard said.

Asaph glanced down, swallowing the lump in his throat. His tunic did not resemble anything a Jewish man on a pilgrimage to Jerusalem would wear. He often wore a Roman-style tunic, and his clean-shaven chin also marked him as someone who copied the Roman way.

"I am not a tax collector," he insisted.

"Your lies say you are," said Black Beard. "Bind him."

As one of the men dismounted and approached, Asaph noticed he had a *sica*, a small, arched dagger, strapped to his waist. These had to be Zealots—devout Jews who despised Rome. Tax collectors were Roman collaborators, so their lives didn't mean much in Zealot hands.

While Asaph prided himself on being one of the Roman lions, he behaved as meekly as a lamb while one of the Zealots bound his hands behind his back, tied a rope to a saddle, and pulled him alongside the horse.

"I have money." He stumbled to keep pace with the horse.

Black Beard glanced over his shoulder from atop his high horse. "What good is offering us money when we can take whatever we want from you?"

"You could ransom me. I'm worth something."

"True. Your head might be worth a few sesterces in the market," one of them joked, and the rest laughed.

Asaph dropped his head, staring at the ground, thankful that the men went slowly, careful not to drag him off his feet. Asaph hoped this consideration was a sign they wouldn't beat him to a pulp and leave him for dead somewhere.

He looked up as a large, black bird of prey hovered above them—a stark contrast against the intense blue sky. He absorbed the scenery on all sides, fearing this would be the last he'd ever see of the world.

The next thing he knew, he found himself praying to God. He didn't pray aloud to prove to these men they had captured a devout Jew. He prayed internally, devoutly, sincerely...and desperately. It was the first time he had prayed, *really prayed*, in years.

Finally, they reached the mouth of a cave, where he spotted another four men crouching by a fire. From the looks of it, they had just finished a meal. Three Zealots stood, while the fourth and oldest remained on his rocky throne.

The eldest had a medium-length beard with a silver stripe running down the middle. He had three distinct furrows on his sun-scorched forehead, with laugh lines branching out from his eyes like someone accustomed to humor. While he might have been robust in his prime, time had taken its toll.

Asaph chewed the inside of his cheek, squinting as he finished studying the man. Beneath the years and the gray facial hair, there was something strangely familiar about him.

"Look what we found!" announced Black Beard, pushing him forward. "A tax collector!"

"In the middle of nowhere?" Gray Beard grinned. "What is there to tax in the wilderness? If you try to tax a jackal, he'll rip you apart."

"Tax us, and we'll do the same," said the young one, who had already dismounted. He pulled out his dagger and strode with the exaggerated confidence of youth.

"I've been trying to tell them I'm not a tax collector. They got the wrong man."

Asaph searched Gray Beard for sympathy. The man returned the gaze with intense gray eyes, but his humor had gone.

"What is your name, tax collector?" he asked.

"I am not a tax collector."

"That is not what I asked. What's your name?"

Asaph decided to give him a false name, but his mind was drawing a blank, and he felt the silence grow.

"Can't you come up with a phony name faster than that?" Gray Beard's grin returned. "Why not just stick with your real name, Asaph?"

Asaph sucked in a short breath. How did he know? He stared at the man, trying to strip away the years and remember where he had seen the face.

Finally, his thoughts clicked into place, like fitting a stone into a wall of lifetime memories, and he remembered. Gray Beard was someone he knew from his hometown in Judea.

Gray Beard was Eliana's father.

JEREMIEL

Jeremiel sat in the middle of the largest room in the home of Peter, a boorish fisherman who was one of Jesus's followers. As throngs of people pushed, trying to find their place, he exhaled, knowing he had a seat of honor, this time alongside other priests.

Peter's home looked out on the Sea of Galilee, which would have been pleasant if the pungent smell of fish wasn't trapped in every corner. Add to it the scent of sweat and desperation as the mob pressed forward, and it was almost unbearable.

Jeremiel eyed the people who came in droves, vying for position, because of the rumors that Jesus apparently healed a leper. Jeremiel had been tracking Jesus's movements throughout Galilee, but he fell ill on the day of the reported miracle, so he didn't witness the act and had a tough time believing it. After the alleged healing, Jesus escaped into the wilderness, making it more difficult to discover his whereabouts or determine his activity.

Now that Jesus was back in Capernaum, on the northwest side of the Sea of Galilee, he made his headquarters in Peter's house. The house was a *bet 'ab* that sheltered other relatives, including the big fisherman's brother, Andrew.

Every inch of the place was packed with people, like sheep jammed into a pen. Even the north courtyard of the home, just outside the room where Jeremiel sat, overflowed with those flocking to see a miracle.

"You have to admit...this is exciting," said Nekoda, who sat to Jeremiel's left, rubbing his hands together.

Jeremiel rolled his eyes. Everywhere he seemed to turn, Nekoda was there, like an annoying stone in his sandal. The same could be said for Nekoda's brother, Chaim, but Jeremiel had more tolerance for Chaim—even sympathy.

As the younger brother, Chaim lived in Nekoda's long shadow. Chaim was shorter and rounder than Nekoda and had inherited his father's oversized head and large ears. The only physical feature that gave him an advantage over his bald brother was a thriving head of black hair. However, Chaim's wild hair only exaggerated his large head.

"When Nekoda was asked to go to Galilee, he insisted I come along to learn," Chaim said. "He's always looking out for me."

Jeremiel grunted. Of course, Nekoda looked out for his little brother. It put him in control.

Nekoda watched, eyes wide. "People are lined up outside."

"And I'm beginning to wish I was outside with them." Jeremiel stared over the tops of the heads, watching the door. "There are too many sick people in this space."

Jeremiel shivered as the uncleanness surrounding them crawled along his skin. What if a leper dared to squeeze into this crowded room, looking to be healed? There would be a stampede, and people would be crushed and killed. The miracle worker, Jesus, would be responsible for their deaths.

"I was there when the leper was healed!" Chaim said. "I never saw anything like it."

Jeremiel rolled his eyes, and Nekoda shrugged with a look that spoke volumes. Clearly, Nekoda was as unimpressed as Jeremiel was.

Once Jesus made his way into the room, many in the crowd began calling out his name, reaching out and begging to be healed. Jesus greeted them silently, staring into their eyes, one after another.

Jesus had just started teaching when something sprinkled on Jeremiel's head. He looked up just in time to see a clump of dirt hit him squarely in the face. Some of the dirt got in his eyes and stung like the devil. He shot from his seat as more dirt showered from the roof.

When Nekoda noticed Jeremiel's dirty hair and clothing, he laughed and stood, trying to help brush it from Jeremiel's robe.

"I can take care of it myself." Jeremiel pushed Nekoda's hand away before glaring at the ceiling. "Someone should remove the animals from up there before they disturb the rest of us."

"Watch out," Nekoda chuckled. "I think you're directly in the path of another downpour."

As more dirt sprinkled from the ceiling, Chaim shook it from his hair, laughing. "I do believe it is raining earth!"

Jeremiel glared. This was no laughing matter, especially now that he realized what was happening. Four men pulled away tiles from the flat roof and clawed through the layer of soil and straw to create an opening. Since they couldn't reach Jesus through the front door, they got creative.

Jeremiel scowled. "Fools! What gives them the right to damage property?"

All eyes went to the ceiling, including those of Jesus, who smiled at the men on the roof.

Just when Jeremiel thought it couldn't get any worse, the four friends began to lower a fifth man on a stretcher made of sheepskin and wool. They had attached ropes to the mat's four corners to lower the sick man through the roof's sizable opening into the heart of the room. Jeremiel shuffled back a few steps when he realized they were about to drop the sick man and his mat right on his head.

With such a big crowd and so little room, Jeremiel wasn't sure how they made space without crushing people against the back walls. Still, they created a small circle around the sick man, who lay on the earthen floor before Jesus.

The crowd hushed as one of the men on the roof called through the hole. "Jesus, please heal our friend! He is paralyzed!"

The word "paralyzed" sent Jeremiel shuffling back two more steps, stepping on someone's toes. When the man behind him shoved him off, Jeremiel nearly tumbled onto the unclean paralytic, whose limbs had been frozen by the judgment of God.

The paralyzed man lay still, only able to move his neck, his eyes darting about, searching for Jesus's face.

Jeremiel's chest tightened. *The man's soul is trapped inside a dead body, as lifeless as stone from the neck down.* He wondered what sins this man must have committed to be struck by such a terrible scourge.

Jesus crouched, lifted the man's right hand, and ran his fingers across the back of it. Then Jesus looked up at the four faces staring down from the hole in the roof.

"Please, Jesus...please," said one of them.

Jesus sent them a smile before staring into the eyes of the paralyzed man. The afflicted man repeated the same refrain: "Please, Jesus."

Jesus put a hand on the man's shoulder. "Friend, your sins are forgiven."

Jeremiel blinked. Nothing would have shocked him more than if the entire roof had caved in on them. Even Nekoda looked stunned.

Jesus speaks blasphemy. Only God can forgive sins! But Jesus says he has forgiven this man's sins, taking on the mantle of the Almighty.

Jeremiel scanned the crowd, wondering who was going to be the first to rebuke Jesus. But everyone seemed too shocked to speak. He decided if no one else had the courage to say something, he would.

As Jeremiel formulated his response, Jesus stood and studied each priest. "Why are you thinking these things in your hearts?" he asked.

So now Jesus claims to read minds? Is there no limit to his arrogance?

"Isn't it obvious?" Jeremiel waved an arm.

Did Jesus have to be told why it was wrong for a mere man to forgive sins? Was he insane? Demon-possessed?

Jesus looked at Jeremiel and smiled. *He smiled!* Jeremiel shook—his heart burning with fury.

"Which is easier: to say, 'Your sins are forgiven,' or to say, 'Get up and walk'?" Jesus asked.

Jeremiel parted his lips to answer, but no words came. It was certainly easier to say, "Your sins are forgiven." But there was much more to true forgiveness than rattling off a string of words. Performing the act of forgiveness meant you had the power to wash away the filth inside a person, but only God had that ability.

"Blasphemer!" someone shouted from the back of the room.

Jeremiel had always been taught there were three ways to blaspheme God. You could attribute evil actions to God, deny the goodness of the Lord, or claim the power and authority of God for yourself.

Jesus had claimed the authority of the Lord.

The Nazarene looked down on the paralyzed man. "But I want you to know that the Son of Man has authority on earth to forgive sins..." He crouched again and stared into the paralyzed man's eyes. "I tell you, get up, take your mat and go home."

The afflicted man took a ragged breath and nodded. He closed his eyes, concentrating, and within moments, his fingers twitched. Murmurs rose from the crowd like a tide.

Jeremiel swallowed, his chest tightening, as he tried to convince himself that he was just seeing things when the paralytic began to move his fingers, like someone working the stiffness out of his hand. Then the man rotated his ankles, cracking joints, and bent his knee, resting his foot on the mat. The crowd rippled with wonder.

Jeremiel scoffed. This was a ruse. He glanced at the four open-mouthed friends on the roof, wondering if it was all an act. Were those four men in on this stunt? If so, they were good actors.

As the paralyzed man stood to his feet with tears in his eyes, one of Jesus's disciples rushed forward to steady him.

He looked up at his friends, waving his arms. "My legs! My arms! Praise God!"

The man threw himself at Jesus and used his newfound arms to hug the Nazarene, squeezing and burying his head in the teacher's chest. He began to weep and shake before he wheeled around, staggering on unsteady legs.

He picked up his mat, as Jesus had commanded, and raised it above his head. "Praise God!"

After taking a step, he hopped from foot to foot, testing out his new legs. On the fourth hop, he lost his balance and stumbled into the crowd. Several men caught him and pushed him back to his feet, and he laughed crazily.

As the man's face lit up with amazement and joy, Jeremiel scowled. How could Jesus claim to forgive sins? This man's sins had bound his arms and legs like ropes. Yet Jesus claimed to have cut those cords, releasing his limbs from bondage. Only the Lord has that kind of authority and power!

Jeremiel wanted to shout, "Blasphemer," but it would have been useless because it would be drowned out by the misplaced jubilation in the room. Even Nekoda and Chaim looked dumbfounded as if they, too, had been taken in by this masterful performance.

Jeremiel bit his tongue, knowing without a shadow of a doubt that Jesus was indeed a dangerous man.

ELIANA

Eliana sensed Calev's fury after she had risked her life to save "that woman" as he kept referring to Keturah. Now, he pushed Eliana to kill Keturah and the dog, for the attacker's blood was not enough.

"Shut up!" Eliana raged at Calev.

Eliana wished she could explain why she bothered to rescue Keturah, but she couldn't. She had been lying on the ground wide awake when she heard scuffling followed by Keturah's muffled cries. She was initially curious when she noticed someone dragging Keturah into the deep darkness. Nothing more.

As she followed from a distance, she could see that the man had a knife to "that woman's" neck.

"Don't save her," Calev warned her.

Eliana shrugged, content with listening and watching. But something changed when the dog, Lavi, emerged from the night and slipped silently to her side.

Eliana gazed into Lavi's eyes and sensed his silent judgment. She looked away and said, "This woman is not part of my pack. Why should I care? Why should I do anything?"

"Yes, don't help her." Calev's dark command rang through her head. Eliana let out an obstinate growl. Why was everyone trying to control her?

"Don't you dare," Calev repeated.

Eliana reacted without another thought, pulling a knife from her robe and hurling herself at the man who abducted Keturah. She was ready to sacrifice herself for Keturah—an idea that shocked and confused her now that she thought about it.

The following morning, when the other traders discovered the man's shredded body in the bushes, it was surrounded by a pack of hungry jackals. The traders assumed he had wandered too far from camp to answer the call of nature, and wild animals had pounced upon him.

No one suspected Eliana's involvement or her dog, Lavi. They had even allowed Eliana to tie a rope around Lavi and bring him along.

"If we run out of food, we can always cook us some dog," one of the traders joked. Eliana tightened her grip on the rope, vowing to kill them if they tried.

The caravan approached the southern gate of Tiberias, the capital city of Galilee, perched on the western edge of the Sea of Galilee. Eliana studied Herod Antipas's newly built city as they streamed between two twin white towers. They moved along the bustling colonnaded street past an enormous theater just to the left.

Keturah leaned close. "Do you know about the graves of Tiberias?"

Eliana frowned. Keturah had been trying to make conversation since the night of the attack. Couldn't she get it through her head that they weren't friends?

Even though Eliana ignored her, Keturah didn't get the message and continued. "They say this city was built over the graves of Jews. That's why many Jewish people will not live here. Does that scare you?"

Eliana cocked her head. Why should she care if the city was built where some old Jews had been buried? Although she grew up Jewish, she no longer belonged to God. She and Lavi belonged to a different pack.

"Nothing scares me," Eliana finally said.

As they moved deeper into the heart of Tiberias, Calev whispered, for what had to be the hundredth time, "The Nazarene is in Galilee, Eliana. Find him and murder him."

"I will," Eliana said.

Keturah turned around and stared at her in bafflement. "You will what?"

Eliana released a soft, purring growl, hoping to scare Keturah. It must have worked. When Keturah adjusted in her saddle and turned away, Eliana sent a satisfied grin at her back.

Eliana raked her eyes over the ground her camel trod over, thinking of the graves buried below the city. This was a city of death, all right. Eliana sensed death rising from the soil like a low-lying fog. Strangely, it felt like home.

SVESHTARI: THREE WEEKS LATER, THE MONTH OF MARCHESHVAN (LATE OCTOBER), 27 A.D.

Sveshtari had shed his armor and strolled the marketplace near the open water, where refreshing breezes swept over him.

Herod had moved his household from the Fortress of Machaerus to the capital, Tiberias, famous for its hot springs. Herod frequented the baths, moving from the warm *tepidarium* to the hot *caldarium* to the cold *frigidarium*. While Herod took full advantage of the health benefits, sweating away his impurities, Sveshtari had to stand guard, sweltering in full uniform and roasting like a pig. This afternoon, however, Sveshtari was glad to be free from the heat of the baths.

He had already made his morning sacrifice to Mars, hoping to find favor with the god of war as a safeguard against Dionysus. For added protection, he wore a woodpecker's beak around his neck as a charm because it was a sacred bird to Mars. Even a bodyguard needed a supernatural protector in a universe where the gods could be petty and violent. He decided that Mars, the god of war, would make the best bodyguard.

Although Sveshtari was on his own time this afternoon, he still found himself drawn into keeping the peace in the marketplace. He'd already prevented a brawl between a shopkeeper and a man who claimed he had been sold a rotten fish.

When a woman's scream sounded to his left, Sveshtari swung around to discover a petite woman clawing at the tunic of a man who carried a squirming dog. The dog's snout had been tied with rope. Otherwise, the furious animal would have torn the man to pieces. Sveshtari sighed, for he had previously dealt with the man, Yosef.

"Give him back!" The woman scratched Yosef's cheek, trying to get him to release the dog. Yosef responded by laughing, then striking the woman squarely in the nose, sending her staggering, blood gushing.

She covered her face, groaning, as Yosef spun around, bumping into Sveshtari's broad chest.

Sveshtari put his hands on his shoulders, holding him in place. "And where are you headed, my friend?"

"None of your business." Yosef tried to wriggle free. While he was big enough to bloody a woman, he didn't have a chance with Sveshtari.

"I make it my business," said Sveshtari. "Whose dog is that?"

"The dog belongs to Mars. I am sacrificing him to a god, so you better not stop me!"

The last thing Sveshtari needed was to anger Mars, the god he had just bargained with to obtain protection from Dionysus. He very nearly let the man go free for that reason alone.

"He lies," came another woman's voice. It sounded surprisingly familiar.

Sveshtari searched the crowd for the speaker, stunned to see Keturah come into view.

"Ke—" he started to say but was unable to finish, his chest tightening with emotion. She had promised to come to Tiberias, but he doubted he would ever see her again.

"That dog belongs to me and my friend, Eliana," Keturah said, motioning toward the small woman with a bloody nose. Her calm voice gave him pause. Wasn't she shocked to see him? He gave a quick shake of his head, remembering the matter at hand.

"This is your dog?" Sveshtari asked Keturah, tightening his hold on Yosef.

"It's *mine,*" Yosef said, jutting his chin.

"No, it's not!" said Keturah's friend with a bloody nose. She lunged to gouge Yosef's eyes, but Sveshtari caught her by the wrist with his free hand, holding her back.

As the petite woman squirmed in his grip, Keturah pointed at the dog. "The dog saved my life. He saved both of our lives!"

Keturah moved close enough that Sveshtari caught the fragrance of her perfume—the same cinnamon smell he had inhaled so many times before. He released the bloody woman's wrist, aching to touch Keturah, but they were in public, and he still had hold of Yosef with his other hand.

"She lies!" Yosef held the animal close. "This dog is my sacrifice to Mars! If you don't let me drain its lifeblood, you will be punished by the gods!"

Sveshtari tossed up his hands and shook his head. He had already saved Keturah, displeasing Dionysus. If he rescued this dog, which was to be sacrificed to Mars, would he make an enemy out of yet another god?

Suddenly, Yosef snatched the woodpecker's beak dangling from Sveshtari's chest and tried to drive it into his neck. Sveshtari grabbed his wrist, breaking it with a snap before smacking him in the forehead with an open palm like a battering ram.

When the thief hit the ground, the mangy animal broke free and bolted for Keturah's friend—proof that the dog belonged to her.

Sveshtari hustled Keturah from the marketplace, leaving Yosef writhing on the ground. They found a secluded spot at the sea's edge, looking across to the hills on the eastern side of the lake—gray terrain with splotches of black. Gullies and rills sliced down the hills like wrinkles on an elephant's hide.

Keturah took Sveshtari by the hand. "I told you I would come to Tiberias to find you."

"With Herod in the city, it is not safe for you to remain here." Sveshtari looked over his shoulder. "If he finds out you are still alive..."

"But I want to be with you," her soft voice urged.

Sveshtari drew her close and said nothing.

"I'm not going to leave you again." Her eyes welled with tears. "So don't ask me to."

Sveshtari exhaled. "You don't have to go far to be safe. Magdala is a morning's walk from Tiberias, and Capernaum is just beyond that. You can hide in Capernaum."

When Keturah did not answer, he ran his fingers through her hair and wondered how many more gods he would displease for her sake. First, Dionysus. Then, Mars. Pretty soon, all the armies of heaven will be aligned against him.

"I have prayed to Nemesis every day since we parted," Keturah said. "I have prayed for justice, and if I stay here in Tiberias, I can get my vengeance on the man who killed my father. I will kill Rufus."

Sveshtari had hoped she had given up her insane plot to kill the body-guard that Sveshtari blamed for her father's death.

"I can kill him for you," he said. "No need to bloody your hands."

"But I *must* bloody them. Rufus killed my father. I must be the one to kill him."

Sveshtari sighed. "Even if you could kill him in Tiberias, it would be difficult to escape punishment. But I could lure him to a smaller city, away from Herod. If I could get him to Capernaum, there would be less risk of getting caught."

He could feel the pulse of excitement in Keturah's body. As she pulled back, her eyes lit up like two torches. "Could you do that for me?"

"I could."

In truth, he had no idea how to fulfill such a promise, but he would worry about that later. Right now, his only concern was satisfying Keturah's wishes and trying not to anger any more gods and goddesses.

JEREMIEL

Jeremiel had stopped for one of his three-times-daily prayers. He bent forward before a stone wall, eyes closed, hoping someone was close enough to hear his eloquent prayers.

When he opened his eyes, he found himself staring at a yellow scorpion a hands-breath away, burrowed into the wall. It had eyes in the front and on top of its head and two large claws, hinged and blood-red at the tips.

With the scorpion's deadly tail hooked over its armored body, poised to strike, Jeremiel cringed and immediately stopped praying. He probably wasn't in immediate danger because the scorpion would have to leap through the air to sting him. But he still drew back from the wall.

Jeremiel wondered if the scorpion was a sign from God. The Lord once told the prophet Ezekiel that the Israelites were a rebellious people and that living with them was like residing with scorpions. Was the Lord trying to say that he was also living among scorpions, and it was his job to speak the truth to them?

The scorpion's tail dipped as the six-legged miniature monster retreated into the crevice, deeper into the shadows. Jeremiel looked around, wondering if anyone had seen him in prayer, but everyone seemed oblivious as a large crowd streamed away from the center of town. Something was happening, and he could only suppose that Jesus was at the center of the commotion. Jesus's healing of the paralyzed man had brought even more fools to Capernaum.

"What's happening?" Jeremiel asked a passerby.

"Jesus is back—and he's having a feast at Levi's house!"

Levi? Talk about scorpions. Levi, or Matthew as he was known in Greek, was a tax collector, yet Jesus had the audacity to make him one of his followers.

Jeremiel hurried forward, following the crowd and wondering if this would be an opportunity to speak the prophetic truth to Jesus and his disciples.

Jeremiel lived a life of separation, observing sharply defined boundaries. The Law set boundaries throughout his day, instructing what he could eat, touch, and even the people with whom he could associate. As a Pharisee—a "separated one"—Jeremiel was careful never to mix the clean with the unclean. He separated clean and unclean people, as well as clean and unclean food. He would not even eat bread if it were cooked using wood from a tree worshipped as an idol. Jesus, on the other hand, carelessly strolled across the boundaries of the Law, dining with sinners and tax collectors. It was scandalous.

Levi's house was just as crowded as Peter's on the day Jesus healed the paralyzed man. People spilled out the front door into the garden. Even if there had been room inside Levi's house, Jeremiel wouldn't have crossed the threshold to dine with a tax collector. He would remain holy—set apart.

"Have you heard what they are eating in there?" came a voice to Jeremiel's left. He turned to find Chaim, Nekoda's brother.

Jeremiel shook his head, afraid to hear.

"Breads, fruits, and wine. Walnuts and lamb and pheasant. *Pheasant!*"

Jeremiel scowled. Pheasant was the costliest of birds. Prophets were called to fast, not feast.

When the banquet inside began to break up, one of Jesus's disciples emerged. It was Peter, the barrel-chested fisherman. The disciple had a bulbous nose, a beard peppered with flecks of gray, and a head of hair as unruly as the waves of the Sea of Galilee.

Jeremiel struck quickly with a question. "How could Jesus eat with tax collectors and sinners?"

"Ask him yourself," the fisherman said, pushing through the crowd.

When Jesus stepped from the house, the crowd pressed in so tightly that Jeremiel couldn't get close enough to ask, but he didn't have to. Other Pharisees, better positioned, fired off the very same question.

"Why do you eat and drink with tax collectors and sinners?"

Jesus stopped and turned. "It is not the healthy who need a doctor, but the sick. I have not come to call the righteous, but sinners to repentance."

"John's disciples often fast and pray, but yours go on eating and drinking!" shouted another Pharisee.

Jeremiel grunted. He wanted to ask the same thing, but he wasn't getting the chance to make his voice heard. Still, he was glad someone had asked. After all, John the Baptist fasted and lived on locusts in the wilderness. How could Jesus consider himself a true prophet if he and his disciples gorged on lamb, fruit, and pheasant?

"Can you make the friends of the bridegroom fast while he is with them?" Jesus answered. "But the time will come when the bridegroom will be taken from them; in those days they will fast."

Peter continued to clear a path so Jesus could move on, leaving Jeremiel dumbfounded. It sounded like Jesus described himself as a bridegroom, but why?

Jeremiel scratched an itch under his sleeve, and his finger grazed across a spot where there didn't seem to be any feeling. The patch of numb skin seemed almost foreign as if it belonged to another body.

Suddenly, everything around him faded. The Nazarene, the disciples, and the mad followers of Jesus all vanished like a mirage as Jeremiel focused on his arm, his mind racing.

This couldn't possibly be happening. Jeremiel tried to convince himself it was his imagination, but he knew the signs! As a priest, he knew them like the back of his hand.

Jeremiel's hand shook as he peeled back his large, flowing sleeve. Heart pounding, he couldn't force himself to look. His fingers blindly strayed across the dead patch of his arm before he finally gazed upon it.

Jeremiel couldn't have been more shocked if a scorpion had flown at him, driving its stinger into his face. He was paralyzed by fear. There, as clear as the sun, was a small, scaly patch of white skin on his forearm, a pale and ghostlike lesion.

Before anyone could see, he yanked his sleeve down, hiding the white scales, and hurried away from the throngs of people.

"Jeremiel! Jeremiel! Where are you going?" Chaim's cheerful, annoying voice rang out.

Jeremiel ignored him and staggered away from the crowd, away from Jesus, away from Chaim, away from his old life. There was no denying it. His world had just burst at the seams. That scaly lesion was the first sign of leprosy. He was a dead man.

6
LUKE, CHAPTER 6

ASAPH

A SAPH HAD HEARD THE rumors since he was a boy—the ones claiming that Eliana's family fled their village in the middle of the night to escape the Romans. If the stories were true, he had always assumed the Romans caught up with Eliana's father long ago. But here he was, sitting before him in the flesh.

Eliana's father, Judah, had aged thirty years, but he looked robust for a man in his sixties. Asaph and Judah sat alone by the crackling campfire, filling in the blank spaces of their past. Asaph's hands were no longer tied because Judah had ordered it so.

Eliana once told Asaph how safe she felt with her father—a strong, steady presence. He knew exactly what she meant. As a boy, Asaph had always wished his father could be more like Judah.

"Where is Eliana living?" he asked. If Judah survived, surely so had his daughter.

But even in the dark, Asaph could see Judah's eyes go hollow. "I just hope she is. Living, that is."

Asaph was afraid to ask anything more. Silence filled the space between them like black smoke. They stared into the fire until Judah finally cracked the silence.

"We were living in a cave near Bethlehem shortly after we fled the village. Eliana went out to see the shepherds one morning, as she did so often, but she never returned."

"Brigands?" Asaph held his breath.

Judah nodded. "One of the shepherds was found dead—by the sheepfold, where Eliana was last seen headed. I stole a horse that day and spent a year trying to track her down. But it was no use."

"I'm sorry," Asaph said. "I cared for your daughter."

Judah let out a strangled moan before whispering, "I failed my girl."

Asaph wanted to tell Judah that a father couldn't be at a daughter's side every moment of every day to protect her. But Asaph knew any assurance would do nothing to soothe him.

So, Asaph said something entirely different—something that shocked him.

"With your permission...I would like to try to find Eliana."

Asaph didn't know where that insane idea came from. He had planned to lie low in Jerusalem for a few weeks and then venture back to Jericho and return to tax collecting.

As Judah leaned closer to the fire, the flames illuminated his face. He stared at Asaph long and hard. "But you're a tax collector," he said as if a tax collector was incapable of noble deeds.

"I was also Eliana's friend."

Leaning back into the shadows, Judah sighed. "I don't know if this is just your way of getting us to let you go—"

"It isn't a trick. I cared for her very much."

For once, he wasn't lying.

Judah scratched his beard. "I don't like you exploiting my daughter's disappearance for your gain."

A flutter of panic passed through Asaph. "Believe me, I would never do that. I mean what I say. I want to try to discover what happened to her."

Judah pulled out his knife, and for one heart-stopping moment, Asaph thought he would use it on him. Instead, Judah carved a circle in the dirt at his feet. "If life hadn't made some strange twists, Eliana might have become part of your family."

Asaph's throat tightened. He had often wondered the same thing. As a young boy, he dreamt Eliana might someday become his betrothed. But no one uttered the words aloud, least of all Eliana's father.

"If I had had the chance, I believe I would have asked for your permission to take her as my wife." Asaph dropped his eyes with a sigh.

Judah jammed the knife into the center of his circle. "Why do you think you can find her if I was unable? It's been thirty years!"

"As a tax collector, I know something about slave trading. And yes, the odds are against me after so many years. But if Eliana hasn't been sent to a distant land, there might be a chance."

Asaph didn't even speak of the other possibility—that Eliana was long dead.

"You realize you are digging into an old wound." Judah slid the knife across the dirt, cutting into the circle.

"I'm sorry."

"Don't be." Judah shrugged. "We all need a good bloodletting now and then."

Rising, he tossed some sand onto the dying embers of the fire. "Would you really give up tax collecting to do this?"

"I would." Asaph hoped his honesty showed.

Judah stared at him for a beat before sending him a curt nod. "Let me sleep on it. I'll leave you unbound and provide a blanket you can use tonight. If you are still here when the sun rises, I will know you are a man of your word. If you are gone, I will know you are still a tax collector and a liar."

"Thank you," Asaph said as the old lion went to fetch him a blanket.

JEREMIEL

Jeremiel stared at the lesion on his right arm, familiar with the sight. As a priest, people often came to him for inspection. If a sore burrowed beneath the skin, he would declare it leprous, pronounce the victim unclean, and send the person into isolation for seven days prior to reexamination.

Although Jeremiel did not believe his lesion went that deep yet, it was still his duty to isolate himself to be sure. So, he packed some cheese and bread to wander into the wilderness alone. Once there, his lesion would either shrink or the disease would slowly ravage his body.

Before leaving Capernaum, he took a moment to sit and pray, only a stone's throw from the synagogue, where Jesus was teaching. He pulled back his sleeve, revealing his lesion, and pressed gently against the surrounding skin.

The numbness is spreading. Jeremiel covered his arm, his stomach sinking. This was not a good sign.

Then he heard a noise from inside the synagogue and wondered what Jesus had done or said this time to create a stir. Jeremiel had sent dire warnings about Jesus back to the Temple in Jerusalem. Caiaphas, the high priest, responded by sending additional priests to verify his reports.

"How have I sinned, Lord?" he muttered.

Like sin, leprosy sank deep into the body, eventually erupting on the hands, the legs, and most horrifying, the face. Nodules and bumps would eventually ripple across his face like stony ground. Leprosy took on a monstrous shape as it ate away at the body like sin devouring the spirit and the soul. It was an external manifestation of internal rot.

But Jeremiel had always striven to be pure and unblemished, and God would not cast away a righteous man. Only one thought gave him hope. He remembered how Moses had demonstrated God's power to Pharaoh by placing his hand inside his cloak. When he removed it, the hand had become leprous. After Moses slipped his hand back inside his cloak and pulled it out a second time, the leprosy was gone.

Maybe God was using him, like Moses, to demonstrate His Almighty power; perhaps this *wasn't* a punishment for his sins. It was the only possible explanation for being afflicted with leprosy despite living a virtuous life.

When the commotion grew louder, Jeremiel jerked his head toward the sound. Jesus strode out the front door of the synagogue with a crowd swarming at his sides like roused bees.

"You cannot heal on the Sabbath!" shouted a Pharisee—one of the men recently sent to Capernaum by Caiaphas. "You could have waited until the day had ended before you healed that man."

"The Son of Man is Lord of the Sabbath," Jesus said.

Had Jesus healed someone inside the synagogue on the Sabbath? Again? He was deliberately provoking the people.

Unconsciously, Jeremiel tugged at the end of his right sleeve, ensuring that his lesion was concealed. When Jesus locked eyes with him and headed in his direction, Jeremiel stood and looked over his shoulder. Should he run?

He planned to sever himself from people, but now, an entire crowd was coming for him. Unsure of what to do, he froze.

"The Son of Man is the Lord of the Sabbath," Jesus said, repeating his blasphemy. When he stopped a few paces from Jeremiel, he said, "I ask you, which is lawful on the Sabbath: to do good or to do evil, to save a life or to destroy it?"

Jeremiel paused, wondering if he should reply. "It is better to do neither. Do not do evil nor heal on the Sabbath."

"But doing nothing when you could do good is to do evil," shouted one of Jesus's disciples from the crowd. Jeremiel couldn't tell which one.

Jesus watched Jeremiel, probing like a priest. *Did he know about his disease?*

Something came over Jeremiel. He couldn't be sure, but he sensed that Jesus was waiting for him to ask for healing. He knew, with strange certainty, that Jesus would heal him, even on the Sabbath, alleviating Jeremiel's problem in an instant. Just like that—as simple as smothering a small flame. Just say the word, and Jesus would heal him.

Was this a test from God to find out if he would indeed keep the Sabbath holy? Would his sin run deeper if he asked to be healed on the Sabbath, and would his leprosy worsen?

It would be *so easy*. With one touch from Jesus, he would be clean. But sin is always easy; resisting evil is hard. It's more difficult to walk against the wind than with it.

"Look at my hand!" a man shouted, wiggling his fingers like a newborn. "You saw with your own eyes that my hand was shriveled, but now my joints move like new."

Jeremiel sucked in a breath. The man's face showed utter delight in having a hand that worked as God designed. What could be so wrong with that?

Jeremiel could receive the same sort of healing. *Just ask. Just say the word*! He was like a starving man, while Jesus offered him a steaming bowl of food. Jeremiel stared into Jesus's eyes; the prophet was still waiting for him to ask.

Jesus's eyes went from Jeremiel's face to his right arm, where the lesion lurked beneath his sleeve.

Then Jeremiel remembered the woman with the snakes, whom he had seen plying her trade close to the Temple in Jerusalem so long ago. She, too, claimed to offer healing. But it was a pagan claim—a serpent's desire. He sensed an invisible snake slithering across his shoulders, sending a shiver down his back. The snake was sin, the snake was temptation, and it coiled around his neck.

Jeremiel turned and fled from temptation, away from Jesus and the desire to break the Sabbath for his gain. Surely, God would reward his courage. Surely, the Almighty would recognize his spiritual perfection and remove his skin's physical imperfection.

The day's heat hung in the evening sky. By the time he reached the city gates, sweat trailed down his forehead, and he fell to his knees, gasping.

ASAPH

When morning arrived, Asaph stayed true to his word and did not run. Even if he had wanted to escape, he would have been too exhausted.

After sleeping on the ground, he woke up weary, with aches running up and down his side. He was used to a cushioned bed with his slave girl there to provide him with a pitcher of water when he awoke, followed by an elaborate meal. This morning, it was as if dirt had infiltrated every part of his body. His dry mouth seemed coated with dust.

Asaph rose to his elbows, eyeing Eliana's father. "Shalom."

Judah was already crouching by the morning fire, where water and warm bread awaited. Like any good Jew, he treated the bread with reverence, breaking it rather than slicing it with a knife. The men fed on barley bread, not as lavish as a loaf made from wheat, but Asaph was so hungry that he would eat anything—except more dust.

Judah handed him a piece with a stern look. "I have decided to provide you with a donkey and basic supplies. When do you hope to begin your search for my daughter?"

"In three days." Asaph bowed his head in subservience.

Three—the number of completeness. Three sons of Noah—Shem, Ham, and Japheth. Three Patriarchs—Abraham, Isaac, and Jacob. Three divisions of the Jewish people—Koven, Levite, and Yisrael. Three daily prayers—Shacharit, Mincha, and Maariv. Three Pilgrimage festivals—Passover, Shavuot, and Sukkot.

Three days for Asaph to prove himself to Judah.

Judah poked the fire, not answering immediately. "I may need more time to consider your motives."

So much for choosing a symbolic number. For the remainder of the morning, Judah put Asaph to work on the most menial tasks, such as cleaning up after the animals. But Asaph was determined not to complain, despite the stink, heat, and flies. At midday, when the sun beat down the hardest, another group of men rode into camp, and Asaph watched from a distance. He had already taken the horses and camels to the nearest watering hole for the first of their twice-daily watering. Now, he was collecting dung from the animals and setting it aside to dry for fuel.

Surely, Judah would see that he must be trustworthy if he spent three days doing this kind of work without fleeing.

Asaph ran a hand across a horse's flank when loud voices burst from the nearest cave. Judah was in a heated discussion with one of the newcomers, the tallest of all the Zealots present. The man kept shooting glares in Asaph's direction.

Asaph leaned closer to the horse, continuing to run his hand against the smooth coat, and swatted away flies in tandem with the horse's tail. Perhaps this new Zealot, the tall man, saw Asaph the same way—as a pest that needed swatting.

Asaph watched from the corner of his eye as the stranger approached. His dark brown cloak billowed in the dust-filled breeze, revealing a sword at the man's side. Asaph's heart rate spiked, but he tried not to display any sign of fear. He continued to groom the horse, turning to greet the man when they were within arm's reach.

"Shalom." Asaph smiled and held out his hands in peace.

"Shalom," said the big man, swinging his right fist in a wide arc like cutting a stalk with a scythe.

There was no time to dodge the fist. It crashed against Asaph's jaw, and he lost consciousness before he hit the ground.

KETURAH

Keturah put a hand to her chest as she gazed at the throngs who packed the mountainside outside of Capernaum—all drawn here by one man, the one they called Jesus of Nazareth. His ministry had its headquarters in Capernaum, in a fisherman's home.

The slope, wild with flowers, was packed with those looking to be healed. The sick hobbled on crutches or were carried on stretchers by family and friends. Some showed terrible disfigurements, such as the man with an arm twisted and spindly like the branch of a tree.

"There he is!" Eliana pointed at Jesus, who stood on a level spot, looking down on the masses.

Keturah and Eliana had come north from Tiberias because Eliana wanted to track down the prophet Jesus. Sveshtari convinced Keturah that she ran the risk of recapture by Herod if she stayed in Tiberias, so she agreed to the trip. She and Eliana had set off together, with Lavi at their side for protection. Keturah only had to wait for Sveshtari to lure Rufus to her—to serve him up for the pleasure of her vengeance.

Keturah took in the stunning scenery. The Sea of Galilee gleamed at the foot of the rolling slopes, with rows of trees and vines bursting with life—walnuts, grapes, olives, and figs.

"The fruits here are famous," she told Eliana. "The rabbis won't even allow these fruits into Jerusalem during feasts because they're afraid people will come to enjoy the food instead of savoring the sweetness of the Lord."

When Eliana acted like she didn't even hear, Keturah wasn't surprised. Eliana was increasingly agitated every step closer to this Jesus of Nazareth. By now, she was constantly fidgeting. While Keturah was used to Eliana's muttering, the woman's ramblings had become harsher and sharper.

"Shut up!" Eliana waved a hand in the air while using her free hand to reach for the knife strapped to her waist.

Keturah cleared her throat, sure that Eliana wouldn't harm her. But she quickened her step all the same, putting some distance between them.

The three of them, Lavi included, had become a unit of sorts, and while they hadn't known each other long, Keturah was oddly protective of Eliana. She even thought Eliana was beginning to enjoy their friendship.

As Jesus's voice broke through Keturah's thoughts, the trio hurried forward and found a spot on the lush, green grass within hearing distance.

"Blessed are you who are poor, for yours is the kingdom of God," Jesus called out. A gentle wind came from the west, smelling fresh and fragrant. "Blessed are you who hunger now, for you will be satisfied. Blessed are you who weep now, for you will laugh. Blessed are you when men hate you, when they exclude you and insult you and reject your name as evil, because of the Son of Man."

The words flowed over Keturah like a sweet breeze. She inhaled them, letting them resonate, when Jesus abruptly moved on to less comforting words.

"But to you who are listening I say: Love your enemies, do good to those who hate you, bless those who curse you, pray for those who mistreat you. If someone slaps you on one cheek, turn to them the other also. If someone takes your coat, do not withhold your shirt from them. Give to everyone who asks you, and if anyone takes what belongs to you, do not demand it back. Do to others as you would have them do to you."

Keturah's heart turned to stone. Words of forgiveness were easy for Jesus to say. His mother hadn't been poisoned by palace intrigue. His father's throat wasn't slit at the feet of Herod. What did he know about enemies?

Closing her eyes, she tried to summon Nemesis, the goddess of justice, whose mission was to even the scales. When someone kills, you kill. When someone uses a knife to murder your father, you wield your blade in revenge. It was the way of Nemesis.

"Nemesis be my sword. Nemesis be my shield."

When Keturah opened her eyes, she noticed Eliana staring up the hillside toward Jesus. Eliana had stopped muttering for a change and seemed more focused as if she were looking at reality instead of the visions that constantly danced around her.

Jesus motioned toward a fig tree. "No good tree bears bad fruit, nor does a bad tree bear good fruit. Each tree is recognized by its own fruit. People do not pick figs from thornbushes, or grapes from briers. A good man brings good things out of the good stored up in his heart, and an evil man brings evil things out of the evil stored up in his heart. For the mouth speaks what the heart is full of."

Keturah tried to close her ears to these words. Her desire for revenge was the fruit she desired, no matter what Jesus might say. Revenge was justice, and justice was *good* fruit, so when the time was ripe, she would kill the man who murdered her father.

"Jesus speaks lies," Keturah said.

Eliana glared back at her and stuck out her tongue. When Lavi rested his head in Eliana's lap, Eliana ran her fingers across the dog's head, his closed eyes fluttering at her touch.

Keturah stomped away, unwilling to listen anymore.

ASAPH

Asaph woke to a face full of water. When he drifted back to consciousness, he found Judah standing over him, holding a pitcher. It took Asaph a moment to recall where he was and what he was doing, and then he remembered the last thing he saw—a man's fist coming out of nowhere.

Raising himself, he looked for the man who had waylaid him and found him standing at a distance, still scowling.

Judah extended a hand to Asaph. "You have to admit you had that coming."

"Why? Because I was once a tax collector?" Asaph rubbed his aching jaw as Judah helped him to stand.

"No. Because you once tormented this man."

Asaph's brow furrowed. He didn't even know him! Did he?

Judah motioned toward the man. "You don't recognize Gershom?"

Gershom?

It took a moment for Asaph's mind to wrap around that name, but his eyes lit with understanding when it did. Gershom, Zuriel's best friend, had once tried to goad him into hitting Eliana with a rock.

"You mean the Gershom from our village?"

Judah nodded. "The same."

Asaph stared at the large man who had struck him. Seeing the child behind the large, bearded brute was challenging, but he could spot some similarities. Asaph nodded. Yes, he could believe it was Gershom, one of the boys that he lorded over. The fellow had undoubtedly filled out over the years. His arms were like tree trunks.

"What's he doing here?"

"I recruit from many villages. Does it surprise you that I recruited from ours?"

Asaph started to smile but winced as pain shot across his jaw.

Judah tossed a glance back at Gershom. "You're lucky. Gershom wanted to slit your throat. Be happy it was only his fist."

"I'm not sure I'd call it luck." Gershom's fist was as solid as stone. Asaph wondered if Judah knew that Gershom once tried to pressure him into hurling a rock at Eliana. But he decided it wouldn't be wise—or honorable—to bring up distant sins.

"Yes, I'd say you're very lucky. He is adept with the blade." Judah motioned at Asaph's jaw. "Anything broken?"

Asaph tested his jaw once again and cast another glance at Gershom. Did the man do anything but glower? "I don't think anything is broken. But I wonder if I should leave camp before my three days are up. I'm not sure it's safe sharing the same camp with Gershom."

Judah bit his lower lip and pondered Asaph's words. Then he heaved a sigh before laying down the law. "You will leave when I decide."

A chill traveled up Asaph's spine. So, he would have to share the camp with a man who wanted him dead?

But it got worse.

Judah stared into the distance. "Gershom and I have been talking. When you leave, he is to go with you."

Judah's words hit him almost as hard as Gershom's fist.

"Go with me? *He wants to kill me.*"

"Gershom has given me his word. He will not harm you."

"And you believe him?"

"He is a man of his word. If he says he will not harm you, he won't."

"Tell that to his fist."

"I know him like a son. He will not break his word."

"But why send both of us?"

"Gershom is more experienced in the wild. He will keep you alive."

A man who wanted him dead would keep him alive? That was hard to believe.

"He, too, is committed to your mission," Judah said. "Gershom once loved Eliana."

"Gershom?"

"Why should you be surprised that Gershom, like you, had been thinking about his betrothal day?"

"But if he finds out that I also once loved Eliana, it will just give him another reason to kill me in the night."

"He gave me his word he would not harm a hair on your head. So, I have made my decision. When you leave us, you go with Gershom."

Asaph and Gershom exchanged glares. Gershom certainly didn't look like a man who would help Asaph survive in the wild. The "wild" was in his eyes.

JEREMIEL

Jeremiel was alone. Physically alone. Spiritually alone.

The sky was dark blue in the distance, almost black, with blue threads streaking from the bottoms of the clouds, revealing far-off rain. Still, he was confident he could cross the Sea of Galilee before a storm hit. He took a boat to the opposite side of the lake to put a safe distance between himself and the people of Capernaum—to separate the clean from the unclean.

He still could not believe he was now counted among the unclean, clothed with shame.

By the time he reached the eastern shore, the storm had dissipated into a dreary gray, and the wind had also died out. He set up camp in a limestone cavern near the small village of Gergesa. Also near his cave was a cemetery, where white stones stuck out from the ground like the fingers of a giant thrusting up from Hades. Leprosy was a living death, so setting up camp on the edge of a cemetery was only fitting.

From now on, he would live on the outskirts of death.

During his first night in this forsaken place, he was sure he heard someone moan in pain. It seemed to be coming from the tombs, although it was difficult to judge the direction of the sound.

Not too far off, the clinking of stone against chain rattled through the air. It reminded Jeremiel of a prisoner trying to use a rock to break his shackles. He wondered if God had sent a demon to torment him—as if leprosy was not terrifying enough. Evil spirits dwelt where there was desolation and death, and cemeteries were ideal haunts.

He spent the next day in the hot afternoon sun, praying, lamenting, and tossing ashes on his head. His leprosy was a smoldering fire that only prayer could extinguish. So, pray he did.

He had not eaten anything for a day, but the hunger pains had subsided—for now. During his first day in the wilderness, he obsessed over the lesion on his right arm, analyzing it for any improvement. But today, he hadn't checked it since morning. He was too afraid.

When night arrived, the moaning returned, and he arose and ventured to the cave's opening. The large moon cast a bright light on the tombs down the slope. Something moved among the graves, rattling chains.

He squinted through the dark and noticed *two* demons or monsters or whatever they were weaving among the tombs, each oblivious to the other. One carried a large stone, using it to pound his chain, grunting with every downward strike.

The second man maneuvered around a large, white tombstone and stopped short, staring at the man beating the rock against the chain. When the one holding the rock spotted the intruder, he screamed and hurled the stone at the other unfortunate creature, missing its target. The second man scurried away to hide behind a tombstone on the opposite edge of the cemetery.

It reminded him of two animals fighting over a small piece of dead territory. Jeremiel realized he fit right in with these monstrous men.

Praying that his fellow phantoms would let him be, Jeremiel backed into the cave, disappearing into the darkness as if the cave were the mouth of a whale, swallowing him whole.

SVESHTARI

Sveshtari had one boy by the arm, while Rufus had another by the ear. As they dragged the two rowdies out of the theater, neither resisted, aware that if they did, Herod's bodyguards had the authority to hit them so hard that it would start raining teeth.

The young boys, slaves in Herod's palace, looked about twelve. Their crime? The pair erupted into a fight amid the audience at the theater in Tiberias. It was Rufus and Sveshtari's job to take care of the fracas.

However, the brawl was probably the most entertaining part of the show this afternoon.

Sveshtari helped to maintain order during several recent plays, but this one was particularly dull. What did Plautus call it? "Murder by monotony." The writer had killed his own story.

Still, their job was to keep order, even when the fighting kept a bored audience awake. So, they dragged the boys from the theater and released them with a warning and a shove. The two boys took off running like wild animals released from a trap.

"I remember being like them at one time," said Rufus, staring wistfully after the boys.

Sveshtari grunted. "Except they're much luckier. I wouldn't have been let go so easily when I was young. I wouldn't have gotten off without a good beating."

"True." Rufus turned to face Sveshtari. "However, I am not sure it would be a good idea to beat a slave boy who knows things you wish to keep secret."

Here we go again. Sveshtari balled a fist. He had managed to stay out of Rufus's path for a while, but today was not one of those days.

"Are those boys spying for you?"

"They see things, but I wouldn't call them spies. The older one, Tullius, told me something curious he had recently seen."

Sveshtari raised a brow, refusing to take the bait. "Tullius has dung for brains."

Rufus laughed. "True, true. But even a boy with dung for brains knows what he sees." Rufus paused, savoring the added drama as he tormented Sveshtari. "He told me he recently saw Keturah on the streets in Tiberias."

Even as panic rushed over him, Sveshtari shrugged and maintained a bland expression. "Like I said, the boy's a fool. Seeing dead people."

"He even saw you talking with Keturah. Do you often talk to dead people?"

"He was mistaken. In their robes and veils, all women look alike."

Sveshtari tried to keep calm, but his jaw began to twitch, a tell-tale sign of agitation. Surely, Rufus could see it.

"You set Keturah free," Rufus said.

Sveshtari fought the urge to strike Rufus right then and there, keeping his fists lowered.

"Herod commanded you to kill her, but you didn't, did you?" Rufus laid a hand on Sveshtari's shoulder as if they were the best of brothers. "But don't worry. I haven't told anyone you freed Keturah, least of all Herod. He would have your head if he knew. Tullius won't talk either, not without my approval."

Sveshtari waited for the demand that would surely follow.

Rufus leaned in close. "But I do expect a reward for keeping Tullius quiet."

"There is nothing to reward. Keturah is dead. Tullius lied." Sveshtari's voice was almost a growl.

Rufus lifted his hands, palms outward. "Don't get excited. I'm just reporting what Tullius saw."

"Keturah is dead by my sword. I know when I have killed someone."

Once again, Rufus put a hand on his shoulder. "Listen, I understand that you need to keep up this false front, claiming you carried out your duty. I would do the same, Sveshtari. So, I will make it easy for you. Think it over, and I will send Tullius to you tomorrow to collect the money I expect. You don't have to admit to me verbally what you did. Just pay up, and I will remain quiet."

Sveshtari glared at Rufus, who met his gaze evenly.

"Just don't kill Tullius, or I will have no choice but to let Herod know what really became of Keturah," Rufus said. "Now come. We still have a job to do."

Hatred boiling, Sveshtari took a deep breath and stared out on the city of Tiberias, clustered between the theater and the Sea of Galilee. He watched Rufus saunter back to the theater with a jovial whistle and imagined knocking out a few of his teeth. But as much as he wanted to destroy Rufus, he understood that the real force behind this blackmail was Dionysius. He sensed the god watching him. Dionysius was playing with him like a cat with a mouse, biding his time before finishing him off.

7

LUKE, CHAPTER 7

KETURAH

W HEN KETURAH AND ELIANA reached the banks of the Sea of Galilee, they encountered a group of fishermen pulling in a dragnet. Keturah observed the men toil while Eliana tossed a stick into the water and watched Lavi dive in to retrieve it.

Keturah agreed to walk the shores of the Sea of Galilee because Eliana hoped they would encounter Jesus teaching there—as he sometimes did from a small boat. Eliana had become obsessed with the prophet since hearing him speak. The teacher's words affected Eliana for the better, so Keturah begrudgingly agreed to accompany her to the Capernaum shore, where they found the fishermen, but no Jesus.

Lavi emerged from the lake, shaking off the water and sending droplets in all directions—all over the two women. Keturah squealed, leaping to her feet as Eliana laughed hysterically, covering her face.

Using her sleeve to wipe her face dry, Keturah sat down and watched the fishermen standing on the shore as they pulled on the enormous dragnet. Because the net was immersed by weights, it took twelve men pulling ropes to haul the catch onto land.

The Sea of Galilee teemed with life. Hundreds of fish flopped around, trying to twitch their way back into the water. Then the men went to work separating the bad from the good, tossing the unclean fish into the sea—those without scales or fins, like eels, catfish, rays, and lampreys.

"Keturah!"

Keturah snapped out of her thoughts and spun, eyes going wide when she saw her former mistress, Joanna, waving as she approached. Keturah looked around to make sure Joanna was alone. If she had been with anyone else from Herod's palace, Keturah would be dead.

Keturah stood, her heart in her throat. The last time they had been together, Joanna was screaming bloody murder, and Sveshtari was carrying Keturah in a blood-soaked blanket slung over his shoulder.

Keturah rushed across the beach as Joanna wrapped her in a scented hug and kissed her cheeks.

"I have prayed every day that you made it to safety," Joanna whispered, pushing a stray hair from Keturah's eyes.

"But what about you? Why are you in Capernaum?"

"To hear Jesus."

Keturah had a hard time maintaining her smile. She was getting tired of all the talk of Jesus.

Joanna put both hands on Keturah's shoulders and beamed. "I think he is the one we have been waiting for. He healed me!"

"I didn't know you were ill."

"I hid it well. But Jesus delivered me."

Keturah didn't believe it for a moment, and she fought the urge to roll her eyes. Hoping to change the subject, she motioned toward Eliana, who stood by the rocks with Lavi at her side.

"This is Eliana and her dog, Lavi. Eliana, this is Joanna, my mistress."

"No longer your mistress," Joanna corrected her. "In my eyes, you are free."

Keturah blinked, unable to speak. She long dreamed of being free, but now the words had been spoken. Yet without parents, without a husband, was she really free? She was alone. An unmarried woman without family was vulnerable. It was just another form of bondage.

"I, too, am free." Joanna's face glowed. "I'm free, thanks to Jesus."

Eliana ventured closer. "So, you believe Jesus is the Messiah?"

Joanna grinned; she always had the most motherly smiles, as comforting as a blanket warmed by the fire.

"Yes, I believe." Then Joanna returned her gaze to Keturah. "Do you realize that Herod's household is now in Tiberias? Dangerously close."

"I know," said Keturah. "But I can't hide in caves all my life."

"Maybe you should travel to a more distant land. Egypt perhaps? When Jesus was a child, his family fled there for safety."

Keturah scowled. *Why does everything come back to him?*

"If you remain here, someone from Herod's household will surely spot you," Joanna persisted. "I really think you should leave for Egypt."

"That would be impossible—for now."

Keturah was not about to reveal that she wanted to remain close to Herod's household to kill Rufus.

"Have you met Jesus? Have you talked to him?" Joanna asked.

Jesus again? "We have only heard him from a distance."

"What do you think?"

Keturah shrugged. "He does good things."

"But Jesus is so much more than that! You must meet him! Today, he is coming to Capernaum. Join me, and I'll introduce you."

"But I am just a slave."

"No longer a slave," Joanna reminded her. "Besides, Jesus talks freely with slaves."

"And I'm a woman."

"If you recall, so am I, and I'm still Jesus's friend. You must've seen that he interacts with women."

Of course, Keturah was aware he talked with women, even teaching them. How could she not notice such unconventional and shocking behavior? But she was reaching for any excuse to avoid meeting him. Jesus might take one look at her, piercing her soul, and tell her she needed to forgive her enemies, including the man who murdered her father.

"Oh please, Keturah, you *must* meet him! And you too, Eliana. Can you come with us?"

Keturah would have thought Eliana would jump at the chance to meet Jesus in person—to touch the hem of his robe. But from the look on her face, you'd think Joanna had just asked her to enter a den of lions.

"No!" Eliana's face suddenly twisted into something animal-like, baring her teeth like a wolf. "No, no!"

Eliana took off down the shoreline, leaving Lavi to scamper after her. Joanna turned to Keturah, waiting for an explanation.

"Eliana has problems." Keturah's face softened. What more could she say?

ELIANA

A howl echoed inside Eliana's mind. She didn't *hear* the howl. She *sensed* it, as if a wild creature had lodged itself inside, shrieking. She pressed her temples as her skull began to throb.

A part of her wanted so badly to be near Jesus—to see his face up close, to smell the scent of his clothes. But she was afraid of what she might do to him. She still had the knife strapped to her waist, and Calev's voice pushed her to use it on Jesus.

If she got within an arm's length of the Nazarene, Calev's voice would strengthen. She didn't dare go near Jesus because she wasn't sure if she could trust herself.

Eliana sprinted toward the fishermen, who hauled in another catch. She slowed and stared at their net, sympathizing with the fish. She was caught in Jesus's dragnet, hauled in from the sea, and was collapsing inward, barely able to breathe—like a fish trying to live on land. While Jesus had given her new hope, breathing in this hope was killing her. She couldn't bear to be hurt again.

As a young girl, she overflowed with promise, but now she feared the weight of disappointment would crush her. She wasn't made for this evil world.

One of the fishermen stopped sorting fish when he noticed Eliana glaring at him. His warm eyes searched hers for a moment before he said, "Shalom." Smiling, he tossed an unclean fish back into the water.

Eliana stood still, thinking of the knife strapped to her waist—an equally unclean object. She closed her eyes and absorbed its impurity. The safest thing she could do was hurl the knife into the sea, so Eliana pulled it from its sheath and stared at the water.

The fisherman went wide-eyed when he noticed the blade, nudging another man at his side. The other man stopped working and cocked his head as Eliana made a move to hurl the knife into the lake but stopped mid-motion.

"Don't," Calev's dark voice whispered. "Keep the knife. You'll need it."

Sweat beaded on her forehead, and her stomach rolled from just touching the knife, just having it in her hands. It was as if every part of her compelled her to expel everything evil, but she couldn't force herself to hurl the knife into the sea. Calev wouldn't allow it. So, she sheathed the blade and started running again.

She didn't have to look back to know Lavi was still behind her, still following, still loyal.

JEREMIEL

When Jeremiel opened his eyes to a new day, his dry mouth ached for water. He craved food but had little energy to eat, drink, or even sit up. His soul was bowed down to the dust.

He eventually forced himself to rise, but he resisted examining his forearm for fear that the army of his disease had continued its steady march across his skin. When he shuffled to the lip of the cave, he stared down at the tombstones, but there were no signs of his fellow monsters—the two men who haunted his nights.

Turning his gaze to the main road leading out of Gergesa, he spotted a lone figure making his way toward him up the rough terrain. It was difficult to see who it was, but he prayed it might be Jesus, come to give him a second chance. The Sabbath had long since passed, so he could now accept his healing power. But as the figure neared, his heart sank when he realized it was Nekoda's brother, Chaim.

"Unclean!" Jeremiel called out. "Unclean!"

He pulled the edge of his tunic over his mouth, but Chaim continued to approach.

"Unclean!" *Doesn't the man have ears to hear?*

"Save your breath, Jeremiel. I am coming to you, whether you like it or not."

Grunting and straining, Chaim climbed the slope leading to Jeremiel's smoldering campfire in front of the cave. Sweating heavily, Chaim sat on the other side of the circle of rocks where Jeremiel had made his fire the night before.

"Nekoda said you left the city and were out here alone, so I had to see for myself," Chaim said, catching his breath.

"Didn't you hear my warning? I said 'unclean.'"

Chaim laughed. He was worse than Nekoda, never taking things seriously. "What did you do to become unclean? Touch an insect?"

Jeremiel raised the sleeve on his right arm, revealing the white lesions. There were now two.

Chaim's grin vanished instantly. "Oh."

"You should go now that you understand the danger."

Even though he should know better, Chaim just sat there, staring at the lesions. Any sane person would have kept his distance from a leper.

"How did Nekoda know I was here?" Jeremiel asked.

"He keeps watch on many people."

Jeremiel was not surprised. All good politicians have hired eyes everywhere, and Nekoda was a master politician.

"We were worried about you, so I came to find out why you fled from Capernaum." Chaim looked around at the desolate surroundings. "I was hoping you went away to pray and fast. But now I understand."

"If you understand, why do you remain so close to me? Don't you care about your safety?"

Chaim just shrugged. "Sometimes I wonder."

"Wonder about what?"

"I wonder why God hasn't smitten *me* with something like leprosy—or worse."

What could be worse than leprosy?

"Why would God smite you?" Jeremiel's voice ached with genuine compassion. He had a soft spot for Chaim, who did not share his brother's ambitions.

Chaim stared at the palm of his hand, where dirt lined the creases of his skin, and rubbed away some of the soil.

"I suppose we have all done wrong," Chaim said, evading Jeremiel's question. "We all deserve to be smitten as you were."

Jeremiel disagreed. He didn't deserve this but said nothing.

Chaim lifted his head to meet Jeremiel's eyes. "I certainly know that I have done much wrong."

Jeremiel wasn't going to beat around the bush. "What did you do?"

Chaim looked away. "I have offered lambs as sacrifices for my sins, again and again, but it's never enough. How many lambs must die for my sins?"

"As many as it takes," said Jeremiel.

"But it's never enough."

Again, Jeremiel wondered what this man could have done to feel such guilt. "Chaim, tell me. What did you do?"

Again, Chaim did not answer.

Chaim's eyes went to the two lesions, which Jeremiel unconsciously scratched. Jeremiel yanked the sleeve over his arm again, hiding his shame.

"What did *you* do to deserve those sores?" Chaim asked.

Jeremiel wanted to scream, "I did nothing!" But he was silent.

"Can Nekoda or I do anything to help you?"

Besides leave me alone?

"What is there to do? I must continue to inspect the disease to see if it is spreading."

"Oh." For what had to be the fifth time, Chaim's gaze drifted to Jeremiel's arms. "I am sorry."

"Tell your brother I am at peace with God," Jeremiel lied. "Go back to Capernaum and sacrifice a lamb, and then ask the Lord for forgiveness for whatever it is you have done."

Chaim nodded. "Come with me. Maybe Jesus will heal you."

Jeremiel bit his tongue to keep from arguing, even though Chaim suggested the very thing he desired. "Jesus's words are dangerous."

"But he can heal."

"So can Beelzebub."

Chaim nodded again and stared into space. Finally, he stood to leave but turned, suddenly looking fatigued. "All of this blood...all these sacrifices. Do they ever end?"

Jeremiel shook his head no.

Chaim stared as if waiting for a more complete answer. Getting nothing, he exhaled a soft "Shalom" before he hiked down the slope toward Gergesa.

SVESHTARI

Sveshtari approached the throne.

Herod Antipas modeled his royal seat after Solomon's. Six steps led up to it, each with a pair of golden lions facing each other. The throne itself was made of ivory, with a golden footstool.

As Sveshtari moved up the stairs, he glanced at the golden lions positioned to pounce—a reminder of the power of the man seated at the top.

When Herod had ordered him to appear, Sveshtari prayed to Mercury that it had nothing to do with Keturah. He had paid Tullius and Rufus their demands to buy time until he could figure out what to do about them. Sveshtari would be surprised if his blackmailers spilled his story so soon. They were hungry for more payoffs. Still, maybe they decided to report his love affair with Keturah before he could silence them.

Once at the top of the stairs, Sveshtari bowed before the throne. Rising, he found Herod resting his chin on his hand, bored. Two more golden lions, larger than the others, flanked the throne.

Herod compared himself to a lion, but Sveshtari thought of him as more of a fox. A lion was regal. A fox was covert and cunning. Definitely a fox.

With a generous exhale, Herod suddenly flicked away a fly. "Have you ever strangled a man, Sveshtari?"

An odd question. Was it a test of some sort?

"Yes, tetrarch. I have."

"Did you enjoy it?"

"It got the job done."

Herod straightened, then slumped, frowning, as if struggling with some great puzzle.

"Which is better—strangling someone or sticking them with a sword?"

"It depends on the situation."

"No, no, no. I don't mean which one is more effective. I mean...which one gives you more pleasure?"

"I take no pleasure in the act of killing."

A look of disappointment crossed Herod's face.

"But I do take great pleasure in defending you, tetrarch," he quickly added. "That gives me the greatest reward."

"Fine, fine, fine, you redeemed yourself there. I have someone I want you to assassinate, and I know you are good at your job. I saw how efficiently you work when killing Obed. He was dead before he hit the floor."

Sveshtari searched Herod's eyes. "Who do you want me to kill?"

Sveshtari hoped it would not be John the Baptist, who was still imprisoned in the Fortress of Machaerus. He had come to like John, an earthy and honest man.

"I have in mind a new prophet in the region—not too far from here. Claims to be the Messiah. The Chosen One."

"And what is his name, my lord?"

"Jesus of Nazareth. Although you can't find him in his hometown of Nazareth. He's in Capernaum."

Capernaum: the city where he had sent Keturah.

"He makes his base of operations in the home of a fisherman named Peter. He is surrounded by twelve or thirteen men and is often mobbed by crowds who come to be healed. It might be difficult to catch him alone to slip a blade between his ribs, but you'll find a way."

"I'm sure I will, tetrarch. I won't let you down."

"I am confident you won't, Sveshtari. Act as decisively as you did the night Obed tried to kill me. Jesus is an even greater threat than Obed. This man thinks he is a king, and there's only room for one on this throne."

"I shall leave for Capernaum immediately."

As Sveshtari descended between the gallery of lions, he let out a silent sigh of relief. Herod still did not know about Keturah. He looked up, thankful for an answer to prayer. And while he wasn't especially fond of killing people whose only crime was blasphemy, he supposed Herod had a right to hold on to his throne, using any means possible.

KETURAH

As Jesus entered Capernaum, crowds continued to grow. People flocked to him with all types of illnesses, from the horrific to the mundane. The healthy also gathered around him to either hear his teaching or challenge him.

The crowd flooded the streets, which wound through a cluster of flat-topped, square homes near the Sea of Galilee. Jesus stood at the core of the crowd, with his disciples forming a human barrier around him to keep him from being crushed by the mob.

"It's going to be too hard to get close to the teacher," Keturah said, still looking for an excuse not to meet Jesus.

"Nonsense!" Joanna motioned her forward. "He'll make a space for me. He always does."

Keturah grimaced, her stomach churning at the thought of looking into the teacher's knowing eyes. Until now, she had seen him from a safe distance.

"Will your friend Eliana be all right?" Joanna asked over her shoulder as the two started toward the crowd.

Keturah paused to remove a stone from her sandal. "Eliana can take care of herself. She's a strange woman but very resourceful. And Lavi is with her. She'll be back. She's done this before."

"I've been praying for her. But I really wish she could have met Jesus. He can heal her."

Keturah doubted *anyone* could heal Eliana, but she kept those thoughts to herself. When they reached the crowd, they found Jewish leaders surrounding Jesus, but the conversation did not appear to be heated.

"Please come and heal his servant," one of the Jewish leaders asked the teacher.

"This man deserves it because he loves our nation and has built our synagogue," chimed in a second man.

Joanna turned toward a woman in the crowd. "What's happening?"

"A centurion's servant is gravely ill and about to die," the woman said, her face filled with concern. "The centurion seeks healing for his servant, and the Jewish leaders are pleading on his behalf."

Keturah wasn't sure which was more impressive—that a group of Jewish leaders did this for a Roman centurion or that this centurion cared so much about his servant. His slave.

When Keturah was enslaved, Joanna cared deeply for her. But that was Joanna. She was a far cry from a Roman soldier who made his living killing people.

Joanna put a hand on Keturah's shoulder. "I know this centurion. He's a Gentile, a God-fearer. He's a good man who helped to build the synagogue near Peter's house at the edge of the water."

A God-fearer was a non-Jew who accepted the one God but didn't fully embrace being Jewish. But God-fearer or not, he was still a centurion—and still dangerous.

When the crowd began to move again, Keturah kept her distance, afraid to get too close. It appeared that Jesus planned to visit the home of the centurion, an unclean Gentile, which must have worried his disciples. Even though the centurion had donated money to build the synagogue in Capernaum, he was still unclean in Hebrew eyes. Would Jesus dare to enter the man's home?

"Why is the centurion living in an out-of-the-way place like Capernaum?" Keturah asked Joanna. "Where are his troops?"

"He's retired."

Keturah hoped that meant he was just a harmless old man. Roman soldiers were not allowed to marry, but this centurion might have taken a wife in retirement. Maybe he had been tamed.

As they moved through the city, five Jewish men rushed to greet Jesus and bowed before him.

"He sent us to speak with you," said one of the men. "We are friends of his."

Keturah assumed they were talking about the centurion again.

"He asked us to send you a message," said another. "He said, 'Lord, don't trouble yourself, for I do not deserve to have you come under my roof. That is why I did not even consider myself worthy to come to you.'"

Keturah wondered if it was true that the centurion used the word "Lord." Even Jesus's disciples usually called Jesus "teacher," not Lord.

"He also asked us to tell you he knows you can heal without dishonoring yourself by entering his home," added the third man. "He said, 'say the word, and my servant will be healed. For I myself am a man under authority, with soldiers under me. I tell this one, "Go," and he goes; and that one, "Come," and he comes. I say to my servant, "Do this," and he does it.'"

At first, Jesus didn't respond. It was so quiet that the only sounds were seabirds squawking.

Was it true that the centurion was simply trying to be kind, giving Jesus a face-saving excuse not to enter the home of an unclean Gentile? Or was he testing Jesus? Was he trying to find out if Jesus could heal without touching his servant or even being in the same room? Healing with the touch of a hand was one thing. Healing from a distance was another.

Finally, Jesus grinned and broke the silence. He threw his arms open and said, "I tell you, I have not found such great faith even in Israel."

The crowd began to murmur, drowning out what Jesus said next. Keturah strained to get closer when the five men turned on their heels and sprinted toward their friend's home, their faces shining with excitement.

Joanna sidled up to Keturah. "Jesus told the men that the centurion's servant is healed. The centurion's servant is *healed*! Can you believe it?"

Can I believe it? That was an excellent question.

Keturah was about to point out that no one knew yet whether Jesus healed the servant, but she saw the eager belief on Joanna's face and kept quiet. There was no need to squash her flame of faith.

As Keturah continued to follow Jesus through Capernaum, she wondered if healing someone from a long distance was possible. If that were the case, maybe Jesus could heal Eliana at this very moment. What was the harm in asking? She had become strangely attached to Eliana.

When Jesus glanced over his shoulder ever so briefly, he looked in Keturah's direction, stopping her in her tracks. She laid a hand over her chest, thinking her heart would burst as the crowd jockeyed for position, almost knocking her to the ground.

Joanna took her by the elbow to keep her upright. "What's wrong?"

"Nothing. Nothing at all."

"Come on." Joanna plucked at Keturah's sleeve. "I am staying in the house of Zebedee for the next couple of days. Would you like to stay with us?"

The last thing Keturah wanted was to stay under a roof with more followers of Jesus. She suddenly desired to hear about the old gods, not this new Lord. She could relate to gods who got jealous, spiteful, and vengeful, not a Messiah who asked people to forgive.

Keturah changed her mind. She shouldn't dare approach Jesus, even to ask for Eliana's healing, because he might challenge her to forgive Rufus—and that scared the wits out of her. Besides, she didn't have a heart like that of the centurion or his friends. She didn't even have the faith of a mustard seed, the smallest of seeds.

"I'm afraid I cannot go with you, *Domina*."

"You needn't call me *Domina* any longer. Remember, you are free."

She didn't feel free.

"Stay with me, at least for a couple of nights," Joanna urged.

"I must leave Capernaum to find out what happened to Eliana."

Keturah wasn't about to tell Joanna that she was leaving to kill Rufus. She had waited long enough to get her vengeance. Sveshtari said he would lure him to Capernaum, where she could murder him. So far, however, there was no sign of Sveshtari or Rufus.

Her path was clear. Tomorrow morning, she would travel from Capernaum to Tiberias, no matter the risk of entering Herod's capital city. She would pray to Nemesis and to Night, the mother of Nemesis.

Then she would kill Rufus and be done with it.

ASAPH

Asaph never experienced this kind of freedom.

As a tax collector, he had power, but it was always tied to his tollbooth. Here, he was in open space, winding through the rolling hills of Galilee amid an armed contingent of Zealot freedom fighters. He sensed a united purpose in the rebel strength of the Zealots, and it gave him a renewed outlook.

Asaph straddled a large horse as he rode beside Judah. Staying close to Judah meant that Gershom would be less likely to attack him.

Asaph looked over his shoulder at Gershom, who traveled three horses behind, and found him still glowering. Asaph shook his head. You would think the man had other things to occupy his mind than hatred. They had been on the road for several days, yet Judah still hadn't sent Asaph on his search for Eliana.

"What do you know about Jesus of Nazareth?" Asaph asked Judah as their horses sauntered toward Capernaum in the province of Galilee. The Zealots were heading there to learn about a new prophet that some called the Messiah. Jesus was his name, a common name, so it meant nothing to Asaph.

Judah loosened his horse's reins. "They say he's a miracle worker. And he calls himself the Son of Man."

The Son of Man. Now *that* meant something.

"You mean like in Daniel's prophecy?" Asaph stared at Judah, eyes wide.

"That remains to be seen."

As a boy, Asaph heard the men of his village often argue about the prophet Daniel's vision—about the four beasts coming out of the sea. Some claimed that the fourth beast—the most terrifying of all—was Rome. In Daniel's vision, this ten-horned beast crushed its victims with large, iron teeth. But Daniel proclaimed that God would judge the fourth beast, destroying it forever, and give dominion to one like a Son of Man—the Messiah, they claimed.

"As I looked, thrones were set in place, and the Ancient of Days took his seat. His clothing was as white as snow; the hair on his head was white like wool," Asaph said from memory. "His throne was flaming with fire, and its wheels were all ablaze. A river of fire was flowing, coming out from before him."

It was startling imagery.

Judah's band of Zealots approached the city as the sun set, smearing the horizon with yellow and red. Asaph caught his breath. It had been ages since he laid eyes on the Sea of Galilee. Dramatic strips of thin clouds, some red, some smokey gray, streaked across the sky. The lake reflected red, just as the Nile must have looked after Moses turned it to blood.

Judah withdrew a short sword, or *gladius*, from his saddlebag. It had a grip fashioned from bone and a blade sharp enough for shaving. The sun flashed silver on the steel as he pulled it from its scabbard.

"This is what we will use to defeat Rome," Judah said. "And if Jesus is who he claims to be, he will lead us."

Judah returned the sword to its scabbard with a metallic clink. Then he leaned from his horse and handed it to Asaph. "You will need this while hunting for my daughter."

"Thank you." Asaph craved such a blade even more than all the precious pottery in his collection back in Jericho.

Judah smiled at him, sealing the bond between them.

As they reached the outskirts of Capernaum, they spotted a lone figure wandering from the city. It was most likely an Essene monk seeking solitude in the wilderness. But as they neared the lone figure, it became clear from the person's clothing and shape that it was a woman. Whoever she was, she'd made a grave mistake leaving the city at sunset. A dog followed at her heels, but it would not be enough protection against a pack of jackals, a pride of lions, or a band of robbers.

The woman did not look up. She stared at her feet and muttered—her headdress covering her face from view.

Judah frowned and raised his voice. "Being out of the city at night alone is dangerous."

The woman ignored them. Asaph noticed she had a knife strapped to her waist, and her dog let out a low growl while the woman trudged past them as if they didn't even exist. Judah halted his horse and watched her pass.

"Woman, did you hear me? Come with us, and we will offer you protection."

The woman let out a hollow laugh and kept walking.

Asaph stared at her back, wondering if they should force her to the city for her own good.

"Lord, save her," Judah said, his raw voice barely carrying in the breeze as she disappeared into the blood-red gloom.

Judah made a clicking noise to his horse, steering it toward the city. With a final glance over his shoulder, Asaph followed as the Zealots neared Capernaum, hoping to see Jesus come daylight.

8

LUKE, CHAPTER 8

ASAPH

A SAPH, GERSHOM, AND JUDAH found Jesus standing in a boat by the shore, straddling the seat toward the back where fishermen normally operated the rudder. With its single mast in the center, the small fishing vessel floated parallel to the beach, crowded with men and women, young and old, some of them standing knee-deep in the water. Jesus's followers formed a barrier to keep the crowd from climbing into the boat and swamping the teacher.

It was the same man.

Asaph passed through the crowd, reasonably confident that the man teaching along the seashore was the same one he had seen John baptize in the Jordan River. He couldn't be sure, but the closer he got to Jesus, the more certain he became.

Asaph muscled his way through the crowd alongside Judah and Gershom. Judah had asked Asaph to come with him to see Jesus, delaying his mission to find Eliana. Still, he welcomed the chance to form a stronger relationship with Eliana's father, especially after overhearing Gershom's complaint that Asaph had become their leader's favorite.

"A farmer went out to sow his seed." Jesus's voice rang far and clear, thanks to the amphitheater acoustics created by the rolling terrain facing the water. "As he was scattering the seed, some fell along the path; it was trampled on, and the birds of the air ate it up. Some fell on rock, and when it came up, the plants withered because they had no moisture."

Asaph shrugged and exchanged a look with Judah. Jesus spoke in riddles.

"Other seed fell among thorns, which grew up with it and choked the plants. Still other seed fell on good soil. It came up and yielded a crop, a hundred times more than was sown."

As Jesus stood in the boat, the vessel shifted and sloshed in the water, but he remained steady, raising his arms. "He who has ears to hear, let him hear!"

People needed more than ears to hear this message, Asaph thought. They needed a scholar to decipher Jesus's mysterious words.

"Are the seeds he speaks about the seeds of rebellion?" Asaph leaned in, whispering to Judah.

The rebel shrugged and scowled. "I wish it were so. But unfortunately, I have been learning some discouraging things about this man. Come. We have heard enough."

Judah, Asaph, and Gershom fought their way back through the crowd, although most people cleared a path voluntarily after one look at the swords strapped to their waists.

Judah led them through the narrow streets to a small, square home with three rooms, one reserved for animals. Barabbas, another rebel, was staying there for a few nights.

Asaph looked him over, thinking the man's name was curious. Barabbas was also called Jesus—Jesus bar-Abbas—with "bar-Abbas" meaning "son of the Father."

While Barabbas and the Nazarene shared the same name, that's where the similarities ended. Barabbas had a more rounded, weathered face, with a scar flowing down his left cheek.

"Jesus of Nazareth is not the Messiah," Barabbas announced after Judah, Asaph, and Gershom had settled on the ground before him. "Some claim he is here to raise an army to overpower the Romans, but he won't be able to by talking about turning the cheek to your enemy or giving your coat to those who steal your shirt."

Barabbas, who reclined before a low table, reached for a piece of bread. "He said we should love our enemies and do good to those who hate us—to pray for those who abuse us. But the Romans devour our people like bread."

Barabbas ripped apart the bread in his hand, his fiery eyes dancing around the table before biting into a piece and passing the other half to Asaph.

Judah scratched his head. "Jesus of Nazareth said we should do good to those who hate us? Did we come all this way just to hear a fool?"

Asaph glanced at Gershom sideways, unable to imagine doing good to him. Jesus must not know the human heart, or he would never suggest such a thing.

"Turning the other cheek," Barabbas scoffed. "If someone strikes us on our cheek, we strike back twice as hard. Then we drink his blood."

Barabbas gulped his wine, licking the droplets from his mustache and handing the goblet to Asaph.

"How could he gain so many followers with such a message?" Asaph lifted the cup to his lips, imagining it contained Gershom's blood.

Judah shrugged and shook his head. "I am sorry to say that even Simon has gone over to Jesus."

Asaph passed the cup to Judah. "Simon Peter, the big fisherman? He was a Zealot?"

"I'm talking about someone different. This other Simon was once a Zealot."

"Sharpen your blades, friends." Barabbas grinned. "The one good thing about Jesus of Nazareth is that he distracts the Romans. This could be a good time for us to act."

Asaph smiled in agreement. But what kind of action did Barabbas intend? Judah had yet to reveal their plans.

Glancing around the table, Asaph nodded. This was so much better than serving as a tax collector. The power of taxation was intoxicating, but this kind of power was an even more potent drug. Let Jesus of Nazareth lead his sheep over the edge of a cliff. He preferred Jesus bar-Abbas.

KETURAH

Keturah kept her distance.

Dressed in rags she obtained from a beggar woman in exchange for her robes, Keturah huddled in the corner of the market, knowing people would treat her as one who is invisible.

Just down the colonnade, Rufus and two other soldiers stood guard at the theater entrance, keeping the peace while the tetrarch attended performances in Tiberias. But Keturah hadn't expected Rufus to be standing at the main entrance, so easy to reach.

So easy to kill.

Keturah had slipped the blade inside the foul-smelling sleeves of her beggarly clothes, the steel knife cool against her skin.

When laughter bellowed from inside the theater, she figured it was either a highly successful comedy or a highly unsuccessful tragedy. Rising to her feet, she wandered down the bustling street, making a slow pass by Rufus, trying to stay hidden among the crowd. Noticing his eyes on her, she kept going without even a sideways glance.

When she was beyond the guards, she shot a look over her shoulder and found him still staring in her direction. This gave her a jolt. Keturah ducked into an alleyway and pressed her back against a crumbling wall, her heart racing. Had he recognized her? No, he couldn't know it was her beneath the ragged head covering, with the cloth drawn across the lower part of her face.

Keturah slid down the wall beside a woman making baskets. She glanced at the woman with a weak smile, drawing her knees to her chest. She dropped her head to her knees, stared at the ground, and muttered prayers to Nemesis, holding out her palm as a beggar woman might do.

Taking deep breaths, she tried to get her nerves under control. When someone placed a cool coin in her palm, she looked up and was taken aback to see Chuza smiling down at her.

Chuza: Joanna's husband. The head of Herod's household.

"Keturah?" Chuza gasped, leaning in for a closer look.

Keturah dropped her head and closed her eyes as if blotting out the world would hide her from Chuza.

"Who is Keturah?" She lowered her voice, trying to disguise it.

Even with her eyes squeezed shut and her head down, she sensed Chuza crouching to her level.

No, no, no. Her mind raced.

He put a hand to her chin and raised her head. She had no choice but to open her eyes. When she connected with his gentle gaze, she almost melted.

"How can this be, Keturah? I thought you had died." He rubbed a thumb along her jawline. Since Chuza was not a devout Jew like his wife, he had no qualms about touching another woman's face.

Keturah studied Chuza's solemn, narrow face. Joanna must not have told her husband what happened on the night Sveshtari supposedly "killed" her.

"I bled, but I lived," she said.

"The bodyguard failed to kill you? He actually failed?"

Keturah couldn't miss the suspicion in his voice. She then realized how unbelievable it sounded that a trained soldier could fail in such a simple task.

"He left me to die beyond the city walls. But I lived."

As Chuza ran his eyes across her rags and nodded, she prayed that her horrifying condition backed up her incredible story. It was an easy assumption that after the brutal attack by Sveshtari, she spiraled into a life of begging on the streets.

But would Chuza report her to Herod? And would such a revelation put Sveshtari's life in danger? Bodyguards who fail in such a simple mission as killing a slave would lose their position, if not their head.

"Please tell no one I'm alive," she whispered, looking both ways. She was asking a lot from the manager of Herod's domestic affairs.

He sighed with a shake of the head. "I still cannot believe it."

"After I tended to my injuries, I wandered to the King's Highway and was picked up by spice traders. I traveled here to Tiberias with them." At least part of her story was genuine. Chuza would never demand to see proof of a scar or wound—although Herod was another story.

"Joanna will be pleased. She was so upset when you were...killed."

"Tell her that I love her with all my life and would be willing to serve her again, *Dominus.*"

Please do not report my existence to the tetrarch. She searched his eyes, imploring him to honor the bond between her and Joanna.

"Is there a problem?"

When Rufus's voice sounded behind Chuza, Keturah ducked her chin. If Rufus recognized her, she was dead.

She waited an eternity for Chuza's response. Would he give her up to the guard? And if he did, would she have a chance to drive her knife into Rufus as he apprehended her? She closed her eyes and thought of all the ways she could die. It was a wonder anyone made it to old age.

"There is no problem here, Rufus. I know this beggar. She is from my hometown of Sepphoris, and I have not seen her for fifteen years."

With the tension boiling over, Keturah kept her head bowed, her face concealed.

Chuza continued his deflection. "Please. No need to concern yourself. I can deal with this woman."

"Very well," said Rufus.

Keturah heard his footsteps moving away, and she sensed Chuza crouching back down.

"Thank you for not betraying me." Her whisper gave away the tears she was holding at bay.

"I am sorry about your father." Chuza's words triggered a surge of sadness. "I wish I could have helped your father, talked to him about his suspicions. Then maybe I could have prevented his death at Sveshtari's blade."

Blood throbbed in Keturah's ears as if a giant had both hands on the sides of her head, slowly crushing her skull. She blinked, unsure she heard Chuza correctly.

"What did you say?"

"That I wish I could have helped your father."

"Did you say you wish you could have prevented my father's death at *Sveshtari's blade?*"

Chuza slowly nodded.

"Sveshtari?" Her throat constricted. "He was the one who killed my father?"

"You didn't know?" Chuza stood with a sigh, rubbing the back of his neck, frowning.

Keturah slowly shook her head. Chuza must have seen the mixture of horror and hatred on her face.

He sent her a look of sympathy. "Sveshtari had no choice, Keturah. He stood only a few paces from your father. Of all the bodyguards, he stood the closest. He had no choice."

Of course, he had a choice!

She scrambled to her feet. "He could have injured my father, not killed him."

"If he had only injured your father, Herod would have made sure your father's death was slow. With Herod, quick deaths are the most merciful."

He was probably right, but that did not change the enormity of the revelation. *Sveshtari had killed her father!* And he had lied about Rufus.

The throbbing at her temples continued, and her back teeth began to ache. But a strange calmness suddenly settled on Keturah's shoulders as if the goddess Nemesis stood behind her and had placed her hands on her shoulders. She imagined Nemesis's large, eagle-like wings gently flapping, raising goosebumps along her arms.

"I must leave," Chuza said, interrupting her thoughts. "But be safe. And be certain: I will not reveal anything about you to Herod."

"Thank you." Keturah smiled, which seemed to reassure Chuza.

"Please flee this city. Head to Capernaum—or better yet, Egypt."

"I will, *Dominus.*"

After Chuza left, she staggered away, occasionally bumping into people on the street, who reacted with disgust at her foul clothing. As she stumbled along, she wondered if she was losing her mind. Would she wind up like Eliana? Was she halfway to being possessed?

"Nemesis be my protector. Nemesis be my sword."

She vowed to return to Capernaum because there, she would find Sveshtari. She would find him, and she would kill him.

Keturah pulled her headdress tightly over her face, despite its horrible odor, and she moved along the main road, past the bathhouse, past pens of sheep and goats. As she looked at the Sea of Galilee off to her right, she wondered if it might be safer to go by water. Joanna had given her some money, and she had enough left to commission a boat.

She wheeled around when she spotted two approaching soldiers, praying they didn't notice her. Instead of a boat, she should find a caravan heading from Tiberias to Capernaum. It was riskier, but—

A hand clamped down on her shoulder and squeezed so hard that pain shot down her arm. She grunted as the person spun her around and yanked off her headdress, throwing her off balance.

Her eyes widened. It wasn't Rufus, thank the gods. But it was another one of Herod's guards, Lucanus.

"I thought I recognized you," Lucanus said, his eyes flashing with something she couldn't quite interpret.

Her throat went dry. How many times could she be noticed without it getting back to Herod? She tried to break his grip, his hands digging into the flesh of her upper arms, but it was futile. He laughed at her helplessness.

"You're the slave girl whose father tried to murder the tetrarch. You're supposed to be dead."

"You must be mistaken, *Dominus*. I'm not a slave."

"*Dominus*?" He raised a brow, his eyes tracing every inch of her before pulling her close and whispering, "You speak like a slave."

Keturah would have liked to wipe the smug grin from his broad face. "Free women also know how to speak to one in authority."

She yanked one arm free when he finally loosened his grip, but he held tight to the other with a challenging stare.

"That's right. I do have authority over you." Lucanus wet his lips, his eyes darkening with desire.

Keturah knew that look. The last thing she wanted was to discover how he planned to use his authority. She reached for the knife in the folds of her garment, but Lucanus snagged her by the wrist, twisting her arm until the blade fell to the ground.

Although Lucanus released her wrist, he kept her close, gripping her opposite arm. "I can do whatever I wish with you, and who would know? You're dead, after all."

He bent to retrieve the knife, scrutinizing it with a mischievous grin before dragging her down the street. "I can see you're going to be quite a bother to deal with. So, I might as well make some extra coin before I return to my duties."

Up ahead, through the jumble of people on the street, sounds of a nearby slave auction grew louder the closer they got. Her heart fell when she realized Lucanus was about to sell her back into slavery.

JEREMIEL: SEVEN MONTHS LATER, THE MONTH OF CHISLEV (LATE NOVEMBER), 28 A.D.

The windstorm struck without warning. It came out of nowhere, as they often do, but Jeremiel knew its source. Chaotic gusts swept down from the high places, blustering east to west. Leaves swirled inside his cave as a gale roared to life.

Curious, Jeremiel ventured a few steps out of his cave to see what was happening and was nearly blown off his feet. Bracing himself against the outside of the cave, he looked out onto the Sea of Galilee. Wild water churned, and white-tipped waves rose and fell, pounding the shore.

He narrowed his eyes and made out a small fishing boat, struggling to stay afloat as it rode the waves. The small crew was caught unaware by the fast-approaching windstorm.

The boat looked to be traveling from Capernaum on the northwestern side of the lake to the eastern side. Most likely, it was headed toward Gergesa, just down the slope from Jeremiel's cave.

Jeremiel ventured farther outside and sat down, watching the unfolding drama as the wind scattered dirt, twigs, and leaves around him. He closed his eyes and inhaled, breathing in the mighty power of God, when a deafening crack broke his concentration.

A large branch crashed in front of the mouth of his cave, and Jeremiel jerked, looking at the distance between where he sat and where he stood only moments ago. He might have been crushed if he hadn't moved.

Jeremiel raised a fist at the dark sky and shouted at the tempest, reciting one of his favorite Proverbs. "When the storm has swept by, the wicked are gone, but the righteous stand firm forever!"

That's when he decided to test the Lord. If God judged him as truly wicked, then the Lord would use this storm to sweep him away. But if he were righteous, he would stand firm. If God wanted to punish him, let the Lord hasten to destroy him with one blast of wind rather than let his body rot slowly with this disease.

Jeremiel stood, focusing on the frenzied waves crashing and foaming against the small boat. As waves spilled into the vessel, threatening to swamp it, he lifted his face to the sky, arms wide, quoting the words of Jonah.

"Then the Lord sent a great wind on the sea, and such a violent storm arose that the ship threatened to break up!"

He recalled how Jonah told the sailors that the Lord had sent the storm to punish him for disobedience. Then Jonah volunteered to be tossed into the sea—a sacrifice to save the ship.

A roar of wind shook Jeremiel from his thoughts. He squinted at the boat flailing on the Sea of Galilee and wondered who had sinned that God would want to blot them out with this windstorm. Did the vessel carry another Jonah, and would he sacrifice himself by hurling himself into the waves to prevent the boat from going under?

By now, the wind was so violent that Jeremiel staggered forward, nearly blown over. Jaw clenched, he planted his front foot firmly on the ground and braced against the wind pushing from behind. He would not be leveled. He would not be crushed.

"From deep in the realm of the dead I called for help, and you listened to my cry!" Jeremiel recited the same prayer that Jonah spoke after the great fish swallowed him. "You hurled me into the depths, into the very heart of the seas, and the currents swirled about me; all your waves and breakers swept over me!"

The wind intensified, howling and tearing at him and trying to lift him from his feet. But he stood firm. A thick cloud of dust billowed, blocking his view of the lake, let alone the boat. That little vessel must have taken on so much water that it had sunk by now. He imagined the men thrashing on the surface of the water or dropping into the heart of the sea with no great fish to rescue them.

Jeremiel could no longer distinguish the sky from land or sea. The entire world became a cloud of whirling dust, and Jeremiel was caught in the core of the storm. But he remained standing because he was righteous. He would not be counted among the wicked!

The wind howled so loudly that when Jeremiel tried to shout more of Jonah's words, he could barely hear himself. So, instead of using words, he screamed, matching the wind strength for strength. And when he thought he could cry out no more, the wind stopped. It happened in an instant as if someone had suddenly shut a door on the wind, and everything went silent.

As the dust settled, Jeremiel swallowed, trying to rid his mouth of the dust and grit. He strained his eyes, trying to see what had become of the boat. He assumed it would be completely gone—the wicked wiped away by the storm, as the Scriptures said. At the very least, it would be partially submerged or overturned, with the men clinging to the hull for dear life.

But when he spotted it, still afloat, he did a double take. It looked like the mast, the cross sticking from the center of the boat, had snapped at the top. But other than that damage, the vessel was whole, and the crew was still crowded inside the tiny boat as if there had never been a storm! How could they have possibly survived?

Lifting his arms, he raised his eyes to the clouds and shouted the final words of Jonah's prayer: "When my life was ebbing away, I remembered you, Lord, and my prayer rose to you, to your holy temple. Salvation comes from the Lord."

Jeremiel had survived this test from God. Like the fishing boat, he had not been swept away with the wicked.

Jeremiel caught his breath. *What if all of this—the leprosy and the storm—is simply God's way of showing me that I am truly righteous? That I could survive any storm, including the one raging on my body? What if the storm was God's way of cleansing me? What if I raise the sleeves of my robe and see that my leprosy is gone?*

He reached for his sleeve but hesitated. He sighed, afraid to look. But the little boat had survived, hadn't it? That was a miracle. Perhaps it wouldn't be the day's only miracle. He closed his eyes and said a prayer, edging his sleeve up with renewed hope, revealing a long stretch of healthy skin.

He smiled—but only for a moment.

As he continued to pull back his sleeve, the first lesion appeared, then the second...and then a third! He dropped his head and closed his eyes.

The leprosy was not gone. In fact, it was spreading.

SVESHTARI

Under Herod's orders, Sveshtari commandeered a boat and reached the other side of the Sea of Galilee before the sun had fully set. After the storm had died, other boats brought people from Capernaum to Gergesa to follow Jesus.

When Sveshtari climbed out of the vessel on the eastern shoreline, the sun was just beginning to disappear beneath the horizon—its large, red half-circle splashing the undersides of the ragged clouds with orange and red light.

He trudged through shallow water, cool around his bare ankles, and approached the rocky land. Dressed in plain clothes instead of the military trappings of his position, Sveshtari planned to act with stealth, not brute force. However, he still carried a knife and sword.

Because of the savage windstorm, Sveshtari had naturally thought he would have to wait until morning to cross the lake. From the western side, he'd seen that Jesus's boat had been caught by the ferocious winds, and he wondered whether the storm might save him the trouble of killing the Nazarene. Surely, the waves would capsize their boat, so he was stunned when the wind stopped abruptly, and he spotted the boat still afloat.

"You are Keturah's lover, are you not?" spoke a soft voice from behind.

Sveshtari turned to discover the same middle-aged woman who traveled with Keturah to Capernaum. She clambered out of a boat, followed by her dog.

"And you are...?" He fumbled for her name.

"Eliana. But surely you must remember my dog, Lavi. You saved him from that man." Her eyes lit up with appreciation.

"Ah, yes. Are you a follower of Jesus?" Sveshtari studied her disheveled appearance, wondering why she was here.

"I follow no one," she said as the light in her eyes died.

"And yet you came across the lake to see Jesus?"

She stared into the distance. "He interests me." She found his eyes and bore into them. "But what about you? Why have you crossed the lake?"

"I am Herod's eyes and ears. He likes to keep track of the prophets in his land."

The sunset bathed everything in unearthly yellow tints, offering enough light to reveal Jesus and his disciples heading toward the small village of Gergesa. Sveshtari turned from Eliana and hiked in their direction, wondering if the lack of crowds on this side of the lake would make it easier to kill the prophet without being discovered. It should be easy to find out where Jesus planned to spend the night and murder him in his sleep.

Sveshtari was so caught up in his thoughts that he didn't realize Eliana was following him until she stepped on the back of one of his sandals. He tossed a dirty look over his shoulder and growled, but she didn't apologize or even seem to notice what she had done.

"What about Keturah?" Sveshtari tossed the question to Eliana over his shoulder as he kept walking. "What does she think about Jesus?"

"She worships Nemesis. She thinks Jesus talks too much about loving your enemies."

Sveshtari was glad to hear that Keturah did not have high regard for Jesus. After killing her father, the last thing he wanted to do was kill a prophet she followed and respected.

Sveshtari noticed that Jesus and his disciples skirted what appeared to be a cemetery on the edge of Gergesa. Up on a bluff, overlooking the cemetery, was a small farmstead with a pen that housed a multitude of pigs. Several farmers sat on stones, looking down on Jesus and his small band of disciples. It all made for an eerie picture with the tombstones glowing in the sunset light.

"How did you meet Keturah?" Sveshtari cut his eyes at Eliana when she came up alongside him.

"I was with the caravan from Jericho, and we—"

Eliana stopped, her eyes wide. An imposing figure emerged from behind a nearby tombstone and bellowed at the top of his lungs as he ran at Jesus, holding a massive stone with his arm cocked.

Instinctively, Sveshtari pulled out his sword. The screaming man, who looked as thick as a block of stone and equally strong, appeared to be intent on murder. He dragged a length of broken chain attached to his ankle, and it jangled against the rocks in his path.

Again, it looked as if someone or something was planning to do Sveshtari's job for him. First, the storm, and now this crazed man. It seemed as if all of creation conspired to destroy the man from Nazareth.

ELIANA

"Kill Jesus, now!"

Calev's command throbbed in Eliana's head and was almost as shocking as the scream echoing through the cemetery. She looked around, searching for the source of the cry, when someone raced from behind a tombstone, preparing to throw a large stone. In the eerie light of the sunset, bold colors burst around this man, making it seem like he was on fire.

Despite Calev's command, Eliana's gut instinct was to warn Jesus. "Jesus, watch out!"

Eliana shook her head. It didn't make sense. She had crossed the lake with the renewed vow to kill Jesus, yet the moment he was under threat, she leaped to his defense.

Looking down at her right hand, she was shocked to see herself holding her knife, which had been hidden in the folds of her robe. She didn't even remember pulling it out.

From the astonished look on Sveshtari's face, he was also shocked to see a blade suddenly appear in her hand. But most surprisingly, it dawned on Eliana that she had pulled out the knife intending to *protect* Jesus, not murder him.

"Use it! Kill Jesus, kill him!" Calev's voice had a frantic edge to it as she shook her head, trying to dislodge his presence.

"Shut up!" Eliana screamed at the sky.

"I didn't say anything," Sveshtari said.

With his sword drawn, Sveshtari increased his stride. They made a comical pair, marching toward Jesus side by side, Sveshtari with his large sword and Eliana with her tiny blade.

As they closed in, the attacker slowed, approaching Jesus more cautiously. The closer he got to the prophet, the more the man's legs began to shake before they ultimately gave out, and he crumpled at Jesus's feet as if shot by an arrow.

The man rolled in the dirt, foaming at the mouth and screaming. Jesus approached and crouched to his level as the man beat himself like he was putting out a fire.

When Jesus extended a hand, Eliana perked an ear but couldn't hear what he said. Finally, the man began to slowly gain control of his convulsing body, groaning and pushing to his knees. He looked at Jesus through hooded eyes. Spittle hung from his beard, and he panted like a winded dog.

"What do you want with me, Jesus, Son of the Most High God? I beg you, don't torture me!"

Torture him? Jesus wasn't even touching him.

"What is your name?" Jesus's voice was full of authority.

The man raised his body, but even the slightest movement had Eliana grasping her knife a bit tighter, hoping he wasn't about to spring upon Jesus. His breathing became more rapid and labored, and blood trickled from the corner of his mouth. He appeared to have bitten into his own tongue.

"*Legion,*" the man moaned.

The very word sent a wave of coldness over Eliana, and she began to shiver uncontrollably.

A Roman legion was just under 6,000 men. How many demons were speaking as one?

"Legion," he repeated, his voice hissing.

Suddenly, the man's body contorted, and he collapsed to the ground, striking his forehead against a stone until blood flowed.

"Don't throw us into the Abyss!" the man shouted. "What do you want with us, Son of God? Have you come here to torture us before the appointed time?"

"Leave this place," Calev suddenly said inside Eliana's head. "Get away from Jesus."

Eliana frowned, confused by Calev's contradictory command, telling her to attack Jesus one moment and flee the next. But Eliana was too mesmerized to pay Calev any heed. While the wild man was on the ground, his arms twisted into an almost impossible shape. But finally, his rapid breathing quieted.

"If you drive us out, send us into the herd of pigs," the man begged.

Eliana followed Jesus's gaze as he looked up at some squealing pigs penned on a bluff. The pigs started darting about as if they sensed something not of this world.

"Run away," Calev whispered, trying to reason with her. "Jesus is dangerous. He will kill us if you stay here."

"But you said you want me to kill him," Eliana said aloud.

Sveshtari shot her a puzzled look.

"Not now," Calev said. "Wait for a safer time. Jesus is too dangerous."

Eliana struck herself on the side of the head. "Quiet!"

Meanwhile, the strange story continued to unfold before them.

"Send us among the pigs," the big man said to Jesus. He bowed, his nose touching the ground. "Allow us to go into them."

Jesus stood, held out his right hand, and said, "Go!"

The demon-possessed man fell onto his back, writhing as if wrestling with an invisible force. Simultaneously, the pigs up on the bluff began to squeal even louder. The three farmers, who had been standing at the edge of the bluff looking down at Jesus and his disciples, suddenly rushed toward the pen, flailing their arms and shouting.

Eliana had never heard pigs create such a ruckus, an unnatural mix of guttural grunts and high shrieks. At Jesus's command, the pigs lost all control, crashed through the wooden pen, and thundered down the steep slope.

All eyes moved from the demon-possessed man to the swine on the bluff. By now, there was little light left from the sunset—just enough to see the ghostly image of hundreds of pigs charging down the slope out of control. One of the farmers leaped into the mix, trying to hold them back with outstretched arms, but he would have had more success stopping a landslide with his bare hands.

The man was trampled.

"No! No!" one of the farmers bellowed as the leading edge of the pigs tumbled over the brow of the bluff, diving toward the black water below. Hundreds of squealing shadows followed, plunging like a waterfall of animals. Two other farmers chased the stampeding pigs, trying to save some stragglers at the back, but the animals were too strong, too out of control.

A crowd of onlookers rushed to the shore for a better view of the pigs as they fell, a half dozen or more at a time. Most of the animals sank like stones, while some tried to swim with their snouts raised to the sky. They paddled farther out to sea until they disappeared beneath the dark waves.

Eliana had been so captivated by the commotion that she hadn't even noticed what was happening with the large man from the tombs. When she finally returned her attention to Jesus, she gasped. The man, once possessed, was now sitting, looking around as if he had just awakened from a deep sleep. Jesus crouched beside him, a hand resting on his shoulder.

"RUN!" Calev's voice was like a thunderclap.

Jesus turned and looked at Eliana intently as if he, too, could hear Calev. That's when she knew what she had to do.

She turned and ran for the edge of the water. She must kill Calev. And the only way to destroy him would be to destroy herself. She would run into the water and not stop until the waves buried her. She would join the pigs and drown.

Sveshtari

Sveshtari plunged into the water, vowing not to let Eliana die as she disappeared under a wave.

Maybe he was acting on his bodyguard's protective instinct, or maybe he was driven by the guilt of so many deaths at his hands. Whatever it was, when trouble struck, he moved without a thought—just as he had when he had executed Keturah's father.

"Neptune, help me," he said aloud, calling on the god of the sea as he reached under the surface and felt around in the dark water. Eliana couldn't have gone far, but it would be impossible to find her in the growing darkness if he didn't do it soon.

Since the water was only to his waist, he dove beneath it, searching with arms wide, before heaving upward, gulping air the moment he broke through the surface.

Sveshtari scanned the water as a chill ran down his spine. He had to move forward, which meant deeper waters, and he didn't know how to swim. If Eliana had reached the place where the water was above his head, he would not be able to do anything to save her.

A grunt sounded to his right, and Sveshtari spun, only to see the ghostly shadow of a pig trying to tread water. The animal soon disappeared beneath the black water with a horrid squeal.

Ducking underwater again, he touched something and yanked his hand back, unsure what it was. Was it a pig or Eliana? He rose from the water and stared at the moonlight shimmering on the water, thinking it may not have been human.

He had heard stories about spirits walking on the bottom of the lake. Could he have touched the cold hand of a demon?

He shivered once more, his skin crawling at the thought of encountering something lurking in the lake. Swallowing his fear, he reached under the water and clasped what seemed like a human arm. He winced, forcing himself to hold on. When it jerked, he gasped. If it was Eliana, she was alive. For now.

The water was up to his mouth, as his heavy robes tugged at him, limiting his movement. He yanked Eliana's arm, but she struggled and almost broke free, pulling him into deeper water.

Sveshtari coughed and dragged in a lungful of air, expending most of his energy standing on tiptoes to keep his nose above water. He almost lost hold of Eliana when a wave pounded him, submerging him for one terrible moment. He was sure he would drown, unable to keep any part of his head above water.

Eliana seemed lifeless, floating like seaweed. He was about to pull her to the shore when he lost his footing and went completely under. With the weight of his clothing, he was sure he was a dead man, destined to roam the bottom of the lake, never to rise again.

Then two strong hands took him under the armpits and yanked him backward. He resurfaced, gasping and coughing and spitting out water. The sky was pitch black, and all around him was confusion and noise, The only thing he was sure of was that he was still clinging to Eliana's arm.

He was pulled ashore by the hands of experienced fishermen accustomed to hauling heavy nets. When he caught a quick glimpse of the men who saved him, he strongly suspected they were Jesus's disciples.

Then he was lowered onto hard ground, still spluttering and exhausted, every muscle in his arms and legs burning with pain. He rolled onto his side and found Eliana lying next to him while her dog Lavi licked her face.

Eliana looked like a corpse washed up on the beach until she twitched and moaned, rolling to her side and vomiting water, some of which hit Sveshtari in the face.

But at least she was alive. And so was Sveshtari.

"Father, hallowed be your name, your kingdom come. Give us each day our daily bread...." Shadows of people knelt around him in prayer.

When Eliana opened her eyes and stared at Sveshtari, she was so close that he contemplated pushing some hair from her face.

She looked dazed, but her expression soon changed as her eyes hardened and her top lip pulled tight, exposing the roots of her teeth. Sveshtari drew back, thinking she would bite him.

"Why did you stop us?" she asked. "Why did you save us?"

"I did it for Keturah. You're her friend."

"You should have let us perish. We had to die to save Jesus. Why didn't you let us die?"

This made no sense at all to Sveshtari. How could her death save the prophet? And why was she speaking of "us"? Then Eliana's eyes rolled back, and she began convulsing. For a moment, Sveshtari wondered if he had pulled a demon from the water after all.

ELIANA

Eliana plunged into herself. Lightning-fast images played behind her eyes as she saw memories of her childhood friends—Zuriel, Asaph, Gershom, and other village boys—stoning her to death.

They hurled stones, cursing her for what she had become during her years as a slave. They called her foul names because she was unclean, and she surrendered to the abuse as the rocks crashed against her legs, arms, and sides of her head.

But one man stood tall among those stoning her. He stepped out from the pack with a calm smile, saying, "You shouldn't have tried to kill me, Eliana."

"Calev?"

In all her life, Calev had just been a voice in her head, but now she saw him face to face. He was a handsome, clean-shaven man with unsettling violet eyes. All the boys who encircled her stopped throwing stones, and they turned to Calev, waiting.

"You shouldn't have tried to kill me," Calev repeated. "Thou shalt not murder."

"But that's exactly what you have always asked me to do. You have always commanded me to kill for you."

"I always commanded you to kill, but for your sake, not mine, Eliana." He spoke so calmly, so matter-of-factly. "I have always done it for you. The first person I asked you to kill was your slave master. He deserved to die. I was just protecting you."

"But what about Keturah? You told me to kill her."

"I knew Keturah would put you in danger. I knew she would be attacked by the caravan trader, and you would try to help her. I wanted to protect you from that danger. You almost died that night."

"You also told me to kill Jesus. Why would you ask me to kill someone I don't even know?"

"Because I knew you would meet him, and he would put your life in danger. I know that most of his disciples will eventually die terribly, and I didn't want you to be one of them. So, you see, I'm protecting you, Eliana. That's what I have been doing all along. Your father was not there to protect you. You only had me."

Eliana saw herself falling to her knees before Calev and weeping. It was true. Her father had failed to protect her. She would never forget the first night after they fled their home—how the Roman contingent came so close to discovering them. That was the first night Calev had spoken to her.

"I comforted you in the dark," Calev said. "I was there for you when your father wasn't. Your father put your life in danger because of his hatred for Rome. He should have cared more about you than he did about his cause."

Calev was right. Her father had put her in danger. If not for her Abba's mission against Rome, she would not have been in the hills of Bethlehem on that day thirty years ago. She would not have been captured by brigands, and she would not have been sold into slavery.

"I should have told you to kill your father," Calev said. "Then all your troubles would have ended. That was my only mistake."

Each of Calev's words was like a stone, striking her where she was most vulnerable. She felt herself crumbling, a fortress under siege. Calev was relentless.

"I have been your only protector, Eliana. It's been me all along. Your father put you in danger. Keturah put you in danger. And Jesus will put you in danger if you're not careful. So, save yourself and kill Jesus."

She lifted her head and saw Calev smiling back at her, making a clicking sound with his tongue against the top of his mouth. All the boys, the wild ones who surrounded her, began to hurl their stones once again.

Eliana fell face-first into the dirt, and the stones kept coming.

JEREMIEL

Jeremiel saw it all. From his perch near Gergesa, he watched the boats reach shore by the cemetery. In the dying light of day, he saw Jesus and his disciples step from the first boat. Then more boats followed because wherever Jesus went, crowds sprouted.

Crouching behind a large stone, he watched as a wild man rushed forward to attack Jesus. Then the pigs started going berserk on the bluff. As the bizarre scene unfolded, Jeremiel slowly moved down the slope, closer and closer to the excitement. He stopped to hide behind boulders, but no one noticed him skulking in the falling darkness.

As he drew near, a woman ran into the water as if directed by the same power that had destroyed the pigs. A man and a dog jumped in after her, and then several of Jesus's disciples hauled them out before they drowned. One of the disciples was Simon Peter, the sturdy fisherman.

Rather than catching Tilapia, Peter was fishing for people this night, hauling a man and a crazed woman to shore where they flopped like fish—or at least the woman did. If Peter separated the clean from the unclean fish, as a good Jewish fisherman did, he should have thrown them back into the water.

But who was he to talk? He had leprosy! He was every bit as unclean as this demon-possessed woman. Maybe he should hurl himself into the sea like the girl and be done with it.

The woman lay prone for a moment, convulsing, when Peter or one of the other disciples—he wasn't sure which—put a hand on her shoulder. Jeremiel gasped at the bold move. Didn't Peter realize he'd made himself ceremoniously unclean by touching such a woman?

When Peter bowed his head, Jeremiel moved closer, hiding behind some brush where he could hear bits and pieces of his prayer—but he couldn't quite hear everything. Jesus stood in the background, calmly observing the scene unfold as a stream of agitated people from Gergesa approached to observe what was happening.

"In the name of Jesus, the Christ, be gone!" Peter's words carried loudly, leaving no doubt about what he said. Jeremiel cocked his head with a frown.

In the name of Jesus, the Christ?

Jeremiel fought the urge to scream, *Blasphemer!* How dare that man pray in the name of Jesus? Who did he think he was? Who did he think *Jesus* was?

But the words seemed to affect the woman. Her screams carried in the breeze, sending shivers across Jeremiel's skin. A ripping noise carried through the air, like the tearing of a large curtain. She writhed in pain as if something was being torn from her body.

The man who had saved her from the sea pinned her to the ground. Otherwise, the woman might have leaped to her feet and tried to hurl herself into the water again.

Then something cracked. Jeremiel jerked at the sound. Was it one of her bones? Had she convulsed so roughly that she broke it? He drew back as she foamed at the mouth and screamed again.

Then all was silent. When the woman lay perfectly still on her back, Jeremiel wondered if she were dead. Had they killed her? Or did she die of terror?

ELIANA

He's gone.

Eliana didn't know precisely how, but Calev had fled her body.

While there had been many times when she didn't hear his voice, this was different. Even on those occasions, she always sensed him lurking in the recesses of her mind. It was like entering a dark room when you knew someone was there. They don't make a sound, even a whisper, but their presence is tangible. That is how it had been with Calev. Until now.

She opened her eyes to find two rugged men staring down at her with wonder. She should have been afraid, but somehow, she wasn't. One of the men, Keturah's lover, had pulled her from the water. What was Svehstari doing out here on this beach?

The other, kneeling over her, was one of Jesus's disciples, a man called Simon Peter. She had never met or spoken to him, but she knew it was him.

"He's gone," she said, sitting up and looking at Peter.

At first, he seemed surprised—as if he couldn't believe it. Then he broke into a smile, and he reared back, laughing.

A cool breeze coming off the lake raised goosebumps on her wet arm. She breathed in the cleansing wind, letting it pass across her and through her. Then she, too, smiled as wide as the Sea of Galilee.

9

LUKE, CHAPTER 9

ASAPH

A SAPH AND GERSHOM BROKE from the rest of the group several days later, leaving Capernaum by donkey. They chose the large Damascus breed, favored for its speed. These donkeys were beautiful specimens—white, long-bodied creatures with elongated ears. But most importantly, they were capable of going long distances without water, second only to the camel.

Gershom rode in front, which suited Asaph fine. Letting Gershom lead the way meant the man couldn't hurl a knife at his back. It also meant talking was difficult, so they moved in silence, the only sound being the rattle of their equipment.

In their search for Eliana, they targeted a string of cities along the Sea of Galilee south of Capernaum, beginning with Gennesaret. In each city, they visited slave markets, inquiring about Eliana. After the first two cities, Asaph began to understand the futility of their mission. Hunting for a forty-two-year-old woman, who had disappeared as a ten-year-old girl, was like looking for a needle in a haystack that had been piled on the ground thirty years ago and scattered to the wind.

On the first few nights, Asaph had difficulty sleeping because he expected Gershom to kill him before he woke. They communicated only when necessary, using grunts instead of words in most cases. But after a week of silence, Asaph started to go mad. He had to talk, even if it was to Gershom.

Asaph side-eyed him one morning as they traveled south from the Sea of Galilee through the Jezreel Valley in Samaria. "Why did you insist on going with me?"

This wasn't the first time he'd asked the question, but he'd yet to receive an answer. It wasn't until the third time that Gershom finally responded.

"Because I don't trust you!"

"You think I might run off on Judah?"

"I *know* you'll run off." Gershom's voice lowered to a growl.

"Then you don't know me."

"You were a brute as a boy and a tax collector as a man. What else is there to know?"

Asaph fumed. He may have been a bully as a boy, but at least he had never struck a girl with a rock—as Gershom and Zuriel had tried to do.

"I'm not the one who wanted to stone Eliana," he snapped.

Gershom brought his donkey to a halt and turned it around with a tug of the reins. His hand went to the sword at his side, his eyes daring Asaph to make a move. Asaph swallowed. Maybe he'd gone too far, but he would not show fear.

"I never threw a stone at Eliana," Gershom said. He still had his hand on his sword as he came alongside, but he didn't unsheathe the weapon.

Asaph knew he should let the matter drop but couldn't resist. "You did nothing to stop Zuriel from trying to strike Eliana with a stone. *I did.*"

Gershom gave Asaph a poisonous glare. Gershom's donkey shuffled its feet on the stony ground, as agitated as its rider.

Asaph's eyes drifted down to Gershom's right hand, which was now wrapped around the hilt of his sword. Then, slowly, Gershom loosened his grip and reached for the sling strapped to his waist.

Was he going to hit him with a stone instead? That would be a fitting tactic for a man who once considered stoning an innocent young girl.

Asaph nodded at the sling. "What do you plan on—?"

"Shhh," Gershom hissed. "Not another word."

Asaph was about to snap back at him when he noticed Gershom staring at something behind him. He spun in his saddle, craning his neck, and spotted a lion loping in their direction, closing the gap between them like something out of a bad dream. But this was no illusion.

Asaph's heart thudded against his rib cage. He glanced at Gershom, who had already dismounted and grappled with his donkey's reins as the animal strained to break free.

Gershom motioned toward him. "Off your donkey. Hold the reins."

Asaph did so, sensing his donkey getting ready to bolt. As the massive lion approached, their donkeys skittered, trying to pull away, but Asaph held firm and whispered soothing words.

By this time, Gershom had his sling in hand. Asaph eyed the weapon, hoping Gershom knew what he was doing. Gershom retrieved a large stone from a sack attached to his side. It was perfectly round, like a bird's egg, but as heavy as gold.

The lion was male, with a shaggy black mane. While the animal wasn't in a full sprint, it maintained a steady, threatening gait. Asaph knew better than to run but wondered if they could use the donkeys as bait while he and Gershom escaped.

The donkeys began to bray, with one trying to nip Asaph's hand. But Asaph held firm. They couldn't afford to lose their means of transportation. While he had never faced a direct lion attack, he had been told that most lions resort to mock charges. However, this did not appear to be one of those because it did not involve a lot of zigzagging and pawing of the ground. The lion maintained an unrelenting approach. Either way, it was vital not to run.

The lion bared its teeth, releasing a deep, barrel-chested growl that rattled Asaph's bones—another bad sign. Lions growl as they attack.

Asaph stood on his toes, shouting at the top of his lungs, holding the reins tight with one hand and waving his free arm—anything to make himself look larger to scare away the animal. Out of the corner of his eye, he noticed Gershom winding up with his sling, swinging it in a figure-eight pattern before releasing the cord with an overhand fling. The rock sailed straight but high, whistling right over the head of the lion.

Asaph groaned. Which one would the lion tear apart first? Asaph decided to go for its eyes if it attacked, then gouge and punch it in the snout.

Don't run, don't run, he kept telling himself.

Meanwhile, Gershom—who seemed strangely calm until now—began frantically digging into his pouch for another rock, spilling several to the ground. The lion's growl grew in power and ferocity.

Asaph noticed a nearby stone, large enough to do some damage. He picked it up and hurled it at the lion, but his pitiful throw fell far short. As if mocking him, the lion kept coming, its odor more pronounced with each step.

Meanwhile, Gershom reloaded his sling, swinging it in circular motions while studying the beast and taking aim. Handled properly, a rock could fly as fast as an arrow—fast enough to penetrate the skin and break bones, but your aim had to be true.

Now! Asaph thought.

When Gershom released the sling, the rock whistled past Asaph, striking the lion between the eyes, Goliath style, breaking its skin and gashing its face. The lion slowed, staggering sideways and roared as blood gushed down its snout. Struggling to stay upright, the beast regained its balance and kept coming.

Asaph hurled another rock, although tossing a stone by hand could not come close to matching a sling. With the lion stunned and staggering, Gershom had time to reload and send a third rock flying. It struck the lion's right eye, burrowing into the soft tissue.

The beast's legs finally gave out, and the lion slumped with a mournful roar. It struggled, trying to push back up onto its front legs, but couldn't. As more blood spilled, matting the lion's fur and masking its face in red, Asaph's knees went weak—the tension of his body giving way to dizzying relief. He fought to maintain his balance as he stared at the mountain of lion flesh, no longer moving. The donkeys, still frantic, nearly pulled him off his feet.

Gershom carefully approached the motionless animal, drawing his sword and finishing off the lion, putting it out of its misery.

Still clutching the donkeys' reins, Asaph backed up and dropped onto a large boulder to keep from fainting. He met Gershom's measured gaze as the man wiped his sword clean with a rag. The lion's life was in the blood, but now it pooled in the sandy soil beneath its head. Flies had already begun to gather around the carcass.

"Remind me never to criticize you about throwing stones ever again," Asaph joked, returning his gaze to Gershom's hard stare. He did not seem amused.

Gershom turned his back and continued to clean his blade before sheathing it and taking back his donkey's reins.

Together, they traveled across Jezreel Valley, leaving the lion's body for the birds and beasts—and flies. They passed between mountains on either side, moving deeper into Samaria, where they would continue their hunt for Eliana in the next city.

The next morning, Asaph opened his eyes to find Gershom standing over him, staring. He shot upright and scooted backward, his eyes darting to Gershom's sword to ensure it wasn't drawn.

Gershom laughed. "What do you think—that I kill people in their sleep?"

"You startled me, that's all."

"Get up. It's about time you knew how to use one of these."

Gershom dangled a sling in front of him. "The next time we encounter a lion, I don't want to be the only one defending us. When was the last time you used one?"

"It's been a long time."

In truth, he had *never* used one.

"Did your father show you?"

"You should know the answer to that question, Gershom. Don't you remember him?"

Asaph's father had spent a fair amount of time beating on him and his three brothers and two sisters. A father like that wasn't about to take the time to teach them how to use a weapon like a sling. He might be afraid his sons would use it against him.

Gershom nodded slowly, lost in thought. "I do remember your father. Sorry."

He spoke as if he genuinely cared.

Asaph stared out into the cloudless morning sky. They had slept in a cave outside Lebonah, their latest fruitless stop. Asaph exhaled, trying to shake the disappointment of his childhood. Eliana had been a bright light in his dismal world. He had to find her.

"Here." Gershom nudged him to get his attention. "I have several slings. You can borrow this one."

"Thanks."

Taking the sling, Asaph rose to his feet, dusting off his robe.

"Check your wingspan." Gershom nodded at the weapon as if Asaph was supposed to understand. Asaph blinked, unsure what he was asking.

Gershom rolled his eyes. "How in the world did you ever lord it over us as a boy? Don't you know anything? Do this."

Gershom spread his arms, stretching the sling across his chest, waiting until Asaph did the same.

"Your sling should be about the length of your wingspan. That looks good. Now slip the knot over your finger."

A knot was at one end of the cord, but he didn't know which finger to slip it over, so he randomly chose one.

"Not that one," Gershom scolded. "Putting the loop over that finger takes away considerable accuracy. Put it over your pointer finger."

You could have told me that from the start. Asaph frowned, but it seemed that Gershom enjoyed having the upper hand, correcting his mistakes.

"Now pinch the other end between your pointer finger and thumb."

Asaph did as instructed, but once again, he failed the test.

"You're supposed to pinch the knot! The knot!" Gershom pointed, jabbing his finger.

"I got it, I got it."

"You have to do it right, or you might as well throw the stones by hand," Gershom said. "And knowing how you throw, I wouldn't recommend it."

Asaph wondered when Gershom would make that observation. He had always been sensitive about his awkward throwing arm.

"Let's give it a try now."

Gershom set up a target, about fourteen cubits away, by propping a piece of wood against a boulder. "Give it a shot. Do the figure-eight windup."

Asaph placed a smooth stone in the sling pouch and swung it in a figure-eight pattern. On the first try, he nearly hit himself in the face. On the second try, he accidentally let go during the windup, and the stone went awry, almost hitting Gershom.

Gershom jumped back with a pointed look. "I will assume that was not intentional."

It took another four tries before Asaph got the windup right, finally releasing the rock with an overhand fling. Still, it missed the target by quite a distance.

"If you were aiming at an elephant, you wouldn't have hit it." Gershom couldn't contain his laughter.

Asaph's face burned hot. He ducked his head, thankful that at least Gershom was smiling. By the sixth outrageously poor throw, even Asaph couldn't help but grin, more than willing to laugh at himself if it meant making Gershom happy. A cheerful Gershom was less likely to murder him in his sleep.

As Asaph continued to practice, he relaxed, and his slings improved, only missing the target by a little.

"That's enough for now, but you're actually showing promise," Gershom said with a clipped nod.

Asaph stared at him for a moment, unable to believe his ears. Almost hitting the target was a minor miracle. It was a *major miracle* that the two of them were finally speaking.

Asaph offered the sling back to Gershom, but the man waved him off with a shake of the head. "Keep it. You will need it to practice every morning and evening. Within a week, you might be on target."

Asaph tucked the sling beneath the rope around his waist. "Thanks."

On instinct, Asaph shot out his right hand, offering to shake. Gershom stared at the hand, his smile vanishing as if he had been offered a rotten fish. Exhaling, Gershom reached out and gave him a firm but quick handshake before they parted, spinning toward their donkeys.

Without another word, they climbed onto their animals to resume their travels. While neither could tolerate each other much, it was an improvement.

SVESHTARI: SIX MONTHS LATER, THE MONTH OF SIVAN (EARLY MAY), 29 A.D.

Sveshtari and Lucanus, a fellow bodyguard, marched through the dark, damp halls of the prison below the Fortress of Machaerus. Two more guards trailed behind, carrying torches. The light caught a few rats in its glow, but the fat, black creatures fled into the shadows.

Finally, Sveshtari and Lucanus reached John the Baptist's cell, where the prophet sat on a stool in a corner. The prophet raised his head, his long, straggly hair dangling in front of his face as the torchlight danced into his cell. Even in the dark, it was easy to see that John had lost considerable weight.

"Herod's stepdaughter is very anxious to meet you," Lucanus said to the Baptist as Sveshtari stood in the background, listening with arms crossed.

Lucanus wore a smirk that reminded him of Rufus, which was no surprise. Lucanus was a pupil of the older, more experienced man who had just been elevated to captain in Herod's guard.

"Just get on with it!" Sveshtari stepped forward.

Lucanus shot him a look of warning before turning back to the Baptist with a faux smile. "There's just one small problem, John."

John sat, uninterested, and gazed past Lucanus.

Sveshtari narrowed his eyes. Was John the Baptist staring at him? Surely not. But it was difficult to tell exactly where he was looking with hair covering much of his face.

"She wants to meet *your head* but nothing more." Lucanus slid a finger across his neck, snorting at his own joke. There was an awkward silence before one of the other guards realized a chuckle was in order.

"The lady wants your head on a platter, served at a banquet upstairs. But look on the bright side. You'll finally be getting out of this prison cell. You just won't have the chance to stretch your legs."

This time, the other guard knew enough to laugh on cue.

Sveshtari walked away with a snarl, unwilling to witness the beheading. He had seen enough of them in his lifetime. He was used to the whims of tyrannical rulers, but he thought Herod was going too far. At a banquet, Herod had agreed to give his stepdaughter, Salome, whatever she wanted. When she asked for the head of John the Baptist on a platter, Lucanus asked if he could have the honor of carrying out the execution.

Gladly, thought Sveshtari. His emotions had been a jumble since Herod had shifted his household from Tiberias back to the Fortress of Machaerus.

The move had happened so quickly that Sveshtari never had time to carry out Herod's order to kill Jesus. But after witnessing Eliana's healing on the beach near Gergesa, he was no longer sure he even desired to carry out the mission. At this point, he assumed Herod had forgotten he had sent him to kill Jesus because he made no mention of it.

The drawback of leaving Tiberias, however, was that Sveshtari was unable to say farewell to Keturah. Even more troubling, he didn't know where she was. He asked Joanna if she had any idea what had happened to Keturah, but she had no clue.

So, Sveshtari had done considerable brooding since coming to the Fortress of Machaerus—this desolate outpost on a hilltop.

And now this...

He wondered if the murder of John the Baptist might trigger a Jewish rebellion. And all because an insane tetrarch had promised his stepdaughter whatever she wanted at a banquet.

Laughter echoed through the subterranean chambers. Sveshtari glowered. Lucanus was probably parading around with the Baptist's head on display.

Later that evening, Sveshtari stood guard at the eastern entrance to the fortress alongside Lucanus. While he said nothing about the beheading, Lucanus must have sensed his disgust.

"I did not like the scorn you showed me earlier today," Lucanus said, eyes straight ahead. They stood side by side, with two arms lengths between them.

"And why should I care what a gallows-bird like you thinks?" Sveshtari was in no mood for fools.

"Because I can make your life difficult. I know people." Lucanus turned to face him, waiting for Sveshtari to do the same. "You have gone soft, Sveshtari. You don't even have the stomach to stay and watch a man lose his head."

Sveshtari lunged before Lucanus even knew what hit him. He shoved the guard against the stone wall, and Lucanus grunted at the back-bruising impact. Sveshtari took him by the chin, pushing the guard's head against the wall, squeezing so tightly that he wondered if he might snap his jawbone.

Using his other hand, Sveshtari latched onto his neck, and Lucanus's face turned crimson as he struggled for air. When Sveshtari thought the man was almost on his last breath, he released him.

Lucanus gasped and rubbed his throat, his murderous stare speaking volumes. Sveshtari sized him up, thinking he'd have to watch his back going forward, or Lucanus might run him through with a sword.

"I know about you," Lucanus spit back after getting his voice back.

Sveshtari laughed.

"I know you didn't carry out your orders to kill Keturah." Lucanus moved so close that Sveshtari could smell the spices on his breath. "I know she lives because I saw her in Tiberias before we came here. But I didn't report her existence to Herod, nor did I tell him that you allowed her to live. So, you should be grateful."

Sveshtari kept his eyes fixed forward, trying to conceal his shock. He held his breath. Had Lucanus really seen Keturah?

"Where is she?"

Lucanus smiled, taking two steps back—out of range of Sveshtari's hand. "Now I have your attention."

"Is she alive?"

"She was when I sold her."

"You sold her?"

Lucanus unsheathed his sword, and so did Sveshtari.

"So where is she?" The heat of Mercury washed over Sveshtari. Mercury was the god who had lopped off the head of Argus—the guard with a hundred eyes. Sveshtari was tempted to do the same to this guard.

"How am I supposed to know? I sold her. She's gone! And if the gods are just, her new master will eventually tire of her and feed her to the jackals, as you were supposed to!"

Lucanus had barely finished his sentence when Sveshtari swung his sword. The younger guard tried to block it with his blade, but Sveshtari was quicker than any of the guards. That's why Herod favored him. Sveshtari's judgments were swift and severe.

Stunned at his speed and reckless anger, Sveshtari looked down at Lucanus's head, rolling around by his feet like a ball. Sveshtari noticed blood spatter on the fortress wall and glanced around, hoping no one witnessed the killing. Thankfully, the hour was late, and there were no sounds from the fortress.

How would he explain the sudden decapitation of his fellow guard? He could tell the tetrarch that Lucanus had been drinking and tried to attack him and that he had killed him in self-defense. Herod would want to believe his favorite bodyguard.

But what about Rufus and the slave boy, Tullius, who knew the truth about him and Keturah? He continued to pay for their silence, month after month, but how long could that go on? Herod had left Rufus in charge of a unit of soldiers back in Galilee, but what would Rufus think when he found out Sveshtari killed Lucanus? Would he reveal everything?

Sveshtari's shoulders sagged, and he leaned against a wall. All he wanted was to be with Keturah, no matter what the gods thought. She was out there, a slave again, and he decided he had to find her. But first, he had to stage his death.

Sveshtari tucked Lucanus's head into his saddle bag. Then, taking Lucanus by the legs, he dragged the corpse beyond the fortress walls and into the darkness where he had once pretended to dispose of Keturah's body. Next, he switched uniforms with the dead man—not an easy task. Fortunately, he and Lucanus were roughly the same height, so the new breastplate fit fine, although it was a bit snug.

Sveshtari twisted off his ring, placing it on Lucanus's finger. Then he clamped his sword in the headless man's still-pliable hand and took Lucanus's weapon. Although he hated to part with his sword, one wrong detail could crucify him.

Sveshtari stood for a moment with his hand on his saddlebag, thinking of the head inside. A single jackal howled in the wind, with a few others joining the chorus. After securing a horse, he would feed Lucanus's head to the jackals sometime during the night. People would blame his death on Lucanus and alarms would sound for his capture.

Once Sveshtari was on horseback, he galloped toward the King's High-way—the same route Keturah had taken. The irony wasn't lost on him that he and Keturah had both "died" in the Fortress of Machaerus. It was a strange way to feel united with the woman he loved.

JEREMIEL

Jeremiel brushed his hand across his face, feeling leprosy's disfigurement. The tips of his fingers ran across bumps and crevices, like running his hand across rocky ground.

Jeremiel had become weary of living on the edge of a cemetery, which reminded him of his impending death, so he crossed over to the west side of the Sea of Galilee where he found refuge in the Cliffs of Arbel—majestic hills that provided a panoramic view of the Sea of Galilee. The mountaintop was the only beauty remaining in his life.

Although Jeremiel was cut off from all human contact, he was aware of some Zealots hiding in the caves of the Cliffs of Arbel, not far from his dwelling. They spotted him a couple of times, but they never came close enough to speak. For the most part, they left each other alone.

Even on the mountain, Jeremiel performed all the ritual washings required of a devout Jew. He washed his hands when he woke every morning, before and after every meal, and whenever he touched the inside of his ear, took off his shoes, or came in contact with a ritually unclean animal or insect. Normally, he would also ritually wash his hands after trimming his hair, but he hadn't bothered to cut it for a long time. With his horrific face and long hair, he must look wilder than John the Baptist.

But at least his hair was clean from regularly performing a *tevilah*, a total body immersion in a spring-fed pool near his cave. That's when he discovered that the leprosy had progressed, ravaging his face. When he immersed himself, he caught his reflection. At first, he thought a monster stared back at him until he realized it was his image.

That was the day he died.

Any time a Jew contacted a corpse, he was ritually unclean until he underwent a red heifer ceremony. A priest would sprinkle an impure person with a mixture of pure water and the ashes of a sacrificial red cow without blemish—a heifer that has never been used to do work. Only then would he be clean.

But what if you have *become* the corpse? What if you have died the death of leprosy?

Jeremiel closed his eyes. Nothing could ever make him clean. He was forever blemished, and if he had a way to send a note to his family back in Jerusalem, he would inform them of his death.

Jeremiel had memorized extensive portions of the Torah, Nevi'im, and Ketuvim, his thoughts dwelling on the Book of Job more and more each day.

Mortals, born of woman, are of few days and full of trouble, Job said. *They spring up like flowers and wither away; like fleeting shadows, they do not endure.*

A shadow. Jeremiel could relate. He was just a dark stain on the ground.

Who can bring what is pure from the impure? No one! Jeremiel hung his head, recalling this passage.

He was destined to be impure for the remainder of his days.

At least there is hope for a tree: If it is cut down, it will sprout again, and its new shoots will not fail. Its roots may grow old in the ground and its stump die in the soil, yet at the scent of water it will bud and put forth shoots like a plant.

Jeremiel had no such hope. When he dies and is laid low, he will breathe his last and be no more. As the water of a lake dries up or a riverbed becomes parched and dry, he will lie down and not rise. Till the heavens are no more, he will not awake.

ASAPH

Asaph and Gershom worked their way through the crowded lower market of the walled city of Sepphoris. Over the past six months, they had gone on two missions to find Eliana—and returned to the Zealot camp empty-handed.

Today marked their third attempt to locate Judah's daughter, this time in Sepphoris. The air was saturated with the smell of incense and spices as Asaph studied the many tables where tradesmen sold their goods—beakers, jewelry, glass bottles, clothing, flax, pickled and dried fish, furniture, and perfumes.

They also sold human beings.

As a former taxman and the one-time owner of several slaves, Asaph knew the business well. He entered the slave market with an air of authority and knowledge, with Gershom at his side.

"You are doing much better with the sling," Gershom told him as they moved through the crowd.

"Your help has made the difference. Thank you, Gershom."

Since Gershom had been giving him regular practice sessions with the sling, the tension between them had lessened—although they were still far from friends. Gershom made that clear. But at least they were not outright enemies.

Asaph cut a look at Gershom. "Do you think Judah will ever let me participate in a raid? I could be of help."

"It's possible." Gershom shrugged. "You've come a long way."

"Thanks." Asaph hid a grin that tugged at the corners of his mouth. That was high praise coming from Gershom.

Asaph nodded toward the platform. Several male slaves stood on the *catasta* with placards hung around their necks, providing information about their many features.

"Are you interested in a strong, healthy male?" asked a slave trader, sliding next to Asaph. He pointed to a boy no older than twelve. "This boy is fair and handsome from the top of his head to the bottom of his feet. And he will be yours for 8,000 sesterces."

Asaph maintained a stoic expression and turned away, but the trader persisted, nipping at his heels. "This home-born slave is prepared to serve at his master's nod. He knows a little Greek; he is suitable for whatever task you want. With this wet clay, you can make whatever you please. He can even sing something untrained but sweet."

Asaph looked down his nose at the man, narrowing his eyes. When a trader gushed, it was a sign they were trying to get rid of inferior stock.

"You used resin on this one, didn't you?" Asaph motioned to another male, this one in his twenties.

"Not at all. He has always been well fed."

Grunting, Asaph moved on. He was sure the young man had been given resin from the terebinth tree to relax his skin. That way, he could more easily be fattened. Before the fattening, he had probably been starved.

Asaph knew all the tricks. He knew some slave dealers would make boys look younger by giving them blood, gall, and liver of tuna.

"None of the other dealers would give you such a deal, but I will offer you this boy for 7,000 sesterces," the trader continued. "Take it now before the deal is off the table."

"I am looking for a female."

"Oh. I see." The trader's eyes lit up. "I have beautiful girls."

"I am only interested in one by the name of Eliana. She would be about forty years old."

"You want an old woman?" The trader stared at him as if Asaph had lost his mind. "Are you trying to save money? If so—"

"Do you know any slaves by the name of Eliana?"

The slave trader scratched his head and led Asaph and Gershom into an adjoining room, where slave girls stood on *catastae*, most of them much too young to be Eliana, all heavily caked in makeup.

"What is her name again? Eliana?" the slave trader asked before addressing his slaves with a wave of his arm. "Do any of you answer to the name of Eliana?"

The women exchanged glances, and a couple of them shrugged.

"Do any of you know a slave named Eliana!" Asaph called out. "She's about forty years old!"

"Excuse me, *Dominus*, but I know an Eliana of that age," came a woman's voice to his right.

When one of the slave women standing on the nearby *catasta* lifted her hand, it was as if a statue had suddenly come to life. She was young and pretty, in her twenties, but her lovely face had been marred by the letters TMQF tattooed across her forehead. The letters stood for *Tene me quia fugi*—"Arrest me, for I have run away."

"The Eliana I knew was a former slave." The girl's soft voice barely carried over the market noise.

"How do you know her?" said Gershom.

"We met in a caravan. She was on the run."

Gershom and Asaph exchanged looks. Then Gershom turned to her and said, "We need to be certain it's the same person. Tell me something about her."

The slave girl didn't miss a beat. "When she was a girl, her family fled to Bethlehem, where she was captured by brigands. Her father was a Zealot."

Asaph stood motionless, mouth hanging open. There couldn't be more than one Eliana with such a story. His heart began to race.

"How much for this woman?" Asaph asked the trader as he motioned toward the slave girl. According to the placard around her neck, the girl's name was Keturah.

"14,000 sesterces."

Asaph whirled around. "You must be out of your mind! This slave girl has obviously escaped in the past. She's not worth half that!"

"For a private sale, you should expect higher prices than at auction."

"But that's ridiculous, even for a private sale."

The slave trader spread his arms. "But look at her beauty and youth. You could have that tattoo removed, and you wouldn't mar her too badly."

"8,000 sesterces," Gershom said, jumping into the negotiation.

"You are a highway robber," the trader countered. "Nothing less than 12,000."

"9,000 sesterces." Asaph crossed his arms.

The trader grinned with a half-shrug. "Nothing less than 11,000 sesterces. I would be a fool to go any lower."

"10,000 sesterces," Gershom added.

"Sold!"

As Asaph pulled out his sack of coins and placed them in the trader's sweaty palm, Gershom took the slave girl, Keturah, by the hand and helped her from the platform.

After they exited the market, Gershom leaned over and asked, "Where and when did you last see this Eliana?"

"I was with her a year ago in Capernaum," Keturah said.

Asaph stopped in his tracks. "Capernaum!"

They had been in Capernaum with Eliana's father around that time. Eliana had been right under their noses!

"Do you think she's still there?" Gershom asked, his stern eyes searching hers.

"Perhaps. Eliana loves the teachings of a prophet named Jesus. If Jesus is still in Capernaum, then Eliana probably is."

Again, Asaph was flabbergasted. They had listened to Jesus speak in Capernaum around that time, so who knows how close Eliana might have been. They had been hunting for her across the land, and she could have been only cubits away all along.

As Asaph, Gershom, and Keturah made their way for the city gate, two men stared at them and approached with swords drawn. But why? Did these men know they were Zealots?

"Act normally," Gershom whispered from the side of his mouth.

"Are they coming for you?" Keturah looked at the ground, avoiding eye contact.

"Turn. Quickly." Asaph reached for his sword, but before he could unsheathe it, someone pressed a blade to his back.

"I wouldn't do that," said a familiar voice from behind.

Asaph and Gershom came to a sudden halt.

"Take your hand off your weapon."

Slowly removing his hand from the hilt of his sword, Asaph's mind raced. He knew the voice but from where?

With arms raised and hands open, Asaph slowly turned and exhaled as a sense of dread lodged in the pit of his stomach. It was his childhood nemesis, Zuriel.

"Well, if it isn't my closest and dearest friends—Asaph and Gershom." Zuriel grinned, flanked by four men.

This was not good odds, especially when Zuriel's blade was only inches away.

"I'm surprised you've become friends with this snake," Zuriel said, shaking his head at Gershom.

"We're not friends," Gershom growled.

"In that case, you won't mind if we take Asaph off your hands. You and your slave girl can go. We have no business with you."

Asaph's knees went soft as Gershom gave him a parting scowl and took Keturah by the arm. They disappeared into the crowd, leaving Asaph to the mercy of this madman. Asaph scowled. He expected more loyalty from a fellow Zealot, especially since Gershom had finally shown him some respect.

"I spotted you entering Sepphoris this morning, and I couldn't believe my good fortune." Zuriel touched his blade to Asaph's chest, applying a bit of pressure over his heart.

"When I spread the word that the tax farmer from Jericho was in Sepphoris, it wasn't hard to recruit a few of my friends." Zuriel put even more pressure on his sword. Soon, the blade would push through his clothing, maybe even his flesh. "My friends were all eager to show a taxman what they thought of him."

"You can't kill me in a marketplace." Asaph glanced around. People stared at them as they passed, but no one made a move to interfere. Drawn swords had a way of silencing others.

"That is why we're taking you somewhere more private."

Asaph looked for a way of escape, but he was hemmed in on all sides by the five armed men.

"Move!" One of the men prodded him with his spear, and this time, the spearhead cut through his clothes, breaking the skin.

Asaph's eyes darted around, looking for anyone to connect with. When he noticed a young man watching nearby, he shouted, "Please help! These men are going to murder me!"

Asaph begged with his eyes just before the flat side of a blade crashed against the back of his head, and all went black.

A throbbing pulse rang in his ears when Asaph finally regained conscious-ness. He moaned, clutching his head as he lay on the ground.

"Good, good, you're awake!" Zuriel's sandaled feet came into focus. "You should be conscious when we kill you. I want you to see the rocks when they begin to fly."

Rocks? Asaph propped himself on his right elbow, taking in his surroundings. They had hauled him behind an isolated storage building without another person in sight. The five men circled him, each holding large stones in one hand and swords or spears in the other.

Asaph rubbed the back of his head and climbed to his feet. "What is it with you and rocks?"

"Call it justice," Zuriel sneered. "I know you always loved Eliana. It's why you never let me hurl that rock at her so many years ago. Now, I get to hurl this rock at you instead. You will be the substitutionary sacrifice, taking Eliana's place."

"You're insane."

"No. Just angry. If I could find some dogs to attack you, I would do that instead—just as you had a dog attack me as a boy. But these will have to do."

Zuriel jostled the rock in his right hand and grinned.

"Who gets to throw first?" one of the other men said.

"No one throws until I do!" Zuriel stared them down, his face flushing.

As the others stepped back with a nod, Zuriel moved closer.

Asaph tried to back away, knowing that the closer Zuriel came, the more force would be behind his rock. When one of his tormentors shoved him from behind, Asaph shuffled right and then left.

Zuriel paused, watching Asaph bounce from one foot to another. Then he laughed. "I didn't know you could dance!"

Asaph's face flushed, and his chest tightened. He thought about making a run for it, but his attackers stood ready, swords in hand. He wouldn't make it three steps before they'd be on him. He might try rushing Zuriel before he could release his stone. That, too, would end in his death, but maybe he could at least take Zuriel with him to Hades.

The other option was negotiation. Zuriel was a businessman.

"Wait," Asaph said when Zuriel cocked his throwing arm. "I'm still a taxman, Zuriel, and I can make your business thrive, free from taxes!"

Asaph glanced around at the other men. "I can help all of you if you let me!"

When the men exchanged looks, Asaph thought he had their attention—until Zuriel busted out laughing. "It's so nice to see you beg! But we all know taxmen lie. Sorry, Asaph."

As Zuriel lifted his arm, preparing to throw, a stone zipped from beyond the circle and smashed him in the head. He dropped to the ground.

Asaph gasped. It happened so fast that no one knew what was going on. Turning to his left, he spotted Gershom loading his sling, with Keturah secured to his waist by a rope.

Zuriel was sprawled out on the ground, either out cold or dead, when Gershom's second stone struck another man's skull, sending two others fleeing. That left one man, who turned toward Gershom, lunging at him with a sword. Sidestepping the attack, Gershom drew his sword with lightning speed, as the pair squared off, blades clanging with every contact.

Asaph scanned the ground, pounced on a rock near Zuriel's body, and hurled it at the attacker. It flew past the man's skull, nearly striking Gershom instead.

Asaph cringed. "Sorry."

Gershom was too busy to respond, battling sword to sword with sparks flying, but he had a hard time maneuvering with Keturah tied to his waist. Asaph snatched up a stone, rushed forward, and rammed the last attacker from behind, cracking his skull with a jagged edge. This time, even Asaph couldn't miss.

"Let's go!" Gershom took Keturah's hand and pulled her along. Asaph snatched up his sword—the blade of Eliana's father, which had been stolen by one of the attackers. Then he sprinted after Gershom, who was already nearing the city gates.

"Thanks," Asaph said to Gershom when they were safely out of the city and on the road leading to Capernaum.

"I didn't do it for you." A scowl remained etched on his face, like the perpetual expression of a statue.

"Then who did you do it for?"

"For Judah. I gave him my word I would keep you alive. Otherwise, I would've probably *helped* Zuriel stone you."

"Oh." So much for Gershom showing him respect.

"I'm sorry I had to tie you." Gershom sent Keturah a gentle expression, his voice softening as he loosened the knot at her waist. "I couldn't take the chance you would flee during the fight."

Keturah gave a clipped nod. Asaph could tell she was trying to act brave, but her fear showed in her eyes. It was as obvious as the tattoo on her forehead.

ELIANA

They kept coming—too many to count. It was a beautiful spring day, and the countryside near Bethsaida, on the northeastern side of the Sea of Galilee, swarmed with people coming to hear Jesus—and to be healed.

For Eliana, her life made a complete reversal that evening at the cemetery near Gergesa. Calev had been cast out forever, his throne overturned.

By this time, she was convinced that Jesus of Nazareth was the Christ, coming to end Roman rule and save the Jewish people. In the months she had been following him, she had seen miracle after miracle—although she didn't need any more proof. One miracle was enough, especially since it happened to her.

The last time she was this happy was the day outside Bethlehem when she sprinted up and down the hills after seeing the baby in the cave. Now, on this day, she found herself staring at the very same woman she had met there—Mary, the mother of Jesus.

When she spotted Mary several days ago, Eliana thought she looked familiar but couldn't place her. It wasn't until she overheard Mary telling someone her son had been born in a Bethlehem cave that the years suddenly melted away, and Eliana's eyes were opened. Mary was the same woman who let her hold her newborn son.

Eliana thought about approaching Mary, but surely, she wouldn't remember her. Many people must have visited the cave that day. Besides, what would she say to the mother of Jesus?

"Come sit," said Chaim, appearing at her side with a welcoming grin.

Eliana started to leave because she knew it was wrong for an unmarried man to be on intimate terms with an unmarried woman. They shouldn't even be talking openly.

While Eliana still had trouble talking with men after the way she had been treated over the years, Chaim put her at ease. He was cheerful, although she sensed a dark stream beneath the surface.

"Please stay." Chaim's eyes implored hers. "You have a way of fleeing whenever we speak."

"I'm sorry, but..." She dropped her gaze to the ground. Didn't he understand her reasons? Lavi whined, leaning against her leg as if sensing her concern.

"Haven't you been around Jesus long enough to see?" Chaim motioned her forward, walking beside her, while Lavi ambled along on the other side. "He talks with women, even Samaritan women."

Eliana frowned. That still didn't make it any easier.

"Let us move a little closer because Jesus is getting ready to speak." Chaim pointed to a spot near the teacher. "Lavi can sit between us if that will make you feel better."

Eliana forced a smile. She waited for Chaim to move, so she could walk behind him, as society called for, but he waited for her to walk alongside him. She was uneasy at this intimate gesture but didn't want to offend Chaim, so she stepped forward, head down.

"The crowd is agitated," Chaim said, eying the growing throng. "They are furious that Herod killed John."

"Is it true how the Baptist died?"

Chaim sighed. "They served up his head at a banquet."

Just the thought made Eliana sick.

"Chaim! Chaim!" A voice boomed from behind.

The pair turned as Chaim's older brother, Nekoda, approached, dressed in his finest white and purple robe. Expensive finery.

"What do you think you are doing?" Nekoda's smug voice seethed from his tight lips as he eyed them.

Nekoda, a member of the Sanhedrin, the Jewish high court, addressed Chaim like many older brothers did—from on high.

"We are off to hear Jesus speak." Chaim shrunk before his brother.

"You are forgetting the matter we were going to discuss."

To Chaim's credit, he stood his ground. "I'm sorry, brother, but I never agreed to discuss anything. You *told* me we were going to talk, but I never agreed."

"So, I'm asking you now. Let's talk."

"I am here to listen to Jesus speak."

"But this is more important, and you know it."

"I don't do everything you command, Nekoda."

Chaim once told Eliana he wished he had the strength to stand up to his brother. She was thankful he was showing some backbone.

Nekoda's wary eyes flicked in her direction. "This is not the place to be discussing our business."

He put a hand on Chaim's shoulder, steering him away, but Chaim shook loose. When Nekoda tried again, Chaim swatted away his hand like he would an insect. "I said not now!"

Nekoda's eyes narrowed. "We *will* talk later."

As Chaim walked away, his older brother added, "You still need my money to survive, don't you?"

Chaim stopped in his tracks. He nodded and glanced over his shoulder. "Not any longer."

"Have it your way then. You're on your own." With that, Nekoda was gone, disappearing into the multitudes.

Eliana said nothing, knowing better than to intrude. But Chaim laughed off the confrontation with one word: "Brothers."

Once they found somewhere to sit, Eliana took in the spring scents and the lush grass on the hillside where thousands now gathered. Jesus moved as he taught, so all could hear him preach. Like Moses on a mountain, Jesus spoke on a hill. And just as Chaim had promised, he made sure Lavi sat between them as they listened.

When Jesus finished, the sun neared the horizon, and hunger began to nip at Eliana's stomach. Surely, those around her were just as ravenous. She wondered if they had time to get home for their meals before dark. If they were anything like her or Chaim, they hadn't brought food for the outing.

"He's right, you know," Chaim said when Jesus had finished speaking.

Eliana's face softened. "Jesus usually is."

"No, I don't mean Jesus. I mean my brother. He said I still need his money to feed myself."

"But Jesus feeds us. He is our manna."

Eliana and Chaim turned their attention back to Jesus, now talking calmly to his disciples, who seemed agitated. Then Jesus laughed, motioning toward a young fisher lad with a wicker basket.

As one of the disciples took the basket from the boy, his face filled with distress. He showed its contents to Jesus with a shake of his head. Then the rabbi laughed again, reached in, and pulled out a loaf of barley bread along with a tiny, dried fish.

Next, Jesus broke the bread, offering pieces to his disciples. Eliana and Chaim watched, eyes fixed on what should now be an empty basket.

Eliana gasped as Jesus withdrew another barley loaf, placing more broken pieces and fish in the disciples' baskets. He did this again and again. There seemed no end to the food as the disciples went off to distribute bread and fish to the hungry thousands.

Eliana and Chaim looked at each other, eyes filled with wonder. Then Chaim burst out laughing at the sheer audacity of it all.

When it was their turn to receive their bounty, Eliana stared at the small fish and piece of barley bread, unsure if it was a dream. Barley bread was the food of the poor, but when she placed a bit on her tongue, it tasted like a feast for a king. She gave half of her bread to Lavi, who gobbled it up in agreement.

Eliana was reminded of another feast for a king that had recently taken place—the banquet of Herod Antipas, where a girl's whim led to the death of the prophet, John the Baptist. Yet, in this banquet on the hill, a little boy's basket of food gave life to multitudes. The contrast was striking.

When she told her thoughts to Chaim, he exclaimed, "Eliana, you amaze me."

As Chaim stared at her, his face shining, Lavi barked and wiggled between them. Eliana turned away, blushing at his persistent gaze.

Before nightfall, someone in the crowd began to sing. One by one, each cluster of people picked up the song, for the words were familiar to most—a Psalm of David. As Eliana rose to her feet, Chaim quickly followed, standing at her side.

As she began to sing the words she learned as a child, a force suddenly ran up the entire length of her body, from her toes, up her spine, to the tingling top of her head.

"Therefore let all the faithful pray to you
while you may be found;
surely the rising of the mighty waters
will not reach them.

"You are my hiding place;
you will protect me from trouble
and surround me with songs of deliverance."

The words broke her down, like the breaking of a loaf of barley bread.

KETURAH

Keturah had no idea how they would find Eliana in such a great multitude. The hillside outside of Bethsaida swarmed with people. While the crowds were large the last time she heard Jesus speak, the numbers were staggering today.

"Are you sure she would come here?" asked Asaph for the third time.

"I told you, it's the most likely place."

As they moved through the crowd, Keturah noticed a woman staring at the letters TMQF tattooed on her forehead. She thought she had pulled her headdress down to cover them, but it slipped to reveal her forehead. Keturah stuck out her tongue at the woman, then laughed out loud when she realized she had done what her friend Eliana did so often when riled.

On the road to Bethsaida, Keturah told Asaph and Gershom how she met Eliana. They asked all sorts of questions, some shockingly personal, but so far, Keturah had asked next to nothing about their relationship with Eliana. It wasn't proper to ask such questions of these men, especially since they were kind enough to purchase her and then tell her she was free. By this time, however, she sensed that Asaph and Gershom might not mind a question or two, so she decided to test the waters.

"How do you know Eliana?"

"None of your business." Gershom shut her down instantly, his jaw clenching.

Asaph, however, answered easily and politely. "We both grew up with Eliana as children." Asaph paused, searching the crowd. "Her father sent us out to see if we could locate her."

"Her father is still alive?" Keturah hurried after them as they moved past another small group eating some bread and fish.

"He is," said Asaph, glancing over his shoulder at her.

"And he's still searching for her?"

"A father never gives up hope. He—"

"You've said enough." Gershom stopped, his stone-cold eyes speaking volumes. "She doesn't need to know anything else."

Keturah's heart went out to Eliana's father. How difficult it would be for him to learn what had happened to his little girl after all these years. She wondered if Eliana's father might wish she had died peacefully somewhere rather than discover she had been so abused that demons slipped through the cracks in her mind.

Clearly, Asaph and Gershom knew nothing about Eliana's current condition. In their minds, she was a healthy girl, not someone tormented by devils. Keturah wondered if she should warn them of Eliana's spiritual state, but maybe it would be best if they discovered it themselves.

As they moved through the crowd in silence, Keturah noticed that everyone seemed well-fed—with baskets of bread and small fish being passed around from group to group. How could humble fishermen feed a crowd this size when it must have cost hundreds of denarii? Perhaps Jesus had attracted quite a few wealthy followers to pay for such a feast—people like Joanna.

Suddenly, a group to their left began to sing, inspiring others to pick up the song, like signal bonfires spreading from mountaintop to mountaintop. The words rang out across the hillside.

A few people even rose to their feet to sing, lifting themselves from the crowd, and that's when Keturah spotted her. A middle-aged woman was among the first to rise, just off to their right.

As Keturah hurried in the woman's direction, Asaph and Gershom followed.

"Do you see her?" Gershom asked.

Keturah rushed forward in desperate silence.

"Do you see her?"

Keturah still ignored Gershom's question. She saw the woman in profile, unsure it was Eliana until she was almost upon her. The woman sang loud and clear with her arms raised and face lit up. Clearly, it was Eliana, but something about her was different. Something had changed.

"Therefore let all the faithful pray to you
while you may be found;
surely the rising of the mighty waters

will not reach them.

"You are my hiding place;
you will protect me from trouble
and surround me with songs of deliverance."

When Eliana turned and stared at Keturah, the darkness behind her eyes was gone. She was beaming. Keturah had always sensed a second personality lurking behind her eyes, but now it seemed like a singular soul stared back at her.

Eliana glanced at Keturah's forehead, where her headdress had slipped again; the letters TMQF announced to the world her shame. In the past, those letters would not have incited any sign of sympathy from Eliana. But this time, Eliana's face dropped, and her eyes welled.

Then Eliana's eyes locked with hers, and the two women burst into tears. As Keturah fell into Eliana's embrace, her heart filled with the knowledge that she had gained the sister she'd always wanted but never had.

Keturah couldn't stop the tears, but she didn't care. They were like Living Water, cleansing her. She clung to her friend, her throat constricting, her spirit soaring. She marveled because the Eliana she knew would have never embraced her like this. Something drastic had happened. Something had shaken her world, turning it right-side up.

"I don't understand." Keturah pulled back between sobs, searching her face. "Is it really you, Eliana?"

"It's really me." Eliana choked, her words barely audible.

"But how...?"

Eliana shook her head and embraced her again, but Keturah pressed. "How...?"

Again, no answer. Keturah held her friend tighter as Eliana's body shuddered with emotion.

Finally, Eliana managed one word. "Jesus."

ASAPH

As the two women broke their embrace, Asaph watched, wondering if Eliana would recognize him. Yet her eyes flitted over them as if he and Gershom were perfect strangers.

"Are these friends of yours?" Eliana asked, cocking her head.

Keturah glanced from Eliana to Asaph before returning her attention to Eliana. "They told me they were friends of yours when you were children."

Eliana looked positively puzzled—and a bit startled. A dog appeared at her side, letting out a low growl of warning.

"You don't remember me?" Asaph hoped his voice would give a clue—although he realized that was an unlikely hope. The last time they had talked, he was ten, and she was nine.

"I'm sorry." Eliana intensified her stare, studying every feature of his face.

"I knew you as well." Gershom stepped forward, almost trodding on Asaph's toes.

Eliana's eyes remained clouded by the fog of time. "You seem familiar, but I'm sorry. I just do not remember."

"I understand." Gershom's tender tone had Asaph doing a double take. Gershom almost seemed an entirely different man.

"I'm not sure I would have recognized you if Keturah hadn't pointed you out," he added.

Eliana forced a smile, then looked to Keturah, her eyes pleading for help.

"You still have eyes like the fish pools in Hesbon," Asaph said, grinning. He moved alongside Gershom, trying to steal back her attention. "Can you still run like a deer? You were always faster than me."

Eliana snapped her head in Asaph's direction, her eyes narrowing as she stared at him. Asaph could see the exact moment when the click of recognition lit her eyes with warmth.

"Asaph?"

He broke into a grin, extending his arms to the side. "It is me."

When Eliana's look of puzzlement transformed into a broad smile, Asaph forced himself to stay put. He wanted to rush forward and embrace her as Keturah had done, but the rules of society kept him rooted. Still, he leaned slightly forward, his body acting on instinct.

"And I am Gershom." Asaph's rival drew Eliana's gaze back to him in a tender tug-of-war.

"You two are still friends after all these years?"

Asaph shrugged. Of course, they were not friends, but she didn't need to know that.

"And who are these men?" said a stout man with a thick head of curly black hair. He stepped beside Eliana, a move that was every bit as protective as the dog's. Was this her husband?

"These are old friends," Eliana said. "Asaph and Gershom, this is another friend—Chaim."

Asaph was happy she labeled Chaim as a "friend," but he could sense that Chaim desired more.

"But how...?" Eliana motioned toward Keturah.

"It was Asaph and Gershom who purchased me and freed me," said Keturah, dropping her eyes to the ground.

"Purchased you?"

"It's a long story."

"We found Keturah while looking for you," Asaph said. "Your father sent us out to search for you."

"My father is alive?" The blood drained from Eliana's face.

Keturah caught her by the arm for support. Chaim also held on to her, but Asaph suspected he did it for the physical contact.

"My father is alive?" Eliana repeated, breaking away from Chaim to look at Keturah in wonder.

Asaph hid a grin at Chaim's dismay. "I am happy to say he is," Asaph said. "He never gave up on you."

"But where is he?"

"In the caves in the Cliffs of Arbel," Gershom said, stepping closer to the women, edging Chaim out of the conversation.

Eliana straightened, biting her trembling lip and staring into the distance. The cliffs were not far away, a little to the south on the lake's western side, near Magdala.

"We must go see him." She spoke as if she wanted to drop everything and leave this very moment.

"I will take you there." Chaim made himself known again, breaking into the conversation.

"As will I," said Gershom.

"We all will," said Keturah, shooting Chaim a look of warning and pulling Eliana close.

Just then, the dog stood on his hind legs, resting his paws on Eliana's side as he licked her face.

"Thank you." Eliana petted her dog as a tear slipped from the corner of her eye. Brimming over, her eyes looked even more like the fish pools of Hesbon. "Asaph and Gershom, thank you for bringing Keturah back to me. You are good friends."

Friends.

Asaph hoped someday they would be more. But for now, that word would have to do.

JEREMIEL

Jeremiel crouched by the pool, dipping his container into the water to pour some over each hand three times. He had almost finished with the ritual cleansing when two women's voices sounded nearby. Jeremiel darted behind a rock.

Peering around the edge of the stone, he spotted three men and a dog accompanying the two women up the steep terrain toward the caves.

The Cliffs of Arbel were honeycombed with caves at different levels of the mountain. From below, it looked as if monstrous insects or worms had burrowed into the side of the cliff, leaving gigantic tunnels. The higher caves made formidable fortresses for Jewish rebels.

The five figures and the dog moved along the base of the cliff, their voices carrying in the spring air. The beginning of the climb up Mount Arbel was strenuous but not insurmountable. Still, the trek from the base would be grueling and treacherous the rest of the way up. He wondered if they would dare go any farther.

Curious, Jeremiel scurried from stone to stone, progressing closer each time. Their voices became louder, yet he was still unable to make out their conversation. The group stopped to sit and take sips of water from their pouches, and then they continued the climb, weaving through the ragged rocks. Was one of them Chaim? It was hard to tell from a distance.

As Jeremiel continued to follow, a clump of soil slid beneath his sandal, and he lost all footing, crashing to the ground. In his peripheral vision, he could see the climbing party turn and stare. Like a scorpion in a crevice, Jeremiel scrambled for cover, pressing his back against a large rock. He heard footsteps approach.

"What are you doing? Stay away from that thing!" boomed a man's voice.

That thing. That's what I've become. That's what I am.

10

LUKE, CHAPTER 10

ELIANA

Eliana was strangely drawn to the man hiding behind the stone. She couldn't explain it, but there was something oddly familiar about him.

"Stay back. It might not be safe," said Chaim, hurrying alongside, followed by Asaph, Gershom, and Keturah.

Noticing a flash of silver glinting in the sun, Eliana saw that Asaph had pulled out his sword.

She stopped in her tracks. "Where did you get that?"

"Your father gave it to me."

"May I see it?"

After a moment of hesitation, Asaph handed her the sword. As Eliana turned it over in her hands, memories came flooding back. She shook her head, unable to believe she held the very same blade her father had once used. They were on their way now to see her father on the Cliffs of Arbel, but his sword made the dream of reuniting with him all the more real.

Eliana stared at the large white rock that the man had ducked behind. The oval boulder, about the length of two men, looked like a huge egg lying on its side. She thought about the man on the other side, wondering what it was about him that spoke to her.

She nodded at the sword in her hands before handing it back to Asaph. "Put it away. You won't need it."

"How do you know? You know nothing about this creature."

"I know he's not a creature."

As she rounded the large stone, the gaunt, hollowed-out man came into view. He had hair down his back, a long beard, and a strip of cloth around his mouth and nose, revealing only his eyes and forehead.

"Shalom!" Eliana said as she moved even closer.

The man pressed his back against the boulder as if trying to disappear into the rock. She braced a hand on the stone and slowly moved forward. Her dog, Lavi, was at her heels, panting.

"Unclean! Unclean!" the man shouted, clamping a hand over the fabric covering his mouth.

"Stay back!" Asaph reached for Eliana, but she moved too quickly. "It's a leper!"

"Unclean!" the man shouted again.

"Jeremiel?" Chaim narrowed his eyes, searching the man's face.

Eliana turned. "You know this man?"

Chaim nodded.

Although the mask concealed most of the leper's face, she could make out enough to see nodules erupting from his cheekbone and encircling his left eye. She stepped forward.

"Stay back!" Jeremiel scooted farther away.

Chaim sidled up beside Eliana. "What are you doing on this side of the lake, Jeremiel? The last time I saw you, you were in the caves near the cemetery outside of Gergesa."

Eliana's heart skipped a beat. "Near the cemetery?"

For Eliana, the cemetery outside Gergesa was holy ground. It's where she had been raised from the dead. She had died in the hills outside of

Bethlehem, where the brigands had captured her, and ironically, she had been reborn in a cemetery.

"You were in the cemetery near Gergesa?" she said to Jeremiel. "I was healed there."

The man scuttled back three more steps. He nodded. "Yes, I was there. That was you?"

"That was the *old* me. I am created anew." She moved three paces closer, and Jeremiel backed away two more steps, crab-like. "Please. No closer. It is not safe."

She knew the rule. You should get no closer to a leper than the length of a man—much farther if the wind is blowing toward you. Jeremiel's face was covered from the nose down, but there was something familiar about his eyes.

"Do I know you?" she asked.

"No," Jeremiel answered in haste. His response was too quick, and it made Eliana wonder why.

She reached into her satchel, slung over her right shoulder, and pulled out a piece of bread.

"Are you hungry?" She held it out.

The man was skin and bones. Surely, he needed food.

"I'm not an animal to be fed," Jeremiel growled.

"Men have to eat too."

Crouching, Eliana set the piece of bread on a small stone partially submerged in the ground between them.

Keturah, who had been silent the entire time, finally spoke up. "Please, Eliana...Your father...We need to leave now to see your father."

Eliana nodded over her shoulder, but before she got up to leave, she turned to Jeremiel. "I will leave this food for you."

"Let's go." Asaph motioned for her to follow.

Then, on impulse, she did something insane. Before she knew it, she found herself unslinging her waterskin and pouring some of her precious water on Jeremiel's dusty feet. She knelt, shaking her hair loose, and dried his feet with her long strands.

"Stop!" Keturah shouted. "What are you doing?"

Eliana thought she'd upset Jeremiel—that he was going to run. But he stared at his feet in stunned silence, his eyes welling with tears.

"Thank you," he whispered.

"Shalom."

Eliana stood, joined the rest of her group, and went back to climbing the mountain, fully prepared to see her father. Lavi trotted alongside, occasionally pausing to turn and bark at Jeremiel.

JEREMIEL

As the strange woman walked away, Jeremiel dropped onto a rock and buried his face in his hands.

"Jeremiel! Jeremiel!" Chaim called out to him from a distance.

Looking up, Jeremiel pulled the cloth tighter on his face because it had slipped, revealing more of his monstrous deformity. Chaim stood at a safe distance.

"Is there anything I can do? Do you need anything?" Chaim leaned forward, straining to hear whatever would come as a reply.

"Just your prayers," Jeremiel said.

"Anything more? I can bring more food."

"Your prayer is my food."

Nodding, Chaim started to ask something more but caught himself, finally offering a simple farewell. "Shalom, Jeremiel."

When Chaim turned to join his group, Jeremiel raised a hand. "Wait!"

Chaim paused.

"Zealots are up in those caves. Be careful," Jeremiel warned.

Chaim smiled. "Thank you, but we will be safe. We're on our way to see one of the freedom fighters. Eliana's father is their leader."

Eliana. That was the woman's name! This was the same woman he had tossed from the caravan—and from the Temple grounds.

At least it was the same woman on the surface, but her personality was different now that the demon had been cast out. Whatever had been living inside her, a spiritual tapeworm, had been removed, and she had regained her senses. Although, would a sane woman wash his feet and dry them with her hair?

With Chaim's final "Shalom," Jeremiel leaned against the stone, overwhelmed by shame. Eliana had risked her life to wash his feet—completely unafraid to touch his decaying skin. And yet two years ago, he would have been furious if this woman had so much as brushed against him.

He pulled back his sleeve, uncovering an entire line of nodules that slithered across his skin in a narrow, snake-like row. He pinched his forearm, but the center was completely numb. He balled his fist and beat on his arm repeatedly until it bruised, yet he still felt nothing.

He dropped his head with a moan. Why had God singled him out for punishment? Was it because of what he had done to Eliana—casting her out of the Temple and forcing her out of the caravan?

Was that it, Lord?

Clutching his stomach, he dropped to his knees. "I'm sorry, Lord! I'm so very sorry."

Jeremiel beat his hand against his chest—a sensation he could still feel. At least he hadn't gone completely numb.

ELIANA

There he stood: her father.

Eliana breathed deeply as she studied his face. Her father stood inside the cave, where the shadows ended and the light began. Although he had aged thirty years, he seemed stronger than she would have guessed—not stooped under the weight of time.

His hair, still partially black, contrasted with his beard, which was striped with gray. His skin was a deeper shade of copper than she remembered, and he had two scars that were not there before.

When Asaph told her that her father was one of the freedom fighters holed up in the Cliffs of Arbel, she couldn't believe it. Her father was still alive, still fighting the Romans? It was as if thirty years hadn't even passed.

He moved swiftly for an old man as they simultaneously rushed toward each other, folding into one another, arms tightening.

Eliana gasped. The strength of his arms reminded her, once again, how he used to whirl her around when she was a child, back when she believed he would never let go. Now, as they embraced, she didn't want him to ever let go again.

Her father pulled away, still clinging to her hand, and they stared at each other. She blinked, studying the gentle curves of his face—the slight wrinkles around his eyes. The right words escaped her—the ones she'd practiced for years if she had this opportunity. Yet, now, she was unprepared. What could she say to a father she hadn't seen for this long?

"I missed you," she finally said. They were obvious words, but they had to be spoken. They were a start.

"I missed you more than a lost limb." He chuckled when she glanced at his legs and arms. "Just a metaphor. I'm all here."

"So am I."

Eliana was suddenly aware they were alone in the cave, which stretched back into darkness. A few other men had been present when she entered, but they cleared out—giving them privacy. Chaim, Asaph, Gershom, and Keturah also remained outside the cave, their voices drifting from a distance.

Eliana chose one of several flat rocks, set up in a circle, and sat while her father positioned himself next to her, still holding her hand. She wondered if he, too, didn't ever want to let go again.

"When I heard you were still alive, it was one of the greatest days of my life—as wonderful as the day you were born," her father said.

"Yes. I have been reborn."

Her father focused on their clasped hands, fumbling for words. "One of my men also said you had been healed."

Eliana beamed at the chance to talk about the Messiah. "I was healed in the name of Jesus. Have you heard Jesus speak?"

"I have."

She saw the flicker of disapproval.

"You don't like what Jesus has to say?"

The last thing she wanted was to stir up controversy in this reunion, so she immediately regretted asking the question. But her father's response was gracious.

"How can I ever disapprove of someone who healed my little girl?" He rubbed his calloused thumb along the back of her knuckles.

Eliana sat up straighter, beaming. "Actually, it was one of his disciples who healed me. But without Jesus, it would not have happened."

"Which disciple?"

"Peter. The big fisherman."

Another smile, this time accompanied by a light laugh. "I like that one. He has fight. I could see him being one of us instead of one of them."

One of us? One of them? She wanted to tell her father there were no "us" and "them." *Everyone* was looking for the same thing. Everyone was searching for the Messiah—even the Gentiles, although they may not know it.

"I assume you have many questions," her father said, turning away. "About your mother and brother..."

Eliana put a hand on her father's cheek and turned his face toward hers. Tears blurred her vision. "Asaph told me about their deaths. I only wish I could've seen them one more time."

"I'm so sorry." Her father leaned his forehead against hers, and they wept silently.

Leaning back, Eliana wiped her eyes. "You must have many questions...about what happened to me in the hills outside of Bethlehem."

His face froze with an almost child-like fear.

Eliana thought about how it would affect him to learn her story. He probably had mixed emotions. When he tentatively nodded, she said, "I will tell you someday. Not today."

The tension released in his face, and she drew in a breath, thankful she chose to wait.

"I always imagined the worst." His soft voice seemed hollow, his spirit brittle.

"Some things cannot even be imagined."

Her father dropped his gaze to their hands as an awkward silence filled the cave. Eliana did the same, thinking his hands still seemed oversized, even though she was no longer a small child when everything seemed larger.

"I'm sorry," he whispered. "I should have been there to protect you. I should have found you." His voice cracked on the last few words as he broke down, heaving heavy sobs that were years in the making.

Eliana wrapped him in her arms. The roles were suddenly reversed.

"You can't stop every sin. No father can."

"But I should have found you." He pulled back, lifting her chin. His eyes poured into hers. "I should have."

Eliana gazed back, her eyes brimming. Considering how long she had been in Egypt as a slave, it would have been impossible for him to find her. Egypt is a vast land.

"I don't think anyone could have found me no matter how hard they looked."

"Where were you?" he asked.

She wanted to say, "In the abyss," but those were the last words a father wanted to hear. So, again, she said nothing. It was better that way.

KETURAH: ONE MONTH LATER, THE MONTH OF TAMMUZ (EARLY JUNE), 29 A.D.

It was like an army heading into battle without visible weapons. Jesus had attracted the usual massive crowds—thousands eager for healing. Keturah heard he was traveling to Jerusalem, but first, he was sending out dozens of people ahead of him—to clear the path, like a hundred John the Baptists.

While Eliana remained with her father in the Zealot camp in the caves, Keturah planned to travel south with Jesus's followers, which will bring her closer to the Fortress of Machaerus. There, she could find Sveshtari.

Sveshtari, the liar. Sveshtari, the murderer.

There was safety in numbers, and you couldn't find a larger crowd than those moving in the wake of Jesus. She found refuge with Joanna, who followed Jesus at every turn. As a wealthy patroness, Joanna made sure Jesus's people were housed and fed.

Keturah sat beside a patch of rockrose flowers, which painted the hillside purple, the color of kings. Some called Jesus a king, so these flowers were only fitting. Other patches were the yellow of thorny broom. In Egypt, yellow stood for all things imperishable and indestructible. Egyptians believed the gods had skin and bones made of gold. For instance, Isis, the goddess of kingship, had yellow skin, and her name meant "throne."

As Keturah looked across the hill, she envisioned the purple and yellow flowers as two armies representing two drastically different worlds. The army of yellow flowers represented the old gods battling a battalion of purple flowers, representing the kings of the Jewish world. It made for a stunning battlefield.

As Jesus moved among the flowers, he prepared to send his army of followers south from Galilee into Samaria.

"When you enter a town and are welcomed, eat what is offered to you," Jesus told the people he was sending forth. "Heal the sick who are there and tell them, 'The kingdom of God has come near to you.' But when you enter a town and are not welcomed, go into its streets and say, 'Even the dust of your town we wipe from our feet as a warning to you. Yet be sure of this: The kingdom of God has come near.' I tell you, it will be more bearable on that day for Sodom than for that town."

Keturah may not be Jewish, but she knew the story of Sodom. Fireballs from heaven destroyed that city of sin. She could understand God's justice and wrath because she, too, wanted things to be set right. She craved justice in the name of her father, who was murdered, and in the name of her mother, whom she was convinced had been poisoned. She wanted it so badly that it hurt.

Keturah watched from the side of the hill as Jesus sent out people, two by two. That was a strange way of sending an army into battle. A general didn't split his army into pairs. It looked more like a spy mission.

No wonder Eliana's father, Judah, didn't trust Jesus's ways. Judah raised a *real army* in the mountains, equipping them with knives, swords, and other weapons he pilfered from the Romans. Meanwhile, Jesus sent out his soldiers without sandals, marching into war in bare feet! It was the most ridiculous thing Keturah had ever seen.

She wondered what Eliana saw in Jesus, but she supposed she might also follow a man if his disciples healed her. Over the past week, Keturah even found herself a bit envious of Eliana—something she would never have imagined six months before.

Eliana's life was slowly coming back together, like bones knitting together to form a new person. First, Eliana was healed and then reunited with her father. And now three men, Chaim, Gershom, and Asaph, were obviously smitten with her. *Three men!*

For Keturah, on the other hand, everything was falling to pieces. She lost her mother, then her father, and now Sveshtari. *Three losses!*

She pulled her headdress lower to ensure it covered the tattoo on her forehead. In her peripheral vision, she noticed a man in the crowd studying her. Did he assume she was a runaway?

She swallowed and averted her eyes. Although Asaph told her he would find a way to remove the tattoo, for now, she was still a marked woman.

Keturah stood and started for Capernaum, slowly picking up speed. She glanced over her shoulder, spotting the same man close behind, eyes fixed on her. She gasped. It was Rufus, the man Sveshtari blamed for her father's death, who sometimes worked as a *fugitivarii*, a slave hunter. She prayed to the gods he wouldn't drag her back to Herod to be executed.

She quickened her step, wishing Asaph and Chaim were with her for protection, but Asaph was still in the mountains with Eliana's father, and Chaim was in Bethsaida, doing business with his brother, Nekoda.

When she peered over her shoulder again to find Rufus still behind her, his narrow-set eyes dead-set on her, she bolted. So did he.

People stopped and gawked. A woman being chased by a man could mean only two things. Either a husband was chasing down an adulterous wife, or a slave was trying to escape. Both scenarios looked bad for the woman. It *always* looked bad for the woman.

Keturah was almost to the gate leading into Capernaum when a man reached out and caught her by the headdress. Keturah broke loose, leaving her head covering behind in the man's hands. Her forehead was exposed, revealing to the world the tattooed letters: TMQF. "Arrest me, for I have run away."

When several men, moving from all sides, converged on her, she pivoted, looking for a way out of the closing net. She ran to her right, but someone stuck out their leg, tripping her. She flew forward, hands outstretched, and hit the ground with a thud.

Then someone yanked her back by the hair, and she cried out. It was as if her hair was being torn out by the roots, her scalp burning with tiny needles of pain shooting beneath the skin. She got up on her hands and knees as someone—she supposed it was Rufus—continued to yank her hair.

Laughter erupted from the crowd as a man kicked dirt into her face. That's when the first stone flew, striking her left shoulder. The second bashed her just above her nose. Warm blood streamed from her nose just before another jagged rock pitted her back.

SVESHTARI

Sveshtari spotted Jesus teaching a large crowd just outside of Capernaum. He hoped to find Keturah mixed in with the masses because he had found her there before. Earlier in the day, Keturah's former mistress, Joanna, revealed to him that Keturah was free again, purchased and released by a man named Asaph.

Once Jesus finished teaching, a young man stood up from the crowd and asked, "Teacher, what must I do to inherit eternal life?"

"What is written in the Law?" Jesus replied. "How do you read it?"

The young man thought for a second. "'Love the Lord your God with all your heart and with all your soul and with all your strength and with all your mind'; and 'love your neighbor as yourself.'"

Sveshtari was only half listening as he moved through the crowd, searching for Keturah's face. Jesus launched into a story about a man who had been beaten by robbers and left by the side of the road to die. A priest and a Levite passed up the poor man, but a Samaritan took pity and stopped to bandage his wounds.

Sveshtari had absorbed that much of the story when he finally spotted a familiar face. It was Joanna, and she hurried up to him, looking upset.

"Sveshtari, I am so happy to see you. Come quickly."

"Where is Keturah? Is she all right?"

Joanna didn't answer, but her eyes widened with alarm. She motioned him beneath a sycamore tree. By the time he joined her, Joanna was crying.

"They've taken her. She's been captured!"

"*Who's* taken her?"

"Herod's men. Rufus. One of Herod's servants witnessed it and told me what had happened."

Sveshtari cursed the name and wished he had taken care of Rufus when he had the chance.

"How far have they traveled?"

"He's keeping her in Capernaum—in the home of a wealthy Roman."

"Quickly. Take me there."

The sky had clouded by this time, and it began to drizzle as they moved through the streets of Capernaum, weaving among the flat-roofed homes and pens of animals, mostly goats and sheep. Joanna led him into the wealthier end of the city, where the homes grew larger and more opulent.

"There." Joanna pointed at the largest dwelling encircled by a wall. Rising above the wall was an upstairs cluster of rooms, forming an L-shaped second story.

A wall encircled the entire compound, and the outer door was locked. So, Sveshtari swiped a box from a nearby stable and used it to climb the wall. Before throwing his leg over the stone barrier, he glanced at Joanna, who had her eyes closed, most likely in prayer.

He would accept whatever prayers he could get from whatever god. He had already made enemies with many traditional Roman gods, so perhaps the Hebrew God would be more understanding.

Landing in a crouch inside the compound, he paused and scanned the area. It was strangely quiet and deserted. He moved down a short path, open to the air and sandwiched between two buildings. Then he made a left turn and nearly ran into a slave girl, who screamed and dropped a serving tray.

Sveshtari darted into the shadows and slammed his back against a wall, praying that her scream hadn't alerted the household of his presence. While the slave girl ran away, she didn't call out to warn anyone.

When no one came running, Sveshtari breathed a sigh of relief. Had he arrived at the right time when Rufus and the others in the home were gone? He looked at the second floor and wondered if Keturah might be bound with rope in an upstairs room.

Sveshtari sprinted up twelve exterior stone stairs, taking them two at a time, and shoved open the door at the top of the staircase. The room was empty. He barged into an adjoining room, but still no sign of life. Then he heard a growing commotion, but it didn't seem to be coming from inside the compound. It was coming from the streets.

He stuck his head out the window and spotted a mob moving down the road, approaching the house. A poor wretch with a *furca* strapped to his back fell to his knees. Like outstretched wings, the man's hands were tied to the ends of the beam of wood mounted on his back.

When several people hauled the poor slave to his feet, the person's delicate features came into view, revealing a woman. Sveshtari gasped as she raised her head, and he got a better look.

"Keturah," he whispered.

Sveshtari was down the stairs and out the front door, moving like a flash of fire and ready to burn Rufus alive. Rage pulsed in his veins. Rufus was making Keturah pay for her escape from the Fortress of Machaerus in the most humiliating way—with the *furca*.

By this time, the crowd had reached the house and taunted Keturah, some spitting in her face, others hurling insults. Her right eye was bruised and oozing blood. Sveshtari's hand went to his sword, tempted to throw himself into the mix. All he could think about was taking out as many as possible before they inevitably killed him.

"No, Sveshtari." Joanna appeared at his side, putting a soft hand on his arm and nodding at his sword. "That's not the way to save her."

Sveshtari ground his teeth. She was right, of course. He finally gave a sharp nod and sheathed his sword.

He should wait until Rufus brought Keturah back into the compound, where the odds would be much more in his favor. But it was torture to stand by and watch. He grunted in response but obeyed, hanging back in the crowd, making sure Rufus didn't catch sight of him.

Keturah exhaled another painful moan as they pushed her forward, ripping the shoulder of her robe. She raised her face, blood trickling down her forehead. That's when he spotted the tattoo: TMQF. *Tene me quia fugi.* "Arrest me, for I have run away."

Sveshtari gripped the handle of his sword once more. It took all his strength to stand by when everything told him to take action.

Joanna cut her eyes at him. "Trust me."

While he hated doing nothing, he listened to Joanna's wisdom and hung back as the crowd pressed on.

Sveshtari blended in behind the mass of spectators, breathing so hard that his chest ached. He leaned over and closed his eyes, trying to calm his nerves. He had to keep his head if he wanted to pull Keturah from this fire.

When a roar went up, Sveshtari raised his head, searching for Keturah, but she had fallen again under the weight of the beam. A one-eyed old man with barely enough teeth to bite into a piece of bread started to dance, laughing at Keturah. Sveshtari curled his fist, wishing he could knock out the man's remaining teeth, leaving him no option but to gum his food for the rest of his life.

Rufus pointed at two women in the crowd. "Help her to her feet!"

Sveshtari followed Rufus's line of sight and swallowed, eyes wide. Rufus had singled out Joanna, who had ventured too close to the chaos. Sveshtari prayed Rufus didn't look too closely and recognize her.

Head down, Joanna sidled up to Keturah, helping her to her feet and whispering something in her ear. A look of recognition flashed across Rufus's face, and he began to scan the crowd. Before Rufus's gaze landed anywhere near him, Sveshtari ducked into a stable, praying to the Hebrew God that he hadn't been spotted. He leaned against a beam, squeezing the hilt of his sword.

"Quickly, to the house!" Rufus's command sounded over the crowd's commotion.

Sveshtari peered around the stable door. The crowd surged toward the stately home where he had been only moments before. When Rufus led Keturah toward the door on the southern side of the house, Sveshtari snagged a ladder from the stable, plunged into the street, and sprinted for the opposite side of the compound.

Slamming the ladder against the wall, he scaled it like an agile animal, climbing onto the roof as a pungent odor hit him. He must be over the stable. Eyes watering, he drew his sword, lying flat and crawling forward to peer over the edge.

Looking across the courtyard, Sveshtari counted four men standing next to Rufus, swords drawn and on alert. One appeared young, inexperienced, and afraid—a weak link that would help Sveshtari fight with five-to-one odds.

"Put her in the stable!" Rufus flung his hand at two of his guards. "But keep the *furca* in place. It will be difficult for her to run with that thing on her back."

As two guards hauled Keturah into the stable, the others stayed at Rufus's side. Splitting the opposition would work to Sveshtari's advantage. He pressed flat against the roof, praying to the Hebrew God that they wouldn't spot him.

Once they entered the stable, he acted swiftly. Dropping from the roof, he landed with a thud in the shadows of the open courtyard and rushed into the dim interior of the stable.

Sveshtari snuck up behind one of the guards, who never had time to turn before Sveshtari made sure he never moved again. The second guard was quicker, spinning around and bringing his blade straight down toward Sveshtari's head. If Sveshtari hadn't danced to the right, the blade would have split his skull. It split the air instead, and Sveshtari lunged forward with his Roman *gladius*, burying his thrust in the guard's gut. The man staggered back, tumbling into a mound of hay.

Keturah didn't say a word as he cut away the leather straps that bound her hands to the wooden beam. When he finally released one of her wrists, she raised her dead eyes and bored holes into his. What had they done to her?

He shook off the thought. There was no time. He struggled to release Keturah's other hand when the other two guards charged into the stable, swords drawn. Sveshtari used Keturah as a weapon—or at least he used the beam, which was still connected to one of her hands. He swung the beam—and Keturah—in a circle, slamming the *furca* into one of the guard's heads, taking him down instantly. This left him one-on-one with the remaining guard, who stopped in his tracks.

"Think about it," Sveshtari said, nodding at the three guards sprawled on the ground, either dead or out cold.

The final guard spun on his heels and darted from the stable.

"Wise choice," Sveshtari said as he cut Keturah's second hand loose. Taking that hand, he led her into the courtyard—no sign of Rufus or the fourth guard. Rufus, being the coward he was, probably left for reinforcements.

"We must get out of here before Rufus returns with more soldiers." Sveshtari tugged Keturah toward the exit.

Back in the marketplace, they weaved through the streets and narrow paths, yet Keturah still said nothing. Not a single word. It was as if he were leading a corpse through the street.

When they turned another corner, a few people stared at Keturah's forehead.

The tattoo! He had forgotten all about it.

Pulling her into an alleyway, he found a merchant selling colorful scarves. Sveshtari tossed a coin at the merchant and grabbed a scarf, tying it around her forehead.

Then she fell into his arms, a movement born of sheer exhaustion. While it wasn't a romantic gesture, he tightened his embrace and kissed the top of her head. "No harm will come to you again."

Of course, he ignored the part of him that told him he couldn't make such a promise. From now on, they would both be hunted, which meant they had to keep moving, always looking over their shoulders.

But for now, Keturah was in his arms. Sveshtari didn't want to break away from the embrace, his nose buried in her hair. Even after all she had endured, her hair carried the same scent of cinnamon. He savored the smell and kissed the top of her head.

Then he felt a sting, like he had been bitten by a snake. As he pulled away, warm blood spread through his garment. Keturah glared—the dead expression behind her eyes had been replaced by fire.

Keturah had just stabbed him.

II

LUKE, CHAPTER 11

ASAPH

A SAPH SAT ACROSS FROM Eliana near the mouth of the cave, one among many carved into the sides of the Cliffs of Arbel. The sword that Eliana's father gave him lay crosswise on his lap. He glanced from it to the scenery, keeping Eliana in his peripheral vision.

The Sea of Galilee stretched before them like a colorful painting. It was a sun-drenched day, with breezes snapping at his hair, which now reached his shoulders. Asaph had even grown a beard, abandoning the clean-shaven Roman look. He was beginning to resemble a true Jewish freedom fighter.

Asaph was also starting to think like one, which posed a problem. He found himself caught between Eliana and her father, Judah. He wanted so badly to please both, but that was not remotely possible.

Eliana's eyes locked on his weapon. "The sword is not the way."

"Sometimes there is no other way."

"Jesus is the way."

Asaph had to consciously keep from snorting, knowing that if he insulted Eliana's rabbi, it might push her into the embrace of Chaim or Gershom. Anyone could see both men were set on Eliana, and Asaph was afraid that either one of them might soon ask Judah for his daughter in marriage.

The thought of losing her tied Asaph's stomach in knots. He couldn't lose Eliana—not again. At the same time, he desired to please her father, who had little patience for the teachings of Jesus of Nazareth. Judah believed in a God who laid waste to the mountains and the hills, making them smoke.

"The Zealots and Jesus are not so different in their ways," Asaph said to Eliana. "One of his disciples is a Zealot."

"*Was* a Zealot," she pointed out. "People change. Even tax collectors."

Eliana smiled when she said it, but the words stung. Asaph never discussed the tactics he had used to collect money, but Eliana must have known.

"I am not that man any longer." Asaph looked at his hands, refusing to meet her gaze.

"For that, I am pleased. My father has been a good influence in many ways."

When he looked up, he caught her staring at his sword. "But not in all ways?"

Although Eliana and her father had argued about Jesus and the Zealots several times, Asaph could tell she was trying not to be critical. "I love my father, despite our differences."

But could you love me, despite our differences?

Asaph dug his toe into the thin layer of dirt on top of the solid rock. "Sometimes force is necessary. It was necessary on the day Gershom and Zuriel struck you with rocks."

He thought that recalling how he protected her from Zuriel when they were children would remind her how much he cared for her, but it backfired.

"Gershom never tried to strike me. It was Zuriel." She cut him down with a look.

"Yes, but Gershom tried to force *me* to strike you."

"People change. If I can't forgive after thirty years, I have not listened to one word that Jesus spoke."

"I am sorry." Asaph slumped. "I should not have talked about that incident."

Finally, a smile broke through Eliana's stern expression. "Believe me. I was grateful for what you did for me that day—although I admit I was a little frightened by the force you used."

"I was alarmed too. But I was doing it for you." His voice softened.

"I know." Again, her eyes went to the sword. "But you don't have to use this sword for me. And you don't have to use it for my father's cause."

"The world needs swords to bring forth judgment unto truth."

Truth be told, if he knew without a doubt that casting aside his sword would convince Eliana to become his wife, he would toss it off the edge of the cliff at this very moment. While he was confident Judah would give Eliana's hand in marriage, he couldn't be sure about her *heart*. Did she care for him? Could she see herself as his wife? Many men would negotiate the marriage contract with Judah without worrying about Eliana's heart, but it was important to Asaph.

Asaph had become closer to Judah, who recently asked him to join their next raid on a small Roman contingent. It was a sign of Judah's blessings. Asaph was now part of the unit—something he had desired for these past months.

But it put him squarely between Eliana and her father.

"Jesus pierces hearts without the need of a sword," Eliana said.

"Some people's hearts will never be changed."

"I changed."

Now it was Asaph's turn to smile. "It's hard to argue with that."

"Then don't."

"Why don't you want me to go on this raid?"

He hoped she would express fear for his safety—or give some hint that she cared for him.

"It's not the way of Jesus."

The wind went out of his sails.

Jesus again. With Eliana, *everything* was Jesus. Asaph nodded slowly.

Eliana was too infatuated with Jesus to give Asaph any thought. And at that moment, he knew, without a doubt, he would lift this sword and ride with Judah. For the first time in his life, he would become a lion.

KETURAH

As the knife slid in, Keturah could not believe she had done it. Even until the last moment, she was unsure she could go through with it. But when Sveshtari took her into his embrace, all she could think was that this was the man who killed her father so quickly and callously.

Nemesis, the angel at her back, helped her to stealthily remove the knife strapped to Sveshtari's waist while lost in his embrace. Then she thrust it through his robes and into his skin. Blood had to be spilled. It was the only way to find peace and redemption. *Sveshtari's* blood had to be spilled.

But was it enough?

After all, she had only stabbed him in the thigh. She had not thrust the knife into his gut as she initially planned.

Keturah backpedaled as Sveshtari roared, his jaw slack. He stared in disbelief at the blade protruding from his left thigh. Blinking, his gaze moved from the knife to her. The knife hadn't gone in too far; Keturah had held back because she thought he might bleed to death if she drove it in deeply.

At first, she thought Sveshtari would slap her across the face, and if he had been any other man, she would be dead by now. She almost wished it would happen.

"Go ahead. Kill me." Keturah raised her accusing eyes to meet his shocked expression.

Sveshtari stared again at the knife, mesmerized by the oddity of a handle protruding from his thigh. If he was in pain, he did not show it. Then he met her challenging stare and sighed. "So, you know what happened to your father?"

"Yes."

She clamped her lips, thinking Sveshtari was behaving remarkably restrained, and wondered why he couldn't have shown similar restraint when it came to her father. Why couldn't he have stabbed her father in a less vulnerable spot, as she had done?

"You didn't try to kill me," he said, pointing out the obvious.

"I considered it. I didn't know until moments before I drove in the knife."

Keturah kept her distance as she eyed Sveshtari, unable to get a good read on him. Although she knew him well, she'd never tested how far she could push him. If his anger flared, she needed to stay far from reach.

"Blood had to be shed," she said, eying his leg with an internal wince. Sveshtari still hadn't removed the blade.

His white robe, bunched around the entry point, had already soaked through in red, the stain blossoming before her eyes. Her brow wrinkled. Would he bleed to death?

But Sveshtari did not seem too concerned. He had probably received much worse wounds in battles. Finally, he gave a shrug and grasped the handle with a slight pause before sliding out the blade. As the red stain spread across his robe, Keturah rushed forward, dropping to her knees.

"What have I done?" She removed her head covering and pressed it against the wound.

When she glanced up, he was biting his lip, doing his best to hide the pain. Keturah pressed her forehead to his thigh, tears flowing. She suddenly wanted badly to stop the bleeding.

Keturah wept for what seemed like an eternity until Sveshtari dropped a hand to caress her head, stroking his fingers through her hair. She sucked in a breath.

"You were justified," he said. "Blood had to be shed. Blood always must be shed, and I deserved it."

Keturah looked up at him, blinking. Had she heard him right? With her hands firmly on his thigh, she said, "Enough blood has been shed, enough blood."

She sniffed, blinking away another round of tears, her hand shaking as she lifted a corner of the rag to check the wound. When more blood darkened the fabric, she stared at it, yelling, "Stop!"

Sveshtari must have thought she was yelling at him because he withdrew his hand from her hair.

"Why won't the bleeding stop?" She wiped away more tears with the back of her hand.

"Don't worry, Keturah, it will stop. Believe me. It will."

They remained in the same position for the longest time—Sveshtari standing with Keturah crouched at his feet, putting pressure on his wound.

Finally, Sveshtari gently moved her hand aside and ripped off the hem of his robe, handing it to her.

"Here. Tie the bandage tight. No need to keep pressing."

He raised his robes, exposing his thigh, and Keturah gasped at the puckering slit in his skin, with blood still dribbling out. Quickly, she tied the bandage tightly around his leg.

"Why are you even wearing these robes?" she asked, finally gaining some control over her emotions. Sveshtari was not dressed in military fashion; he looked more like a typical Jewish man—very strange for a Thracian soldier.

Then Sveshtari proceeded to tell her his remarkable story. He explained how he had been present for the beheading of John and how Lucanus had boasted about selling her into slavery. He then told how he had killed Lucanus in one blow before disguising the corpse to look like him. He was dressed as a Jewish man to blend in with the crowd.

Sveshtari groaned as he took a seat on a nearby rock. "So, I guess this means we are both dead in the world's eyes. Some people still think you're dead, and now they think Lucanus killed me. It's like we can start our lives anew."

Still sitting on the ground, Keturah stared up at him. "Start anew? First of all, I think Rufus now knows you are alive."

"He saw me?"

"Of course, he saw you. He knows we're both alive!"

Keturah shook her head with a scoff. Did Sveshtari really think she would start fresh?

She leaped to her feet. "I will *never* forget what you did to my father! We are not new creatures! We all have pasts, and I will *never* forget!"

Heart racing, she started to slap him, but he caught her arm, his fingers tightening around her wrist. Might he break her wrist as he did to the man who tried to steal Eliana's dog? She held her breath as they stared at one another, his uncertain eyes searching hers.

"You can never forgive me?" he asked, dropping her arm. "But my blood has been spilled."

"But not enough blood!" She knew she was declaring the exact opposite of what she had said moments before, but logic had no part in her fury. "There can never be enough spilled!"

Sveshtari looked like a rock had fallen on him.

Good. Keturah stomped off, satisfied that her words had wounded him, probably more than her knife.

As she departed, however, she had a strange sense that those words weren't entirely hers. She suspected that Nemesis had spoken, and she was only the mouthpiece for an angry god.

SVESHTARI

Sveshtari wasn't going to humiliate himself by running after a woman. Besides, his leg ached, and his limp would make him look even more pitiful. So, he tried to walk normally and followed her toward the city's edge.

He thought about her exposed head and the message branded on her skin. The last thing he wanted was for Rufus's men to get their hands on her again.

As Keturah exited Capernaum, Sveshtari spotted her moving toward the massive crowds that continued to surround Jesus of Nazareth. He kept his distance, reflecting on how everything in his past was dead to him. Everything that had made up his identity was gone. He was no longer a bodyguard in Herod's Palace, he had angered the gods Dionysius and Mars, and now, he had lost the one woman he loved.

Sveshtari was sure the gods were having a grand time at his expense. He dared to keep himself to one woman, which meant Dionysius would keep punishing him. The gods were probably already orchestrating his arrest for helping a slave escape.

He hurried his pace, ignoring the searing pain that shot through his leg with every step, and disappeared into the crowds that surged around the prophet from Nazareth. The throng was on the move, heading south like an Exodus army.

As dust kicked up in brown clouds, he lost sight of Keturah, who disappeared into a cluster of female followers. Sveshtari watched the multitude of women following Jesus and shook his head. Most rabbis had only men sitting at their feet, drinking up the knowledge, but Jesus was different in so many ways.

When there was no sign of soldiers or pursuers, Sveshtari plunged deeper into the crowd. There had to be a thousand or more on the move.

"Where is Jesus headed?" he asked a short, stocky man, who couldn't help but stare at the blood that had soaked through his robe.

"He is heading to Jerusalem," the man said, putting some space between them. "Do you think you can manage with that?" He nodded at Sveshtari's leg.

"It's nothing." Sveshtari tried not to wince at the latest jab of pain.

By the end of the day, the large group following in Jesus's wake reached the outskirts of Magdala, near the base of the Cliffs of Arbel. Sveshtari had learned that Jesus planned to travel to Jerusalem by way of Perea, bypassing the more direct route through Samaria. But they hadn't made much progress that morning because Jesus kept stopping to teach.

Sveshtari paid no attention to Jesus except when he raised the hackles of the Pharisees and Sadducees who dogged his steps. Those encounters could be highly entertaining—and today was one of those days. Jesus had healed a mute, at least according to the man standing next to Sveshtari, but the Pharisees remained suspicious.

The Cliffs of Arbel made a dramatic backdrop to the unfolding scene. While most people remained seated on the ground, two Jewish priests near the front of the crowd rose to their feet. Jesus stopped talking and gazed in their direction.

"By Beelzebul, the prince of demons, he is driving out demons!" one of them shouted, stabbing the air with his finger.

Jesus paused, letting the silence speak for itself before addressing his accusers. "Any kingdom divided against itself will be ruined, and a house divided against itself will fall. If Satan is divided against himself, how can his kingdom stand?" Jesus again waited.

A good point, Sveshtari thought. *Why in the world would the prince of demons cast out an evil spirit from a man? It would stir up a devil's civil war.*

The Pharisee turned to the crowd, aiming a finger at Jesus once more as if pointing a knife. "I say it again! By Beelzebul, the prince of demons, he is driving out demons."

Jesus gave him a sly smile. "Now if I drive out demons by Beelzebul, by whom do your followers drive them out? So then, they will be your judges." Jesus spoke loud and clear for all to hear. "But if I drive out demons by the finger of God, then the kingdom of God has come upon you."

The Pharisee's bony forefinger wilted at the mention of God's finger. What was a puny human finger in comparison to God's?

"Blasphemy!" the Pharisee sputtered before slamming a closed fist against the palm of his hand.

After several others told the Pharisee to be quiet so the rabbi could speak, Sveshtari sensed a sermon coming. He made a move to leave.

"When a strong man, fully armed, guards his own house, his possessions are safe," Jesus said. "But when someone stronger attacks and overpowers him, he takes away the armor in which the man trusted and divides up the spoils."

Sveshtari paused and sat back down. He was unsure what Jesus was trying to say, but talk of armor and strength caught his attention.

"He who is not with me is against me, and he who does not gather with me, scatters," Jesus declared.

Sveshtari nodded. *That I understand.* Jesus was saying there was no neutral ground, and as a soldier, Sveshtari agreed wholeheartedly.

Sveshtari smiled as he pictured two armies charging each other from opposite sides of a battlefield, with a Pharisee standing between them, raising his hands, and declaring, "I am neutral!"

But there was no neutral ground on a battlefield, which meant the Pharisee would soon be crushed—overrun by *both* armies.

You must choose sides.

That was probably the first thing Jesus ever said that made complete sense to Sveshtari.

That night, Sveshtari set up his campfire in the center of Magdala. With all the people following Jesus, there was no room in the local inn. Actually, there had been one room available, but Sveshtari insisted the innkeeper give it to a pair of women following Jesus.

Staring into the fire, Sveshtari rubbed his stomach, still hungry after a small meal of fish and bread. As he did, he noticed a friend of Eliana and Keturah emerge from the darkness and sit on the ground just a few handbreadths away. Chaim was his name—the brother of a Sadducee priest.

Sveshtari had talked to Chaim once, but he didn't know the man, so he found it curious they were suddenly sharing a campfire.

"Shalom," said Chaim. He had noticed Sveshtari looking at him.

"Shalom." Sveshtari conceded to the Jewish form of greeting.

"I never had a chance to thank you, Sveshtari."

"For what?"

"For what you did for Eliana. For pulling her out of the sea."

Sveshtari nodded, embarrassed by the gratitude. "It was just a reflex action. Besides, Jesus's fishermen should get all the credit."

"Both you and the fishermen saved her life. Thank you."

Sveshtari nodded again, hoping Chaim would change the subject. After an awkward silence, he got his wish.

"Did you hear Jesus speak today?" Chaim put his elbows on his knees and leaned in, eyes intense.

"Some of it. I enjoy his wordplay with the Pharisees."

"He said that whoever isn't with him is against him. Do you believe that?"

Sveshtari nodded thoughtfully. "It is difficult to remain neutral, yes. You must choose a side."

"But Eliana tells me you were a Thracian bodyguard working for a Jewish tetrarch under Roman rule. With so many allegiances, how did you know which side you were on?"

Sveshtari tensed. If Chaim knew he had once been a Thracian bodyguard, how many others knew? This kind of knowledge could get him killed.

"You *can't* tell anyone what you know about me."

Chaim must have heard the threat in his growl because he quickly put up a hand and shook his head. "I told no one you were once a bodyguard for Herod. And I never will. I promise."

After a silence, Chaim ventured another question. "So, you really think we must choose a side?"

Sveshtari cut his eyes at him and answered through clenched teeth. "That's what I said."

"Then you agree with Jesus?"

"I do. On this point."

The campfire light illuminated Chaim's face, which displayed a pained expression. Sveshtari cocked his head and asked, "Are you feeling all right?"

"No, no. Must be something I ate." Chaim paled as he turned to the side, eyes filled with worry.

"Or something you've done." Sveshtari knew a guilty conscience when he saw one.

Chaim flinched. Sveshtari was tempted to ask Chaim what he had done, but the man seemed to be suffering for it already. And to be honest, he really didn't care. Chaim's problems were his own.

"I think it's something I ate," Chaim repeated before excusing himself and slipping away into the dark.

KETURAH

"For your sake, you should try to forgive him," Joanna urged.

"For *my* sake?"

Keturah had come to Joanna for sympathy. Instead, she was getting a sermon. Her old friend spent too much time listening to Jesus.

Joanna found rooms in the village of Magdala, at the foot of the Cliffs of Arbel, and invited Keturah to stay with her. A single oil lamp sat on the low table before them, with Joanna and Keturah resting lengthwise on cushions.

"Your anger is poisoning you," Joanna said. "You nearly killed the man you love today."

"He is not the man I love." Keturah's eyes hardened.

"If Rufus had been the one who killed your father, and if you had your chance, would you have driven the knife into his stomach?"

"Of course."

"Then why didn't you do the same to Sveshtari? Something altered your aim. What made you drive the knife into his leg?"

"I don't know. I'm a fool."

"You must feel something for Sveshtari. Why else would you have held back?"

Keturah groaned, her back still aching from the beam being strapped against it. She touched the tender spot above her cheekbone, where a stone had struck her, and said nothing in response.

"Jesus says that our eyes are the lamp of our body." Joanna passed her hand slowly over the lamp, causing the flame to bend in the breeze.

"Do we have to talk about *him* again?"

"Hear me out, Keturah. Our eyes are lamps in a dark world. But I don't see any light in your eyes. Only darkness and blood."

"That's all I feel," Keturah whispered.

Cold darkness coiled inside, shivering up her back, and she began to shake. Joanna removed her shawl and came around to place it gently over Keturah's back. As she did, Keturah kept her eyes on the lamp light, a yellow-tipped, small white flame swaying from side to side, flickering in the breeze, then nearly extinguishing.

Keturah had no idea how long they sat in silence before they both retired to their rooms for the night.

She fell asleep quickly—and woke to a thumping on the front door. She had no idea how long she had been asleep or whether she was still dreaming. When the pounding came again, this time more insistent, she sat up and wiped her eyes. She shivered, hugged herself, and listened as all went quiet. She wondered if the unwelcome visitor had given up and left them in peace.

When the pounding returned even louder, she crawled out of bed, threw on a cloak, and stumbled into the main room. "All right, I'm coming!"

Joanna materialized moments later, also throwing on a cloak.

"Who is there?" Joanna asked, standing at the door, trying to keep her voice down.

"It's Chaim."

"Chaim?" She frowned and sent Keturah a look. "You know it is not proper to come to our rooms in the night."

"But this cannot wait." His voice was hurried and urgent.

As Joanna eased open the door, a flicker of light moved through the doorway, and Chaim entered with a lamp. Keturah pulled the shawl tighter around her shoulders.

"What could be so important that you would come here in the dead of night?" Joanna closed the door, her voice barely over a whisper.

"It's my brother." As the flicker of light bounced off Chaim's features, Keturah saw the alarm in his eyes.

"Did something happen to Nekoda?"

"No. It's what he has done. He went to the Roman soldiers in Capernaum and told them about Eliana's father and the freedom fighters up on the cliffs."

Keturah stood a little straighter, her lethargic mind suddenly sparking to life. "And why would your brother, a Sadducee, do something like that?"

Chaim looked down at his feet. "As an exchange for favors. It's not the first time he has supplied information to the Romans."

"What are you saying?" Joanna sucked in a breath.

"Nekoda serves as the eyes for the Roman authorities, keeping watch on his Jewish brethren."

"And you knew this?" Keturah snapped, stepping forward and pointing in accusation. "Surely, you didn't learn this about your brother just now. Why didn't you speak up sooner?"

Chaim dipped his head even lower as he shuffled from foot to foot.

"What do you think the Romans plan to do about the Zealots in the cliffs?" Joanna asked.

Chaim finally lifted his head, his eyes filling with regret. "Kill them all."

Keturah gasped. "When will they attack? Do you know?"

"Just before first light."

"You mean the Roman soldiers are going to scale the cliffs? Tonight?" Joanna snatched up her sandals and began to put them on.

"They are going to lower soldiers down from the top—in baskets. And the night is quickly fleeing. It is almost morning."

"We have to act now to warn Eliana and her father," Keturah said, also putting on her sandals.

"Eliana? You mean she's still with the Zealots?" Chaim's voice rose.

Keturah flung her hands in the air. "Of course she is!"

"But I thought she was only staying a couple of nights with them."

"You thought wrong." Keturah made a move for the door, but Chaim blocked her way.

"Where are you going?" he said. "You can't scale the cliffs in the dark."

"She must be warned!" Keturah glared, stepping past him. "I thought you cared for Eliana!"

"I will climb the cliffs. You stay here." Chaim followed as Keturah darted for the door.

"We must be wise about this," said Joanna, hurrying to stop Keturah. "Let Chaim go with Sveshtari because he should be accompanied by someone with military knowledge."

"I will *die* before I ever ask Sveshtari for help," Keturah snapped. Just the mention of his name triggered an overwhelming rage.

Keturah dashed past Chaim, yanking open the door. Joanna reached for her cloak, but Keturah tore away and sprinted into the darkness.

Lifting the hem of her robe, she ran faster than ever, oblivious to obstacles in the dark. She knew she was being a fool, but she didn't care. She would do this on her own. She would climb the mountain. In the dark. Without Sveshtari's help.

SVESHTARI

Sveshtari and Chaim clambered up the side of the mountain in almost total silence. Since Chaim was not as nimble or fast, he dislodged rocks along the way, sending them tumbling downhill. Chaim's steps were labored and his speed excruciatingly slow. But Sveshtari had no choice but to wait for him because Chaim knew where the Zealots were hiding on Mount Arbel.

Chaim and Joanna contacted him earlier that night, telling him of the danger facing the Zealots and asking him to deliver a warning to the Jewish freedom fighters.

"Do it for Keturah," Joanna had requested. "Do it for her friend Eliana."

Sveshtari thought Keturah should have come to him for help, but he understood why she hadn't. If he carried out this mission, maybe Keturah would finally find a way to forgive him. That was his hope, at least.

Sveshtari bounded to the next ledge, then paused, motioning for Chaim to catch up—as if his frantic waving would magically make him climb faster. While Chaim scrambled forward, panting like an old mule, dawn was fast approaching, and so was the Roman attack. They were running out of time.

A little farther up the side of Arbel, they came across the bodies of two Zealot sentries. That could mean only one thing: Romans were nearby. Putting a finger to his lips, Sveshtari urged Chaim forward with a look, and they pressed onward, steadily climbing.

Soon, they spotted a Roman guard standing on a ledge, his distinctive form silhouetted by the moonlight. Sveshtari glanced around, considering his options, which were few and far between. This was going to be tricky.

He eyed the Roman's armor, which consisted of a thick breastplate and backplate. The soldier's helmet protected most of his head and neck. The only vulnerability was by the ear. To take him out, Sveshtari's timing and effort had to be swift and silent.

Drawing his knife, he motioned for Chaim to stay. Then he maneuvered to the right, hoping to come at the guard from behind. Sveshtari hurled a stone beyond the guard, who immediately spun toward the sudden sound.

Sveshtari pounced, plunging his knife below the soldier's ear while clamping a hand over his mouth.

When it was over, he lowered the dead body to the ground and removed the guard's *gladius*, thinking it would come in handy when the battle struck the caves of Mount Arbel.

As he returned to Chaim, Sveshtari spotted a second soldier rushing toward him, shield forward and sword raised. Since Sveshtari had no armor or shield, a frontal assault would be next to impossible.

Raising his *gladius*, he charged the Roman, a suicidal maneuver if ever there was one. At the last second, he slid to the ground, gliding past the Roman and hacking at the guard's unprotected calves. As the soldier screamed and crumpled to the ground, Sveshtari winced. The Roman's outcry was sure to draw attention, but it couldn't be helped.

Sveshtari sprang to his feet, plunging the sword into the Roman's neck before he could raise further alarm. He then took the dead soldier's *gladius* and offered it to Chaim, who stood in stunned silence, staring at the sword as if he had just been handed the very staff of Moses.

"C'mon," Sveshtari whispered. "Sunrise is almost here."

Sveshtari bounded upward, with Chaim well behind. At this pace, they would never reach the Zealots in time.

12

LUKE, CHAPTER 12

JEREMIEL

J EREMIEL SAT IN THE cave, alone as always. He had not looked into a stream for many weeks because he was petrified to see what his face had become, if he could even call it a face any longer.

He ran his fingers across his chin, memorizing the landscape of his skin through touch alone. Every day his fingers took the climb, beginning at his chin and working their way up the sides of his face, resting on every nodule and bump that had erupted on his cheeks and forehead.

The cave he occupied was not too far from the caves that the Zealots used as their base of operations. And every day, that woman, Eliana, followed the narrow ledge between their respective caves to leave him food. He wasn't sure what was riskier—approaching a leper or navigating the narrow ridges.

Every day, he asked God to forgive him for how he had treated Eliana, and every day he marveled that she would bring food to an unclean man; sometimes, she even brought him scrolls to read.

As darkness set in, Jeremiel set aside his scrolls, lay himself down, and fell into a restless sleep. Like most nights, he woke up sweating—his body blanketed with fear. He was oddly alert as he walked to the cave's opening to sit.

The night was clear, with a crescent moon hanging like an oil lamp in the sky. Below, he could see a sprinkling of fire lights in Magdala—pinpricks in a midnight world. The lights were the only sign that he wasn't perched above a bottomless landscape.

Magdala overflowed with followers of Jesus because the prophet's "army" had marched into the village earlier in the day. Jeremiel was tempted to climb down and ask for healing. He might have, too, if he didn't have a strong sense that God wanted him to remain on the cliffs all day and night.

"But Jesus will soon be leaving the region," he had said out loud to God. "If I don't approach him now, I may never get the chance again."

"Stay."

It wasn't an audible voice that he heard. It was an interior voice, but it was as clear as if spoken aloud. Jeremiel had no idea why God would want him to remain in his rocky aerie, but he obeyed. He always obeyed.

Jeremiel dipped his head in prayer. "And there was evening, and there was morning—the sixth day. Thus the heavens and the earth were completed in all their vast array. By the seventh day God had finished the work he had been doing; so on the seventh day he rested from all his work. Then God blessed—"

Jeremiel opened his eyes and cocked his head at the sudden sound of rocks sliding—small ones, from the sound of it.

He stood, his heart racing. Might it be the striped hyena he had seen roaming the area? These animals were nocturnal.

Then Jeremiel heard a grunt—a very human sound. That made no sense. Who in their right mind would be scaling these cliffs in the dead of night?

Just when he was about to discount it as his imagination, it came again. A human grunt, followed by the tinkle of tumbling stones. Someone was coming, but Jeremiel was strangely calm. There wasn't much that he feared anymore. If you had been struck by the worst thing imaginable—if you were a leper—there wasn't much that could terrify you.

The only thing that ever scared him these days was his reflection. So, he continued to sit calmly at the edge of his cave and waited for whatever or whoever approached.

KETURAH

The lower slope of the mountain rose at a steady incline but not as formidable as the craggy cliff face that awaited Keturah. Still, the slope was littered with stones of all sizes, and she had already tripped twice in the dark. She rubbed her arm, wincing as she grazed a tender spot near her elbow. She'd have quite the bruise, but at least her arm wasn't broken.

As Keturah inched up the slope, she lost her footing and slid on cascading stones, stopping just short of a steep ledge. Catching her breath, she worked her way back to safety.

That was close. She looked over her shoulder, heart pounding, realizing she should have listened to Joanna and asked Sveshtari for help. Keturah shook her head, chastising herself. What was she thinking?

Keturah had been told since childhood that spirits called *numina* lived inside rocks. So, when her foot hit another stone, concentrating a blast of pain at the tips of her toes, she wondered if the stories were true.

She screamed, dropping to the ground and squeezing her left foot. She prayed her cry hadn't woken even more gods, who wouldn't be pleased.

She leaned against a large boulder, her chest heaving, breathing through the pain. She bit her lip and stared into the dark, wondering how she thought she could do this alone. Part of her wanted to turn around and call off this foolish mission. But she wasn't sure whether Joanna had enlisted Sveshtari's help—or if *anyone* was on their way to warn the Zealots.

If Joanna couldn't track down Sveshtari, Chaim would probably try the climb on his own, but Keturah wasn't confident he could do it. Keturah wasn't capable either, but she could not desert Eliana, leaving her at the mercy of the Romans. So, she inhaled and plodded forward, the incline becoming steeper, her legs cramped by exhaustion. She paused to sit on a rock, but only after she excused herself to the god who might live within it.

After a few moments, she continued her trudge, stopping where the cliff rose at a steep angle. She looked up with a sigh. The crescent moon was all the light she had to go by, but her eyes had adjusted to the dark as she probed the ground with her feet, looking for a proper foothold. One consolation was that the uneven jumble of rocks provided plenty of places to put your feet. She leaned forward, getting a firm grasp before crawling up at an angle on all fours.

It was slow going, so she was sure the sun might beat her to the top of the mountain. She prayed she was wrong because the Romans were attacking at first light, and that moment rapidly approached. She stole a glance above.

Soldiers were probably already moving into position at the very top of Mount Arbel, looking down on the cliffs and caves below. They would lower the baskets from there and storm the caves, trapping Eliana, her father, and all his men.

Keturah had no choice but to take the more difficult path up the northern face of Mount Arbel, yet she could not trust any of the footholds or handholds. She gripped what she thought was a solid rock, but when she heaved herself forward, the stone came loose, tumbling out like a broken tooth. She slid about six feet, scraping her side and arm.

Groaning, she lay there panting and holding her arm—the skin scraped worse than before. This was impossible...and foolish. She closed her eyes, wondering if she had gone mad.

When Eliana's smile flashed through her mind, Keturah shook her head, unable to turn back now. Not when her friend's new life was just beginning. So, she continued her climb, inching up like an insect. As she rose higher, she felt a stronger buffeting of the wind. She moved steadily up through a narrow crevice, where she could get a better footing.

Then one of the stones beneath her gave way, and she twisted her foot, her ankle wrapped in a sheet of pain. She screamed and lay on her back, breathing heavily and fighting back sobs.

After a few moments, Keturah tried to rise, but her ankle gave way, sending knife-stabs along the outside of her foot. She buried her head in her arms, waiting for the intense pain to settle. Then she broke down in tears because she wasn't sure if she could maneuver the slope with a sprained ankle. Every part of her ached like a chorus of agony, singing her misery.

JEREMIEL

It was as if the face of the cliff was sobbing as the sound of a weeping woman rose from below, eerie and inexplicable, carried in the wind. But why would a woman be on the Cliffs of Arbel in the middle of the night? Was it a demon luring him to a precipice? Or was he losing his mind?

"Help me, God," a small, distant voice called out.

Jeremiel shook his head. This was just the kind of trap that Satan, the seducer of men, might set.

"Help me, please." Her cry sounded again.

Jeremiel took a step forward. He should at least check out the source of the cries. If Satan were enticing him, he would gladly fight the evil one.

And if he died wrestling with Satan, or *Sammael*, then at least it was a noble way to end his suffering.

By this time, Jeremiel knew the terrain like he once did the streets of Jerusalem. He memorized every twist and turn after climbing across the rocks every day, exploring, and praying. Just like prisoners knew every inch of their cell, he had intimate knowledge of every stone. This cliff had become his prison. Still, he had never ventured so far in the dark.

Slowly, he moved down the cliff, trying to pinpoint the sorrowful sound, but the weeping seemed to be moving about. It first came from his left, then a little to the right. Was the wind playing tricks on him, or was the Evil One taunting him?

"Hello!" He cupped his hands. "Who is there?"

The sobbing suddenly ended, and he heard only the whipping of the wind.

Then: a woman's voice.

"My name..." Her voice trailed, leaving Jeremiel unable to decipher anything more. He felt the tug to investigate.

Jeremiel continued to work his way down the cliff with a skill that surprised him. His muscles remembered every step he had taken by day, and he wondered if he could climb this cliff even if he were completely blind. Someday, when leprosy finally ate away his eyesight, he would go blind, so this was a practice run for that inevitability.

"I turned my ankle!" The woman's voice pierced the darkness. He was moving in the right direction.

Jeremiel's foot dislodged a cascade of rocks and pebbles, and he slid on his back before grabbing hold of an unmovable stone. He paused to catch his breath, unsure where the cliff's edge might be. How close had he just come to sliding into oblivion?

Jeremiel adjusted, trying to lift himself from the rocks digging into his back when a hot stripe of pain streaked from his shoulders to the center of his back.

"I'm over here!" The woman's desperate voice carried in the wind, this time a bit closer and to his right.

He got on all fours, facing the cliff, and moved steadily down the steep slope. He probed the dark with his feet like he was moving down an unsteady ladder with uneven, broken, or missing rungs.

"Are you one of Judah's men?" the woman asked. Her voice was nearby, just down the slope.

At last, Jeremiel could make out the outline of her body, a shadow moving on the ground. She was real, not a figment of his mind or a spiritual mirage.

"I am not one of the Zealots," he said. "What are you doing out here at night? Have you lost your mind?"

A long silence. When the woman finally spoke, her voice carried a hint of fear. "Are you the leper?"

Jeremiel sighed. In the past, he had many identities. Priest. Pharisee. Father. Husband. Human. Now, all were stripped away, leaving one: leper.

"My name is Jeremiel."

"You're Eliana's friend," she said. "I, too, am Eliana's friend. Keturah."

Evidently, he had more than one identity in her mind after all. Jeremiel was not just the leper. He was also "Eliana's friend," which brought some measure of comfort. He felt strangely proud to be thought of as Eliana's friend.

"Yes, I am her friend."

"Then you must warn her...and her father. The Romans are coming."

"Romans? They're coming here? When?"

"At first light."

Jeremiel studied the horizon. The darkness had already begun receding, the blackness slowly draining from the sky.

"How will they attack?"

"From above."

Jeremiel glanced over his shoulder at the higher caves where the Zealots were hidden. While he couldn't just leave this poor woman, he doubted he'd be able to carry her either up or down the sides of the cliff. Besides, she wouldn't want to be touched by a leper.

Keturah must have sensed his indecision. "Go. Warn them, and don't worry about me. It's just a sprain."

"I can't leave you here."

"I'll be safe. When the Romans attack, they won't see me down here."

She was right. She certainly would be safer here than higher up the cliff.

Jeremiel glanced back up at the slope with a sharp nod. "I will send help as soon as I can."

"Thank you."

As the leper turned to begin the slow ascent, the light started to break. *The Romans will attack soon.* Jeremiel picked up his pace, hoping to make it in time, when he noticed movement from above. He watched in horror as the Romans streamed down the cliff on ropes like spiders on threads. Some were lowered in baskets holding several soldiers, while others descended individually.

"Oh God," came Keturah's voice from below. She too could see what was happening. They were too late, and the Zealots were about to be caught in a storm of fury and blood.

SVESHTARI

The Zealots formed a long line of attack, each man carrying two *pila*—javelins they had stolen from the Romans and stockpiled in the cave. Sveshtari, who had been invited to join their battle ranks, was amazed at the number of *pila* the Zealots had gathered. He tightened his grasp on two javelins, each the length of a man and tipped by tapered steel.

Twenty-five Zealots hunched in the shadows, remaining astonishingly quiet. They were poised, listening to the sounds of movement outside the caves—the creaking of wooden baskets being lowered.

The Romans were coming, and they had timed their attack perfectly with the arrival of the light from Apollo's chariot. Sveshtari gripped his spear so hard that his knuckles went white. He thanked the gods that he and Chaim arrived when they did, catching some of the Zealots at their morning meal; most had not even awakened yet.

In little time, the Zealots formed battle lines a few steps inside the mouths of three adjacent caves, hiding in the shadows from the quickly descending Romans. Sveshtari readied his *pilum*, its steel tip sharp enough to penetrate a Roman shield and armor. A man beside him wore a gladiator's "scissor," an axhead worn over the arm like a steel sleeve.

After years of bodyguard duty, Sveshtari had almost forgotten the exhilarating anticipation of battle. He welcomed the explosion of action, although uncharacteristic fears nagged at him, telling him he might not be up to the fight. He had never fought trained Roman soldiers and was out of practice.

Still, they had the element of surprise.

Suddenly, two baskets containing three soldiers each dropped before their cave opening. Sveshtari and the other Zealots released a blood-curdling battle cry and surged forward.

ASAPH

The shock on the Romans' faces was a sight to behold. Asaph and the others at his side surged forward, driving their *pila* through armor, skin, and muscle. The Roman soldiers never even had time to leap from their baskets into the cave. They had planned to pin the unsuspecting Zealots to the ground with *pila* and slaughter them with *gladius* swords. But the tables had been turned.

Because Asaph had little training with the *pilum*, he opted for the weapon that Gershom had taught him to handle—the slingshot. His first rock sliced the open air and disappeared into the dark, hitting nothing. Gershom laughed and shot him a grin.

Gershom should have been paying more attention to the Romans. Asaph's eyes widened at Gershom's folly when a Roman spear came whistling out of the dark. The *pilum* struck Gershom in the right shoulder, breaking through skin, muscle, and tendons. Gershom's grin was replaced by a look of horror as the Roman climbed out of the basket to finish him off with a short sword.

As blood streamed down his back, Gershom switched his sword to his free hand. Stumbling, he swung the weapon as best he could with his weak hand, but it was futile. The enemy moved in for the kill.

Asaph, momentarily frozen by terror, needed to act before it was too late. Loading his sling without a moment to waste, he swung and released, sending a rock—the size of a man's fist—smashing into the enemy's face above his eye. The Roman dropped his sword, staggered back two steps, and vanished. He stumbled off the ledge and into mid-air, falling as if a trapdoor had opened beneath his feet.

Asaph stood, his sling dangling, and exhaled before flashing a grin. He had done it.

Gershom turned, his face pale, and gave Asaph a weak smile before his legs collapsed beneath him, and he crumpled to the stone floor.

SVESHTARI

Sveshtari had always been good with the *pilum*. His javelins found their mark, driving through the chests of two Romans before they could climb out of their baskets.

It was as simple as pinning insects to a board. One soldier crumpled, while the other fell backward out of the basket to meet a much quicker death on the rocks below. The Roman with the javelin skewering his shoulder tried to clumsily climb out of the basket, but Sveshtari cut him down with two quick slashes.

After the Zealots massacred the first Roman line of attackers, those above began to pull back the baskets, now filled with dead men. Sveshtari and others lunged, slashing the ropes and sending one basket crashing below to shatter on the rocks.

With a victorious shout, Sveshtari craned his neck and saw that the same scenario had unfolded in front of the other two caves. The Romans had been soundly defeated.

Catching movement from the corner of his eye, he swung his gaze to the top of his cave and discovered another group descending, this time individually on ropes.

"Romans!" Sveshtari cupped his hands to alert his fellow fighters. The Zealots were not in the clear by a long shot.

He ducked back inside the cave as armed soldiers appeared on the narrow ledge running in front of the caves. Two Romans rounded the corner at full tilt, but four Zealots charged them with shields, hurling one down to the rocks. When another Roman backpedaled, trying to save himself, he grabbed a Zealot by the arm. They both toppled off the ledge, spiraling downward, their cries filling the air.

Sveshtari and his group waited for any others foolish enough to run along the narrow ledge, but they heard no shuffling or approaching steps. There were no sounds but the hard breaths of the men as they braced for whatever came next.

"Stay ready," a Zealot whispered.

After a few more moments, when nothing happened, Sveshtari inched forward to peek outside. All remaining Romans had retreated.

Sveshtari ducked into the shadows. "They're moving away." He could sense the tension releasing.

"They know it would be foolhardy to attack when they would have to move single file along a sliver of a ledge," Judah said.

The Zealots were safe for now, but they couldn't maintain this position all day. The Romans would regroup, find another strategy, and lay siege. At the very least, the Romans would starve them out.

Sveshtari swung around to face Eliana's father, who put a hand on his shoulder. "Sveshtari, we have much to be grateful to you and Chaim for bringing us this warning," said Judah.

"I only wish we had arrived sooner. Maybe we could have prevented the Romans from killing your sentries."

"We have a back door out of these caves. Most of my men will exit that way before the Romans can return, and I urge you to escape with them. You have already done more than I could have ever asked for."

Sveshtari shook his head. "Thank you, Judah, but I will remain here to provide defense until you are safely away."

"I can't ask you to do that."

"I have decided, so I suggest you lead your daughter and the others to safety now. There is no time to argue." Sveshtari stood with legs wide, eyes pointed, and jaw firm.

Judah studied him, taking him in from head to toe before giving a sharp nod. "I am leaving two other men with you to hold off any more Roman surges. But I don't think they will make another assault any time soon. When they try again, we will be gone, and I trust you will be too."

"Agreed." Sveshtari uncurled his fists at his sides, thankful Judah was listening to reason.

"Give us a head start, and then my men will show you the escape route, and you can follow."

After a clasp of hands, Judah was gone, disappearing into the blackness of the cave. Sveshtari turned to face the oval of light. Peering around the edge of the cave's opening, he saw that the ledge was clear.

He didn't expect the Romans to attack immediately, but they would return. That was the only certainty.

KETURAH

Keturah watched everything unfold from the side of the cliff where she lay. It almost made her forget that her ankle had swollen to the size of a beef bladder, pulsating with pain.

Surely, Sveshtari or someone must have warned the Zealots in time because they were ready when the Romans came sliding down the face of the cliff with death-defying dexterity. There had to be well over a dozen Romans who had plunged to their deaths onto the rocks—most of them in the wooden baskets that shattered to a thousand pieces. One thing was certain. The Romans wouldn't give up easily, not after losing so many men.

As the sun rose, she wondered if she dared to scramble down the slope. Although there might be Romans about, staying put could be more dangerous. She couldn't walk, but she might be able to slide down carefully.

As she debated her next step, Latin voices sounded nearby. *Romans.* She swallowed her fear, squeezing her eyes shut, praying they wouldn't see her. She was going nowhere.

Keturah lay on her back in the crevice, shrinking deeper into the narrow slot on the cliff's side. As the voices grew louder, loose rocks tumbled nearby, dislodging beneath the feet of advancing soldiers. She bit her lip, holding back a cry, and moved onto her side. She couldn't fit her entire body into the crevice, so a portion of her hip was exposed. Fortunately, a tangle of vegetation shielded her from view.

"The centurion believes the Zealots had a way out," said one of the soldiers. "But I don't think this is anywhere near where that exit would have led."

They were hunting Hebrews, and if they found her, they would assume she was one of the Zealot women.

As Keturah tried to make herself fit, squeezing deeper into the crevice, a jagged rock jabbed her left shoulder. She stifled a cry. That was all she needed—another wound on top of her sprained ankle, bruised back, and black eye.

Keturah closed her eyes as the footsteps neared, trying to will the soldiers away. Should she play dead? Would they think she had fallen to her death from one of the ledges? Closing her eyes, she prayed to the God of the Jews. What did she have to lose?

When everything went silent, she held her breath, sensing their presence.

"Is she dead?" said one voice.

"One way to find out."

Keturah screamed as a spear sank into her shoulder. The soldier's *pilum* resurrected her from her feigned death. One of the soldiers grabbed her by the hair, yanking her from the crevice and standing her to her feet.

She limped and let out a suffering sob as she found herself facing two soldiers. The younger one prodded her with the butt end of his *pilum*.

She clasped a hand over the cut on her shoulder and glared, wishing she could slam a rock into the man's sneering face. They would make her bleed for it, but what was one more wound, especially when she was about to die?

JEREMIEL

Jeremiel watched from above, behind a large stone. He had been heading back down the cliff, hoping to help Keturah, but it was too late. The Romans who discovered her would surely kill her on the spot.

Just moments before, he had been encouraged because his fellow Jews had driven away the Romans, killing many. But that thrill of victory was gone. Although he never approved of the Zealots' ways, he had always admired their resistance. They were certainly better than the Sadducees, who tried to appease evil and make pacts with devils.

But now, as he watched two soldiers toying with Keturah, he sensed death everywhere. Jeremiel fell face down on the ground and pleaded with God.

How I long for the months gone by, for the days when God watched over me, when his lamp shone on my head and by his light I walked through darkness! Oh, for the days when I was in my prime, when God's intimate friendship blessed my house, when the Almighty was still with me and my children were around me, and the rock poured out for me streams of olive oil.

He didn't dare speak those words out loud, but they raged in his mind.

On my right the tribe attacks; they lay snares at my feet, they build their siege ramps against me. They advance as through a gaping breach; amid the ruins they come rolling in. Terrors overwhelm me; my dignity is driven away as by the wind, my safety vanishes like a cloud. And now my life ebbs away; days of suffering grip me. Night pierces my bones; my gnawing pains never rest.

Jeremiel rose to his knees, scooping dirt from the ground and covering his face with handfuls of dust.

When I hoped for good, evil came; when I looked for light, then came darkness. The churning inside me never stops; days of suffering confront me. I have become a brother of jackals, a companion of owls. My lyre is turned to mourning, and my pipe to the sound of wailing.

Like a jackal, Jeremiel crawled on all fours to move higher up the cliff. He had been reduced to an animal state. The very word "leper" sounded primitive and wild.

He scrambled up, oblivious to everything around him. He was no longer a man. He was no longer a human. He had been changed into a monster, a man-wolf, and he retreated into his cave, leaving the woman behind to die.

KETURAH

One of the soldiers took her right arm and hauled her to her feet. Part of her robe caught on a rock and tore, exposing her calf. The man holding her arm laughed. She spat at him, and he responded with a punch in the face, knocking her to her knees.

"Shall we make sport of her?" the younger of the two soldiers asked.

"No time for that. Kill her now." The soldier wiped her spit from his face, his eyes narrowing.

The young soldier nodded, took a handful of hair, and yanked her head back, exposing her neck. Keturah swallowed, her blood pulsing in her veins. She had only moments left. What would it feel like to die? Would it be like sleeping or waking up...or falling or opening a door? Would the pain be gone forever?

"She deserves to die the way my brothers did today," the younger soldier said. "She deserves to be thrown from the ledge."

So, it would feel like falling.

The oldest of the soldiers jutted his chin at the cliff. "Take her up to the ledge while I keep hunting for Hebrews."

The younger soldier hauled her to her feet and shoved her forward. Keturah fell against the rocks, skinning her left knee.

"Climb," he said.

She looked up to the closest ledge, doing her best to stand. She preferred this death. She would fly, at least for a few moments, and when she hit the ground, there would be instant darkness. That sounded easy enough.

Let it be so.

Keturah was ready to fly. It was time.

SVESHTARI

Sveshtari wanted to hurl his *pilum*, like Jupiter throwing a lightning bolt, straight for the face of the Roman soldier shoving Keturah up the side of the cliff. But the soldier was too far away, so Sveshtari stormed from the cave and hurried across the narrow ledge, hoping to cut off the Roman's path.

By the looks of it, the soldier was going to hurl Keturah to the rocks. The Romans sought one hundred drops of Jewish blood for every single drop of Roman blood. Keturah's blood would soon be added to the Jewish chalice, even though she wasn't a Hebrew.

As he hurried along the ledge, his thigh throbbed where Keturah had knifed him. His gait soon became a limp, but he pushed forward without letting up.

Just when Sveshtari thought his legs would give out, the Roman rounded a corner and came to a sudden halt. Sveshtari blocked his way.

"Not a step closer," the soldier said, putting one arm around Keturah's waist and placing a knife to her neck.

Sveshtari stopped, held up his palms, and spoke in a measured tone. "Let her go, and I will not kill you."

The Roman soldier backed up two steps, dragging Keturah and looking to his right, over the edge of the cliff. Sveshtari followed his gaze. This spot wasn't as high as he assumed the soldier was taking Keturah, but it was high enough to break her to pieces.

Sveshtari watched the soldier sort out his options, a bead of sweat trickling down his brow. The man's eyes darted from the rocks below to the path and tightened his grip around Keturah's waist.

Sveshtari held back a grin. He had the soldier where he wanted him, and they both knew it. If he pushed Keturah over the edge, he would be exposed to the full wrath of Sveshtari. The soldier was physically less imposing than Sveshtari, so he must know he had to keep Keturah alive as a human shield. The boy's only chance to live would be to push Keturah into Sveshtari's arms and run for it.

At least, that was what Sveshtari hoped.

Sveshtari studied the young man, determining the best course of action. The Roman was a rail-thin soldier with panicked eyes constantly darting, checking out his footing on the ledge, checking out the height of the fall, checking out Sveshtari.

Suddenly, the soldier stumbled and almost fell as part of the ledge crumbled beneath his feet. He lunged for the cliff's wall, holding Keturah in place and slamming his back flat against the rock. His chest heaved as he stared over the ledge. During the misstep, his knife slipped and nicked Keturah's shoulder. She let out a cry, blood trickling down her arm.

Sveshtari tried to make eye contact with her, hoping to send a silent reassurance, but her eyes dropped, and she stared at the ground. She had surrendered to death.

"Let the woman go, and you will live," Sveshtari said.

The Roman swallowed, his Adam's apple bobbing. Sveshtari raised a brow and took another step forward, but the soldier lurched back and tightened his grip on Keturah.

A gust of wind lashed the stone ledge, whipping their robes and hair as if they were about to be swept away by a storm. Sveshtari shielded his eyes from the swirling dust as the soldier started to totter. Sveshtari had to act fast before other Roman soldiers came running to assist.

"If you harm her, you will be dead by my hand." Sveshtari shot him a grave look. "I am stronger and quicker. Your only hope is to hand her over and run."

The soldier shook his head. "You'll use your sword when my back is turned."

"I won't leave her side to chase you down, so you will escape with your life. You know that."

The soldier shuffled back another step, drawing Keturah with him. Sveshtari took two steps forward.

ELIANA

Eliana sighed as old fears awakened. The brief battle in the caves brought back traumatic memories of her kidnapping outside Bethlehem—being dragged into slavery and dying a thousand times every day.

Eliana was surrounded by twenty-five men who would die to protect her. Still, the machinery of the Roman army was efficient and terrible, so what good were twenty-five Zealots? The only consolation was that she wouldn't die alone.

Asaph had her by the hand as they hurried through the twisting passageway of the caves of Arbel, with her dog, Lavi, by their side. She had wanted to stay with Gershom, but her father and Asaph would not allow it. She agreed to leave him only because he had a Zealot with medical training tending to him.

As she and Asaph moved swiftly through the caves, torchlights leading the way, she recalled their childhood when they ran through the village. Only this time, they ran with purpose. If they didn't move fast enough, they would die.

The "back door" spilled out of the wall on the western edge of the cliffs, the side farthest from the Sea of Galilee. Eliana's father led the way, briefly exposing them to the morning glare before taking another path that streamed into an entirely different network of caves. There, they found a tunnel into yet another section of the mountain.

Eliana looked around, eyes wide. It was a maze within a maze. The cliffs were so riddled with caves that it would take the Romans days, maybe weeks, to track them.

According to Asaph, they planned to make their way to nearby Magdala when night fell, hoping to blend in with the thousand-plus followers of Jesus. Eliana began to have hope, a dangerous thing.

Once Judah decided they were safe, they settled into the cavern's recesses, and Asaph took a seat beside her, their backs against the cool rock. Lavi curled up against Eliana and closed his eyes.

Asaph adjusted the sword strapped to his waist, and it clanked against the rock floor. He seemed so proud of that sword, so pleased that her father had given it to him.

"Will Gershom live?" she whispered.

Asaph nodded. "I pray so. They will cut the *pilum* down to size, so he can move more easily. But they will not attempt to remove the rest until he is in a place of safety."

"Thank you for defending Gershom."

Eliana had been hidden during the battle but had heard about his heroics. Asaph shrugged, clearing his throat before changing the subject. "Your father is upset that he let you get caught up in this."

"It was my choice to be here. I want to be with my father."

"And he with you. But he realizes he put you at risk by allowing you to stay."

She dragged in a deep breath. "I understand. I realize I cannot live with the freedom fighters any longer."

"None of us can live in these caves now that the Romans have targeted us. We will regroup. Many of these men have families in the nearby villages—Magdala, Arbel, some in Tiberius and Capernaum. Perhaps you could live there with the other wives."

Other wives?

Asaph was getting ahead of himself. She was not his wife yet, not even betrothed. She wondered if he had talked to her father about marriage. Was that why he hinted at his future with her as his wife? She had to let him know of her decision, and now was as good a time as any. He had given her the perfect opening.

"I cannot live in any of those villages. I have decided to follow Jesus as he makes his way to Jerusalem."

Asaph paused and stared, obviously taken by surprise. "How will you live? Who will provide a tent of protection?"

"The followers of Jesus share freely among themselves. No one goes hungry."

"And if you and his followers are attacked? Herod will not tolerate Jesus for much longer. He does not share thrones, so who will protect you then?"

"Jesus said not to fear those who can kill the body."

"You will be willing to die for Jesus?"

"I already know what it is like to have died. His followers brought me back to life."

"But his followers do not carry swords. What would have happened today if we did not have our swords to defend ourselves?"

"God is stronger than any sword."

"God is spirit. And a spiritual sword would have done us no earthly good."

Eliana didn't respond. They sat in silence for a spell.

"Have you spoken to your father about this?" Asaph eventually asked.

"I will. When we reach Magdala at nightfall."

"He will not give you up so easily. He lost you once, and he will have a hard time giving you up again, this time to Jesus."

Was this a threat? She didn't think her father would use force to keep her from following the Nazarene. Or would he?

In many ways, her father was a stranger. She had not seen him for thirty years, and when she had last lived with her father, she had been under his full authority. But now she was part of Jesus's spiritual *bet 'ab*. Did her Abba, her father, still see her under his headship?

"You're all your father has left," Asaph said, locking eyes with her.

Eliana flicked her gaze to the ground. She didn't need the reminder that her mother, who had died of tertian ague, and her brother, who was killed by the Romans, were now gone. She was well aware of how alone her father was.

But was that reason to give up her future to please her father? She met Asaph's caring eyes with a frown. Her father was supposed to be looking out for her, not the other way around.

"Please. Do not tell my father of my plans. Let me speak to him."

Asaph remained silent for a moment before giving a slight nod.

Eliana turned away, hands clasped at her waist, and began to pray. Although her father disapproved of Jesus of Nazareth, would he force her to remain with him? She suddenly feared that by entering her father's camp, she might have walked into a new form of bondage. Jesus had warned his followers of this.

"Do you think I came to bring peace on earth?" he had said. "No, I tell you, but division. From now on there will be five in one family divided against each other, three against two and two against three. They will be divided, father against son and son against father, mother against daughter and daughter against mother, mother-in-law against daughter-in-law and daughter-in-law against mother-in-law."

Jesus had left out one pairing—father against daughter.

JEREMIEL

Jeremiel sat deep in the cave, staring at the circle of light at the edge of darkness. He pulled his knees up to his chest as the words of God echoed in his head.

What is the way to the abode of light? And where does darkness reside? Can you take them to their places? Do you know the paths to their dwellings?

Jeremiel knew precisely where the darkness resided because he was living in darkness, and the darkness was within him.

I am unworthy—how can I reply to you? Jeremiel thought. *I put my hand over my mouth.*

The words of God rolled on.

Where were you when I laid the earth's foundation? Tell me, if you understand. Who marked off its dimensions? Surely, you know! Who stretched a measuring line across it? On what were its footings set, or who laid its cornerstone—while the morning stars sang together and all the angels shouted for joy?

The words of God became an avalanche in his mind, words tumbling end over end.

Who shut up the sea behind doors when it burst forth from the womb, when I made the clouds its garment and wrapped it in thick darkness, when I fixed limits for it and set its doors and bars in place, when I said, "This far you may come and no farther; here is where your proud waves halt"?

Here, on the Cliffs of Arbel, his proud waves had halted.

Jeremiel heard a commotion outside the cave and rose to investigate. A man shouted, and a second voice threatened. Jeremiel crept toward the light, and suddenly, all became clear, like a fog burning away in the morning.

This precise moment was where his meandering thread of life had led, and it all made sense. Although God had *not* called him to be a prophet, he knew why the Lord had given him this disfigurement and why he arrived here at this very moment on this very day.

He peeked around the cave's opening, spotting a Roman soldier holding on to the woman, Keturah. He had his arm around her and a knife at her throat. The voice of the second man commanded the soldier to let her go free. Jeremiel couldn't see this man, but he didn't need to. The confidence in the man's voice was evident.

Jeremiel curled a fist. Here must the Roman soldier's proud waves stop. Here it must *all* stop!

Jeremiel stepped into the morning light, as calm as he had ever been. As he strode out of the cave, he lowered the dirty rag that covered his face, exposing his uncleanness to the light of all creation.

"Let the woman go," he said. His voice was so calm that he almost didn't recognize it as his own.

The Roman soldier looked over his shoulder, eyes wide, taking in Jeremiel's disfigured face. He must have thought a monster from Hades had stepped out of the cave.

"Please, release her." Jeremiel stepped forward, extending his unclean hand to touch the soldier's shoulder. The Roman shrunk back, his eyes filled with horror and disbelief.

Meanwhile, the man on the other side moved closer to the young soldier, who found himself trapped between two ways of death—the sword and sickness.

In his panic, the soldier shoved Keturah over the ledge. Then he spun, rushing toward Jeremiel, who ran to meet him, wrapping him in an unclean embrace, the open sores of his face pressing against his skin.

When a sharp sting bit Jeremiel's body, he knew the soldier's knife had entered his flesh. The soldier tried to break free, but Jeremiel held on for his life. The Roman screamed, stabbing him again and again, as if trying to cut through a stranglehold of vines, but Jeremiel remained calm.

Jeremiel prayed and thanked God for sending him here at this moment, on this day.

He felt two more stabs and then another, then another, but Jeremiel still refused to let go. He became the soldier's second skin. As the Roman tried to run, he stumbled, and the two of them staggered sideways, Jeremiel never letting go.

Suddenly, they were both in the air, face to face. Jeremiel saw the blue sky spinning, then the rocks, and he released his hold on the young soldier, extending both hands to his sides as if flying. He tumbled head over heels and caught one final glimpse of the Sea of Galilee sparkling in the distance before everything became a blur.

I know that you can do all things; no purpose of yours can be thwarted...

Jeremiel's final thoughts were blessed by peace. As the ground rose up to embrace him, there was no pain, and at last, he found his way out of darkness.

SVESHTARI

Sveshtari caught Keturah around the waist.

The Roman soldier had been so distracted by the leper that Sveshtari managed to edge closer while he wasn't paying attention. If he hadn't been able to move within reach, Keturah would already be dead.

As the Roman shoved her toward the edge of the cliff, Sveshtari caught her and pulled her to him, away from the precipice. His back slammed against the rock wall, and he pulled her so tightly against his body that he was afraid he would crush her.

"Are you okay?" He could barely get the words out as he reacted to what unfolded before his eyes.

The leper clung to the Roman soldier, who repeatedly stabbed him, but the unclean man never let go. When the two of them staggered toward the edge, Sveshtari tucked Keturah's head into his chest to keep her from seeing. But she shook loose and turned just in time to see the leper and the soldier tumble into open air.

Then she turned back to Sveshtari and buried her head in his chest with a quiet sob.

Sveshtari knew they should return immediately to the safety of the caves, but he couldn't let go of Keturah. It had been so long since he'd embraced her like this, and he wasn't sure if she would ever allow it again.

"I'm sorry," he whispered. "I am sorry for all I have done."

She remained motionless, with her face buried in his chest. When he kissed the top of her head, and she still didn't react, he released a slow breath. *At least she didn't spit in my face.*

The spell was soon broken as voices erupted from below.

"We must go," he whispered, leading Keturah along the narrow path of the ledge.

Two Zealots were waiting for them when they arrived back at the caves. One of them stepped alongside Keturah, putting an arm around her shoulder and drawing her into the cave.

The entire time, Keturah kept her head down. The only sounds she uttered were groans as she walked. She was having trouble putting weight on one foot. So, once they were away from the precipice, Sveshtari lifted her into his arms and carried her.

The Zealots led them to a tight opening in the back of the cave, where they squeezed through the narrow door, entering a wider hall that led to another tunnel. One of the Zealots carried a torch, and the light led them through the darkness.

KETURAH: ONE WEEK LATER

Sveshtari wiped some blood from Keturah's forehead. She glanced away, thinking she must look terrible. Her black eye had faded to a yellowish splotch, while her arms and back still ached. Her ankle fared the worst. It was still difficult putting weight on it, but that wasn't the extent of her pain.

"Ouch!"

"Sorry," said Sveshtari.

He pricked the tattoo on her forehead with a pin, wiping away more blood—all in preparation for an ointment that he guaranteed would remove the words.

When the bleeding stopped, he applied another coating of the ointment.

"You're sure this will work?" she asked.

"It's better than the alternative."

Keturah winced. The alternative was to scrape away the skin, layer by layer, until the ink was eventually gone. Not only did it sound excruciating, but it would leave a scar. However, a scar was preferable to this tattoo, which would attract pursuit and punishment for the rest of her life. This tattoo, this "stigma," had to go.

"Six days from now, we apply another dose," he said.

"And how many will it require?"

"The man said the tattoo would be gone in twenty days—without a scar."

After Sveshtari wrapped her forehead in a linen bandage, they hiked to the banks of the Jordan River, where they hoped to find Eliana, Asaph, and Chaim.

Sveshtari and Keturah blended in with the followers of Jesus, who occupied a small village not too far south of Tiberias. Both were disguised as Jews, which meant Keturah had to remove her nose ring and earrings and hope her piercings healed quickly.

Jesus was working his way south to Jerusalem, although so far, it had been slow going as the teacher stopped to preach in various synagogues. But they were expected to leave soon for Scythopolis, a route that hugged the Jordan River. Keturah would ride a donkey because her ankle wasn't strong enough for her to walk.

All the Zealot fighters had vanished since the battle on Mount Arbel, most disappearing into the wilderness. Only Judah remained to be near his daughter.

Eliana. Keturah shook her head. To think that she was afraid of Eliana only a short time ago when they met in the caravan. When they first forged a friendship, death lingered in Eliana's eyes. Now, she studied her friend, who sat on the grassy hillside, listening to Jesus speak, and wondered how it could be the same person. Eliana's eyes had once been filled with murder. Now, her gaze reflected wonder.

Jesus walked amidst the crowd. "Therefore I tell you, do not worry about your life, what you will eat; or about your body, what you will wear. For life is more than food, and the body more than clothes."

Do not worry about your life? Keturah wished it were possible. Her life, especially in the past two years, had been one constant worry. Today, she was concerned that the Romans would track her down, forcing her back into slavery—or that Herod's men would find her and kill her.

"Consider how the wild flowers grow," Jesus continued. "They do not labor or spin. Yet I tell you, not even Solomon in all his splendor was dressed like one of these. If that is how God clothes the grass of the field, which is here today, and tomorrow is thrown into the fire, how much more will he clothe you—you of little faith."

"I have heard enough," Sveshtari whispered into Keturah's ear. "Can we go somewhere and talk? I can carry you."

For days, Sveshtari had been trying to rekindle what they once had. But Keturah decided she would rather sit here next to Eliana, Asaph, Chaim, and Lavi. Her friends.

"I'm staying," she said. Sveshtari bristled and frowned, but then he heaved a big sigh and sat back down. Keturah cast a glance in his direction and smiled to herself. He wouldn't give up on her, and strangely enough, she found that comforting.

ELIANA

It was another warm, blue-sky afternoon. Eliana lay on her back, her head propped on a smooth stone, with Lavi sprawled across her. Her dog's heartbeat thumped against her chest.

Eliana turned and smiled at Keturah, who sat cross-legged nearby, with Sveshtari at her side. Always at her side. Next to him were Asaph and Chaim.

Eliana stared at the clouds drifting overhead. Both Asaph and Chaim obviously wanted her as their wife. But was she too old for marriage? She wasn't sure.

The only thing for certain was that she would follow Jesus, even to Jerusalem, even into the heart of Herod's power. So were hundreds of others following in his wake.

"If you go to Jerusalem with this teacher, you will find only trouble," her father warned her.

"Maybe. But I will also find Truth."

Jesus ended the day as always—with teaching.

"When you see a cloud rising in the west, immediately you say, 'It's going to rain,' and it does. And when the south wind blows, you say, 'It's going to be hot,' and it is. Hypocrites! You know how to interpret the appearance of the earth and the sky. How is it that you don't know how to interpret this present time?"

Eliana, still on her back, cocked her head and stared at the blue sky. It would indeed rain when clouds appeared in the west because storms usually swept in from the Great Sea. But understanding the truth about Jesus was much more difficult.

Who was this Jesus? A King? A Messiah? Eliana thought so. But what did that mean? Some saw the Messiah as a warrior King, but Jesus was anything but a warrior. She had never seen him carry a sword.

"Consider the ravens." Jesus lifted a hand as a black bird flew overhead. "They do not sow or reap, they have no storeroom or barn; yet God feeds them. And how much more valuable you are than birds! Who of you by worrying can add a single hour to your life?"

Eliana closed her eyes, letting those words sweep over her like a fresh breeze. Although there were many things to fear, Jesus was right. God fed the birds, and he would do the same for her.

She made a vow. Today, she would not fear the future or regret the past. Today, she would simply pray. Today, she would enjoy the company of her friends and her teacher's words.

Sensing a shadow cross her face, Eliana opened her eyes and spotted someone standing over her. The sun cast a shadow across the person's face, but she could tell it was a woman from how she was dressed.

When she sat up, the woman's face became clearer. Eliana gasped. It was Mary, the mother of Jesus.

Eliana scrambled to her feet, brushing the dust from her robe. Since joining Jesus's followers, Eliana hesitated to approach Mary, unsure of what to say. She didn't know if Mary would even remember her. Now, here she was—the mother of the Bethlehem child.

Just as Eliana feared, she had no words. She stood slack-jawed, eventually sputtering, "Shalom."

Mary smiled. Beamed, actually. Like everyone, time had eroded Mary's youth as steadily as the rain had beaten away at the Cliffs of Arbel. But, also like the cliffs, the erosion had created a different kind of weathered beauty.

"Shalom." Mary's warm brown eyes shone with kindness. "I have seen you several times over the past week. And every time I do, you remind me of someone. Do I know you?"

"We met a long time ago. In fact, it was the very week your son was born. I was a little girl when I came to the cave. I held your baby boy in my arms."

Eliana felt like a fool as the tears suddenly welled up in her eyes. She tried to talk through the tears, but she was a mess.

"I held him in my arms." Eliana wiped her eyes with the sleeve of her robe. "I'm sorry...I'm sorry for crying...but I held him, and now he is the protector of my heart. He is the one."

Eliana buried her face in her hands, unable to get out any more words. Mary put her arms around her as if she were a child.

After Eliana had been taken by brigands that day near Bethlehem, she craved the arms of her mother. This was the first time she had been embraced by a mother, any mother, in thirty years.

"I'm sorry," Eliana repeated, staring at her feet and wiping her eyes with her fingertips. "I feel so foolish, crying like this. But it's been so hard."

"I know, daughter. Life is hard."

She called me daughter.

"I do remember you," Mary added, patting her back. "You were the same little girl who followed me to the home of Elizabeth."

Eliana looked up, her lips parting. The tears still stung her eyes as she stared in amazement. She was shocked that Mary's eyes also brimmed with tears, like the Pool of Siloam.

"You remember?" Eliana asked.

"I will never forget that day—and I never forgot you. You made me feel happy just seeing you smile."

Eliana tried to smile now, but it was difficult through the tears. "Can I ever be that girl again?"

Mary seemed taken aback by the question. She stared at her so intensely that Eliana had to drop her head. The heat of a blush passed across her face.

"The seed is always there. The seed can still produce good fruit."

"But I'm old," Eliana said.

"If you plan to live forever, what is 'old'?"

Eliana smiled, unsure of what to say next.

"Your son saved me," she said.

Mary stared into Eliana's eyes intensely before breaking into another smile. Then Mary gave Eliana another hug, triggering another gush of tears.

Holding her tight, Mary prayed: "*Mi sheg'molayikh kol tov, hu yigmo-layikh kol tov. Selah.*"

It was a prayer for those who had survived danger: "He who has bestowed upon you every goodness, may He continue to bestow upon you every goodness. Selah."

Mary's embrace was long and warm. As the two women parted, Eliana watched her go until she vanished into the crowd. Then, Eliana crouched to stroke Lavi's soft fur, closing her eyes and savoring the westward breeze.

Today, Eliana was at peace. Jerusalem was still a long way off.

AUTHOR'S NOTES

I STILL REMEMBER THE first time I watched the movie *Ben-Hur* in the theaters as a child. Two scenes remain vivid in my memory. The first was the bloody death of Messala under the wheels of the chariots. (I remember my mother telling me I could turn away and not look at the gory spectacle.) The other scene was Jesus giving water to Ben-Hur.

While Ben-Hur was a fictional character, his story weaves in and out of the historical narrative of Jesus, presenting the tale of the Christ through fresh eyes. It had a profound impact on me.

Therefore, in writing *Thrones in the Desert*, I decided to present the Book of Luke through the fresh eyes of five fictional characters. These characters weave in and out of the Book of Luke, with the twelve chapters of *Thrones in the Desert* following the trajectory of the first twelve chapters of Luke. The second book in this series, *Swords in the Desert*, will follow the last twelve chapters of Luke.

Jesus's dialogue comes directly from the New International Version of the Bible. Similarly, much of the dialogue of other Biblical figures—from Mary and Elizabeth to John the Baptist—is from Scripture. But there are a few exceptions, where I put fictional dialogue in the mouths of Biblical figures, such as Eliana's final scene with Mary. However, I tried to keep the fictional dialogue to a minimum when it comes to people from the Bible.

My intention was not only to look at the Book of Luke through fresh eyes. It was to draw people back to the source, the Scriptures, to encourage people to read the story of Jesus with the same wonder of someone discovering the story for the first time.

In writing this novel, I learned more about the Bible and the culture of the times in a couple of years than I had in my previous twenty. Much of this learning came from classes that I audited at Urbana Theological Seminary, particularly those taught by Professor Ken Cuffey. I also had the joy of taking the trip of a lifetime to Israel, under his leadership. In Bethsaida, a portion of a cobblestone road remains from Jesus's time, so we literally walked on stones that Jesus once stepped upon.

Another major influence was Seth Kerlin, my pastor at Cornerstone Fellowship in Urbana, Illinois. Seth's sermon series on Luke inspired me to choose that book out of the four Gospels in the first place.

I should note that I based the battle on Mount Arbel on an actual incident, as reported by the Jewish historian Josephus. In *The Wars of the Jews*, chapter 16, he describes how Herod the Great (the Herod at the time of Jesus's birth) attacked robbers in the caves by lowering "the most hardy of his men in chests, and set them at the mouths of the dens." The soldiers killed the robbers and their families. I borrowed this incident to create my fictional climax.

My goal, Lord willing, is to continue to follow these fictional characters into the Book of Acts, which Luke also authored. While some characters will die and others spring up, I envision following these characters and their descendants into the rich history of the Church.

There are many sources for this novel. In addition to the NIV, here are some of the key resources that I used.

Chronological Aspects of the Life of Christ, by Harold W. Hoehner. Academie Books, 1977.

The City in Roman Palestine, by Daniel Sperber. Oxford University Press, 1998.

Daily Life in the Time of Jesus, by Henri Daniel-Rops. Servant Books, 1961.

Every Living Thing: Daily Use of Animals in Ancient Israel, by Oded Borowski. Altimira Press, 1998.

Herod Antipas: A Contemporary of Jesus Christ, by Harold W. Hoehner. Zondervan Publishing House, 1972.

Holman Bible Atlas, by Thomas V. Brisco. Holman Reference, 1998.

The Life and Times of Jesus the Messiah, by Alfred Edersheim. Hendrickson Publishers, 1993.

Lexham Geographic Commentary on the Gospels, Barry J. Beitzel editor. Lexham Press, 2017.

The New International Commentary on the New Testament: The Gospel of Luke, by Joel B. Green. William B. Eerdmans Publishing Company, 1997.

New Testament History, by F.F. Bruce. Doubleday, 1969.

Policing the Roman Empire: Soldiers, Administration, and Public Order, by Christopher J. Fuhrmann. Oxford University Press, 2012.

The Slave in Greece and Rome, by Jean Andreau and Raymond Descat. The University of Wisconsin Press, 2006.

Slavery in the Roman World, by Sandra R. Joshel. Cambridge University Press, 2010.

The Wars of the Jews, by Flavius Josephus, Translated by William Whiston. Thomas Nelson, 1998.

The World Jesus Knew, by Anne Punton. Monarch Books, 1996.

SWORDS IN THE DESERT

Coming Soon

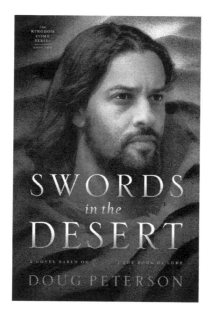

Follow Eliana, Asaph, Keturah, and Sveshtari through the second half of the Book of Luke.

ACKNOWLEDGMENTS

It started with a sermon.

Several years ago, my pastor, Seth Kerlin, did a year-long sermon series on the Book of Luke, immersing our congregation in the Gospel. This was the kernel of my idea to write my first Biblical novel. Seth also sat down with me to talk about the Book of Luke, giving me my first lesson on King Herod, the king when Jesus was born, and his son Herod Antipas, the tetrarch when Jesus died and rose again.

Thank you, Seth, for triggering the idea—and for giving me the name of my Thracian bodyguard, Sveshtari.

Next, I offer my thanks to the Urbana Theological Seminary and Professor Ken Cuffey, who took me deep into the New Testament. His insights were invaluable. Thank you, Ken, for also reading through the manuscript and correcting me when my history went awry. (I take responsibility for any errors and inaccuracies that remain.)

Meanwhile, my wife, Nancy, has the patience of a saint. I lost count of the number of times she read drafts of *Thrones in the Desert*, consistently giving me wonderful big-picture feedback.

I also thank Vern Fein, the poet laureate of his street in Urbana, who gives me unflagging encouragement when we meet regularly to talk about writing. He too reviewed the manuscript, as did my sister Kathy, brother Ric, and mother Irene, as well as Heath Morber and his son Cavan. Thank you for your faithfulness.

After I ran the novel past my team of readers, I turned to Kim Hough, who does a thorough and masterful job of editing, as she has done for three of my books. Also, thanks to Santiago Romero for your beautiful map; and to Kirk DouPonce for another amazing cover and back cover design.

In addition, thanks to Vincent Davis II, who helps me promote my novels and knows more about Amazon algorithms than anyone I know.

Finally, I give joyful thanks to the Father, who invites us to share in the inheritance of His holy people in the kingdom of light. "For he has rescued us from the dominion of darkness and brought us into the kingdom of the Son he loves, in whom we have redemption, the forgiveness of sins." (Colossians 1:13-14)

May your Kingdom Come.

—Doug Peterson

ABOUT THE AUTHOR

 Doug Peterson is the award-winning author of 84 books, including seven historical novels, 12 comic books (and counting), and over 40 children's books for the best-selling VeggieTales series.

Doug's passion for writing can be traced to grade school, when he ran his own media empire, publishing the monthly *Peterson Popper* magazine and *The Weekly Waste* newspaper (with a circulation of 3). By the time he was in fourth grade, he had written and bound dozens of his own books, including such classics as *20,000 Leagues Under a Swimming Pool* and *In Cold Ketchup* (real titles).

Doug graduated in journalism from the University of Illinois in 1977 and did a short stint as the editor of a small Wisconsin weekly newspaper. (Their motto: "This is Wisconsin, so we pay you in cheese.") Fearing that he might be forced to root for the Packers, Doug and his wife returned to the University of Illinois in 1979, where he began work as a science writer and half-time freelance writer.

Doug's VeggieTales book *The Slobfather* won the 2004 Gold Medallion Award for preschool books, and he was co-storywriter for the best-selling video, *Larry-Boy and the Rumor Weed*. His popular short story, "The Career of Horville Sash," was made into a music video featuring Grammy-winner Jennifer Warnes, and he co-wrote "Roman Ruins," an episode in the bestselling line of How to Host a Murder party games.

Doug has a love for history, so he made the transition to historical novels with *The Disappearing Man*, published by Bay Forest Books in 2011 and chosen by Canton, Ohio, for its One Book, One Community program.

Doug's historical novels center on the theme of freedom. Three novels feature true stories of the Underground Railroad: Henry "Box" Brown, a slave who mailed himself to freedom; Ellen Craft, a slave who escaped by pretending to be a white man; and Harriet Tubman, the most famous conductor on the Underground Railroad. He also has two Civil War novels and a novel based on the rise and fall of the Berlin Wall.

A versatile writer, Doug co-authored two stage plays—one based on Dietrich Bonhoeffer, the Church's voice of resistance in Germany during World War II, and the other about the improbable friendship between Benjamin Franklin and evangelist George Whitefield.

Most recently, he was hired to write an extensive series of comic books on American history, illustrated by Marvel artists. His non-fiction work includes the popular book *Of Moose and Men*, co-written with Tennessee comedian Torry Martin, and *Back to the Futures*, co-written with economist Scott Irwin.

Doug has also been a science writer for the University of Illinois at Urbana-Champaign for over 40 years. He has been married for 47 years and has two sons and four grandchildren. He and his wife live in Champaign, Illinois.

OTHER TITLES

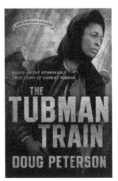

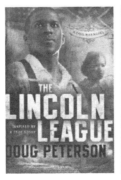
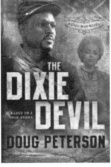

Made in the USA
Middletown, DE
29 September 2025

18481903R00194